PRECIPICE

A NOVEL BY

TOM SAVAGE

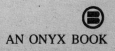

AN ONYX BOOK

ONYX
Published by the Penguin Group
Penguin Books USA Inc., 375 Hudson Street,
New York, New York 10014, U.S.A.
Penguin Books Ltd, 27 Wrights Lane,
London W8 5TZ, England
Penguin Books Australia Ltd, Ringwood,
Victoria, Australia
Penguin Books Canada Ltd, 10 Alcorn Avenue,
Toronto, Ontario, Canada M4V 3B2
Penguin Books (N.Z.) Ltd, 182-190 Wairau Road,
Auckland 10, New Zealand

Penguin Books Ltd, Registered Offices:
Harmondsworth, Middlesex, England

Published by Onyx, an imprint of Dutton Signet, a division of Penguin Books USA
Inc. This is an authorized reprint of a hardcover edition published by Little, Brown
& Company. For information address Little, Brown & Company, Inc., 34 Beacon
Street, Boston, MA 02108.

First Onyx Printing, May, 1995
10 9 8 7 6 5 4 3 2 1

Copyright © 1994 by Tom Savage
All rights reserved

PUBLISHER'S NOTE
This is a work of fiction. Names, characters, places, and incidents either are the
product of the author's imagination or are used fictitiously, and any resemblance to
actual persons, living or dead, events, or locales is entirely coincidental.

For my mothers—both of them

Marion Eleanor Savage Phillips
Mother
(1917-1958)

Lesley Savage
Mom

. . . Behold me, what I suffer
Because I have upheld that which is high.

SOPHOCLES
Antigone
translated by Edith Hamilton

BEFORE

THE FIRST THING he noticed was that the front door of the house was standing wide open. Then he heard the humming.

Afterward, whenever people asked him about it, he always remembered that it was unusually warm; the kind of day, he would tell them, that made him wish his uniform were not quite so heavy. The sun bore down on his back and seemed to permeate his clothes. On a day like this, even without the jacket, he would break into a sweat within the first five minutes of his shift, and by the time he got home in the afternoon he would be drenched. His wife always forced him to remove his shirt and trousers right there in the living room, and she'd take them immediately to the washing machine in the basement. The good thing about this was that it enabled him to steal a cold beer from the refrigerator and plunk himself down on the couch in his underwear. Sometimes he made it through such a day just dreaming about sitting there in his shorts with the little electric fan aimed at his naked belly, drinking from that frosty bottle. . . .

At this point in the narrative he would pause for a moment, and his audience would invariably smile and nod in sympathetic appreciation. Then the smiles would fade as they became aware of the change in his mood, the expression that came into his eyes and the subtle, almost imperceptible deepening of his voice. By the time he continued they would be watching him in silent anticipation, knowing yet dreading what was to come.

On this particular warm Tuesday morning he had paused on the sidewalk in front of the pretty white house on Pine Street, sighing. His home and his bottle of beer were still some six hours away. He slung his heavy canvas bag from his shoulder and rummaged through it. He knew he had something for number 46 today. Looked like a couple of bills. He found the mail, wiped his brow, and trudged up the pathway to the porch.

This week wouldn't be so bad, he thought. Four days instead of five, yesterday being the holiday. Next month, at his wife's insistence, he was going to ask for a neighborhood farther from the post office. Then they'd give him a truck to drive around in. He was getting much too old for the foot brigade. . . .

So fixed was the routine of his so-called appointed rounds that he'd already dropped the mail into the box before he happened to notice the door. Coming from the dazzling sunlight into the shade of the porch had dimmed his eyesight temporarily.

Oh, well, he thought. None of my business. . . .

He'd almost turned around to retrace his steps down the walk when he stopped short, arrested by a faint sound from inside the house. He stood on the threshold, scanning the shadows beyond the open door, looking for the source of the soft, high-pitched humming he'd heard a moment before. He recognized the tune, some kids' thing—"Frère Jacques," that was it. . . .

"Hello," he called from the doorway.

The humming continued.

Then his eyes adjusted, and he made out the dark interior of the room.

The moment he saw her, he knew something was wrong.

She was about six or seven years old, he decided. He had no children of his own, and he'd never been particularly good at guessing their ages. She was sitting on the floor in the center of the living room, dressed in a white nightgown. She was staring vacantly ahead of her, and she clutched something to her as she rocked slowly to and fro, humming.

He knew the young woman who lived in this house by sight. Sometimes she greeted him at the door with a warm "Good morning," and he would hand her the mail. But she didn't seem to be around this morning. So why was the door open? And why was the child sitting there in her nightgown at eleven o'clock? Hadn't school started today . . . ?

"Mrs. Petersen," he called, aware of the hoarseness in his own voice.

The girl did not look up, did not seem to hear him. He searched his mind for her name—he was sure he must know it—but a peculiar dullness was already beginning to set in. He couldn't think clearly. . . .

"Little girl," he finally managed to croak.

No reaction. She sat there, rocking and humming.

There were strict rules in his profession. He would never have dreamed of crossing the threshold, of entering someone's premises, until he saw what it was the little girl was holding in her hands.

Then he saw the blood.

Before he was aware of having moved, he was across the room and kneeling in front of her. He reached out with his shaking hand and touched her face. Only then did she stop humming and look up at him.

"Have you hurt yourself?" he whispered.

He reached over to take the enormous knife out of her hands. She pulled away from him. There was a nasty bruise on her left temple, but otherwise she did not seem to be hurt. He looked down at the blood on her hands and on her nightgown, realizing with a sudden, cold certainty that it was not hers.

"Where's your mommy?" he asked as gently as possible.

She watched him for a moment. Then, as if he no longer interested her, she clutched the knife to her little chest and began to rock again, humming under her breath.

He rose to his feet, gazing around him. There was broken glass everywhere on the carpet. A huge breakfront stood against one wall, doors open, glass shattered, interior gaping. The coffee table in front of the couch was lying on its side, and the bowl of flowers and two ashtrays that had obviously once rested on it had rolled away to lie in various other parts of the room. All the window shades were down. The air conditioner in the far window hummed softly, but the open door had defeated its purpose. The air inside the house was warm and thick, almost stifling.

He raised a hand to his tightening chest as he looked over at the empty dining area and, beyond it, the open door to the empty kitchen. Then he turned to face the archway that led to the other rooms. If he stood still, he knew, he would begin to hyperventilate. He was fifty-seven years old, and twice already he'd come dangerously close to a heart attack. He must move, must act.

Leaving the girl in the devastated main room, he walked slowly, cautiously into the dark hall beyond the archway.

"Hello," he called again, but by now he knew that no one would answer. The silence in the house was almost palpable.

He glanced around at the four doors, three of them closed. The open door was on the left, at the end of the hall, and the only illumination was the sunlight that poured through it from the bedroom beyond. Looking down, he saw the tiny, bloody footprints on the white hall carpeting, leading from that room to the living room behind him. Even now he was aware of the vague, unpleasant smell.

He willed himself to move. It seemed to take him forever to walk the few feet to the bedroom doorway. He closed his eyes, took a deep breath, and stepped inside.

She was lying facedown in a patch of sunlight next to the bed. Her nightgown—white, like her daughter's—and the carpet around her were soaked with blood. There were dark brown stains everywhere: on the bed, the walls, the mirror above the vanity table. Blood covered her outstretched hands and matted her pale blond hair.

The stench was overwhelming. He had clamped his hand over his mouth and pinched his nostrils, preparing to kneel down next to her, when he realized the futility of his action. Mrs. Petersen had been lying here for several hours. . . .

The sudden footfall behind him made him gasp and whirl around. The child stood in the doorway, the knife grasped in her left hand. As he watched, she slowly raised the knife in front of her. Involuntarily, he brought his arms up to protect himself. Oh, dear God, he thought. A little girl. . . .

The two of them stood there facing each other, silent, frozen, a grotesque tableau in the little bedroom of the pretty house on Pine Street. Sunlight poured in through the windows, hot against his neck, gleaming on the blond hair and the slick puddles at his feet. Something in the child's expression, or, rather, her lack of expression—he always had trouble describing it, although he never forgot it—caused him to slowly lower his arms to his sides. It's the surprise, he remembered telling himself. I'm still taking it all in, assessing the damage, the calamity of it, and I'm not reacting properly. Besides, the very idea is ridiculous. She can't be more than seven. . . .

Then, at last, the oppressive silence was disrupted. The little girl blinked once, licked her parched lips, and spoke in a soft, dull whisper, staring not at him but at the empty space somewhere beyond his shoulder.

"Mommy's dead," she said. "I killed her."

The knife fell from her hand as her eyes glazed over and her tiny body slumped to the floor.

The first wave of shock washed over him, and later he would not recall his next actions clearly. He must have moved. The child was now in his arms, and he was running down the hall into the living room. Phone, phone, he must find a phone. . . .

The telephone was on the living-room floor, partially concealed by a stray throw pillow from the couch. He held the girl with one arm and reached down with the other. The receiver was dead. The coiled cord leading to the main body of the phone had been severed.

He dropped the useless instrument, cradled the child against him, and lurched through the open front door. Out, out into the clear air, the bright sunlight, away from the smell and the blood and the knife. The girl must have awakened, he supposed. The sound of terrified screaming filled his ears as he staggered down the pathway to the sidewalk.

Only later, when the neighbors began to appear, running toward him from their houses; when they finally took the unconscious child from him; when the wail of a hundred approaching sirens slowly entered his consciousness, did he become aware that the screaming he heard was his own.

He always ended there, with that little flourish, slowly grinning at the astonished expressions that invariably came to the faces of his listeners, unaware that his blithe smile was born not of humor but of his own acute embarrassment. He told the story many times, whenever people asked, less and less frequently as time passed and everyone began to forget about it, until eight years later, when his wife died and he retired from federal employment. After that, for reasons of his own, he stopped repeating it altogether.

PART ONE

GODDESS OF THE MOON

ONE

TUESDAY, AUGUST 6

THE IDEA OF MURDER, once formed in her mind, simply would not go away. She'd been working on the plan for quite some time, waiting—patiently, she thought—for just the right opportunity to set it in motion. She'd tackled the situation as she would a crossword puzzle, or one of her beloved anagrams or word-association games. When she'd at last figured out the ideal solution, she'd jumped right in. She'd cleared the field, so to speak, and now she was—slowly, painstakingly—baiting the trap. It was going to work; she had no doubt of that. It was why she was here now, today. And it was apparently going to be easier than she'd expected. . . .

Kay watched the girl from her chaise longue in the shade of a palm, trying to decide on the best way to approach her subject. She was grateful for the cool, concealing shadow. The intensity of the midafternoon sun on a cloudless day was something that even seven years of living in St. Thomas had failed to make less painful. That's what you get, she mused, for allowing your husband to talk you, an Irish redhead, into moving to the tropics. Not so bad, really, as long as you could lie in the shade with a tall glass of rum punch within easy reach. She took a sip: Dutch courage. She'd always been shy around people she didn't know. She hated breaking the ice, which is what she would have to do. She would have to get off of this chair and walk over to the girl, engage her in conversation. Present her case, as her late first husband would have said. Her new husband, Adam, was not a lawyer.

The girl stood before her easel near the shoreline, digging her bare toes into the warm white sand and contemplating her half-finished watercolor. If she was aware that she was being watched, she gave no sign of it. To all appearances, she had nothing on her mind but the elusive hues of the rich blue, wind-whipped Caribbean she was trying to capture with the artificial, oddly inadequate spectrum in the gleaming silver tubes of her paintbox. No shady palms for her: she welcomed the sunlight bearing down on her naked limbs, the breeze in her hair. She seemed perfectly at ease, a perfectly capable young woman. Her only problem, it would seem (if you were to ask the woman watching her), was keeping the watercolor pad from taking flight down the beach, leaving her and the bare easel to cope as best they could. She held a medium-sized brush in her left hand, and with the right one she absently adjusted the bra of her bikini. Then the hand traveled up to capture a stray lock of her dark, shoulder-length mane and push it behind her.

She's really quite a lovely young woman, Kay decided. Tall—just about the same height as Kay herself, who was five-eight—and possessed of that willowy grace one usually associated with dancers. Looking down at her own body, Kay shook her head and let out a long sigh. It was hard to feel willowy after one had borne a child. Lisa was twelve years old now, nearly thirteen, and Kay had never been willowy in the first place. Oh, well, heigh-ho. . . .

The girl, seemingly oblivious of Kay's scrutiny, dropped the medium brush into the jar of cloudy, blue-violet water on the tray table that the hotel management had so kindly provided. She picked up a long, thin detail brush and placed the wooden end between her teeth. She chewed absently, gazing out over the water.

With the ingrained practicality of the rich, Kay wondered just what this was going to cost. She wasn't sure how much to offer. The girl was obviously well-off: nobody flew to St. Thomas, even in off-season August, and took a room here at Bolongo Bay Beach Club unless they had a few bucks. Kay was a member of the club, entitled to all privileges of pool and dining room, chaises and tennis courts and all the rest. If her dues were any indication, she could well imagine what they asked for a room with a balcony overlooking the bay. But then again, Kay also knew that someone else had paid for the girl's vacation. She would never have even entertained the notion of offering the girl employment if it hadn't been for the conversation she'd overheard at lunch the day before. . . .

There had only been a few people dining on the small, split-level deck above the pool. There were not many rooms in the hotel, and hardly any of the club members came to the beach on weekdays. Most of them, unlike Kay, had jobs.

She and the girl had caught each other's eye and smiled politely as the girl was seated at the very next table. Kay considered, briefly, inviting the girl to join her. The girl was a painter and Kay was a collector: they could pass the time discussing art. But just as Kay was about to make her move, a tall, blond young man in a black T-shirt and Speedo bikini arrived at the girl's table.

"Hello again," he said. "May I?" He looked down at the empty chair across from the girl.

She glanced up, startled but apparently not annoyed by the intrusion. "Sure—Bob, was it? I'm sorry, I—"

"Yeah, Bob," he said, lowering his lanky frame into the offered seat. "The only other guest in the hotel, it seems. Unless you count those two." He jerked a thumb at a young honeymoon couple who sat entwined a few tables away, and he and the girl laughed. "They're not very sociable, except with each other. Everyone else around here is about a hundred years old." He looked over at Kay and grinned charmingly. "Hi!"

"Hello," Kay said, smiling, before looking back down at her menu. A hundred years old, eh? Cheeky sonofabitch.

Kay was forty-five, and just beginning to take the arrogance of youth personally.

"You're Diana," he continued, turning his grin back to the girl. "The other day you said that you graduated from Yale or some such place three years ago—"

"Harvard." She laughed. "Four years ago."

"—and you're a painter. What—other than the fact that every view on this island looks like it should have a calendar hanging under it—brings you to St. Thomas?"

The girl did not answer him immediately, Kay noticed. She merely shrugged one of those "beats-the-hell-out-of-me" shrugs.

"My mom's idea," she said at last. "Her treat, actually. I'd never be able to afford this by myself."

"Ah," Bob replied. "And why did she send you here?"

The girl smiled. "Oh, the usual. I've just come through . . . a bad time. A man."

"Oh." This was not part of Bob's plan. "Divorce?"

"Sort of," the girl said, her smile widening. "He refused to get one."

Bob, his hopes obviously renewed, leaned forward. "Well, men aren't *all* that bad. Take me, for instance. I'm here for a few more days, and—"

"Look," she said, fixing him with a level, no-nonsense gaze. "I don't want to seem rude, but could we just have lunch?" Then she disarmed her words with a light laugh.

Kay smiled to herself. Smooth move, Diana, she thought. Polite but firm. Just as my mother taught me. We have Similar Backgrounds. Excellent. Kay couldn't fault Bob for trying. She looked over, then, with pretended indifference. He was handsome—well built and tanned and engaging. Rich, too, she guessed. About the girl's age, perhaps twenty-five. Hell, if she, Kay, were twenty years younger, she'd be delighted by such attention. The girl must still be hurting from the married man to so flatly refuse such a specimen. This, for some reason, made her seem all the more interesting to Kay.

Most young men, Kay reflected, would have taken the girl's refusal as a cue to try harder, to waste more time attempting to force their unwanted erections, so to speak, upon her. Bob, to his credit, conceded with grace.

"Okay, lunch," he said, grinning. "On me. I insist. Then I'm out of your life."

They ordered then, and made polite conversation. Later, just as Kay was finishing her own repast and preparing to return to the chaise longue, she overheard the most interesting part of their dialogue.

"So," Bob said between bites of a club sandwich, "when do you go back to—wherever?"

"New York," the girl replied. "I'm here another week, then . . ." She trailed off, gazing out at the view.

"Hmm. Not looking forward to the real world?"

The girl shook her head slightly, still watching the bay beyond the pool.

"Hell," she sighed, "I wish I didn't have to go back at all. Not yet, anyway. If I could find some kind of job and a place to live, I wouldn't mind staying here for a while. . . ."

At that moment, it seemed to Kay, the girl looked

briefly over at her and smiled. Then she resumed her contemplation of the distant waves.

Kay rose and walked past their table and out onto the beach, the seed of an idea already planted in her mind.

Now, remembering the girl's words from the day before, Kay sat up on the chaise and steeled herself. How difficult could it be? The girl had wished for a job and a place to live. If she'd been serious in her wish, she'd get it. If not, so what? I can always get somebody else. With this resolve, Kay stood up and walked slowly down the beach toward the lone figure at the easel.

The girl noticed her approach. When it became obvious that the woman was coming up to her, she paused at the end of a brushstroke and turned to face her. Nice-looking, she thought. Mid-forties, maybe a little younger. Good figure. Sensible black one-piece bathing suit. And that hair! Bright, shimmering red, in a soft halo around her face. And, of course, the milky, freckled skin to go with it. She reached up to her own hair, currently dark brown, and once again pushed it out of her face. . . .

Kay arrived before the younger woman and presented her best how-do-you-do smile.

"Hello," she said. "Mind if I have a look?"

The girl regarded her for a moment, then shrugged and stepped aside from the easel.

It was the water in front of them, and over in the right corner was the edge of the point that jutted out from the end of the beach. The colors were right: the many shades of blue and the verdant tangle of seaside foliage. The vivid, glinting white of the sand. But there was something odd about the picture, Kay thought. It was much too— she searched for a word—*controlled*? No, *meticulous*. More meticulous than she had come to expect of watercolor studies on rough canvas. If an artist wanted all those distinct edges—the careful detail in water, sky, and land—he or she would normally choose a different medium. Oil or, at the very least, acrylic. It was pretty enough, if that was any criterion. Competently executed, but not—no, decidedly not the work of a professional. The girl was a talented amateur. Besides, there was something else about it that was—what?

The sudden laugh startled her.

"What's wrong with this picture?" the girl intoned, adding with her grave delivery the unmistakable quotation marks. She grinned.

Kay looked up into the lovely face and smiled her vague embarrassment. "I was just wondering—"

The younger woman nodded."

"Clouds," she said.

The word hung there between them for a moment before its import registered on Kay. She glanced at the watercolor, then up at the perfectly clear blue sky, then back.

Clouds.

She had filled the sky with them. And not just any clouds, Kay noticed. Not the happy white cotton patches or pale streaks of cirrus that could be regarded as artistic license, prettification. Oh, no. The huge cumulus mass dominated the painting, crouching angrily above the subdued, overcast water. How very odd, Kay thought. The girl had taken a beautiful, sunny seascape and rendered it dark and shadowy. *Ominous:* that was the word. Why, it almost looked like the backdrop for a particularly depressing Wagnerian opera. . . .

The young woman was smiling, apparently appreciative of Kay's uncomfortable reaction. She put down the brush and stuck out her left hand.

"Diana," she said. "Diana Meissen."

Kay reached out instinctively with her right hand. Oh, dear, there was really no way to shake properly. She took the girl's hand rather uncomfortably and gave it a brief squeeze.

"Kay Belden—*Prescott!* I beg your pardon, Ms. Meissen. You see, Belden was my first married name. I'm a widow. I've recently remarried, and I'm still getting used to . . . oh, well, Kay Prescott. Please call me Kay."

She trailed off lamely. Why on earth had she done that? Great, Kay! Your Freudian slip is showing. What a dumb, knee-jerk sort of thing to do! It wasn't just her embarrassment at meeting strangers; it was this girl.

If there had been an awkward moment, the young woman didn't seem to have noticed.

"Call me Diana," she said. "As you can see, I'm what you might call an interpretive artist."

The two women regarded the watercolor, laughing.

"Well, Kay drawled, "it's a very interesting interpretation."

"The Pessimism school: that's what my art teacher called it. I'm the opposite of an Idealist; you know, those painters who can take *anything* and make it look like a

Hallmark card. I take a beautiful day and make it look like, I don't know . . ."

"*Tristan und Isolde?*" Kay suggested. "Why do you do that, do you suppose?"

The girl grinned. "You sound like my analyst."

"You're right." Kay replied. "Sorry. I guess you just express yourself in dark tones. There's no law against it. You obviously like art that makes a statement."

They laughed together again.

"I suppose," the girl said. "You know that painting *The Scream*? It's one of my favorites. That little figure in the foreground with its mouth wide open, lost in that vast, oppressive landscape. That incredible sense of alienation, of absolute, cosmic terror."

"Ah, yes," Kay said, nodding. "Mucha."

The girl glanced up sharply. Then, slowly, she smiled.

"Actually, it's Munch," she said, not unkindly. After a moment's pause, she added, "But I guess you know that."

Whatever doubts Kay might have been feeling disappeared in that moment. Perhaps, she thought, this *is* the right one, after all. She laughed.

"They taught you well at Harvard," she said. "And I do not mean about artists."

The girl's eyes widened momentarily. "How on earth—oh, yes! Lunch yesterday. You were at the next table. Were you eavesdropping, Kay?"

No dissembling, Kay thought. Not with this one. Just get to the point.

"Yes," she admitted with what she hoped was a disarming smile. "A little. Enough to hear you say something that was very interesting to me. It may be of interest to both of us."

They stood there, the painting between them, each taking the measure of the other. Somewhere above their heads a pelican, swooping toward the water in search of prey, began to sound its hunting cry. The girl looked up, squinting against the sun, to see the bird fly down, down, closing in with gathering speed on some already sighted, unsuspecting target. Splash. The graceful white missile crashed into a wave and stabbed its head beneath the surface. The head came up an instant later, flashing silver from its long, sharp beak. With another guttural shriek and a flapping of wings, it zoomed up and away in wet, white triumph. She watched it disappear and turned back to the woman facing her.

"You've been watching me for three days," she said. "Now that I've passed your little test, or whatever it was, perhaps you'd like to tell me what this is all about."

Kay blinked. All right, she thought. Score one for you, young lady. She put on her warmest, friendliest smile.

"It's about a drink," she said, gesturing toward her shady chaise longue up the beach. "A few minutes of your time. I have a proposition for you. It's about my daughter, Lisa. And my husband. And Cliffhanger. Let's get out of this sun. I'll help you carry your things—"

"Excuse me," the girl interjected. "What did you say about a cliffhanger?"

Kay grinned as she picked up the paintbox. "Not a cliffhanger. Just Cliffhanger. It's the name of my house.

I'll explain. Come along, Diana. You may want to hear my offer."

The girl smiled to herself as she picked up the pad and the easel and followed the woman up the beach.

The two women lay side by side under the palm tree. They were sipping rum punches, and Kay was smoking a cigarette.

"I'm looking for a companion," she said, exhaling a stream of mentholated smoke and flicking the ash of her Virginia Slim into the sand. "A sort of au pair, I guess. Kind of a secretary. Not exactly a governess. The last girl who held the position referred to herself as a production assistant. Dear Sandra, such a peculiar sense of humor. I think she had dreams of being in the movies, poor thing. Well, she's gone now."

The young woman looked over at her. "Hollywood?"

Kay laughed and reached for her drink. "Hardly that! She was not what one could call a pretty sight. But she was forever reading those horrible fan mags, you know, from the checkout counter at Woolworth's. Debra Winger Having Tom Selleck's Baby. Madonna Kidnapped By Aliens. She was with us nearly two years, and she insisted on discussing these things at the dinner table. I thought I'd go mad."

"So you fired her."

"Oh, no," Kay said. "Nothing like that. I had no *real* complaint about her. She seemed to like her room at Cliffhanger—room and board, incidentally, plus salary— and she was obviously fond of Lisa. I assumed everything was fine. Well, never assume. One day about a week ago she came to me and said she was leaving. Just like that. It was rather odd, actually. She said she'd had some sort of windfall, come into a lot of money. I wasn't aware of any rich relatives lurking in the background; she never spoke of a family. Well, good luck to her."

The younger woman shrugged and gazed out over the water.

"So," she said after a while. "Room. Board. A salary— how much, by the way?"

Kay told her. She did not tell her that it was twice as much as she had been paying Sandra.

"Hmm," the girl replied. "Very nice. I would be your daughter's companion—"

"Yes."

"—and your secretary?"

"Sort of. Not much, really. Social engagements. Help out with the odd party. A little correspondence. What did they tell us in school—I'm a Vassar girl, by the way—'light typing'? In my day we learned steno, but I don't expect that of you."

"Then you won't be disappointed," the girl replied.

They laughed again. Kay rolled over on her side and faced the younger woman.

"I like you, Diana. I'd a feeling I would. It's so nice to talk to an intelligent girl, one who isn't simply rattling off movie gossip. You're not particularly *passionate* about art, are you? I mean, I hope I haven't just traded Debra Winger for Edvard Munch. . . ."

"You haven't traded anything for anything. Not yet, anyway. I haven't agreed—"

"Of course," Kay said. "Tell me, were you serious yesterday when you told that young man about wanting to stay?"

The girl was silent for a moment. She took a sip of her drink, weighing several things in her mind. At last she said, "Yes, I think perhaps I was."

Kay studied her face. "Was it that bad?"

"What?"

"The man. Darling, we're girls here. Men can be the creeps of all time, especially the ones who turn out to be married. I learned that at Vassar, don't you know. Was he just awful?"

The girl turned slowly to confront her. "Yes, he was—is—awful. And I feel more strongly about him than I've ever felt about anyone else."

"Oh, dear," Kay said. "Well, you're not running back to New York, are you? No chance with him, I suppose?"

For the second time that afternoon, Kay was surprised by the girl's sudden laughter.

"By that you mean, am I going to go flying off at a moment's notice and leave you searching for another au pair? No. If I agree to take the job, I'll take it. As for—the man, well, I'll just have to wait and see what happens."

"Yes," Kay said. "Well, it's none of my business. I hope it all works out for you. In the meantime—"

"In the meantime," the girl said, "tell me about Lisa."

The shadows of the late afternoon lengthened, and the shimmering heat rising from the fine white sand began to disperse. The breeze from the sea came steadily to shore, washing gently over the two women who were now the sole occupants of the beach. The rustling in the fronds above their heads; the steady, muffled roll of the breakers; the occasional shrill cry of the gulls. And over all, the soft sound of Kay's voice.

"We moved to St. Thomas when Lisa was six. She was born in the States, but she's practically a native Virgin Islander. Fred, my first husband, was a lawyer, and he got a job offer with a firm down here. He's gone now. Five years ago. He was flying over to Puerto Rico. A business trip. Well, Lisa looks like her father, and she got her red hair and green eyes from both of us, and she has his brains, thank God! The three of us had such a wonderful time together at Cliffhanger."

"Cliffhanger," the girl echoed.

Kay laughed. "Oh, wait till you see it! It really is the most gorgeous house in the world. Anyway, three years ago I met Adam Prescott, who'd just arrived here. He was kind and attentive and wouldn't take no for an answer. You know the type: rich playboy-dash-sportsman, spectacularly handsome, divorced, et cetera. We were thrown together, actually, by a well-meaning friend of mine who's a bit of a yenta. You'll meet Trish, I expect. She's a doll. So, Reader, I married him, as Charlotte Brontë once observed. He moved in with us at Cliffhanger, and the last three years have been a damn sight better than the time right after Fred was . . . anyway, Adam has a sailboat, and I'm active with the local Arts Council. I also play bridge two nights a week. People on this island give a lot of parties, and we're expected to give them, too.

"That's where Sandra of Hollywood came in. I realized that with Adam and me out and about so much, Lisa was spending too much time home alone. She has her little friends from school, of course, but even so . . . I advertised locally. 'Young woman, responsible, educated, suitable,' tra la la. You should have seen some of the responses I got! An inordinate number of the young people on this island—I don't mean natives, we're talking Statesiders—well, we used to call them hippies, but I guess I'm dating myself. Anyway, I settled on Sandra, and she and her lifetime subscription to *People* magazine joined the ménage. Now I need someone to replace her, and I can't bring myself to run another ad. I shudder to think, right? Then, the other day I saw you here on the beach, painting. I said to myself, 'Now, there's a presentable young lady with a decent background.' So, there you have it. Fade to Black, as Sandra would undoubtedly say."

She looked over at the younger woman, trying to gauge whether it was working. Hard to tell, really. The girl lay on her chaise, casually playing with the straw in her drink. At last she raised her eyes to Kay.

"Adam Prescott," she said slowly, as if trying the name on for size.

Kay forged ahead. "Oh, he's great! I wonder where our lives would be without him. He's so very *capable*, you know, as some men are. I'm very fond of him. My life now is extremely pleasant."

34

The younger woman nodded, thinking that it didn't sound very much like love. . . .

Kay leaned forward.

"Doesn't sound much like love, does it?" she said, startling the girl, causing a deep red flush to suffuse her face. "Well, my dear, it is. I—I love him. Not the same as Fred, of course, but I suppose we only get one Fred in a lifetime." She stopped suddenly, watching the other woman. "Why am I going on like this? I barely know you, and here I am—I don't seem to mind at all talking to you about my most—"

They regarded each other.

Kay smiled and said, "I'd like it very much, Diana, if you could take my offer. Even if it's just on a trial basis. You'll think about it, won't you?"

There was a long pause as each woman assessed the situation. Kay had no way of knowing what the girl was thinking. The girl sat in silence for a while, looking down at the backs of her hands as they rested on the arms of her chaise. Kay noticed the glint of sunlight on the tiny, pale hairs of her forearm. Odd, she thought. Brunettes are forever bleaching or dyeing or otherwise lightening their hair, but this girl seems, for some reason, to have gone the other way. . . .

The girl spoke suddenly, drawing Kay's focus from her dark hair to her face.

"Okay, how about this: why don't you have me over to your house? I'd like to meet Lisa and see how she and I feel about each other before I commit us both to anything. I'm here at Bolongo for another six days. Any day is fine with me."

"Good," Kay said. "How about dinner tomorrow night?"

The girl considered this. Then she said, "Fine."

It was arranged. Six o'clock the following evening. Directions to the house. Dress casual. Dinner at seven.

The sun was beginning to disappear when Kay finally left the young woman and took off for home to tell Adam and Lisa the wonderful news.

"Good-bye, Diana," she called back as she went. "I'm glad I finally got up the courage to approach you. See you tomorrow."

The young woman watched as Kay strode up the beach, past the pool and out of sight. Then she nodded to herself.

Yes. It was apparently going to be easier than she'd expected.

Much easier. . . .

TWO

WEDNESDAY, AUGUST 7

HE WAS THINKING about the plan. He always felt this rush of exultation in the time, the days and weeks, just before. Soon, he thought. Soon. . . .

The water glistened ahead of him and sparkled in his wake. The crisp, clean breeze whipped through his white-gold hair. He was rolling smoothly across the surface of the Atlantic. Stretching his massive frame luxuriously to its full, towering height, the wheel grasped firmly in his powerful hands, he looked up at the gulls circling above: stark white against blue. This was freedom; perfect, suspended, unquestioned. This regal isolation, where only he was God, away from the prying eyes and probing questions of mortals. Heaven. Only him, alone.

"Hey, Adam! How about another brew?"

Well, not exactly alone. The wild, abandoned feeling

was swept away, Paradise lost, in the boiling white foam behind.

He turned his face from the gorgeous horizon to confront the prosaic, eminently negligible visage of Stuart Harriman. Or what was visible of it, at any rate: the round, pink, woodchuck face was currently graced by dark sunglasses and a streak of Noskote on the bulbous pug snout. The neck, as thick as the bald head, disappeared inside a floral island shirt of screaming red, yellow, and green. He was holding up a frosted can in his thick, sausage-link fingers. God, he was ugly!

"No, thanks," Adam growled, forcing himself to smile. Stu Harriman was Kay's bridge partner—his entree into Adam's domain. Kay had insisted that Adam take Stu and his wife, Brenda—another beauty!—for what she called a "spin." He glanced over at Mrs. Harriman, sitting in the stern with his young mate, Kyle. She, of course, was sipping daintily from a can of Diet Coke, smiling at Kyle, at Adam, at the water, at everything. The woman never stopped smiling. Her industrial-sized muumuu matched her husband's shirt. Looking from one to the other of them, Adam decided that the husband was slightly better looking than the wife.

They came about, and Kyle jumped up to secure the sail for the new tack. The boom had swung to starboard, missing Stu's head by inches. Watching the man duck, Adam smiled grimly to himself.

"Oooh!" squealed Brenda.

"Damn near got me that time!" squealed her husband. Kyle caught Adam's eye, grinned, and, as usual, said nothing. He sat next to the dreadful Brenda, calmly smoking one of his inevitable cigarettes. He was a quiet young man, strong and efficient. A perfect mate, really. Adam was glad to have him aboard. His former assistant, Greg, had been a chatterer. Well, don't think about *that*, Adam cautioned himself. This was Kyle's sixth week living and working on the boat, and he was quite an improvement on Greg. In every way.

Adam took the sloop out at least twice a week. Day sails. He was always home in time for dinner; Kay insisted on that. But now, after nearly three years, he still looked forward to being alone, but for a mate, out on the water. Of course, Kay frequently tagged along. She enjoyed sailing, being out on the ocean with him, and she had taken a great liking to Kyle. She'd even invited him to dinner at the house several times. She'd never cared for the vociferous Greg, whose language, more often than not, had bespoken his profession as a man of the sea.

The *Kay* had been her wedding gift to him. He, in turn, had paid for their three-month honeymoon in Europe. The cost, he figured, had been about the same. All those museums and cathedrals and opera houses. Skiing in Gstaad, exploring the Greek islands, walking all over every major city and tiny village on the continent—the woman's energy was limitless. Well, he reflected, it had actually been rather fun. . . .

He checked his Rado—another present from the bountiful Kay. Three-thirty. Time to think about turning back. He could shower and change at the clubhouse and be home by six, as instructed. A guest for dinner. A nice young artist, Kay had told him, whom she'd run into at Bolongo. A new companion for Lisa.

He smiled.

That last one, what was her name? Sandra. Sandy. Like the dog in the funnies. Arf, to say the least. And all that crap about the movies! Adam had little use for films. Eastwood was okay. Schwarzenegger. Chuck Norris. The rest of them could all go take a flying leap.

The plan . . .

He gripped the wheel, trying to suppress another rising thrill of exhilaration. When that didn't work, he forced himself to concentrate on the present. The Harrimans. Oh, God!

Adam sighed: time to head back. He turned to his young mate.

"Prepare to come about," he called.

Kyle immediately threw his cigarette overboard and snapped to attention.

Adam liked that.

"But my dear! I mean, who *is* she?"

"Oh, Trish, don't carry on so. She's a perfectly nice young woman."

"You're taking her into your *house*, Kay. Putting her with Lisa. Shouldn't you ask for *references* or something? You don't know a *thing* about her."

"What's to know? Really, Trish, give me a little credit here. She's staying at Bolongo. The vacation is a gift from her mother. She's an artist. From New York. She went to *Harvard*, for Heaven's sake! She's One Of Us."

Patricia Manning settled her ultrathin model's body more comfortably on the white wrought-iron patio chair, ran red-lacquered, two-inch nails querulously through her short black hair, and fixed her friend with a look that all but shouted her wisdom in these matters. When she finally came up with a suitably devastating retort, she enunciated each word slowly and carefully, as if she were addressing the town bellringer.

"Darling, Lizzie Borden was One Of Us, and I've no doubt she went to all the right *schools!*"

Kay turned from the low gray driftwood fence that ran along the edge of the cliff next to the house and confronted the other woman.

"Lizzie Borden was middle-class at best," she announced. "Besides, it was never proved that she did anything in the first place!"

Trish rolled her impeccably mascaraed eyes and reached up with a bangled hand to play distractedly with the gold pendant on her modest bosom.

"I'll be sure to tell that to the police," she sighed, "when they exhume your remains." She fell back against the chair, the Great Friend who had Done Her Duty.

"You do that, darling," Kay replied, turning back to the view.

The cliff on which the house was situated jutted out into space, surrounded on three sides by a seemingly endless expanse of ocean. Off to the right, past the large resort hotel on the next point, the capital city of Charlotte Amalie rose dramatically out of the harbor. The tiny distant buildings were mere dots and smudges of white and pastel tones, red- and silver-roofed, against a field of vivid emerald green. The greatest concentration of hazy shapes was in the downtown shopping area, just at the water's edge. From there the spots of color thinned, fanning out in all directions: west, toward the airport; east, toward the less-populated "country" outside the city limits; and upward, toward the top of Signal Hill, the island's highest point, looming majestically some fifteen hundred feet above the exact center of the waterfront town, a bright green silhouette against the azure sky. The mountain dominated all: a huge, benevolent giant placed there by God to watch over and protect the little city crouching at its feet.

That's what Kay always imagined it to be, regarding it from this remote perspective. The sight of the city—far away across the harbor, yet oddly close at hand—never failed to instill in her a feeling of security, especially in the two years she'd lived here as a widow, alone with her daughter. However isolated this house was above the sheer, hundred-foot drop to jagged rocks and churning sea, she need only look over at the town to know that she shared this magic isle with fifty thousand others, not to mention the constant stream of tourists.

Kay and her friend turned at the same time, their attention drawn by the pretty twelve-year-old girl who came out of the house through the sliding glass doors from the living room. The child ran lightly across the redwood deck that hung, invisibly supported, over the void, and jumped down the two steps to the flagstone patio. She rushed up, breathless, to the two women.

"Is she here yet?" she cried, unable to contain her excitement at the prospect of new friendship.

Kay laughed and dropped her arm over the girl's shoulders.

"Not yet, darling. In about an hour. Whatever happened to 'hello'?"

"Sorry. Hullo, Mommy. Hullo, Aunt Trish."

"Really, Lisa," her mother admonished. "You'd think you didn't have anyone in the world who cared about you! You have me, in case you've forgotten. And Aunt Trish. And your dad."

Lisa made a face.

"You mean Adam," she said. "He's *not* my dad. And you guys are never around much, anyway."

"Lisa!"

"Well, it's true," the child insisted.

Trish, her languor instantly forgotten, assessed this new situation and found it too tense for her liking.

"Just look at the pair of you!" she gushed in her very best Auntie Mame. "All that incredible red hair! The last time I saw that hair, it was on Piper Laurie."

They both knew the answer to that one. In perfect unison, mother and daughter supplied the punch line.

"What was she doing with our hair?"

They laughed. Trish, not to be outdone, winked lasciviously.

"Making love," she murmured. "With Paul Newman, if memory serves."

Kay clamped her hands over Lisa's ears in mock horror. "Trish! Not in front of the child!"

Lisa shrugged the hands away and grinned up at them. "Who's Piper Laurie?" she asked.

Trish reached over and patted the girl's milk-white, freckled face.

"A beautiful movie star," she said. "Almost as beautiful as you."

Lisa giggled.

"Oh, God!" Kay cried. "More movie stars. We're all beginning to sound like Sandra!"

She smiled, first at her friend and then at her daughter. She leaned down and kissed the child's flaming red hair, the gift from both her parents.

The patio outside the clubhouse was shaped like the prow of a ship cutting proudly through the sand, ringed by incongruous midocean palms and sea-grape trees. There was even a mast rising up, flying all the usual nautical flags. The cars in the parking lot formed a multicolored, metallic wake. The building itself was the cabin of the imaginary vessel. Adam shook his head in disgust. Jesus, he thought. The S.S. *Wishful Thinking*.

He strode into the lobby of the club and looked around. Fairly crowded for a weekday. If the building was a phony craft, this was its phony crew. Overweight, middle-aged men and women lounging on luxurious couches among marble-topped coffee tables and potted bonsai trees. Wicker ceiling fans rotating lazily above, gently stirring the conditioned air. Sailing togs everywhere—striped, boat-necked jerseys, gum-soled decktop shoes, braided white skipper's caps. One face-lifted, siliconed hag even sported a pinafore over her all-too-revealing string bikini. They lay back in plush comfort, conversing softly, clinking the ice in their tall frosted glasses. Home are the rich, bored, drunken sailors, home from the sea. Ha! The closest any of these losers ever got to a yacht was this yacht *club*! A schooner, as far as they were concerned, was something you served beer in.

There were smiles and waves from every part of the room. Oh, sure. If they couldn't be sailors, they could at least pretend to *know* one. Adam gave them all a general smile and wave as he made his way toward the hallway that led to the changing rooms. He just wanted to get out of this haven for rich, white wannabe yachtsmen as quickly as possible. He'd kept his distance from them as much as he could, but Kay was a joiner: the bridge club, the arts club, the beach club, the yacht club. Many of these creatures were her friends, and they assumed— mistakenly—that they were his friends as well. Adam prided himself on his ability to make people like him, even as he despised them. These people weren't sailors: the real sailors were out sailing, for God's sake, not posing in the clubhouse with Bloody Marys in their fists.

Two bikini-clad young women—the only young ones in the place—passed by him on their way out to the beach, smiling and giggling together as they caught his attention. He swiveled to watch their receding forms as they went out onto the deck. With a long, appreciative sigh, he turned his eyes away.

As he crossed the room he noticed the Harrimans, who'd arrived from the beach ahead of him, plunking their

overstuffed bodies down on an overstuffed sofa and calling for drinkie-poos. Brenda's expression: drinkie-poos. He
waved good-bye to them and headed for the showers.

He almost made it. As he passed the last couch, he saw
Jack Breen rise from his place between Nancy Breen, his
wife, and Barbara Conroy, his alleged mistress, and barge
toward him.

"Adam Prescott, you old spotted dog!" he bellowed in
his hearty, alcoholic basso. "Back from the briny? Beautiful out there today, eh? Goddamn baby's ass! How's that
new mate of yours working out?"

Adam steeled himself for inevitable boredom and
grinned. "Just fine, Jack. Thank you for introducing us."

The man winked. "Least I could do, matey. Didn't want
to see you in drydock after that other one took off.
Whozis—Greg. Ever find out what happened to him?"

"Uh, no," Adam replied, leaning slightly backward to
avoid the hot breath: beer and onion dip. "He just seems
to have disappeared. You know how these young guys
are—probably signed up with some pretty headed down
the island chain. He mentioned that he'd like to see more
of this part of the world."

Jack nodded, jabbing Adam a little too hard in the ribs.
"There's probably a woman in it somewhere. Some heiress
with a big boat, lookin' for a strapping lad to play captain.
Oh, to be young again, eh?"

"Yeah," Adam said. "That sounds about right. I wouldn't
doubt it, knowing Greg."

"Can I stand you to a beer?" Jack boomed, shoving his
mug a little too close to Adam's face.

"No, thanks. Got to get home." Adam patted Jack's shoulder, a little too hard, and moved on.

"See ya, mate," Jack shouted after him. "Say hello to Kay for me!" He plunked himself back down between his wife and his very close friend and reached for the dip.

Adam practically ran down the hall to the locker room.

The young woman pulled back the clear plastic curtain adorned with comical blue and lavender fishes swimming among rampant streamers of green seaweed, and stepped out of the tub. The hot shower had been to steady her nerves, and she had let it go on for much too long. A small, discreet note above the sink requested that, due to the premium on water in this part of the world, guests' showers be as brief as possible.

She stood naked before the foggy mirror in the steamy bathroom, inspecting her handiwork. Was everything perfect? It had better be. . . . She reached up with her hand and cleared a patch of the glass. She went through the now-familiar routine with the eyes and leaned in very close to check them. Yes . . . yes, they would do. A hand reached up to unravel the turban from the wet hair. The towel dropped to the floor.

Yes. Perfect.

She regarded the face, the slender neck, the wide shoulders and firm, round breasts. Imagine, she thought: imagine being less than beautiful. It would never have worked. None of this would have been possible. Thinking of her parents, she admitted to herself that her beauty had been inevitable, a foregone conclusion.

No, she decided. Better *not* to think of her parents. Not now, at any rate. . . .

She would wear the little black dress. It was a daring move—a lot of leg and a lot of cleavage. But after a thorough search through all the clothes she'd brought to the island, it seemed the strongest choice. The red sheath was too much, the peach silk not enough, and the blue suit made her look like an airline hostess. Slacks would be wrong, she felt, and jeans were out of the question. When Kay Prescott said "casual," she was not referring to jeans. That left the pleated navy skirt and ruffled white blouse— Gidget Goes To St. Thomas—or the black cocktail dress. She'd brought one other garment with her, but it was hardly appropriate; she was saving it for a special occasion. So, the black it was, with her hair up and a single string of pearls.

She wasn't the sort of woman who normally cared much about clothing, but tonight was special. Very special. She couldn't just look all right; tonight she had to look sensational.

Nodding slowly to herself, she reached for the blow-dryer.

The hot, soothing spray pounded into Adam's flesh. He could feel every muscle, every fiber of his being loosen, relax, release all tension. He never experienced what could be called stress: he had long ago conditioned his body and mind to ignore those particular impulses. That was the road to heart conditions, high blood pressure, ulcers—all those ridiculous weaknesses he would not allow himself. They were the province of the ordinary.

He stepped out of the shower and walked across the white-tiled locker room, drying his body as he went. He paused before the full-length mirror next to his locker.

He was forty-seven years old. He stood six feet five inches tall and weighed 225—and every ounce of it muscle. Well, okay, not every ounce, but more than most. His platinum hair was full and long, with barely a sign of thinning. The most magnificent-looking young man anyone in Farnsworth, Minnesota, had ever seen was actually improving with age.

Age: it was the thing he feared most. Hell, he thought with a wry smile, it was practically his *only* fear. One day, he knew, the advancing years would catch up with him. He would feel it in his joints and organs as the muscle and sinew he had so carefully nurtured started to weaken. His arms and legs and chest would lose their present definition and begin to sag. Well, there was only one way to face that eventuality: with a great deal of money. More than he had now. He would go wealthy, if not gentle, into that good night.

He reached into his locker and took out the clothes he would wear to dinner. Clean socks and underwear, white linen slacks, and his favorite shirt. Crisp, long-sleeved pink cotton with the monogram AP on the pocket. It was quite old, actually, but this particular shade looked good on him. Regarding the monogram, he thought about his name: Adam. He liked it. It was appropriately dramatic, appropriately large. The first person; the father of the world; the ultimate symbol of manhood.

He was pulling on his slacks when Kyle entered the room. The young man went over to a bench, sat down, and removed his sneakers.

"Hi," Adam called, grinning. "I see we've both survived the Harrimans."

"Only just," Kyle muttered as he pulled his tank top over his head. He stood up and dropped his cutoffs.

"Sorry about that," Adam said. "Kay's idea, not mine."

"Yeah." Kyle nodded, stepping out of his underpants.

Adam looked over at the young man and spoke in a conciliatory tone. "Are you free the day after tomorrow? I'll make it up to you. We could go over to St. John. No Harrimans, I promise. I'll bring the beer."

Kyle met the other man's piercing gaze. Then, blushing, he turned away.

"Sure," he said, heading for the shower. "Sounds great."

Adam watched him go. The broad shoulders, the dark chestnut tan on smooth young skin, the white strip of loins and buttocks where bathing suits blocked out the sun. Beautiful, he thought. A body the equal of mine. The body of a twenty-two-year-old.

He listened as Kyle turned on the water. Then he picked up his wallet, removed two fifty-dollar bills, and walked across the room. He tucked the money into the pocket of Kyle's shorts. He'd already paid him for the day, but this was for the extra labor of putting up with Stu and Brenda. He went back to his locker, smiling at the thought of Kyle—later tonight, perhaps, in some pub with his young friends—reaching into the pocket and discovering his serendipity.

He whistled softly to himself as he slowly buttoned the monogrammed pink shirt.

The young woman was negotiating the winding, bumpy route to Kay Prescott's house in her rented car. To keep calm, she concentrated on the myraid flowering trees and plants that seemed to line every road on this island. Red, white, purple, yellow. More red, a particularly large flower hanging heavily from dark green bushes: hibiscus. The purple ones were frangipani. Soon, she thought, I must try my hand at painting them.

Consulting Kay's hastily jotted instructions, she slowed as she reached the left-hand turnoff. A long, narrow gravel drive wound up a wooded hill to disappear beyond a thicket of palm trees. She glanced at the identical brass plaques that adorned the pillars on both sides of the entrance to the drive. The name of the estate was printed in Roman capitals.

She hesitated for only a moment between the stone pillars, her foot pressing firmly on the brake. Then, taking a long, deep breath, she slid the foot over to the accelerator. The pillars glided by, receded.

She was in.

One sharp turn, then another. After that the gravel road straightened, and the way stretched ahead of her in a steep uphill gradient. At the top of this hill would be the cliff, and the house that she had until now only imagined.

What would it be like? she wondered. What would *they*

be like? Would she be welcomed into this home, entrusted with the child, accepted? She'd have to actually *live* here with them: the fact, assimilated long ago as a given, suddenly become real, immediate. She was here now, going through with it. She would live, reside, dwell—

Dwell. "Rather would I dwell . . ."—what the hell was that? Oh, yes: *Antigone.* One of her favorites. She'd recited it in a class at school. Her wicked uncle, the king, had declared her dead brother to be a war criminal. A law had been passed forbidding anyone from burying Polynices in sacred ground, but Antigone defied the proclamation. He was her brother, and they were the children of Oedipus; that was all that mattered to her. Family. . . .

She'd worn a sheet that was supposed to be a toga, and lined her eyes with kohl. Her defiance, her contempt, her hatred had filled her voice with outrage, resounding through the classroom.

" 'Rather would I dwell in the house of mine enemy,' " she'd cried, " 'than honor such an edict. . . .' "

Appropriate, she thought as she drove up the hill and rounded the final curve. The car burst from under the blanket of trees into dazzling sunlight, into the huge clearing. And there it was, at last.

Her first impression of the enormous building before her was of white stucco walls and huge expanses of plate glass, all gleaming in the sun. Sliding doors and picture windows: the architect had taken full advantage of the panoramic view. A large, flat roof, perfect for catching precious rain to add to the water supply. The giant tamarind in the center of the circular driveway, with a beige Land Rover and a beautiful white Mercedes resting in its ample shade. The riot of flowers and the wide carpets of freshly mown grass that rolled away on either side. The house, the lawn, the trees; and beyond them the precipice, and the water stretching out to the far horizon, and behind and around and above it all—up, up as far as she could see—the endless, breathtaking deep-blue sky.

It couldn't be real. No such place could truly exist. Not on this planet.

She parked in the circle, behind the Mercedes, and got out of the car. She stood for a moment regarding the edifice before her, willing her heart to slow its wild pace and her fists to slacken at her sides. Then, resigning herself to whatever was about to happen, she walked across the cobbled path to the front door. This is it, she thought. Here I am.

Cliffhanger.

The sleek red Nissan 300 ZX flashed along the rough country roads on its way home. Adam would not have chosen so bright a shade, but then again, this was not his car. Ostensibly, yes: he had the use of it. But the Nissan, like the *Kay*, had been a gift. The red, she'd told him, matched her hair, and whenever he drove the car he was to think of her.

He remembered her laughter as she'd said that. It was a light laugh, a happy sound. He'd heard it since, of course. Too often.

He frowned as he drove, keeping the speedometer at a

steady, illegal seventy-five. One couldn't christen automobiles as one did vessels. It hardly mattered: the color would serve to remind him that nothing in his life right now truly belonged to him.

That house. She'd lived there with her first husband, for Christ's sake, and *she* had been the one to come up with its cutesy name.

Cliffhanger. The *Kay*. The red-headed Nissan. Everything was Kay's.

But not for long, he thought, downshifting as he came over the last rise before the turnoff that led up the driveway to the house. Oh, no, most definitely not for long! Something was going to change all that, and soon.

The plan. . . .

With a little smile at the corners of his lips that widened as he drove, he turned the car off the main road and glided through the stone pillars with the name emblazoned in brass upon them. The red sports car carried him a very long way that August afternoon, further than he could have imagined—up the winding, palm-lined drive and into history. A history of sorts: the plan, as he called it; the scandal, as others would call it; the series of events that would later come to be known and whispered of as "that Cliffhanger business" by people—local and otherwise—who still have difficulty believing it.

THREE

WEDNESDAY, AUGUST 7
(CONTINUED)

TRISH LIKED HER immediately. At the same time, though, she was aware of that little warning bell that always sounded in her mind whenever there was a prospect of Trouble.

They had heard the car pulling up, and a few moments later Nola had brought the lovely young woman out to join them on the patio next to the sundeck. Trish made the usual automatic note of the pearls (real), the hair (dyed, but becoming), the scent (Bal à Versailles), and the black dress (Alaïa, *definitely*). Big brown eyes, gorgeous figure, sexy as all get-out.

Trouble.

"Lisa, Trish," Kay said, "this is Diana Meissen."

The young woman smiled at Trish, then turned to the

child. "Hello, Lisa. I've been looking forward to meeting you."

"Hi," Lisa replied, a warm blush darkening her cheeks. "Gosh, you're pretty! Can I call you Diana?"

"Of course."

"I'm twelve. How old are you?"

"Lisa!" Kay cried.

The young woman laughed and sat down on a wrought-iron love-seat. "I just turned twenty-six, in April."

Lisa plopped down beside her. "Aries?"

"Why, yes."

"Wow!" Lisa screamed. "Aries women are the strongest in the zodiac! 'Self-sufficient, single-minded of purpose.' That's what it says in my Linda Goodman. I wish *I* was an Aries, but I'm a Leo. August twenty-second." She frowned, letting God and the world know what she thought of Leo.

"But you're the lioness," the young woman told her. "Most dignified, most graceful, and most popular. I'll bet you're an athlete. I'll bet you're the best female athlete at Antilles School."

Trish noticed Kay's surprised reaction.

"How did you know—" she began before Lisa cut her off.

"Yes! You read Linda Goodman, too!"

"Wouldn't read anyone else! August twenty-second. Hmmm. Your birthday is in two weeks. We'll have to do something about that." She caught Kay's eye and winked. Kay smiled.

That clinched it, as far as Trish could see. This one wasn't a movie nut, boring the kid to death with the latest lies about Meryl Streep. This one was on Lisa's wavelength, and the child was already in love. So, for that matter, was Kay.

And that, Trish realized was the Trouble. Hell even *I* like her! Three down, one to go.

Adam.

She was aware that Kay and her other friends regarded her as a somewhat frivolous woman: rich, snobbish, a bit self-centered and pampered. True, all of it. But Trish was no fool when it came to men. Unless, of course, they were men she was in love with. She could number two important politicians, an Oscar-winning actor, a bullfighter, and a Peer of the Realm among the males who had broken her heart. But she was not now, nor had she ever been, in love with Adam Prescott. Unfortunately, Trish had not seen through his initial charm quickly enough. Now, in retrospect, she regretted ever having introduced him to Kay. Well, the damage was done, and it was no longer any of her business. . . .

Even as she was thinking this, the roar of a small, powerful car reached them on the patio. A door slammed, and Adam appeared around the side of the house and came across the lawn toward them.

"Hello," he called. "I figured you'd all be out here." He bounded over to Kay and kissed her lightly on the lips. Then he kissed Trish on the cheek and winked at Lisa. "Hi, baby."

"Hullo," Lisa whispered, not meeting his gaze.

Trish watched with great interest as he at last turned his attention to the new female in his vicinity. The girl stood up, and he presented himself before her. There was, it seemed to Trish, a frozen fraction of a second as they confronted each other.

"How do you do?" he said. "I'm Adam Prescott."

"Diana Meissen," she replied, extending her left hand.

They shook. Then, Trish noticed, he produced his most dazzling, heart-stopping grin.

"Welcome to Cliffhanger, Ms. Meissen."

The girl grinned, too. "Please call me Diana."

Trish looked around at them all. The child, her enthusiasm gone, was gazing out over the water. Kay stood there, smiling her Mistress of Cliffhanger smile, that vacuous expression of those silly women in television commercials who tell you what to use on your kitchen floors. And Adam and the beautiful Diana were grinning at each other.

Oh, yes, Trish thought as she reached for her cocktail. Trouble.

It was the most beautiful house the young woman had ever seen. If she concentrated on that, perhaps her heartbeat would return to normal.

The sun was just setting behind the hills on the other side of the harbor when Kay offered to take her on a tour. She followed the woman up onto the sundeck, the now-faithful Lisa at her side. The native housekeeper, Nola, was setting five places at a table on the deck. The white linen tablecloth was held down by a large, old-fashioned gas lamp in its center, surrounded by a mound of freshly picked tropical flowers. Two torches, one on the wall of the house next to the sliding glass doors and one in a sconce at the corner of the deck railing, whipped and fluttered in the light late-afternoon trade wind. She stared at the torches and the flowers and the gleaming cutlery, then turned around to face the view. She gasped.

Her paintbox held no such colors. The sun was barely visible on the skyline, and the air above and around it was pale lemon and peach. The next layer emanating outward was deep orange and cherry red. Then, extending up and out in all directions, came the shades she remembered from the labels of the tubes, yet so much richer, so much more *alive*: magenta, puce, violet, blue-violet. To the east, in the direction of St. John, the farthest reaches from the sun were already a deep indigo. In moments, she'd heard, there would be a brief, legendary flash of green, but you had to watch closely for it. Then this awesome spectrum would melt away, leaving the entire canvas a deep, velvety black.

Kay led her through the doors into the living room. Almost everything here was white and driftwood gray: the stucco walls and archways at either side; the white leather-covered couches and chairs around the glass-topped, black wrought-iron coffee table; the white area rugs tossed artfully about the gray terrazzo floor; the pale-gray bookshelves and home entertainment center; and the paneled foyer that led to the front door. The two side walls were covered with several large modern paintings, one of which she recognized as a Miró, and every table and shelf was accented with local carvings and statuettes of dark, shiny mahogany. Everything else, front and back, was glass. The huge invisible wall before her afforded a view of the front drive, the tamarind tree, and the forest beyond; behind her, the glass exposed the ocean. She looked up: in the center of the white-beamed, twenty-foot-high ceiling hung an enormous black wrought-iron chandelier, with more than a dozen curved branches all ending in flickering bulbs. The same color metal formed the banister of the staircase against the wall to her left, which led up to bedrooms. Under the stairs was an archway that led to Kay and Adam's suite.

"The house was built thirty years ago," Kay said, "by a retired couple named Harbinger. Harbinger—isn't that perfect? Samuel and Clara. They're buried on the cliff just inside the woods at the far end of the patio. He died about fifteen years ago, and she remained here alone until her death, shortly before Fred and I came to St. Thomas. Their daughter lives in the States, and she had no interest in the place, so she sold it to us. We thought it was so romantic: the life-long lovers resting together on the cliff, overlooking the Caribbean." She paused a moment before adding, "Fred's buried there, near them, a little farther along the cliff. For all I know, Adam and I may end up there as well. He doesn't have any living relatives, and I have no intention of spending eternity in that awful family mausoleum in Greenwich! Oh, well, there'll be time to think about all that. Let me show you the rest of the house."

To their right, a swinging gray door opened into the ultramodern kitchen where Nola bustled about, preparing their meal. It was a gorgeous arrangement of wood hues:

chestnut parquet floor, blond butcher-block counters, natural wicker breakfast table and chairs. The walls were of red brick, and everywhere on them hung glinting brass pots and pans. Beyond the kitchen, she was told, were the pantry, the utility room, and the garage at the corner of the house nearest to the patio.

Kay led her back into the main room and over to the large door between the kitchen and the sundeck. This opened into a lovely paneled room with a large mahogany desk, brown leather furniture, and a beautiful Oriental carpet in a pattern of deep reds and blues. Hundreds of books lined the walls, and in one corner stood a baby grand piano.

"Office," Kay said. "Den. Library. Music room, though none of us plays the piano. It only seems to get used at parties. Do you play?"

"No, not really," the young woman replied.

The master suite on the other side of the living room was as pink as the kitchen and the den were brown. A chintz flower-print spread and canopy dominated the king-size bed. The walls, carpet, and dressing-table skirt were the palest carnation. Doors led to two huge walk-in closets and two marble bathrooms, his and hers.

Lisa ran ahead as Kay led her up the stairs to the second floor. Through an archway was a short hall, glass on one side looking out over the driveway, with four doors on the other side. The first was Lisa's room, a riot of dolls, unsheathed compact disks, discarded clothes, and posters of rock stars, George Michael the heartthrob of the moment. The cluttered, delightful mess elicited a stifled moan from her mother, who quickly closed the door on it and continued down the hall. Next were two large, beautiful guest bedrooms, both in different patterns of white and green, each dominated by a huge mahogany four-poster bed. The final door was hers.

From the moment she stepped into the small, simply but tastefully appointed blue bedroom, with its comfortable double bed, its private bathroom, and its sliding glass door leading out to a tiny balcony with a glorious ocean view, she knew that everything was going to be all right. She could stay here, in this room and in this house, with these people, for as long as it would take. She looked around a moment, nodding to herself, aware that the woman and her daughter were watching her from the doorway.

"Lovely," she said.

Kay Prescott smiled and led them back down the stairs.

"I like the white leather," she told her hostess, running her fingers along the top of a couch.

"Thank you," Kay said. "Of course, it's very practical. For a very good reason. There's still one member of the household you haven't met."

She nodded to her daughter, who grinned, filled her lungs, and shouted, *"Jumbi!"*

Almost immediately, the kitchen door swung toward them and an enormous black and tan German shepherd bounded into the living room and over to Lisa. It leapt up at her, all dripping tongue and wagging tail, emitting little whimpers of joy as the child reached out for a hug.

"This," Kay said, "is Jumbi. She's been with us since—

well, let's see, she's six now. She was originally Fred's pet. Fred named her that, after the creatures of West Indian folklore. You know, mischievous little sprites that terrorize the local populace. This Jumbi is hardly sinister: she's a teddy bear with most people. She lives in the garage, or at least she's supposed to. But I suspect that Certain People smuggle her up to their bedrooms more often than not. I name no names."

She didn't have to. Dog and child were clearly inseparable. Lisa turned to their guest. "Go ahead. Pet her, Diana."

The young woman smiled and stepped forward, her left hand extended.

And froze.

The animal whipped her head around toward the newcomer. Baring evil-looking fangs, she fixed the woman with a gaze of pure hatred and uttered a long, low growl.

Slowly, carefully, the young woman withdrew her hand and stepped backward.

"I don't think Jumbi likes me," she said with a soft, nervous giggle.

"No," Kay agreed. "How strange. You're only the second person I've ever known who causes that reaction in her."

At that moment, Trish and Adam came through the doors from the deck to join them.

"I think dinner should be just about—" Adam began.

He stopped short in the doorway, staring. When he spoke again, it was in a firm, angry voice.

"Get that animal out of here. *Now!*"

After a moment of uncomfortable silence, Lisa frowned

in disgust and led the unrepentant Jumbi out to the garage beyond the kitchen.

The woman named Trish was watching her with obvious interest, and she saw Kay give her husband an annoyed glance. She stood very still, willing her heart to stop pounding. Jumbi. *Great.*

Then Adam grinned, breaking the spell and restoring order, and Nola appeared at the kitchen door to announce that dinner was served.

She barely made it through the meal.

It was sumptuous, or so she supposed. There certainly was enough of it. The courses arrived endlessly: cantaloupe soup; watercress and tomato salad; some type of small local shellfish, the name of which she missed. Roast lamb was the star of the evening, with oven-browned potatoes, homemade mint sauce, and something that Kay introduced as Nola's specialty. It was a native dish called kalaloo, which seemed to consist mainly of spinach, okra, and bits of pork, and it was probably delicious. She somehow remembered—in her breathless, tingling, nauseated attempt at eating—to compliment Nola. But it didn't really matter what was put in front of her: most of it was cleared away untouched.

If Kay or anyone else noticed her lack of appetite, nothing was mentioned. Everyone smiled and chatted pleasantly in low, civilized voices. At least two wines were offered, white for the shellfish and red for the meat, which helped to keep the party going. Trish fired off several one-liners that were presumably amusing, judging from the laughter of the others. Even Lisa seemed to be having a good time, something rare for a child among grown-ups. The young woman observed them all as a stranger would—as if through binoculars, or from another table. Their words did not always reach her ears: she had yet to orient herself to the whistling wind and the ceaseless, rhythmic crashing of the waves against the rocks a hundred feet directly below her chair.

At last her uneaten compote of island fruits was whisked away from in front of her, and her hostess rose, announcing coffee and cordials in the living room. She followed the others in through the glass doors and settled herself on a couch across from Kay and Adam, with Lisa once again at her elbow. Kay poured demitasse, and she was handed a tiny goblet of something-or-other that was excruciatingly sweet and tasted like chocolate. The witty banter continued for another hour.

She felt, all the while, as if she would scream. She was aware of it welling up inside her and pushing at the back of her throat, and it was only by clenching her teeth tightly together that she kept the cry from escaping. Predinner cocktails, two wines, cordial: nothing could make her relax, or cause this first-night assault of terror to abate. Surely they must all be aware that she had barely eaten, barely spoken, barely *breathed*. But on they went, clearly oblivious.

Slowly, during the course of the final part of the evening, the panic began to subside. She knew, in the rational part of her mind, that this would only happen once. After tonight it would be easier. For how long had she been planning it? Now was no time to fall apart and ruin everything, before she'd even officially begun. No: she would get through this. She *must*.

With a charming smile, she looked her quarry directly in the eyes and asked for another drink.

"So, Diana," Adam inquired, "how do you like St. Thomas?"

"Oh, it's beautiful. I've never seen anything quite like it. Of course, I've only been here for ten days. Perhaps the spell will wear off soon, and I'll take it all for granted."

Adam raised his Courvoisier in the girl's direction.

"Beauty," he said, "is something we should never take for granted."

For a brief moment their eyes met. Then she looked away.

Everyone smiled and murmured the usual noises of agreement. Everyone but Trish, he noticed as he surveyed them all. She was staring down into her glass, saying nothing. Yes, his instincts about her had been right. She never failed to make him feel ill at ease, self-conscious, simply by refusing to succumb to his charm. He would have to watch Patricia Manning very closely. . . .

Patricia Manning, very closely watched, stood up at that moment and announced her departure.

"Sorry, darlings. Under normal circumstances, I'd gladly dance till dawn. But my circumstances are anything but normal. I have to be up very early tomorrow. I'm playing— are you sitting down?—golf. At nine o'clock. With Stu and Brenda Harriman. Exhale, everybody. Kay, dear, you've done it again. Hang on to Nola: she's fabulous."

Adam watched as she went over to the young woman.

"It's been lovely meeting you, Diana. We'll see each other again soon, I think."

"I hope so, Trish."

A hug from Lisa, a smile and a wave for him, and at last the woman was gone. Kay walked her out to her car as Adam poured another drink for the girl. She was conversing quietly with Lisa, something about astrology. She seemed to be making a point of ignoring him. He smiled to himself as he reached for the Courvoisier. Those legs, he thought. That black dress is most becoming. . . .

Kay came back into the room.

"Time for bed, Lisa," she said.

"Oh, Mommy," the child whined.

"Now, dear. Say good night to Diana."

Lisa rose and stood before the young woman. "Will you be . . . coming back?"

"Would you like that?"

"Oh, yes! Please say you will!"

Adam and his wife watched as the young woman glanced over at them. Then she smiled.

"Of course I will."

The child grinned and ran over to her mother. "G'night!"

"Sleep tight," Kay said, kissing her forehead.

Then Adam got a surprise. Lisa turned and came slowly, almost shyly, across to where he sat. Leaning over, she pecked him on the cheek. "G'night."

He reached out and ruffled her hair. Looking over the child's shoulder, he noticed that Diana was watching their exchange with great interest. "Good night, baby."

Then the child ran off up the stairs. A moment later, they heard her bedroom door close.

"Well," Kay said, "I think we have some arrangements to discuss. Let's go out on the porch. We don't want to be in Lisa's way."

She led them outside into the cool night air. To their right, the lights of Charlotte Amalie twinkled in the distance. The hotel on the next point glowed brilliantly, and the muffled sound of steel-drum music wafted across the bay.

The girl could move in as soon as she liked, Kay said. The room was ready; it had been vacant for only a week. Adam stood at the railing and looked out at the lights of town, feigning indifference, hanging on their words. When the girl said that she would arrive two days hence, he nodded to himself.

Her sudden laughter caused him to turn around. She was listening as Kay droned on, but she was watching the pantomime beyond Kay's shoulder, on the other side of the glass doors. Lisa had materialized and tiptoed down the stairs. She crossed the room into the kitchen. A moment later she reappeared and ran back the other way and up the stairs, the shepherd at her heels.

"Well,' Kay said when she heard the bedroom door slam, "the coast is clear. Would anyone like something else to drink?"

The girl looked as if she were about to decline, so Adam spoke quickly. "Why don't we all have a glass of Nola's iced tea?"

"Excellent suggestion," Kay said. "I'll just be a minute."

She went inside the house and disappeared into the kitchen. The door swung shut behind her, and they were alone on the deck.

The steel band continued to play in the background, its muted strains just audible over the pounding of the surf below. They turned at the same instant to face each other. Her lips parted, and for a moment he thought she would speak. But she remained silent, motionless, staring over at him, into his eyes. Her hair moved slightly in the evening breeze. He watched her for a moment. Then he stepped forward, closing the gap between them.

And he was in her arms.

He kissed her once, hard, on the lips. Briefly, he allowed himself the luxury of burying his face in her hair. Then, with a quick glance at the kitchen door, he pulled away from her and dropped his arms. They spoke quickly, in urgent whispers.

"I wanted so much to call you—"

"No!" she hissed. "Don't. And for God's sake, stay away from Bolongo."

He reached out and gave her hand a quick squeeze.

"A painter," he breathed. "Nice touch."

She grinned at him then, through the darkness. I can do that, her smile seemed to say. I can do anything. For you.

"A couple of days," she whispered. "Then . . ."

He nodded.

When Kay returned a moment later with the tray, Adam was saying. "She fills the pitcher three-quarters of the way with tea. Then she peels three oranges and throws them in the blender . . ."

69

FOUR

FRIDAY, AUGUST 9

"N O T S O F A S T, darling! I'm still recuperating!"

Trish struggled to make her way through the teeming mass of flesh on Main Street. They had only just finished lunch, and the strain of walking all over the golf course yesterday still haunted her calves. Kay had already disappeared ahead of her.

It was madness to have come here today, especially at this hour. There were four cruise ships in port, and the duty-free shopping the tourists craved was mostly to be done on this relatively tiny four-block strip. The narrow, car-glutted lane was lined on both sides by shops offering everything from native crafts to imported Paris fashions at a fraction of Stateside prices, along with the jewelry and perfume, liquor and cigarettes that everyone insisted on dragging back to Chicago and Des Moines and Oklahoma City by the carload. They pushed and shoved and bullied their overfed, Bermuda-shorted, Foster Granted, Copper-toned hides around as if the island were one enormous white sale. Even so, Trish was enough of an ambassador to smile and beg everyone's pardon as she forged ahead. As far as the Virgin Islands economy was concerned, the daily visitors were bread and butter. Bread and butter, bread and butter: she repeated it under her breath like a mantra, reminding herself all the way. What she *wanted* to do sometimes was clear a path through this rude, sweaty human jungle with a machete.

God, it was hot! Her dress clung to her. The sun bore down on the street, and the famous trade winds had trouble finding their way through these densely packed rows of enormous converted Danish warehouses that were still the town's predominant structures. Here the air was still and thick with humidity. Hard to believe that the water-front was mere yards away. She'd give anything to be home with her feet up, the air conditioner blasting. But no: Kay wanted a new dress—now, *today!*—and when she was in one of these moods there was just no stopping her.

Kay could be such a bore. Why on *earth* did she need a dress? Just because Adam was taking her out to dinner tomorrow night? As if her wardrobe weren't already—well, hey. Why does any woman buy new clothes? Diana Meissen was moving into Cliffhanger today, and Diana Meissen was inordinately pretty, even by Trish's exacting standards. . . .

At last she arrived at the entrance of the shop into

which Kay had disappeared, and she lurched forward into blessedly cool darkness. She looked for Kay, smiling inwardly as her eyes roamed around the cavernous room. Once the proud haven for soon-to-be-shipped crops of cotton and sugar cane, and likely as not the ignominious drop for Blackbeard's fabulous plunder, the massive seaside structure was now a ladies' clothing store.

She spotted her friend through the milling mob, inspecting the dresses on display near the back. Push, shove, elbow, oh!-I-beg-your-pardon, and she was there. The pleasantly chilly, perfume-scented air inside the boutique did its job quickly: her heartbeat slowed and her breathing returned to normal.

Kay was holding a boldly printed red and orange Oscar de la Renta cotton gown up in front of her and gazing at her reflection in a full-length, rattan-framed glass on the solid exposed-stone wall.

"What do you think?" she asked.

Trish stood beside her and took a good, long look. The dark red and burnt orange patches were interspersed with white. Great with the red hair. Sleeveless; cinched waist; long, full skirt. Classic, festive, islandy: yes. Perfect for Kay's figure. And the plunging neckline was just what the doctor ordered.

"Can you try it on?" she asked. "I want to see it."

Kay consulted her watch. "Why not? I don't have to pick up Diana at Bolongo for nearly two hours."

She trotted dutifully off to the nearest cubicle.

Trish smiled to herself. She did not have to see the dress, but she felt, instinctively, that Kay needed to do this. And the crazy thing about it was that Kay wasn't consciously aware of that fact. Trish knew. She'd seen Adam's immediate interest in the girl the other night. But Kay, she also knew, did not suspect a thing. The two women had known each other for seven years, ever since Kay and Fred arrived on the island. It wasn't that her friend was stupid; quite the opposite. But Kay was one of *those* people, the ones who are honest and decent and trusting. They give the people they love a square deal, and they automatically assume that they are, in turn, being given the same thing. It was not in Kay's nature to be suspicious of anyone. She had imbued Adam with Fred's sterling qualities, and for all Trish knew, he possessed them. But she somehow doubted that.

Trish was not a member of Adam and Kay's yacht club. It was a bit too—well, clubby: Hail-fellow-well-met, eight bells and all's well, the sun over the yardarm. Drunks, most of them. But Brenda Harriman was a member, and she had repeated to Trish some gossip she'd picked up there. Adam had been seen, more than once, setting sail with his mate, Greg, and some girl. A redhead, of all things. Of course, she was probably Greg's girlfriend. . . .

She shook her head absently, knowing better than to listen to that nonsense. One of the favorite pastimes of the idle rich on St. Thomas. Besides, it had been months ago. The girl had not been spotted lately, and Greg had apparently left St. Thomas recently. Adam had a new mate now, somebody named Kyle.

I wouldn't be thinking these things, she told herself, if I liked Adam Prescott. If I didn't feel there was something—what?—*creepy* about him. He doesn't seem to have any friends. . . .

Her mother had never told her about certain types of men—actors and bullfighters sprang to mind—but she *had* warned her about the two syndromes to be avoided at all costs: Men With Too Many Male Friends and Men With No Male Friends. Too many meant they wouldn't be around much, and they regarded women in general as Only Good For One Thing. But *no* male friends was *real* trouble. If the other *boys* didn't trust them, there was usually a very good reason. *Cherechez beaucoups des femmes.* . . .

Kay doesn't know these things, she thought as her friend emerged from the dressing room wearing the evening dress. Kay is not worldly-wise. . . .

The sky over Glen Cove, Long Island, had been overcast all morning. There had been several flashes of lightning, and a low rumble of thunder in the distance. When the first large, heavy globules of rain hit the flagstone patio, Margaret Barclay closed the novel she'd been reading and slowly, painfully rose to her feet. Leaning heavily on her cane, she went into the house.

She'd known, from the moist feel of the air in her bedroom when she arose, that it was going to be a restless day. A cane day. Sure enough, the first twinge had shot through her right calf even as she made her way downstairs. She hadn't bothered with breakfast, preferring instead to go straight out back to see to the weeding around her rose bushes. She hadn't got very far in this endeavor: the dark clouds above her began to announce their presence the moment she knelt and reached for the spade with a rubber-gloved hand. The moist air always aggravated her condition, making her act of kneeling especially painful. So much for that idea. . . .

Oh, well, she'd philosophized, the flowers were looking a little droopy. It had been a particularly dry Long Island summer so far. A good drenching might make everything seem a bit perkier.

Everything but her.

She'd stubbornly refused to go indoors immediately. If she couldn't do the weeding, she'd at least get some fresh air. A thorough search through the stack of unread books she'd recently purchased had caused further annoyance: she was in no mood for anything. Finally, in desperation, she'd grabbed the paperback romance Mrs. O'Rourke had left lying on the kitchen counter: *Enchanted Prairie*, by Melissa Mills. She'd always harbored a faint curiosity about this type of literature. She'd hobbled out to the patio with the book and a cup of coffee and settled herself down for however long she'd have before the sky opened.

The novel, like the weather, had immediately made her impatient. When the rain arrived, she rose and entered the house with a vague sense of relief.

The phone in her study was ringing. She made her way to the desk and sank into the padded chair, grateful to remove the pressure from her bad leg. She dropped the book and the cane and reached for the receiver.

"Margaret Barclay," she announced.

"Hi, Mom."

The moment she heard the familiar voice, it flashed in

Margaret's consciousness: the true reason for her foul mood, the anger and frustration she'd been experiencing for the better part of two weeks. She'd actually made it through most of the morning without once worrying about the girl. The sound of her voice immediately corrected that oversight. Forcing a light and, she hoped, natural tone, Margaret went immediately into her Delighted Parent mode.

"Darling! How are you? *Where* are you?"

"Sorry. I guess it's been a couple of weeks. I—I'm in Florida. Visiting some friends. How are you?"

Margaret bit back the urge to argue.

"Oh, I'm fine. The leg's acting up, but it always does when it rains. How's the weather down there in— Florida?"

Florida! Indeed. . . .

"Perfect. Everything about this place is perfect. Listen, I know I said I'd probably be back in a couple of weeks, but something's come up. I—I've been offered a job down here, and I think I'll accept it. Just for a while. . . ."

"A job? What sort of job?"

"With a family. Au pair. Taking care of a little girl."

Margaret raised an imperious eyebrow, but she kept her tone of voice casual. "Do we know this family?"

"Oh, no. Their name is—Goodman. They live in Miami. The girl's name is Linda. She's the sweetest thing! Listen, Mom. I don't have much time. They're coming to pick me up any minute now. I'll call you when I'm all settled in, okay?"

She could ask for an address, she knew, or a telephone number. She had a hundred questions burning in her throat, but she knew better than to ask any of them. In some ways, the girl was predictable. But only in some. . . .

"Very well," she replied, keeping it light. "I look forward to hearing from you. Take care of yourself. And darling, *please* be careful—whatever you're doing."

The girl was not here, thank God, to see the tears in her eyes. She had always been impatient with Margaret's tears. And now her voice was solicitous.

"Is Mrs. O'Rourke coming in every day?"

"Yes, darling. She feeds me and keeps the house clean. She's even helping me with the garden. And Bitsy and Louise come over twice a week for Scrabble. Don't worry about me."

"I'll be back soon enough to play Scrabble with you."

"You always beat me, darling. You and your mania for word games. At least Bitsy and Louise give me a fighting chance."

"Okay. Take it easy with that leg. Don't go entering any marathons."

In spite of herself, the old woman smiled. That girl has her mother's charm! She can always make me laugh. . . .

"I love you, Mom. 'Bye."

"Good-bye, darling."

Slowly, Margaret replaced the receiver.

Her mother's charm. She glanced at the photograph of the young, beautiful blond woman with the merry blue eyes on the desk before her. Her sister had been gone these twenty years. And now, she reflected, the girl calls me Mom.

Enough: she had to think, and quickly. The girl was up

to something. Again. Otherwise, why would she claim to be in Florida? And why the alias? Something must be done, before she gets in more trouble.

Margaret shuddered, thinking of the past. The private day school: thrown out for fighting with the other girls. The boarding schools: flunked. The time she ran away and was found, months later, in that awful house in Haight-Ashbury with the rock-and-roll singer, or whatever he was. The abortion. The methadone clinic. The married men.

The psychologists. The psychiatrists. The priests! Margaret had been desperate. And yet she had never stopped loving the girl, or caring about what happened to her. And she never would. No Barclay had ever walked away from a fight, or deserted one of their own. She would always be there for the girl, she thought as she contemplated the photograph. She owed her little sister that much.

That one doctor, Stein—consulted after the suicide attempt, when she'd been thrown out of Harvard after only two semesters—had made sense of it. He'd told Margaret that the girl was manifesting her rage by means of self-destructive behavior. Losing her parents like that, at such an early age. It had been horrible, the sort of trauma that an adult would have trouble coping with, to say nothing of a six-year-old. He warned that until something made her feel safe and secure, she would probably continue the pattern. He also warned that as she matured, the games would become more complex. More outrageous. And certainly more dangerous.

Safe and secure, She, Margaret, had not been able to provide those feelings. She had not been enough.

A long sigh escaped her lips. She sat, staring at the yellowing photograph of the lovely young woman holding up the beautiful baby girl.

This time, thank God, she had been prepared. She had provided for this eventuality. She didn't know what her niece had in mind, but she would know soon enough. Soon enough to stop it, whatever it was. Before she hurt herself again.

Or someone else.

Margaret shuddered again and pulled her old, ratty gardening sweater more tightly around her shoulders. What could it be? It almost certainly involved a man. The girl had inherited her mother's weakness for beautiful men. And Albert, her father, had been beautiful.

A chilling draft, real or imagined, permeated the room. She sat very still, gradually becoming aware of the torment outside that rattled the windows and flooded the garden, replenishing the roses. Nature took care of some things so easily.

But only some, she thought. The rest is up to us.

With grim determination, Margaret reached again for the receiver and slowly dialed a number in St. Thomas, Virgin Islands.

The young woman replaced the receiver in its cradle and made a last, careful inspection of the room. Had she forgotten anything?

The two open suitcases on the bed were full; she would have trouble closing one of them. She smiled. The suitcases had made Mom nervous when she saw them standing in the foyer in Glen Cove twelve days ago. You just got back from that Caribbean jaunt; where are you off to now? She'd preempted Mom's questions by kissing her lightly on the cheek and dashing off to Kennedy Airport. It was vital that Mom *not* know where she was.

The plan . . .

She shook her head, thinking back over the catalog of crazy stunts and sorry failures that had been her life. But not *this* time. This time I will be successful, so successful that *nobody*—not even Margaret Barclay—will ever forget it.

She loved Margaret, more than anything, but she could not afford to tell her too much. Margaret—Mom—would stop her. And the plan must not be stopped.

The scrapbook, the source of the whole idea, rested on the top of the larger suitcase. She reached down, picked it up, and placed it on the desk of the dressing table. She leafed slowly past the few pages of photographs to the second section. She read and reread the clippings. They were photocopies, of course, recently made: the original scrapbook was safely locked away at home in Glen Cove. All the information was there, all the details of the two surprisingly similar cases. The famous one, twenty years ago, as covered in several New York newspapers. The other was more recent—ten years ago—but information regarding it was much harder to come by. It had occurred in a fairly remote part of Hawaii, on the island of Kauai. The two incidents had provided the necessary modus operandi. Not to mention the inspiration.

The inspiration was perfectly simple: in both cases, the

perpetrators had not been caught, had *never* been brought
to justice.

Now, in the present, the same amount of care was being taken. Everything had been worked out, provided for.
The dates and times, the travel arrangements, the
disguise—and she herself, *alone,* had come up with the final, *Grand Guignol* touch.

The means.

They had planned most of it on the *Kay* two months
ago, making sure that Greg was out of earshot. He had to
be along on their outings, Adam had explained. Beard.
Besides, he'd pointed out, staring into her bright-green
eyes and reaching over to caress her bright-red hair, it was
Greg who'd introduced them in the first place. . . .

She smiled now, remembering. She'd met Greg in Sparky's Waterfront Saloon late one night. She'd been there with
another young woman from her hotel, a plump, frizzy-haired
schoolteacher from Pittsburgh whose name she'd now forgotten. On her third night in St. Thomas they'd been out
pub-crawling, or "man-hunting," as Pittsburgh had tipsily
giggled. She had been told to try Sparky's, and she insisted,
over Pittsburgh's initial protestations, on checking it out.
They'd wandered into the friendly, crowded bar and plunked
themselves down on barstools, directly next to the attractive
young man who had immediately begun the usual staring
ritual. He'd bought them drinks, and within an hour Pittsburgh had been picked up by the bartender and *she* had
made a date with Greg to go sailing on his boat the following afternoon.

The boat, of course, was not his.

She would never forget the moment she first set eyes on Adam Prescott. Even now, just at the thought of him, a raw electric shock formed in the pit of her stomach and moved slowly up her spine to tingle at the back of her brain. . . .

She placed the scrapbook carefully back in the bag and looked around. Yes, she was ready now. She called the hotel office, and a big, friendly native man arrived to take the luggage and the easel down to the front entrance. She followed him, carrying the paint-box. She checked her watch: she still had thirty minutes to wait. She settled her bill in the office and wandered out to the open-air bar beside the pool.

The bartender was just placing the tall, fruit-embellished piña colada before her when her fellow guest, the ubiquitous Bob, slid into the chair next to her.

"Hi!"

She forced a smile. "Hello."

"I see you're not in your Island Period today."

"What? Oh, no," she said. "Just taking it easy this afternoon. I'll paint some more later. What are you up to?"

She wasn't really interested, of course, just killing time. But he *was* rather—well, if she hadn't had the plan . . .

"Nothin' much." He grinned and ordered a Heineken. "But my plans have changed. I'm here a while longer, all expenses paid. That includes dinners, by the way. Interested?"

"Sorry. My plans have changed, too. I'm leaving today."

She didn't tell him about Cliffhanger. The fewer people who knew her business, the better.

"Back to New York?" Bob asked.

"Eventually."

"Uh-huh. Well, *sköl!*"

They chatted pleasantly for a while longer. At last she saw the beige Land Rover pull up in the entrance driveway beyond the office. She stood up.

"Excuse me a moment," she said.

"Sure." The young man grinned.

She walked past the office, picked up her bags, and went over to Kay, who was just emerging from the car.

"Hi," she said.

"Hello, Diana. Ready?"

She nodded. The two women put the luggage and the easel in the back and climbed in. She glanced back over at the bar. Bob was talking to the bartender, and the two of them were laughing. Her departure was going unnoticed. Good.

They traveled along the now-familiar road in the direction of town and turned at the entrance to the driveway. In minutes, they were there.

Kay parked the Land Rover in the shade of the tamarind and turned, smiling, to her new employee.

"Here we are," she said. "I just know you're going to love it here. And I know somebody who's overjoyed by your arrival!"

Yes, she thought, smiling back at Kay Prescott. So do I.

Nola met them at the door.

"Mrs. Prescott, Ms. Manning has called twice in the last twenty minutes. She says to call her the moment you get in."

"Thank you, Nola. Could you get the rest of Ms. Meissen's things and put them in her room?"

"Of course. Welcome, Ms. Meissen."

The young woman smiled and followed Kay into the living room. Kay went over to the phone and dialed.

"Hello, darling," she said into the receiver. "I just left you *seconds* ago downtown. What on earth—" She stopped, obviously cut off by Trish's voice. She listened a moment, her eyes widening in disbelief. "What?! Oh, dear God! When? Oh. It must have been while you were all playing golf. Jesus! I'll be right over."

She hung up and headed for the front door.

"Sorry, Diana. I have to go to the Harrimans' house. They've been robbed, and Brenda is distraught. Maybe Trish and I can help out. When Adam returns from St. John, tell him where I am. I don't know if I'll be back in time for dinner, so go ahead without me."

She ran past Nola, who was just entering with the luggage, jumped back in the Land Rover, and drove away.

The young woman watched Kay disappear and smiled to herself. The Harrimans, whoever they were, had been robbed.

The game was afoot.

She turned around, then, to see Lisa and Jumbi running down the stairs to greet her. The dog stopped short several feet away and refused to advance nearer. Its mistress had no such reservations.

"You're here at last!" Lisa sang out, bounding right up to her.

The young woman smiled.

"Yes," she replied. "I'm here. At last."

* * *

She isn't here, he thought. She's gone.

He'd been waiting at the bar for nearly an hour. Then he'd gone to her room and knocked. No answer. At last he went down to the office.

"Ms. Meissen?" the startled manager said. "Why, she's gone. Checked out about an hour ago. . . . No, she didn't leave a forwarding address. Besides, I wouldn't be able to tell you—"

He ran out to his rented Chevette and raced across the length of the island to the airport.

Departures. He ran from desk to desk, airline to airline, scanning the departure boards for information. Only one flight had taken off since he'd last seen her, a twin-engine Prinair to Puerto Rico. The pretty native girl behind the counter could not divulge passenger names, but she shook her head when he asked the crucial question. No, there had not been a young woman on board.

He checked the waiting lounges, the restaurant, the gift shop. He even had a friendly Pan Am stewardess check the ladies' room. Nothing.

He thought of calling cruise-ship lines, but he knew that those lists, too, were classified.

Finally he returned to the hotel. A small boat or private plane, he thought as he drove. He doubted it, though. Instinct told him that she was still here, somewhere on the island.

He entered his room just as the sun disappeared. He didn't bother to turn on the light. He went out onto the balcony and gazed up at the darkening sky. A cool breeze did little to soothe his hot, flushed face.

Oh, damn! he thought. Now what? He'd finally snagged a decent gig, the first of his fledgling career. His boss had entrusted him with it. *Him!* Not that stupid Russo, who thought he was James Fucking Bond. A special assignment for a special client. A leg job. Babysitting, really. A few weeks, a thousand per and all expenses in some fancy watering hole. Just follow the mark, report whereabouts, and stay put for further instructions.

A thousand per! Enough to pay off a big chunk on the Upper West Side one-bedroom condo he'd just moved into. And that, he admitted to himself, wasn't his only motivation. The mark, it had turned out, was incredibly pretty.

Okay, he'd read the dossier. *Crazy,* but pretty. . . .

He shook his head in a mixture of self-disgust and self-pity. Some detective, he mused. Some goddamned Sherlock! He couldn't even hang on to a perfectly easy tail, an emotionally unstable young woman. She'd simply walked right out of the hotel as he sat there, downing a brew.

With great reluctance, he went back into the room and over to the phone. He was going to be fired. He just *knew* it! He'd have to find another job. Well, he thought grimly, no more waiting tables. No more driving cabs. And no more goddamned singing telegrams! He'd have to find some other way to supplement his acting career. He picked up the receiver and slowly dialed the number in Glen Cove, Long Island.

"It's me again, Miss Barclay," he said. "Robin Trask. I'm afraid I've lost her. . . ."

FIVE

THURSDAY, AUGUST 15

H E W A S O U T again, out on the ocean. *His* ocean.

He waved back at Kyle on the *Kay.* The young man saluted, lit a cigarette, and resumed his work on the ripped sail.

As soon as he was around the point, out of sight of the yacht club, he opened up the engine. He would have to be as quick as possible. As far as Kyle was concerned, he was merely testing the Boston Whaler, making sure it was still in working order. He did this periodically; if anything happened to the *Kay* at sea, the Whaler was their potential survival. There was nothing out of the ordinary in his action. No reason for suspicion.

But he would have to be quick. The boat could only manage about seventeen knots at full throttle. He'd taken that into account, of course. He didn't have far to go.

He followed the coastline, keeping close to shore. Instinctively, he scanned every beach and waterfront condominium complex for bathers or residents taking an unusual interest in the tiny boat as it passed. No: nobody was watching.

Excellent.

It had been one week now since Diana moved into Cliffhanger. She had, as far as he could see, adjusted to life there with remarkable ease. She had immediately gone about the business of making herself indispensable to Kay and Lisa. She and Kay shopped and gossiped and went out to lunch together, and she was teaching the child the fundamentals of drawing and painting. All he heard from his wife and stepdaughter was Diana this and Diana that and I don't know, let's ask Diana. He gleaned that secret plans were under way for Lisa's thirteenth birthday. There was much giggling and whispering among the women. *His* women.

Excellent.

They had not been able to meet alone, under the circumstances, either at the house or away from it. She was always with Kay and Lisa and Trish. And he made sure to spend as much time as possible away from Cliffhanger. Kay, silly though she was, could not help but feel the tension between them if she were given the chance. Lisa was sharp: little got past her. And he'd never trusted Trish Manning in the first place. He and Diana carefully kept their distance from each other.

But it hardly mattered. Their plan—the parts that involved *her*, at any rate—had been discussed and committed to memory two months ago. Phase One had gone beautifully: she'd made it back to the island and into the house without a hitch, and he'd kicked off his part of it with the Harrimans. He couldn't help smiling when he thought about *that*.

Excellent.

Then, of course, there were the parts of the plan that Diana didn't know about.

Like Greg.

And today's little excursion.

And . . .

Four minutes, twenty seconds.

He slowed as he neared his destination. Time for Phase Two. . . .

"Sun—"

"Bright."

"Bright—"

"White."

"White—"

"Snow."

"Snow—"

"Christmas!" Lisa shrieked as she and Jumbi danced across the lawn and disappeared between two trees near the edge of the cliff. "Come on, Diana!"

The young woman followed them. It was difficult for her to keep pace with them, encumbered as she was by sketchpads and paintbox. She entered the woods behind the girl and discovered a narrow, well-worn path that wound down the side of the hill, parallel to the cliff that dropped away some twenty yards to her left.

So this was the promised adventure Lisa had been hinting at all morning. "After lunch," she'd said, her Cheshire-cat grin widening mysteriously. "The most wonderful place! You'd never know it was there unless someone showed you."

They'd fallen into a familiar routine in the past week. In the mornings, as soon as breakfast was done, Lisa jumped on her bicycle and pedaled off down the hill to visit her best friends, two sisters who lived a short distance away on the main road toward town. Twice the other girls had come to Cliffhanger, and the three children had played on the lawn or disappeared into Lisa's room, amid much rock music and high-pitched laughter. Kay used the late morning to correspond—mostly by telephone, but there had been two dictated letters so far. The end-of-month bills were arriving, and it soon became apparent that Kay was grateful to have these taken out of her hands. She merely signed the checks that the younger woman placed before her.

One morning—the day after she volunteered to be Kay's unofficial bookkeeper—the two women had gone into town to shop. Kay had bought a new purse and ordered some personalized stationery. They'd spent a good deal of time in the art gallery at A. H. Riise, where they'd discovered a remarkable similarity in their artistic tastes. Actually, Kay had pointed out what she liked, and the young woman had readily agreed. They'd wandered from the gallery to the store's jewelry section, and it was there that she'd made the mistake of admiring a small, fairly inexpensive amethyst brooch. Before she'd known what was happening, Kay had handed a Visa card to the woman behind the counter, and the pin had been whisked from the display case, boxed, bagged, and placed in her hand.

"That's a bribe," Kay had said, cutting off all protest. "To keep you around for a while."

Then they'd gone to meet Trish for lunch at a lovely little restaurant above Main Street. She had watched, smiling, as Kay and Trish fought over the bill, each woman insisting adamantly that it was her turn to pay.

Every afternoon she was alone with the child. Kay busied herself around the house or went off to afternoon bridge games with Trish and her other friends, and she and Lisa would go out on the deck or the patio with art supplies. Or if the girl was not in the mood for a drawing lesson, there was always the book.

On her third day in residence at Cliffhanger, Lisa had arrived in her bedroom and looked around with undisguised interest at her belongings, zeroing in almost immediately on the large book on the table next to the bed. Not the scrapbook with the clippings and photos: that was in a locked suitcase at the back of the closet. This one was called *Myths of the Greeks and Romans*, and it was one of her favorites. So, naturally, it became Lisa's favorite as well. She'd thrown herself across the bed right then and there and demanded the first chapter, aloud. This concerned Kronos, father of Zeus—who was known to the Romans as Jupiter, she'd explained—and it involved sex, bloodshed, and cannibalism, among other delicious ingredients. Lisa had been enthralled, and now hardly a day passed without the next installment of the most ancient of soap operas.

The book was beautifully illustrated, and Lisa was particularly fond of the "family tree" picture near the front, which delineated the hierarchy of Mount Olympus, complete with little drawings of all the major deities labeled with their Greek and Roman names and their godly functions. She had made a project of memorizing all this double information.

"It's like the Bible, only weirder!" had been the child's glowing review. "Athena/Minerva. Demeter/Ceres. Ares/Mars—is he named after the planet?"

"Nope. Other way around."

"Wow, what funky names! Themis, Aidos, Nem . . . Nem . . ."

"Nemesis," the young woman slowly pronounced for her. "The goddess of retribution. Revenge. . . ."

"Look, Diana," Lisa cried. "One of them has your name! 'Artemis/Diana. Twin of Apollo. Daughter of Zeus/Jupiter'—don't tell me, let me guess: they named *that* planet after *him*!—'goddess of the moon and of hunting; protectress of women.' What does that mean, 'pro-tec-tress'?"

"It means we'd better get out of this room and outdoors into the fresh air for your lesson, or your mother is going to tan our hides."

They'd laughed together then and gone outside. Lisa had taken the book with her, and later that day they'd read some more. She loved the book. She loved the painting lessons. She loved the word-association game they played almost constantly.

She was crazy about her new companion.

Now, in the woods below Cliffhanger, Lisa's new companion glanced around. There was a wide variety of trees all mixed together, growing so close to one another that the leaves and branches above her head formed a thick blanket that blocked out the sun. There were mossy oaks and huge tamarinds like the one in the driveway and tall, slender, silver-barked birches and a plethora of others she could not identify. And everywhere among them, incongruous, the palms and century plants she'd expected. She inhaled deeply: the rich, moist, green scent of forests. It was dark here, dark and surprisingly cool. Hardly anyone's idea of a tropical island at midday, yet here it unaccountably was, another gorgeous St. Thomian surprise. The sparkle of the water glinted through the foliage to her left. As she trailed the elusive figures of the child and the dog, she became aware of the increasing volume of the surf. Then the ground beneath her sandaled feet became sand, and she emerged from the arbor into bright daylight. She stopped, staring, as Lisa whirled around and came back to join her. Jumbi headed immediately for the breaking waves.

"What do you think?" the child asked, giggling at the astonished expression on the woman's face. "Pretty neat, huh?"

They were standing on a tiny, perfectly curved beach, set deep in a little cove next to the base of the cliff, almost engulfed by the thick press of jungle surrounding it. Powder-white sand, electric-blue water, Kodachrome viridian palms and sea grapes. There were rocks at either end of the strip of sand and in the water as well. Large green, slippery formations were clearly visible just below the surface, covered with thousands of spiny, ink-black sea urchins. The cove, with all its attractions, would never be appropriate for swimming. Even Jumbi, prancing in the waves at the very edge, ventured no farther into the water.

"It's beautiful," she whispered.

Lisa laughed, grabbed her hand, and led her out to the miniature shore. From the center of the beach she could see the huge, solid pile of boulders to their left: the jagged, sea-swept rocks at the base of the high, sheer cliff face that loomed up from the water. The house was nestled at the apex high above their heads, with its jutting deck partially visible from where they stood. Her gaze traveled up, up, up to the tiny, distant structure. She shielded her eyes from the glare of the sun, peering up at the corner of the deck. A lone figure stood there, leaning on the railing, looking down at them.

It was Kay Prescott.

As she watched, the woman raised an arm and waved. Lisa screamed and jumped up and down, flailing her arms for the benefit of her mother, that diminutive dot of life on the miniature redwood platform suspended so precariously over the precipice.

She shuddered, thinking to herself, imagining it, the enormous reality hitting her in a rush, at that moment on the glorious beach. A long way, she thought.

A long way to fall.

He checked his watch again. Six minutes.

It hadn't been difficult to find her. She was staying in a small, inexpensive guest house above town, trying to decide what to do with the money. He'd suspected as much. A few casual questions to the right acquaintances, and he'd secured the address. Then it had been merely a question of an accidental meeting on the street just outside the inn, a harmless kiss and a discreet invitation. It was all right now, he'd assured her, now that their business relationship was over. And besides, she *knew* how he'd always felt about her, didn't she? He'd fixed her with a gaze of long-smoldering desire and made a vague grab in the vicinity of her breast. She'd blushed and smirked and agreed to the rendezvous. Making sure there was no one on the street observing them, he'd kissed her again and told her where to be, and when.

And here she was.

Excellent.

He came in to the shore and waited, watching, as she sashayed over to him. She was wearing a short-sleeved white blouse over her black bathing suit. A white silk scarf concealed her mousy brown hair. Hoop earrings, too much makeup, dime-store perfume.

Deborah Kerr, no doubt. *From Here to Eternity.* And he was supposed to be Burt Lancaster.

Fine.

He grinned as he helped her into the boat. He held his breath and kissed her on her pudgy, rubbery lips. Nothing in this world, he thought, could be further from Deborah Kerr. . . .

"You look beautiful," he crooned.

She giggled, fluttering false lashes. "*Merci, monsieur!* Now, just exactly where *is* this special island—this Bali H'ai?"

Oh, Christ! *Not* Deborah Kerr. Mitzi Gaynor in *South Pacific!*

Fine. She could be whoever she wanted to be.

He produced his laziest, sexiest smile. "You'll see."

Eight minutes.

He started the engine and headed the boat straight out, away from the island, toward the open sea. . . .

If it hadn't been for the dog, she probably would never have noticed it.

They were sitting on the sand facing the ocean, and she was showing the child the secret of sketching water, a constantly moving model. The idea was to suggest the movement, to convey fluidity. Lisa, as usual, was getting it right on her first try. She was observant, all right. Very talented, and very clever. . . .

Jumbi had been running at the breakers, barking and wagging her tail, attempting to frighten the water into staying on the sand where she could play with it. As clever as her young mistress, she soon realized that this would never come to pass. In the canine equivalent of disgust, she abandoned her inconstant playmate and ran off down the beach in search of another, more acquiescent friend. They laughed at her antics and resumed drawing.

"I'll start this time, Diana," Lisa said. "Water."

"Wet," came the reply.

"Wet—"

"Rocks," the woman said, glancing off to their left.

"Rocks—"

"Cliff."

"Cliff—"

"Woman."

"*Woman*?! All right, woman—"

"Kay."

"Kay—"

"Adam."

Lisa rolled her eyes and spat out the response. "*Adam*—"

"Eve."

They giggled.

"Eve—"

"Christmas!" the young woman announced, triumphant.

They burst into laughter. Lisa dropped her charcoal pencil and clapped her hands.

"You're wonderful, Diana!" she cried.

At that moment, Jumbi began to bark.

She was somewhere behind them, and the urgency of her yapping made them turn around. They saw the animal standing at the edge of the forest, her attention arrested by something not visible from their perspective. They stood up, dropping the art supplies, and walked toward her.

"What is it, girl?" Lisa asked softly as they approached. "What do you see?"

Jumbi was growling now, standing quite still, watching something in the woods.

When they saw what she was watching, they began to laugh.

It was an iguana, crouching at the base of a nearby tree, frozen in obvious terror. Its huge hooded eyes bulged more than usual, and its scaly gray spines and horn seemed poised for defensive measures. Even as they spied it, the shepherd sprang forward with a snarl.

"Jumbi, *no!*" Lisa screamed.

The reptile collected its wits and took off like a shot, slithering away into the forest with remarkable speed. Lisa reached out just in time to grab the dog's collar and prevent her from giving chase.

As she watched the iguana scurry through the woods, the young woman noticed something she had not previously seen. There, set back among the trees before them, obscured by the foliage, stood a small building. It was no more than a shack, really, perhaps twelve feet by sixteen, built rather crudely of wood.

"What on earth is that?" she asked the child.

Lisa followed her gaze. "Oh, that. Daddy built it a long time ago, when we first moved here. He had a boat he used to keep down here, and that"—she jerked a thumb at the structure—"was for storing stuff. It hasn't been used in years. Mommy sometimes talks about tearing it down, but I think she likes it. I heard her tell Aunt Trish once that she and Daddy used to play there. I think she was talking about sex. Maybe that's why she's never gotten rid of it."

The woman stared at her a moment, smiling at the sudden, inexplicable wisdom of children. Then she stepped forward through the trees. She crossed the short distance to the small, slightly crooked door. There was a hinged bar next to the rusty knob, but the padlock hanging from it was open. She removed the lock, pushed open the door, and went inside. Lisa and Jumbi remained on the beach.

It took a moment for her eyes to adjust to the gloom. The single window high up on one wall had been boarded shut, and the only light filtered through the irregular crevices between the badly aligned planks that formed the walls. A table on one side had been fashioned from a sheet of plywood resting on two sawhorses: it had obviously served Fred Belden as a workspace. Dark patches marred its surface, evidence of long-ago oil spills from some now-defunct outboard motor, no doubt. A lone blondwood oar rested along one wall near a metal folding chair and in a corner stood two red plastic containers for gasoline. Even now the tiny, airless room smelled faintly of diesel.

She was about to turn around and leave the shed when she noticed something in the opposite corner, something that didn't quite fit with the other objects in the place. There, spread out along the wall, were two large white blankets. At one end, against the wall, rested a long, uncased pillow. She stared a moment: something wasn't right. . . .

She knelt beside the makeshift bed and lifted the corner of one white blanket—too white for long disuse. She sniffed. Fabric softener.

The act of pulling away the blanket revealed something else, in the corner next to the pillow. An empty wine bottle and two clear plastic glasses. Next to these was a tiny can that had once contained Starkist tuna. It now housed the remains of several cigarettes. She picked one up and examined it. The elegant green lettering at the base of the filter was singed but unmistakable.

Virginia Slims.

The snapping of twigs outside the door told her that Lisa was approaching the shack. She threw the blanket back over the objects in the corner and rose quickly to her feet. She was just about to turn around when the voice from the doorway arrested all motion.

"You really shouldn't be in here, Diana," Kay Prescott said. "It isn't safe."

The younger woman took a deep breath and turned around to face her. "I was just—"

Kay pointed over at the far wall, just under the window. "See those tracks? Termites. One good breeze and the whole thing will probably come crashing down. You could be seriously injured. I don't have any insurance for that." She smiled, but her tone was firm. "I'd rather you didn't come in here again."

With that, she turned and went out to join her daughter

on the beach.

After a moment, the other woman followed her.

There is a place in every ocean, a certain distance from land, where the water beneath the turbulent surface is deep and freezing cold. It is dark there: the sunlight can penetrate only so far before its power is defeated by the shadows. Men rarely venture into it, knowing as they do that the silence and the stillness are deceptive. There, as everywhere else, a thousand different forms of life have made their home. Most of them are small, peaceful, inconsequential; some are invisible to the human eye. It is not of these that men are afraid, but of the larger ones, the ones that travel in groups, roaming the depths in constant search of sustenance. Their food is at a premium, and when it is found it is attacked and fought over and violently eliminated. The presence of these denizens ensures the secrecy of the place: its mysteries remain its own.

Fourteen minutes.

He cut the engine and sat back, smiling at the girl. She lounged on the forward bench, gazing dreamily around at the expanse of water and the hazy, faraway strip of green that was St. Thomas. She had kicked off her sandals and removed the blouse and the earrings, which lay on top of the straw bag at her feet.

"Alone at last!" she gushed, coloring slightly as she became aware of the intensity of his stare. "But why are we stopping here?"

"I have a surprise for you."

She regarded him with amused skepticism and raised a penciled eyebrow. "Here?! What sort of surprise?"

"Don't worry," he said. "It's not what you think. The boat's too small, and the water's too choppy."

They both laughed.

"I should say so!" she agreed, lowering her tone to a gravelly purr. "Besides, I think it may rain soon. Imagine getting caught in a storm all the way out here! Did you ever see *Key Largo*?"

"Sure." And you're Lauren Bacall, he thought.

She lowered her eyelids. "So, what's the surprise?"

He leaned forward. "See that tarp behind you? Look under it and you'll find a bottle of wine and two glasses."

A slow smile came to her lips. She cocked her head to one side and rested a hand on her bosom. Lauren Bacall, Mitzi Gaynor, Deborah Kerr: she was every magnificent woman she'd ever read about and dreamed of becoming.

"Why, you marvelous, romantic man! You've thought of everything!"

Yes, he thought. I have.

"I want this to be perfect," he whispered.

"Oh, it is!" she insisted. "Its wonderful! I'm having the loveliest time. And now, my lord, lie back while I furnish thee with libations."

She turned around then. She knelt in the bobbing craft, her back to him, and reached down to pull the dark-blue oilskin away from the marvelous, romantic wine.

He reached forward with his right hand, whipped the white scarf from her head, and dropped it onto her other clothes. He grabbed a handful of the mousy brown hair and whirled her around to face him. He had to see her eyes.

"Hey!" she cried, but her voice had the sound of laughter in it. "What are you unnnnn—"

The knife plunged into her throat, through her esophagus, and out the back of her neck.

"—nnngghhhhh. . . ."

Adam gripped the handle and yanked the blade backward, out of her. He tossed it away. He pushed her backward, so her head and the wound were over the side. For one long, exquisite moment he stared into the wild, pained, uncomprehending eyes, until just before they clouded over. Then he leaned back, grasping the edge of the bench for support, and raised his leg. Planting his foot squarely in the center of her stomach, he shoved her over the side. The body pitched backward and down into the water, twisting once as it fell.

She floated for a while, facedown, bobbing gently in the waves. As he watched, fascinated, her left arm straightened rigidly out beside her and the hand balled into a tight fist. Then, ever so slowly, the fingers loosened and opened slightly, and the arm relaxed. The body moved away from the boat, rising on a sudden crest and dropping into the trough behind it. There was one last glimpse of the mousy hair, the bathing suit, the chubby white legs, and then the sea accepted her. Only in those final seconds before she sank had she become aware of what had happened, realized that she was dying. And after that there was nothing, oblivion, and the long descent.

He filled his lungs with fresh sea air, held it for a moment, and slowly exhaled. He raised his face to the sun, allowing the warmth to penetrate and soothe. He relaxed his body, one muscle at a time. The rage evaporated as the first tingling wave of ecstasy washed over him. The reviving wind swept through his platinum hair. He was alone on the surface of the ocean, where only he was God.

Then he opened his eyes and lowered his gaze to the bow of the craft, where she had been kneeling. He had moved swiftly: there was not a drop of blood in the boat.

Excellent.

It was all in the water. It would seep from the wound in her throat and spread outward in every direction. A homing device calling attention to his precious gift, his generous donation to those other gods, the ones that waited below.

He consulted his watch: seventeen minutes and counting.

Excellent.

The engine roared to life. In just under five minutes he was back at the remote cove where he had picked her up. He floated in to shore, grabbed the bag and the clothes, and leapt into the shallows. Her car would be parked around here somewhere. No time to move it, he thought, so improvise. He ran up onto the beach and dropped her belongings a safe distance above the highest tide line.

The straw bag fell over sideways, spilling its contents onto the sand. He bent quickly to retrieve everything and stuff it back inside: compact; atomizer; comb and brush; a pack of Juicy Fruit gum; a fastened manila envelope bulging with something, probably clippings of movie stars; six or seven magazines. *People, Us, Modern Screen, Premiere.* Jesus. . . .

He scanned the palm grove that concealed the beach from the road beyond it: yes, there was her old, battered Jeep, parked in the shadows among the trees.

Excellent.

Six minutes later he was back at the club, tying the Whaler to the stern of the *Kay.* Kyle, he noticed, had finished repairing the sail and was not reattaching it. He was hunched over his task, the inevitable cigarette dangling from the corner of his mouth, oblivious of the outside world. He would not have noticed if Adam had been drenched with gore.

Excellent.

Twenty-nine minutes, eight seconds, from start to finish.

Perfect.

The young man looked up from his chore as Adam climbed aboard. "That was fast. Is she seaworthy?"

Adam grinned.

"And then some," he said.

The sharp cry of a seagull caused him to look up. There was a flock, perhaps a hundred of them, soaring through the clear sky above the boat. Flying off, catching the wind, wherever they wanted to go. Absolute freedom.

God.

He smiled, remembering something from long ago: the birds outside his bedroom window.

SIX

FRIDAY, AUGUST 16

"I DON'T KNOW, Miss Barclay. I'm beginning to think I'm wasting your time and money. Maybe I should just—"

"It's my time, Mr. Trask," came the imperious reply, "and my money. I've just been explaining that to your employer in New York, Mr.—oh, dear, I'm terrible with Japanese names. I can't for the life of me pronounce this—"

"Yakimadoro," Robin said, smiling into the receiver. "You have to say it a few times."

"At least. He said that if it's all right with you, it's all right with him. He also said to tell you that casting calls don't really begin for another month or so, and then he emitted a sound I interpreted as laughter. I infer from that remark that you're an actor, and I don't think Mr. whatever-his-name-is takes your career very seriously. I'm willing to raise your fee to twelve hundred a week. Are you amenable to that?"

He gazed down from his balcony at two pretty, bikini-clad women who sat at the poolside bar, laughing as they sipped tall, fruity drinks. The chair next to them was unoccupied. Twelve hundred, he thought. I've died and gone to heaven. . . .

"I'm amenable," he said. "I'm very amenable, Miss Barclay." Hell, for twelve hundred per, I'm the most amenable out-of-work actor this side of the Rockies.

"Good. Now, Mr. Trask, do you have anything? Any leads?"

Oh, boy. He squeezed his eyes shut, his mind racing. She was pinning a lot of hopes on him, and now she was asking if he had any leads. He didn't have any leads; he didn't have anything that might even *lead* to leads. He had dick, and they both knew that, though the rich lady from Glen Cove would not have expressed it in quite that way. Thank God his boss, the Sarcastic Samurai, and Johnny "Call-Me-James-Bond" Russo weren't here to see him squirming.

Stall, he thought. Buy some time. You'll come up with something. You're an actor, for chrissakes! If you can't *be* a detective, you can at least *act* like one.

"As a matter of fact," he suddenly heard himself saying, "I'm following up on a lead right now. I'm expecting a phone call from a guy—a *source*. Yeah. I should have something for you, um, soon. Can I reach you at this number all afternoon?"

"Of course, Mr. Trask," she said. "I hope it's good news. Otherwise—"

"Hey," he interjected, trying to sound like he was wearing a rumpled trenchcoat, "let's not think about otherwise. Just stay put till you hear from me, okay? And please call me Robin. We're in this together, ya know."

Wow. Humphrey Bogart, please write.

"Very well, Robin. Please find her for me. I can't help thinking something may happen to her. Something terrible. She's a very—she's made mistakes in the past. Stupid, destructive things. When you have a child you love—" There was a pause on the other end of the line. Then she said, "I've buried everyone else in my family, Robin. I don't want history to repeat itself."

Robin Trask, actor and detective, was silent. There was nothing he could think of to say.

He looked out at the beach. A young woman in a pink bathing suit stood in the shallows, holding a little boy above the surface as he made his first, fumbling attempt at swimming. He paddled successfully for several feet before his head disappeared momentarily beneath a breaking wave. She pulled the grinning, sputtering child from the water and held him up, wet and gleaming, to the sun. Their triumphant laughter floated up to the balcony.

Long Island Sound. His dad had tossed him in and fished him out and held him to his chest. Laughing.

"I'll find her," he said, and he hung up the phone.

He carried the instrument back into the room and placed it on the night table next to the manila folder. Then he picked up the file and left the room.

Wandering out onto the beach, he noticed that the two young women he'd seen at the bar were gone. Just as well: he had some thinking to do. He dropped the folder in the sand, shed his shirt, and placed it on top of it. He waded out into the water, dived, surfaced, and rolled over onto his back. He floated in the warm, clear Caribbean, eyes closed, remembering. . . .

Until this, nothing really unusual had ever happened to him. He'd grown up with nice parents in a nice house in Merrick, Long Island. He'd majored in drama at Columbia because it seemed like an interesting, colorful thing to do. He hadn't even fallen in love with it, been "bitten by the bug," until he was actually onstage, in front of people who laughed and applauded. Then, of course, the way was clear. After graduation he'd remained in the city, against the wishes of Dad the accountant and Mom the real estate broker, moving to the fifth-floor walkup on Sullivan Street that he'd shared with two classmates.

In the next three years, he'd been in one off-off-Broadway play, two Equity showcases, and one non-Equity summer stock company in New Jersey that he hoped the union had never found out about. He'd also been—between endless auditions—a waiter, a bartender, a cabdriver, a singing delivery man, a telemarketer, Chucky the Clown in a parade, Chucky the Clown at a child's birthday party, Chucky the Clown handing out pamphlets on Madison Avenue, a shoe salesman, and—for one memorable evening with one of the roommates and another guy he'd met in the Equity lounge—a stripper at Chippendales.

De Niro, he'd decided, had not started this way.

He saw Mr. Yakimadoro's ad in *Backstage* ("Between Engagements? Make Good Money While Putting Your Acting Skills to Good Use . . ."). A private investigator: it sounded romantic, and it beat hell out of Chucky the Clown.

So, Yakimadoro Investigations. It was just the three of them—the boss, Robin, and Johnny Russo—and the secretary, Mrs. White, a black grandmother from Harlem. They worked out of a shabby storefront office next to a Korean fruit and vegetable market on lower Eighth Avenue, one short block from the meat-packing district.

In the next eighteen months, he'd made good money while putting his acting skills to good use. He'd found two missing husbands, one missing wife, one missing bookie (his first and only dead body), and two and a half insurance swindlers (the half-swindler actually had the broken leg he'd claimed though not the amnesia). And all without ever once leaving the tri-state area; it seemed to him, in fact, that he'd spent most of his time in Brooklyn.

The romantic world of private investigation.

He'd saved every dime he could. He was tired of the overcrowded walkup on Sullivan. He'd fallen in love with a reasonably priced, recently vacated condo on West Seventieth that he'd discovered in the line of duty (Missing Husband Number Two). He wanted his own place. He wanted a dog, or at least a cat. He wanted a girlfriend. He wanted an acting career.

He wanted a life.

Then, three weeks ago, two extraordinary things had happened. Missing Husband Number Two, back with his wife and desperate to sell, had accepted his offer of a (low) down payment. Robin had paid the man, signed the papers, and moved his meager belongings to his new home. He was just beginning to wonder where the second payment would come from when his boss had called him into his office and handed him the Margaret Barclay case.

Miss Barclay and Mr. Yakimadoro had a mutual acquaintance who had put her in touch with him. She needed someone to tail her niece, who was apparently going to take off any minute for parts unknown. Miss Barclay wanted the parts to be known. He, Robin, was to be ready to leave at a moment's notice, follow the girl wherever, and report back to Miss Barclay.

Then he'd read the dossier. His assignment was a very mixed-up young lady, a spoiled rich girl with a self-destructive streak—not surprising, considering that business when she was little. Oh, well, for a thousand a week he could handle her.

The moment he first saw her, coming out of the Glen Cove house with the two suitcases and getting in the cab, he knew she was not like any woman he'd ever met. She was beautiful, almost as beautiful as her photograph in the file. Her hair in the picture was nicer than her current red shade, but even so, she was still prettier than most. And there was something about her, immediately apparent, even in that short walk to the cab: an attitude; an en-

ergy level; an aura of excitement, of sexuality. *Something*.
She was the sort of woman who could change his life.

And she had. Because of her he'd been in St. Thomas,
and briefly in Florida. That had been the first stop, nearly
three weeks ago.

He'd tailed the cab from Glen Cove to Kennedy, being
careful not to get too close. Rule Number One: keep your
distance. When she'd alighted in front of Delta Air Lines,
Robin had grabbed his bag and followed.

He'd been in the line behind her when she checked in.
Her reservation—to Miami, as it turned out—was under
the name Selena Chase. She'd flown first class, and he'd
booked passage in coach. Rule Number Two: watch expenses.

Rule Number Three, which was really Number One in
importance: never lose the mark. That had very nearly
happened at the Miami Hilton.

He'd shelled out twenty to the redcap who'd carted her
luggage and hailed her cab, to ascertain her destination.
Then he'd made his way to the hotel and paid more than
he could afford for a room. He'd spent most of the night
and morning in the lobby, his battered suitcase on the
floor next to him, waiting for her to show. She'd never left
the place, as far as he could tell. It was nearly noon, and
he was just formulating an elaborate plan for storming the
front desk and finding out which room she was in
(brother? husband? messenger?), when the tall brunette
in the sunglasses had emerged from the elevator, followed
by a bellhop with her bags, and proceeded to settle her
bill.

He'd barely noticed her. She was out the door and in the taxi before it registered. That walk. And then the suitcases: fairly large, with an intricate brown and beige pattern and the designer's name all over the place. Courréges. He'd made a note of them at Kennedy, when he was behind her in line. . . .

In seconds he was lunging into the backseat of the next cab at the stand, shouting that ridiculous, timeworn cliché at the back of someone's head. He'd been lucky: the head belonged to one Angelo Merino, a hip, handsome nineteen-year-old from the country that had produced Mario Andretti. Angelo had known what to do. There was a desperate man in his backseat and a beautiful woman in a car somewhere ahead of *his* car. It was a matter of national pride. After screeching to a halt behind her cab at the entrance to American Airlines at Miami International, he even refused the fifty.

Robin had spent the entire flight to St. Thomas wondering why she was now traveling as Diana Meissen, and why she'd changed her hair.

He'd followed her to Bolongo and settled in to watch and report. He registered as Robert Taylor—a perfect role model for actors *and* detectives. Besides, the name was close enough to his own, and the initials were the same, just in case anybody happened to notice the RT on his suitcase, his key chain, and his wallet. Rule Number Four: pay attention to details.

After several days of watching her swim, paint, shop, and dine in restaurants, he'd begun to believe that he was being paid a great deal to take a vacation. He'd even gone so far as to introduce himself to her twice—"Hi, I'm Bob!"—as anyone would have, considering they were both tourists staying at the same small hotel. His daily calls to Margaret Barclay had been downright boring, yet she had never once suggested that he relax the surveillance.

In the ten days before her disappearance, Robin had seen her come into contact with only two people aside from himself, and both meetings were apparently accidental.

The first had occurred on her third day on the island. She'd been swimming earlier, and then she'd hopped into her rental (pale-blue Chevette, T-48734) and gone into town. She wandered down Main Street, window-shopping and making occasional purchases. She spent some time in a drugstore, where she bought a tube of Colgate toothpaste, dental floss, Tampax, L'eggs pantyhose (Medium Tan), a lipstick (this involved a long ritual in front of a mirror, and she and the two native girls behind the counter discussed, in great detail, the relative merits of Really Red and Passion's Promise before the latter was chosen, to everyone's delight), a large bottle of Renu Multi-Purpose Solution, a small bottle of Bain de Soleil tanning oil, a huge bottle of Après le Soleil post-tanning lotion, a yellow box of something-or-other by Clairol (he was too far away to read the label), and a package of Daisy disposable razors. A few minutes later she went into a perfumerie called Tropicana and asked for a small bottle of something that sounded like Bollifer Sigh.

Her next stop had been a tourist shop with an Arab-sounding name, where she'd bought two souvenir T-shirts, one of which read "I'm a Virgin (Islander)." The other read "If you love someone, let them go. If they come back to you, they're yours forever. If they don't, hunt them down and kill them." She and the salesman, a swarthy gentleman in a turban, shared a good laugh over that one.

Then he'd followed her down an alley to the Waterfront and into a restaurant called Sparky's Waterfront Saloon. She sat at a small table in one corner of the packed room, and he took the only other available table in the place, across the floor. Several groups and couples concealed him from her, but they also nearly obliterated his view. The restaurant had a nautical motif, running to ropes and barrel-stave tables and dim hurricane lamps. They both ordered lunch. When, some minutes later, he got his next unobstructed look at his mark, she was no longer alone.

She'd been joined by another young woman, a big-boned, rather heavyset girl with pudgy features and dull brown hair. They were chatting amiably as they ate, and Robin assumed that the restaurant's obvious popularity had necessitated the doubling up at tables. He looked around: he was now the only lone diner.

Eight people, tourists, had entered and sat at a large table in the center of the room, cutting off his view entirely. He wolfed down his omelette, paid, and headed for the door, having decided to wait outside the restaurant to resume the tail. On his way across the room, he glanced over at the two women and noticed that the big girl was now holding up an overstuffed six-by-nine-inch manila envelope. As he got to the doorway, she laughed rather loudly and placed the envelope in her purse. His quarry watched this, smiling.

Twenty-five minutes later his girl had emerged from the restaurant, and he had followed her back to the hotel.

That evening, he had reported every unremarkable detail of the day's activities to Miss Barclay, right down to the brand of toothpaste she'd bought. The woman seemed puzzled by a couple of her niece's purchases.

The second meeting had been right here on the beach a week later, the day after he'd joined her for lunch. He'd been sitting on his balcony, rereading *Farewell, My Lovely* and occasionally glancing down at her as she painted by the water. One of the club members—that good-looking older gal, the redhead who'd sat next to them the day before—came over to her. They talked and laughed and pointed at the easel. Then they lay on beach chairs and ordered drinks from the waiter. The conversation, apparently casual, lasted about an hour. The redhead left, and a few minutes later the mark rose, collected her easel and paintbox, and came into the hotel. He heard only one part of the conversation: as the older woman was leaving, she turned—right under his balcony—and called back to the girl.

"Good-bye, Diana. I'm glad I finally got up the courage to approach you. See you tomorrow."

The following evening he had lost her, but only temporarily. At about five-thirty he'd tiptoed to her room and put his ear to the door. Running water, a shower. She was getting ready for something. Thinking he'd have a half-hour's grace, he returned to his room, showered, shaved, dressed in his new lightweight seersucker, and then wandered innocently down to the parking lot to wait. He stood there for a good fifteen minutes before he noticed that her rental car was gone.

He'd panicked, but only for a moment. Some club member had invited the girl to dinner, or perhaps a party. Maybe she was an art lover, or an acquaintance from the girl's first visit to the islands a couple of months ago (Miss Barclay had mentioned a Caribbean trip in the dossier). He kicked himself for his own stupidity in losing her and drove into town for dinner. Hell, he could use a night off, away from her.

He'd dined in a noisy, crowded restaurant on the waterfront called The Greenhouse. Three tourist women at the next table had struck up a conversation with him and invited him to sit with them. It was their last night in St. Thomas, and they wanted to go dancing. They were all slightly drunk, and they made it clear—in a friendly, well-bred way—that they were available to him. One woman, a college girl from New Orleans named Ginger, had attracted him. So he'd gone dancing with them, and had entirely too much to drink.

He'd spent the night with Ginger at her hotel. As he made love to her, it occurred to him that he had not been to bed with a woman in nearly six months.

It also occurred to him that she reminded him of his mark.

When he returned to Bolongo the next morning, he'd seen that the pale-blue Chevette was once again in its usual space. The rest of the day was uneventful: the girl painted on the beach and he sat, hung over, watching her.

Now that he thought of it, he remembered something rather peculiar happening on that day, too. He'd been in the pool next to the bar, hoping vainly that the sun and the chlorinated water would ameliorate the throbbing in his head. At one point, the girl left her easel and came over to the bar. She ordered a Coke and asked if she could use the bar's phone for a long-distance call. Robin crawled nearer in the water and lurked there, mere feet away, as the instrument was placed before her.

Just then, a gaggle of boisterous children had crashed into the water nearby. The girl clamped her free hand over her ear and leaned forward, speaking into the phone. He didn't catch all of what she said, but he distinctly heard her ask the operator for a number in Long Island. She uttered a word that might have been "gables," and something else that sounded like "hospital." A moment later someone came on the line, and she spoke for about five minutes. Then she hung up and returned to the beach.

When he heard her ask for Long Island, Robin had assumed she was calling her aunt. That night, however, Margaret denied having heard from the girl. He'd shrugged it off and, professional detective that he was, forgotten all about it.

The next day, as he sat at the bar, the girl had walked out of the hotel and disappeared.

Robin came out of the water and rested on the sand. As the mid-afternoon sun bore down on him and the tropical breeze dried his body, he reviewed his actions since the girl had vanished.

He'd started with the rental car. He'd traced it to the correct agency and flirted outrageously with the girl behind the counter until she admitted to him—though, she whispered, it could cost her her job—that the car had been retrieved from the hotel parking lot on the morning of the girl's disappearance. The client had settled her bill the day before—in cash.

Margaret Barclay had repeated to him what the girl had told her in their last phone conversation. They both knew it was probably a dead end. She'd claimed to be in Miami when she was actually calling from St. Thomas; there was no earthly reason for them to expect that there was a family named Goodman on the island.

In fact, there were two such families. Unfortunately, neither of them included a child—or anyone else—named Linda, nor had either of them recently hired an au pair. They'd never heard of a Diana Meissen. The name Selena Chase meant nothing to them, either. When he mentioned the third possibility, her real name, they lost patience and insisted that he obviously did *not* have the right Goodman. He thanked them and hung up.

There were only a few major flights from the island each day. He planned each morning and afternoon around his trips to the airport. He watched the amorphous crowds boarding planes and scanned the waiting lounges: nothing. He could only hope she would not embark by some other means.

He made the rounds of hotels and guest houses. He

walked the length of Main Street and wandered through the shopping centers and large gathering places. Every beach, restaurant, bar, and nightclub. And every night, very late, he returned alone to the little room with the balcony to gaze out over the moonlit waves and fall, exhausted and empty, into heavy, dreamless sleep.

It was during this time, this long fugue state that lasted only days but seemed to go on for weeks, that he began to realize that he was alone on the island. He didn't know anyone here, and the strangeness of his surroundings heightened his sense of alienation. As this feeling intensified, so did another that had long been suppressed, unnamed and unacknowledged. For the first time in his life, he admitted to himself that he felt despair.

The word, once spoken, opened up a floodgate somewhere in his soul, and out flowed all the pent-up doubt and fear. He was not a detective, not an actor, not anything. He was twenty-six years old, and there was nothing he could point to with any sense of accomplishment or fulfillment.

If searching for an unknown young woman in an unfamiliar place achieved no other goal, it gave him this: when the assignment was over—when he found the girl or did not find her, when he was back in New York with his parents and his few friends once more within reach—he would have to take stock of his life and see if he could discover what it was that he wanted. He would have to reconsider everything.

But first he would find the girl.

A thrill, almost of pleasure, surged through him. It really was that simple, he thought. A sense of purpose, of something that had to be done. Now. Immediately. It was a step, the first of many, in what he hoped was the right direction. And with the decision came the inspiration: the woman. The redhead, the club member who'd spoken to her on this beach—and who'd probably been with her elsewhere as well. He would get to her and see if she knew anything. A real detective would have thought of that before.

He knew better than to ask the manager, or even the friendly bartender, about the redhead. At this hotel, as at all exclusive places, privacy was respected. But it hardly mattered: he'd seen the woman here before, more than once, and he felt certain that she'd show up again, and soon.

He picked up the folder. He would reread the file and commit the brief details of the young woman's biography to memory. Then he'd go back to his room and call Miss Barclay. Put her mind at ease. There was hope, after all; he was sure of it. He would find her niece for her.

As it turned out, he never did find her.

She found him.

SEVEN

SUNDAY, AUGUST 18

PARIS HAD JUST GIVEN the golden apple to Aphrodite, thus making a botch of the world's deadliest beauty pageant, when a shadow fell across the open book. Startled, the young woman looked up to find that Adam had joined them on the patio.

He loomed over them, his hands in his pockets, his body blocking out the sun. A lazy smile played at the corners of his mouth as he gazed down at the young woman and the child huddled together on the loveseat. They blinked mutely up at him, reorienting themselves to St. Thomas in the twentieth century.

"One of my favorites," he drawled without preamble, prompting her to wonder just how long he'd been standing there. "And a lesson to us all. The wrath of the gods—and *female* gods, at that. The poor man never had a chance.

But even so, he should never have chosen Aphrodite. Not when her fellow contestants were so much more powerful. What do you think, baby?"

Lisa, who obviously did not appreciate his interruption of the story, flinched at the hated familiarity and then shrugged.

"Maybe he thought she was the prettiest," she said.

Adam chuckled. "It wasn't about beauty; it was about power. Three choices: Love, Wisdom, and Power. The Queen of the Gods, the wife of Zeus. I would have chosen Hera in a New York minute. And you, Diana—whom would *you* have chosen?"

She thought about it. Handing the book to Lisa, she rose and went over to the driftwood railing to stand, her back to them, staring down at the water crashing against the rocks far below. It had been three days since the beach, since she found the little house with the blankets and the wine bottle and his wife's cigarettes. This was the first time since then that she'd seen him alone, without Kay. Kay Prescott. His wife.

When at last she turned around and spoke, her voice was colder than the depths of the unquiet sea behind her.

"Assuming I were a man," she said, looking directly into his eyes, "assuming I were Paris, I would have selected the goddess I could not control."

He returned her gaze. "And which of them would that have been?"

She didn't smile, and she didn't back down from the deadlock of their eyes.

"Whichever one of them wanted me the least," she replied.

It was Adam who looked away. As soon as he had done so, she turned to the child. "I think we should get some drawing done this afternoon, don't you?"

Lisa was apparently grateful for the excuse to leave.

"Sure," she said, rising and heading for the house. "I'll get the pads. I'm gonna get a Coke, too. Would you like one, Diana?"

"No, thank you."

The child was at the steps to the sundeck before she remembered her manners. "How about you?" she called back to Adam.

"No, thanks."

The moment Lisa was gone, Adam took a step forward and spoke. "What's the matter with you? You just sounded like—"

"Listen," she said, cutting him off, "we only have a few minutes. Did you make the reservations?"

He stared a moment, then nodded.

"New York on Friday the thirtieth," he said. "American Airlines. Frances will meet us at the Waldorf and take Lisa. Our return is set for Thursday the fifth. School starts that week, but Frances will probably keep her in Greenwich, all things—"

"And you?"

"West Palm Beach, the next day. Saturday the thirty-first. Return to New York on the fourth. I have a room booked at the Waldorf for that night. The next day

Frances brings Lisa there, and then we fly back here. That's what everyone thinks, anyway. . . ."

"What about a car for your stay in Florida?"

"Done. Hertz, right?"

She nodded. "Good. The other car will be in Palm Beach. The two round-trip tickets and the other things you'll need will be in the glove compartment. Miami— San Juan: Pam Am. San Juan—St. Thomas: LIAT. I used the names you wanted. There'll be a car at the airport here. Avis. I used a third name for that. Petrillo: you'll have black hair by then, so I figured you could be Italian. I'll write down the address in Palm Beach where the car will be waiting as soon as I know it."

"Who's putting the car in Palm Beach?"

She waved her hand dismissively. "A friend. A woman I, shall we say, did some time with."

He shrugged. "As long as you can trust her. Listen, there may be a problem."

Her eyes widened. "What?"

"Lisa. There's some question as to whether she's going to Connecticut."

A sharp chill of panic coursed through her. "You said she went every year for Labor Day!"

"I know, but Kay thinks maybe—"

She leaned forward. Reaching up, she clutched his upper arm, digging her nails into his flesh. "I want Lisa out of here. Otherwise, it's off. We'll have to postpone—"

"No," he said firmly. "It has to be Labor Day."

She forced herself to look up at him. The pale-blue eyes stared intently down at her, a study in determination.

She had a sudden vision of them on the *Kay*, two months before, planning everything. He'd had that same look in his eyes then. She knew it had to be Labor Day, and why.

"Okay," she said, removing her hand and lowering her gaze. "Just be sure she's on that plane with you."

He nodded. Then, with a swift glance toward the house, he reached out to stroke her hair.

"I want to see you," he breathed. "Away from here. I want to make love to you."

She pulled away from his touch. "Later. After it's over. We'll have time for all that."

A sudden grin lit up his face. She was acutely aware of his eyes; his platinum hair glinting in the sun; the massive, muscular body inches from hers. She could smell aftershave, something with bay rum in it. He'd tried to make love to her once, on the *Kay*, but Greg's presence had precluded it.

He leaned even closer to her.

"We'll have time for a lot of things," he said, and there was laughter in his voice. "Eleven million things, to be exact. And that's not counting the house."

She regarded him for a long moment. Then her gaze fell to the loveseat beside them, to the discarded book lying there.

"The apple was made of solid gold," she said, "but that meant nothing to the goddesses. They wanted it for other reasons."

His smile faded, and the pale eyes darkened.

"I love you," he said. "You know that."

Now, she knew instinctively, it was her turn to take the initiative. With an effort, she grinned and took his hand.

"Yes," she whispered. "I know. Now get out of here."

He squeezed her hand, and his smile reappeared. Then he turned and walked across the lawn in the direction of the driveway.

She stood there, her hand on the driftwood fence, watching him go. Tall, she thought. He's so tall, so blond, so beautiful. . . .

And such a liar.

Then Lisa was running out of the house and across the redwood deck. She turned toward the little girl, and after a moment she began to smile.

"Patio!" Lisa called as she approached with the sketchpads and the soda can clutched in her hands.

"Yard," came the reply.

"Yard—"

"Lawn."

"Lawn—"

"Mower."

Lisa giggled and rolled her eyes. "Mower—"

"Grass."

"Grass—"

"Green."

"Green—"

The woman thought a moment.

"Jealousy," she said.

"Jealousy," Trish exclaimed. "That's all it is, plain and simple. I just can't *stand* it!"

Kay, lying on the adjacent beach chair under her favorite palm tree, followed Trish's gaze and nodded. The girl in the white bikini running down the beach could not be more than twenty. The long, tanned limbs; the slender waist and generous hips; the glistening braid flying out behind her: if only Sandra were here, she mused. She could tell us which film star that reminds me of. . . .

"I know what you mean," she said. "Don't forget, *I'm* the one with Diana Meissen living in her house."

Trish sat up, swung her legs off the chaise, and leaned toward her friend. "Darling, is something the matter?"

Kay looked over at her friend and read the concern in her expression. No, she thought. I'm not going to tell her about the house on the beach. The whole thing would sound paranoid at best. I am *not* one of those hysterical women, always imagining worst-case scenarios and flying into rages.

She shook her head and forced a smile.

"Bo Derek," she said, watching as the lovely young woman in the white bikini floated by along the shoreline before them. She could almost hear the strains of Ravel above the roll of the surf. . . .

"Well, don't underestimate yourself," Trish said. "If I'm not mistaken, you have an admirer—a *young* admirer— over there by the pool. He's been watching you for the last fifteen minutes."

Kay turned her head for a discreet look. She saw him immediately: tall and lanky, with shaggy, sun-bleached hair, clad only in the brief black Speedo. Their eyes locked for a moment, then he flashed a grin and began to walk toward her.

"Oh, him," she sighed. "I'm afraid not, Trish. Another slave of the beauteous Diana."

The man named Bob arrived next to her.

"Hello," he said. "We haven't really met, but my name is—"

"Bob," Kay supplied, smiling at him.

His eyes widened, and the klieg-light grin returned. "Uh, yeah. Bob Taylor. No relation. I'm staying here at the hotel, and I've seen you around a few times. . . ."

"Kay Prescott," Kay said. "This is Patricia Manning."

"Hello, Bob," Trish cooed, reaching up to smooth a jet-black lock into place.

"Hi," he said. "Sorry to disturb you, Ms. Prescott."

"Missus," Kay said.

"Oh. Mrs. Prescott. Sorry. It's just that I noticed you talking to a friend—an *acquaintance*—of mine—"

"Diana Meissen," Kay said, amused by his discomfort. "Yes."

He nodded. "Yeah, well, she—uh—left before I could give her my number in New York. We're both from New York, you know, and I thought when I got back there myself—"

Before Kay could stop her, Trish leaned forward. "Oh, Diana is—"

Kay's warning glance shut her up.

"Diana is a lovely girl," she finished for her.

He looked from one to the other of them. "Yes, well, I was wondering if you knew how to get in touch with her."

Kay leaned back on the chaise. For no reason of which she was immediately aware, she stretched her long legs to their full length and casually brought up her right hand to rest behind her head. She smiled lazily up at the young man.

Then it happened, just as she had been unconsciously hoping it would. Bob, standing over her, dropped his gaze to rake the length of her body. She could tell that it was an appreciative glance, and she was delighted at the sudden blush as he remembered himself and quickly returned his eyes to her face.

He was the answer to an unacknowledged prayer. She'd been feeling odd in recent days, not at all like herself. She thought of Adam, whose lovemaking had been so cold, so perfunctory, the last few times. Beauty, Adam had said, was something we should never take for granted. She had been feeling unbeautiful, undesirable, but this young man had reminded her. He obviously thought she was attractive.

More important, he thought Diana was attractive.

"You understand, Bob," she said, "that I couldn't just hand over such information—assuming I had it, of course. But perhaps you could tell me how long you'll be here at Bolongo, in case I happen to speak with her."

The young man smiled and nodded. "Sure. I'm here for a while. At least a couple of weeks. It all depends on my—employer."

"What do you do?" Trish asked.

He stared at her a moment. Then he looked up at the rows of condominium projects that lined the hills above the beach. Waving in their direction, he said, "Development. Real estate."

The two women nodded.

"Well," Kay said, gazing dreamily—she hoped—up at him through her lashes, "I'll see what I can do. About Diana."

"Great," he said, fixing her once more with the incandescent smile. "Thank you. It was a pleasure meeting you. Both of you."

With that he turned and loped away down the beach.

Trish sighed, her eyes on his receding form. "My, he certainly has a beautiful—personality. But what's with all the secrecy, Kay? Why didn't you simply tell him—"

"I couldn't," Kay interjected. "I saw Diana with him once. I don't think she'd appreciate my disclosing her whereabouts to him. Not without her permission."

Trish shook her head in disbelief.

"How very peculiar of her," she decided. "What is she, a nun? Let me tell you: if that young man should ever ask, you hereby have permission to disclose *my* whereabouts!"

They laughed together and sipped their planter's punch. Kay lit a cigarette.

"Seriously, though," she told her friend, "you can't be too careful. You never know who anybody is."

Trish gave her a withering glance. "Oh, for sure! His name isn't Bob Taylor and he isn't in real estate. He's actually the Kissing Bandit, preying on rich locals. Hey, maybe *he* pulled off the job at Stu and Brenda's house!"

"Really, Trish! Don't make vulgar jokes about that. It was awful for them. Poor Brenda. All her jewels gone without a trace. Imagine if they'd been home when it happened, instead of playing golf with you. They might have been . . ." She shuddered, just thinking of it.

"Yeah," Trish agreed, sobered by the thought. "But still, it's too bad they didn't discover the jewelry missing until the next day. There might have been a chance for the police to catch the man."

Kay was no longer thinking about that. She was thinking about Bob Taylor. The way he'd looked at her body, and the ardent expression in his eyes when he'd asked about Diana. She reached again for her drink and settled back on the beach chair.

Bob Taylor, she thought. Diana. Yes, they'd make a lovely couple.

She didn't have much time. Kay and Trish would be back from Bolongo by five-thirty, and she was expected to help with dinner. Nola was off on Sundays, so Kay prepared the meals.

She'd seated Lisa at the table on the deck, telling her to sketch the hurricane lamp in its center. Then, claiming allergies she did not possess and the need for a refill on a nonexistent prescription, she'd climbed into the Land Rover and driven here, to the Havensight Mall next to the docks. Not too far from Cliffhanger, and plenty of public phones. There was also a pharmacy that was open on Sunday, in case there were any questions. She found a bank of egg-shaped phone shells at the end of a row of shops. No cruise ships were docked behind the shopping center today, and there were few people about.

Her first call, charged to her Calling Card, was to South Bay Gables, the rest home in Brookhaven, Long Island. She hadn't phoned there in a week, since that last day at Bolongo, and she was anxious for a report. She spoke to a nurse and to the doctor on duty, and both assured her that everything was as well as could be expected. She thanked them and hung up.

She didn't want the second call to ever be traced back to her, so the Calling Card was out.

"Operator, I'd like to place a collect, person-to-person call to Mrs. Juana Velasquez in Jacksonville, Florida."

"Number, please."

She gave it.

"Who's calling, please?"

"Tell her it's Blanca."

She waited, imagining her friend at home in the little house in the unfashionable part of town. She'd been there once, briefly, shortly after Juana and her husband had moved there. If her guess was correct, her friend would be home this afternoon, tending to the baby—her godchild and namesake—and waiting for a Sunday-evening call from Carlos, currently a guest of the state.

Sure enough, Juana answered on the second ring. The baby was gurgling in the background, and she smiled at her friend's sudden, hearty laugh upon hearing the name of the caller.

"*Hola!*" Juana cried. "Where you callin' from?"

"Someplace."

"Okay, 'Blanca.' White girl. I haven' call' you dat in years. Ever since de clinic. Hey, you keepin' clean?"

"One day at a time."

"Me, too. I don' even take *aspirin,* since de baby."

"How is she?"

"She fine. She *big!* You come visit soon, see fo' yo'sel'."

"I will, soon. Promise." She cringed at the lie, even as she heard herself uttering it. "How's Carlos?"

"Ay! *Madre de Dios!* Dat man! 'Nother fifteen mont's."

"It'll be over soon, Juana. Then he'll be home."

"If I let him! Stupid idiot!"

"I hear you. Listen, Juana, I don't have much time. Did you get my package?"

"Uh-huh. 'Bout a week ago. I done like you say. Carlos' brodder, Tino, foun' a good car. I drobe it down dere my-sel'. Here's de address of de parkin' lot."

Good, she thought: an out-of-the-way place off North County Road in Palm Beach. "And the stuff in the glove compartment?"

"All dere, jus' like you say in de letter. Streaks and Tips, black. Mustache an' beard, an' dat stuff you put it on wid, spirit gum. All dem plane tickets, too. Hey, what do I do wid de rest of de money? Tino got de car fo' 'bout twelb hunnerd, an' de odder stuff cost about fifty. You sent ten grand. What's de rest for?"

"My godchild. And her mother."

There was a pause on the other end of the line.

"You some crazy white girl. *Te amo*—Blanca. Dis ting you doin': you ain't in no trouble?"

She blinked, surprised by the sudden tears in her eyes. "No, Juana. I'm not in any trouble. Really. Thank you for everything. I have to go now. I'll be in touch real soon."

"You watch yo' ass. *Vaya con Dios.*"

"I love you, Juana. *Vaya con Dios.*"

She hung up the phone. She raised her hands to her face, wiping away the tears that were now cascading down her cheeks. Then, checking to be sure she was not being noticed, she ran to the Land Rover and drove back to Cliffhanger as fast as she could. She arrived mere moments before the others.

Kay told her about the meeting on the beach that night after dinner, over coffee in the living room. It was one of those oh-by-the-way things that always seemed to surprise her.

"Oh, by the way," Kay said, settling back into the white couch facing her, "we ran into Bob Taylor at Bolongo today."

She had to think a moment to remember who Bob Taylor was.

"Who's Bob Taylor?" Adam wanted to know.

She watched with an odd mixture of annoyance and amusement as he dropped gracefully, effortlessly, onto the couch next to his wife and grinned across the coffee table. Was there a note of jealousy in his voice? No; she was being fanciful. How was Adam to know that Bob Taylor was a handsome young man? For all he knew, Bob Taylor could be an old man in a wheelchair. . . .

"He's not a who, he's a *what*!" Trish exclaimed, thereby enlightening the world in general and Adam in particular. "He's a hunk, a fox, an absolute *sculpture*. And he's *very* interested in finding *you*, Diana. My dear, take a marginally older woman's advice and run—do not walk—to the nearest telephone."

"Well, here's what I was thinking," Kay said, leaning forward as her husband dropped an arm across her shoulders. "The reason I mention it. The you-know-what is Thursday." She glanced up toward Lisa's room before continuing. "Five of her friends are coming, the Hogan sisters and another girl and two little boys. The grown-up contingent is getting a bit coupley: Adam and me, Kyle and some young woman or other, and Trish and Jerry Flynn."

"Lucky man," Trish interjected.

"That leaves you, Diana," Kay explained. "Odd man out. I don't know how you feel about it, but I thought perhaps—"

"I see," she said, nodding.

She did see. Kay was being a clever hostess, balancing the seating at the table in the restaurant following the birthday sail on the *Kay*. These things were important to Kay Prescott, who seemed intent on making everything, even a child's birthday party, a picture-perfect example of domestic bliss. Her every action made the statement "See what I do for my family."

She regarded Kay across the coffee table, thinking—not for the first time—that this woman was probably not unlike her own mother. As she had been. Before.

"Well," she said. "I'll think about it. Is he still at Bolongo?"

"Indefinitely," Trish said, reaching for a bottle of dark amber liquid to top off her glass. "He's here looking at real estate for development, or something lucrative like that.

Although, I must say, he seems terribly young for such an office. Oh, well, my movie friends keep telling me that all the moguls in Hollywood these days are about nineteen years old, so I reckon anything's possible. *Do* ask him, dear. It might be great fun. For *you,* I mean. . . ."

Everyone laughed. She took the opportunity of this light moment to steal a surreptitious glance at Adam. He was leaning comfortably against his wife, his arm draped over her shoulders, playing absently with a lock of her bright-red hair. As she met his gaze across the table, he winked at her and nodded his head.

So. That was that. *He* wanted her to do this thing, too: invite a complete stranger to be her date at the party. Another beard, like Greg on the *Kay* two months ago. She looked into his smiling eyes and spoke, unable to resist the dig.

"You're right about one thing, Trish. He *is* a sculpture. Rather like a god, something in bronze."

She watched, unamused, as the amusement drained from Adam's face. She momentarily studied his large fingers as they twirled Kay's hair, the deep red strands against the deeply tanned flesh, committing that image of casual intimacy to memory. Then she rose to her feet.

She had to get out of that room.

"I'll do the dishes," she announced, reaching down for the silver tray that held the coffee things.

"Don't bother, dear," Kay offered, dropping her hand onto her husband's thigh, a gracious smile on her lips. "I can see to it later—"

"No," she said. "You made dinner. I'll clean up. It's no trouble, really."

With that she picked up the heavy tray and walked through the swinging door into the kitchen. She placed the tray with the other dishes near the sink and leaned forward, her hands pressing down on the countertop. She lowered her head and closed her eyes, waiting for the dizziness and nausea to subside.

With little thought for what she was doing, she reached out with both hands and turned on the faucets. She picked up the plastic bottle and squeezed a stream of clear yellow liquid into the sink. She watched, transfixed, as the water rushed noisily down to mingle with the detergent and filled the stainless steel basin with a rising carpet of pearlescent foam. The hot steam floated upward, assaulting her nostrils with the cloying aroma of artificial lemons. She loaded the glassware in first, plunging her hands down into the scalding water, experiencing that brief, almost pleasant thrill of exquisite pain before her skin adjusted to the temperature. She washed and rinsed, washed and rinsed: glasses, plates, platters. She followed them with the cutlery, thinking all the while of the little smile on Kay's face as she touched her husband, of Adam's face as he twirled his wife's hair. Round and round, between his fingers, round and round. . . .

The little burst of pain made its way through her reverie and into her brain, dispersing the fantasy. She cried out softly and jerked her hands from the water. Looking down, she saw her left hand clutching the handle of the enormous carving knife, and her right hand grasping the blade itself.

Then she saw the blood.

It spread out quickly over the surface of her wet palm, emanating from the long, thin slash that ran along the base of her fingers. She stared, transfixed, as the edges feathered out, mixing with the water on the hand, covering it and dropping slowly, drip, drip, drip, into the sink. The ribbon of red against the soft, white flesh. . . .

The bloody hand reaching slowly out to her, inching its way across the rough pile of the carpet. The soft moaning sound filling her ears, feeding her terror. The cold hardness of the knife clutched in her tiny fingers. The cry of rage welling up inside her. The first wave of merciful shock, dulling her senses, blinding her eyes to the sight as she crouches in the doorway of the bedroom. Blood on the wall, the carpet, the bedspread. Darkness.

The knife fell into the basin, sending a splash of soapy water up into her face. As the jolt of naked, primordial panic shot through her body, her unwounded hand flew up involuntarily to clamp over her mouth, cutting off the scream. The sound that ultimately forced its way out of her throat and past her rigid fingers was little more than a whimper.

"Mommy."

The door swung open behind her. She was no longer alone in the kitchen. She stood frozen, unable to turn around or even think clearly. She held the bleeding hand over the sink, staring down at it as if it did not belong to her, wondering what to do.

"My dear, what on earth . . .?" Kay Prescott cried as she came up behind her. "You're bleeding! Here."

She stood there staring down, hearing the ripping of soft paper, and then she felt the pressure as Kay took her injured hand and pressed the towel to the cut.

"Hold that there tightly," Kay instructed as she pulled open a drawer and rummaged.

She held the paper towel, still stupid, still unable to form a coherent thought. She felt the towel being pulled away by soft fingers, heard the aerosol hiss. Something cool made contact with the wound and then began to burn.

"Ouch," she said.

She heard Kay giggle softly, smelled her fragrance. Opium. Kay Prescott, Adam's wife, wore Opium. When her mind began to function, she focused on the hand holding the spray can of Bactine. Of course this woman would keep Bactine handy: she had a twelve-year-old daughter. Lisa. The fingers clutching the can had long, tapered nails. She recognized the polish as Passion's Promise, the same shade as the lipstick she herself had bought recently. Perhaps in the same drugstore, with the same friendly women hovering over her, advising, helping her to choose . . . .

"What did you do to yourself?" Kay asked, reaching again into the drawer to produce cotton gauze, surgical tape, and scissors.

She shook her head absently.

"It's nothing," she insisted, watching as the woman

quickly and expertly bound her hand. "There was a knife, under the suds."

Kay glanced down at the sink, clearly perplexed. "Yes, but why were you washing the dishes by hand?"

She followed Kay's gaze from the sink to the space down below the counter. Oh, God, a dishwasher. Of course.

Then they both began to laugh.

"Darling, when was the last time you were in a kitchen?"

She felt the flush on her cheeks. "It's been a while."

Kay nodded. "I'm never here myself if I can help it."

"As she stood there laughing with Kay Prescott, she raised her left hand to her chest. The hand touched something small and cold. She looked down.

It was the amethyst brooch.

She mumbled something, some sort of thanks, something about being suddenly exhausted, and left the kitchen. She made her way quickly across the living room and up the stairs, pausing to say good night to Trish and Adam, who sat in uncomfortable silence, obviously waiting anxiously for Kay's return. She stopped once, briefly, at the top of the stairs and turned to look down at the two people seated below her. The last thing she saw was Adam's face as he gazed up at her, glowing in the soft light from the chandelier. Then she turned around and walked down the hall to her room. She closed the door behind her and locked it.

She moved swiftly across to the closet, pulled out the suitcase from behind the hanging clothes, hauled it up onto the bed, and unlocked it. She sat down and leafed slowly through the newspaper clippings in the scrapbook. The old case, twenty years ago, with the photographs she couldn't bear to look at. Tonight she forced herself to study them. Then she turned to the other case, the one in Hawaii. The accompanying pictures were no less horrible, but she stared at them for a long time, feeling herself become filled with the sharp, breathless excitement.

Yes, she thought, poring over the clippings. I can do this.

It had been a bad moment there in the kitchen, with the blood on her fingers. But there would be no more of that: she would close her mind and her heart to the past, concentrate only on *now*. She would do what had to be done, like—

Antigone.

Diana, Goddess of the Hunt.

A slow smile spread across her face. She put aside the scrapbook and reached once more into the suitcase, into the small hidden compartment at the back.

Slowly, carefully, she withdrew the knife.

She held it up before her, watching the long, thin blade winking in the light. She pressed it flat against the side of her face, feeling the ice-cold steel bite into her warm cheek. She closed her eyes and emitted a long, low sigh. Then she opened her eyes and held the dagger out, inspecting the carved brass handle with the intricate design. The designer's name appeared at the base of the handle, where it met the eight-inch blade. Kouronos.

Her smile widened.

It was a Greek knife.

She had gone to a great deal of trouble to find it. It had to be a Greek dagger. A Kouronos. Once, long ago, she had held another just like it.

"Mommy."

She realized, after several moments, that she had uttered the word aloud.

She replaced the weapon in its hiding place, thinking as she did so of Adam. Adam, tall and beautiful, a god disguised as a man. She thought of Kay Prescott, his wife, and of Lisa, his stepdaughter.

Then she thought of Adam's plan.

Labor Day. . . .

As she locked the suitcase and returned it to the closet, she became aware of the soft patter that had begun on the roof above her. She undressed carefully, with only the one good hand for the buttons and the brooch, turned down the sheet on the bed, and switched off the light. She walked across the room, naked in the dark, and opened the sliding glass door. The warm tropical rain splashed down on her as she stepped out onto the balcony above the wet, deserted sundeck. Light shone out onto the deck from the living room, and through the rain she could hear the muffled sound of laughter. Slowly, deliberately, she raised her unbandaged fist above her head and swiftly, violently flung it outward.

The amethyst glinted once in the rainy silver moonlight as it arced and plummeted down, down into the ocean waiting far below, at the base of the cliff.

PART TWO

GODDESS OF THE HUNT

EIGHT

MONDAY, AUGUST 19

IF YOU SURVIVE long enough, Margaret decided, everything eventually happens to you. I am living proof of that.

She was kneeling in the soft black earth next to the rosebushes, thankful for a sunny day, meticulously extracting the offending weeds from the base of one that was particularly besieged. She leaned over to the nearest blossom, blood-red and fairly bursting in the warm morning air. Closing her eyes, she drank in the rich perfume.

Summer roses. How many have I planted in my time? Nurtured, tended, loved: ten thousand? Twenty? More, probably. And that was merely the roses. There had been marigolds and honeysuckle, zinnias, tulips—and violets, her second greatest horticultural passion. She'd even had a go at orchids once, but had found she didn't have the patience for them. Orchids required a certain artistic temperament that she had never possessed.

Her mind was wandering this morning, more than usual. But at least, she thought, I'm aware of the fact. I'm just nervous.

He will be here very soon.

She had thought long and hard before finally picking up the phone and making the call. There were several options open to her, and this had seemed to be the wisest.

Of course, she could just wait for news from Robin Trask in St. Thomas. But the young man, nice as he seemed to be, was not a very competent investigator. Besides, he couldn't know just how worrisome the girl's behavior was. Certainly not from the brief outline she'd provided in the dossier.

No, she could not remain inactive. A passive role had never been in her repertoire.

Nor could she go barging down there. The thought had occurred to her several times a day ever since Robin's report that the girl had vanished. She'd fantasized about it: arriving in St. Thomas and going straight to the local police, locating her niece, and bringing her back to the States. In handcuffs, if necessary. Tell them she was a thief, or an escaped mental patient—

No. Whatever else she was, the girl was a Barclay. Family. Nothing so ignominious, so undignified, could be allowed to happen to her, despite her own undignified behavior in the past. Margaret could suffer disgrace if it was brought about by her niece, but she could never bring herself to be the direct cause of it.

Besides, such an act would end their relationship. The girl would never forgive her. She loved her niece more than anything else, and she feared losing her.

She would never admit that fear, not to another living soul, and certainly not to her niece. It was a weakness, a ridiculous dependency, and she prided herself on her strength. She'd only recently admitted her fear to herself. It hardly mattered. She could always, for the record, fall back on her other phobia as her true reason for not going to St. Thomas.

Margaret was afraid of airplanes. Ever since the crash, some forty years ago, that had claimed both her parents and her young husband, leaving her—barely out of her teens—to bring up her much younger sister by herself. She had been married only a year when the tragedy occurred, and she was seven months pregnant. The news brought on a miscarriage, during which she very nearly died. She'd lain in the hospital wanting to die, trying to will it to happen. The pain of that time had never left her, but neither had she succumbed to it. She'd returned to the house in Glen Cove, to the little sister who needed her.

Once, in the sixties, she'd wanted to go to the surprise wedding of an old friend in Texas. She'd even boarded the United 727 at La Guardia and taken her seat. But the moment the enormous airliner began to taxi down the runway, she'd experienced an overwhelming sense of panic. She'd risen from her seat, taken the nearest flight attendant aside, and quietly but firmly explained the situation. The plane had returned to the gate, and from that day to this she had never flown.

Of course, if it became necessary, she could book passage on a cruise ship. But the shortest voyage available took four days, so, after much thought, Margaret had chosen a third option.

Now, in the garden, she rose painfully to her feet, brushed the dirt from her knees, picked up the watering can, and hobbled slowly into the house to wait for him.

The housekeeper, Mrs. O'Rourke, lowered the silver tea service onto the coffee table between them and left the living room. A moment later he heard the faint sound of a vacuum cleaner. That woman certainly earns her salary, he thought as he settled back on the couch and looked around. It was an enormous house: the big living room with its large, comfortable furniture covered in dark burgundy velvet; the curved staircase leading to the upper floor; the doors to the patio revealing a glimpse of the flagstone terrace and the roses beyond. There was an office next to this room, he remembered, and a dining room and kitchen on the other side. A beautiful gray BMW in the garage. He glanced over at the grand piano covered with silver-framed photographs.

The woman across from him was as he remembered her: handsome, regal, yet somehow also warm and friendly. A woman with an enormous capacity for love.

He accepted the tea she poured, thinking what he'd thought the last time he was here, four years ago. Any child growing up in this lovely house with this lovely woman should feel secure, well adjusted, happy. But he knew from his practice that people rarely responded as expected.

Dr. David Stein had just turned fifty, and people were still a constant source of surprise and fascination to him. His wife was always laughingly reminding him that this was why he'd become a clinical psychologist in the first place. He remembered the young woman, this woman's niece, quite well. Very beautiful. Very friendly, when she wanted to be. But he'd always had the impression that, even alone with him, she was not very forthcoming. She had secrets that nobody shared.

He adjusted the wire-rimmed bifocals on his round, friendly face and ran a hand through his thinning black hair. Then he settled his stocky, worsted-covered body more comfortably on the couch.

"So that's where it stands now," Margaret told him, continuing the conversation that had been interrupted by the housekeeper's entrance. "She's called twice, both times very briefly, both times claiming to be in Florida with a child named Linda Goodman and her family."

There was a princess phone on the end table next to her couch. She pointed to it. "See that little wire sticking out at the side? I told the Nassau County police that I've been receiving anonymous calls threatening my life. The second call, two days ago, was from a public phone at a mall in St. Thomas. She's there somewhere. And she's presumably going by one of two names, Diana Meissen or Selena Chase. She has dark hair and brown eyes—don't ask me why! On her third day down there she bought a large bottle of contact lens solution and a box of what was obviously hair coloring. She apparently plans to keep the charade for a considerable amount of time. She'd just dyed her hair in Miami, so why another box? And why a large bottle of solution, when small ones are available? Why lenses at all, for that matter? She has perfect vision."

He smiled. "Perhaps *you* should hire yourself out as a detective."

"I'm worried, Dr. Stein. Of all the people I consulted, you were the one who made the most sense. She's been fine—really!—since you worked with her four years ago. In fact, about three years ago she became positively serene. She got a part-time job and enrolled in acting classes in the City. I asked her at the time what had brought about her change in attitude, and she said, 'At last I know what I want to do, and how to do it.' I assumed she meant the acting lessons.

"Then, a few months ago, she got it into her head that she wanted to see the West Indies. She took off for the Islands, and she was gone for over a month. When she returned, she was very excited about the trip. There was something peculiar, though: she'd dyed her hair bright red."

"She'd never done that before?" the doctor asked.

"No, never. And something else: the airline ticket she'd used to come back from the Islands. She left it on the coffee table when she got home. The name was written on the Pan Am envelope in huge black letters: Selena Chase."

Dr. Stein leaned forward. "Did you ask her about it?"

He watched as Margaret began absently twisting her fingers together.

"No," she whispered. "I learned long ago that there's no point in interrogating the girl."

He nodded: he'd learned that himself. He glanced down at the file on the coffee table, his own transcripts of his sessions with the girl four years before.

"And the red hair?" he asked.

"She kept it that way until she took off three weeks ago. She *said* she was on her way to Florida, but by then I'd engaged Robin Trask to follow her. She dyed her hair brown and went to St. Thomas. I'm very worried, Dr. Stein."

"So you called me," he said.

"Yes. I thought perhaps you could find some pattern to all this, something that might indicate where she is or what she's doing."

He sat back on the couch and thought for a moment before answering. How had she done this? How had she managed to get him involved before he'd even agreed to take the case? He and his wife were leaving in a week for a long-awaited vacation in Europe.

Oh, well, it hardly mattered: he was involved now. Extraordinary woman. . . .

"All right," he said, leaning forward again. "Here's what we know. Refresh my memory if I leave out anything pertinent."

Margaret sat there gazing out at her garden, watching the shadows lengthen from late afternoon to dusk, listening as the doctor recounted the story. Now and then she supplied a detail, but mostly she remained silent.

Margaret's sister, Madeleine, fifteen years her junior, had married a man named Bert Petersen when she was nineteen. He was a twenty-year-old Merchant Marine she'd met at a dance, big and handsome and friendly, and Margaret had thought him entirely unsuitable. A poor boy marrying a rich girl. A poor boy who hadn't even gone to college. A laborer. But Madeleine had always had a streak in her that her sister found rather perverse: she shunned the rich men of her acquaintance, dismissing them as soft, self-absorbed, boring. True enough, Margaret supposed now, and Bert was certainly handsome, with a definite strength that could only be described as masculine. Madeleine had been immediately, overwhelmingly attracted. Margaret wondered if she would so quickly disapprove of him now, but she had been younger then. At any rate, her low opinion of him had changed a year later, when the child was born.

The young family lived in Islip, Long Island, not too far from Margaret, who had never remarried. She saw a great deal of Madeleine and Bert, often staying in their house or going out with them in their little sailboat. Margaret forgave her brother-in-law for stealing away her only sister, and everyone doted on the beautiful child.

Doting on her was probably mistake number one, according to Margaret. Even before the events that destroyed her family, the little girl had shown signs of being terribly spoiled. She screamed and cried when she didn't get her way, and she frequently flew into destructive rages. Bert was away with his business more often than not, and when he was around he paid scant attention to his daughter. Madeleine was much firmer with the child, and the child obviously resented it. She had announced to Margaret on more than one occasion that she hated her mommy. She would sit on the front steps of the house for hours, waiting for her father to return from his long trips. When he at last arrived, the girl would follow him everywhere.

Madeleine remained stoic about her daughter's obvious favoritism. She insisted to Margaret, smiling, that it was a passing phase. She cheerfully went about the business of disciplining her daughter, and the child loudly went about the business of resisting.

Margaret, however, was ecstatic. In addition to her sister, she now had a young brother-in-law who seemed to like her and a niece whom she adored. She became part of an extended family, and they were her world.

That world came to an abrupt end late one rainy September night in Islip, when the child was six years old. Bert was away, and Madeleine and her daughter were alone in the house. . . .

At this point in the story, Margaret covered her eyes with her hand and held her breath. Dr. Stein, noticing this, skipped over the events of the robbery and murder of Madeleine Petersen and the subsequent fate of her grieving husband.

It hardly mattered. The facts, such as they were, were available from police and media reports of the time. The robber, who had been terrorizing the town, leaving several homes bare and three people dead—four, if you counted Bert—was never brought to justice.

There was really no point in going into all of it now: this was the blank space in his sessions with the young woman, anyway. She apparently had no memory of the night in question or of the next week, which she spent in the hospital. Neither had she, in her conversations with the doctor, once mentioned her father's apparent suicide some six months later. All she seemed to recall were the dreams that had plagued the rest of her childhood, horrible dreams of an enormous black figure with a knife coming toward her. A large black man, or someone wearing a black stocking mask.

Dr. Stein had offered to help her confront the past, four years ago, in the wake of her own suicide attempt. She had refused hypnosis, refused to discuss it at all.

Now, seeing the worry on Margaret Barclay's face, he continued the recapitulation.

After the incidents with her parents, the girl had been brought here to live, and Margaret had legally adopted her. Even then she was willful and rebellious. Recurring nightmares. Disruptive in classrooms: by the age of sixteen, she'd been in and out of more schools than Margaret could remember. Fighting with other children, especially those who knew about her parents and teased her. Children could be so cruel. One bad time at a convent school with a nun, who required brief hospitalization after the girl attacked her.

Then, when she was sixteen, something happened to change her, quiet her down. She was getting ready to leave for boarding school in upstate New York at the time, the school from which she would graduate a year later. For reasons unknown to her aunt, she suddenly became very serious and applied herself to her schoolwork. She improved her relationship with Margaret. For the next three years, her world was relatively sane.

Upon coming of age, she inherited a great deal of money. Not as much as it might have been: after his wife's death, Bert had gone on a six-month tear of drinking and gambling before meeting his own fate. By the time he was through, at least half of his wife's fortune was gone. Still, his daughter's inheritance was considerable.

One year later, at the age of nineteen, the girl went crazy again. It was more insidious this time, more overwhelming. She was in the middle of her second semester at Nassau Community College. Living with Margaret in this house, commuting to classes, doing quite well in all respects. Margaret had grown used to having the girl with her, to their sharing meals, planning weekends, talking together long into the night.

One sunny April day, the girl announced to her aunt that she was quitting school and going off to see the world. She'd bought a plane ticket to Hawaii and was leaving the next morning.

Nothing Margaret said could dissuade her: she took off the next day for Honolulu. She phoned the minute she was once again on solid ground, knowing as she did that

Margaret was fearful of her flying and would stop worrying only when she knew her niece was no longer airborne.

Dr. Stein consulted his notes and resumed, "About a year and a half after her disappearance to Hawaii, you received a call from the San Francisco police."

Margaret sat rigid, her fingers gripping the arms of her chair.

"Yes," she said after a moment. "She'd been living there for some fifteen months, with a group of hippies she'd met in Hawaii. In some communal house in Haight-Ashbury. The house had been raided for drugs and several of its occupants arrested, including the man with whom she'd become involved. Some sort of singer, and twice her age. One of the men in the house was a police plant, or whatever they're called. He told them that my niece was not involved in selling drugs, but that she was—she was an addict. The police found her home address and called me.

"They sent her home with a detective I hired to escort her. She was ill. She weighed about eighty-five pounds when she arrived. I knew nothing about these things, about heroin and cocaine and what have you. With the help of the family doctor, I put her in a clinic here on Long Island. She was there for four months. As soon as they'd let me, I went to see her every day. She was miserable, sorry for what she'd done with her life. It was an awful time for her, for both of us—"

Dr. Stein raised his hand to stop her. There was no need for her to go on: he knew the rest. In addition to her other problems, the girl had been two months pregnant.

Margaret, on the advice of doctors and going against her every belief, had consented to what they called termination of pregnancy. An abortion. But she agreed with the experts that it would be impossible for her niece to carry the child to term, under the circumstances.

When the girl was released from the clinic, she expressed a desire to complete her interrupted education. She wasn't yet sure what she wanted to do, exactly, but she wanted to go back to college. The best college possible. She studied diligently and scored high on her SATs, and Margaret promptly used every contact and old family friend to get her into Harvard. It took a while to arrange, but finally, at the age of twenty-two, the girl went to Boston.

Once again, it lasted only two semesters. She flunked most of her courses, and the dean Margaret spoke with reported a history of absence from classes and inattention. *Disaffected:* that was the word the woman used. The girl didn't seem to care about anything. Furthermore, the dean informed her, there were rumors that the girl was carrying on with a married professor, a man twice her age, notorious as a libertine. Margaret, fearing the reappearance of drugs, had the girl brought home.

Forty-eight hours after her arrival in the house, Margaret found her on the floor of the upstairs bathroom, the empty pill bottle lying next to her. A doctor in Boston, unaware of her history, had prescribed Seconal for her nightmare-induced insomnia. The figure in the black mask had apparently returned.

The paramedics arrived just in time.

That was when Dr. Stein first met her. Margaret's friend Elizabeth, better known as Bitsy, knew his wife. He came here to the house, as Margaret was unwilling to let the young woman go out by herself.

He remembered the day clearly: his arrival in this house and its odd sense of silence, of shadowy darkness. The polite formality of this handsome woman as she introduced him to her niece.

He'd been struck by the girl's beauty, and by her air of tragedy. There was something intense about her that reminded him of the Greek plays he'd read in college. They talked for weeks about her parents, her recurring nightmares, her lost child, and her impotent rage, which so often resulted in erratic behavior and unhappiness. He explained to her the particulars of manic-depressive psychosis. He suggested further hospitalization. No, she insisted, she would take charge of her life without more doctors, and certainly without more drugs. After two months, she stopped seeing him.

He spoke to Margaret, but there was nothing they could do, short of having the girl declared incompetent and forcing her to receive treatment. This Margaret refused to do.

Her condition gradually improved. All else aside, he now reflected, the girl was a survivor. She calmed down, took a part-time job at a local clothing store, and began acting classes in the City. She occasionally saw another young woman, one she'd met in the clinic. This girl's name was Juana, and she was the first real friend Margaret's niece had ever had. Margaret did not care for the loud, vulgar young woman, but she appreciated Juana's steadying influence.

By the time Juana married her boyfriend—apparently some sort of petty criminal—and moved to his hometown in Florida, the girl seemed to have become calmer than she'd ever been. She went to visit her friend in Jacksonville the next year, when Juana's baby was born. She'd become a friendly, caring, normal human being, or so Margaret had thought.

Then, recently, the old patterns had surfaced again. About three months ago, the girl had quit her job and taken off for the West Indies, returning with a new shade of hair and a disturbing, feverish sense of purpose. She'd thrown herself into the acting classes as never before. Then, three weeks ago, she'd announced that she was going to Florida.

Margaret had assumed she was going to visit her friend, but Juana's name was never mentioned. It had seemed to Margaret that her niece might very well be on the verge of another manic disappearance. Bitsy—again—had come through, putting her in touch with Yakimadoro Investigations.

Then, two days ago, Dr. Stein had received another urgent call from the woman in Glen Cove.

It was now early evening, and he would have to leave soon. His wife was expecting him for dinner.

They regarded each other across the coffee table as he thought back over all his previous visits to this house. The sessions with the girl had all taken place here, in the living room. He looked down at the folder next to him, the sketchy details of a troubled life.

The figure in the mask. The aura of Greek tragedy. The love of puzzles: anagrams and word games. The desire to become someone else: hair dye and false identities and acting lessons. The episodes of mania, followed by near-catatonic depression. The two instances—ten years ago, when she was sixteen, and again three years ago—when she had lapsed into some odd condition of serenity, even euphoria. The drugs, the abortion, the attempted suicide. Affairs with much older, usually married, men. Over all, her reticence: her fiercely guarded privacy, her unwillingness to communicate with her aunt, with him, with anyone. She was apparently repeating an elaborate pattern, over and over. She wasn't hopeless, wasn't incompetent—not yet. Find the pattern, find the solution. He would have to do something nobody had yet done.

He would have to invade her privacy.

He glanced over at the staircase, then stood up and faced her. "Would you take me upstairs, please, Margaret? I've never been up there. I want to see her bedroom."

She asked no questions. Without a word, she rose from her chair and led the way up the stairs and down the hall. She opened the door, switched on the light, and stood just inside the doorway, watching as he walked past her and into the room.

Blue. It was his first, overwhelming impression. The walls, the bedspread, the rug next to the bed, the curtains at the large window on the far wall. Deep, clear blue. The color of the sky and of water. The color that was said to be best, psychologically, for interior decoration, with its calming, soothing effect. He stared around at the blue, wondering if it had done the room's occupant the slightest bit of good.

He went over to the window and looked out. It was twilight now, and he could barely make out the dark shape of the tall tree just beyond the pane. The lights of the house next door winked through the leaves and branches.

There were several furnishings in dark brown wood: a bedside table that held an alarm clock, a blue-shaded lamp, and a blue telephone; a large bureau next to the window (he pulled open all the drawers, which contained clothing); a hope chest at the foot of the bed, filled with sheets, blankets, and an eiderdown comforter. But the side of the room that most interested him had three bookshelves running nearly the entire length of the wall, with an old-fashioned mahogany writing desk beneath them.

The two upper shelves contained a wild assortment, a mélange of seemingly unrelated literature: novels, plays, poetry. Robert Frost and James Michener and Agatha Christie, Hawthorne, Delderfield, Anne Tyler, the Brontës. Toni Morrison leaned against Jackie Collins, who propped up Mary Renault. Anthologies of playwrights: Williams, Shaw, Chekhov, Neil Simon. No rhyme or reason; a wide range of moods.

The bottom shelf, just above the desk, was a different matter entirely. It was her reference shelf, the permanent collection. The *Random House Encyclopedia*; *Webster's Ninth*; Uta Hagen's *Respect for Acting*; the complete works of Shakespeare; Roget, Bartlett. The Bible, King

James version. At the extreme right end was a comprehensive collection of the principal Greek dramatists: Sophocles, Euripides, Aeschylus, Aristophanes.

The last book on the shelf was a hardcover with a shiny new black dust jacket. Dr. Stein reached for this and pulled it down. On the front of the jacket was the beautiful, familiar painting of Perseus riding the winged Pegasus, his bow at the ready. A recent edition of what was obviously an old favorite. He nodded, smiling: it was an old favorite of his as well.

Edith Hamilton's *Mythology*.

As Margaret watched in silence, he opened the volume and riffed through the pages.

She had used a yellow marker to highlight passages.

He looked up from the book and met the gaze of the woman in the doorway.

"Diana," he said. "What was the other alias?"

"Selena," Margaret told him. "Selena Chase."

He nodded. Then he closed the book and held it up. "Mind if I borrow this?"

Margaret shrugged. "Whatever."

Then he turned his attention to the desk. It was an old piece, what used to be called an escritoire. There was a slanted lid in front that swung down to become the writing surface itself. Inside, there were little drawers and shelves and pigeonholes. He saw pens and blue stationery—pale blue, the color of her eyes—with her name and address engraved in royal blue at the top of each sheet. Old envelopes were shoved into every possible cranny: letters from Margaret and Juana, bills, checks, tax information.

He replaced the lid. No, what he was looking for was not there: he hadn't really expected to find it. She would have taken it with her. A diary, if she kept one, was something she would use every day.

He was about to turn away and leave the room when his attention was arrested by something he hadn't noticed before. There, under the slanted lid, at the bottom of the desk, above the legs, was a large drawer, which he tried and found to be locked.

He pointed at it and turned to Margaret. "What's in there?"

She came up beside him and looked down at it, shaking her head. "I have no idea. I'm not accustomed to going through people's things. Then again, I've never had my telephone tapped, either, to say nothing of engaging detectives to spy on her. She's got me doing a lot of things I would never normally consider."

He nodded, knowing that she was thinking about the abortion.

"Well, you're about to do one more. Where's the key, do you know?"

"No. It would be a little skeleton thing, if I remember correctly. This desk was my mother's."

He reopened the lid and searched briefly through the drawers and pigeonholes. "Nope. She probably has it with her. There's something in this drawer that she doesn't want anybody to see. . . ."

He reached in his back pocket for his wallet. He selected a thin, sturdy plastic credit card and slipped it into the crack at the top of the drawer, just above the keyhole. He wiggled it for a moment. With a small click, the drawer slid open.

"One of my patients showed me how to do that," he said, grinning. "Never mind what I was treating *him* for."

"She'll know we've been in here," Margaret said.

"No," he said, pointing. "When you want to close it, just depress this spring lock at the top here with a card or a knife and slide the drawer back into place."

She nodded distractedly, unable to conceal her anxiety.

They stood there, leaning forward, staring down at the large, heavy volume bound with tasseled gold rope that lay inside. He reached down and slowly pulled it out. He held it up and opened the cover as Margaret peered over his shoulder.

The first twenty pages or so were photographs: her parents, Margaret, a man and a woman whom Margaret identified as the girl's maternal grandparents. Herself as a baby: studio portraits, Christmas snapshots, in a mall with her mother, on a sailboat with her parents and Margaret, cradled in her father's arms. Taped to one page, between photos, was a tiny lock of pale gold hair. Her first steps, with parents grinning proudly. On a pony at the age of three or four, with Bert's steadying hand on her little leg. A birthday party: blowing out five candles, watched by several other delighted children. A final shot of her between her smiling parents in front of a pretty house. She would have been about six. . . .

Then Dr. Stein turned the page.

"Oh, dear God," Margaret whispered. She shut her eyes tightly, turned away, and went to sit on the edge of the bed.

He stared down at the clippings, aware of the yellowing paper, the screaming headlines, and the strong odor of rubber cement.

"FIFTH ROBBERY—WOMAN DEAD!" the first headline proclaimed, followed by, in smaller letters, "Third Victim of Islip Burglar. Mailman's Grim Discovery. Child Attacked, Hospitalized."

The following pages were a veritable history, every printed word on the subject, accompanied by photographs of the girl with her head bandaged, Madeleine in life and death, the postal employee who'd found them the next morning, and the shocked, devastated Bert. "SEARCH CONTINUES." "HUSBAND OF ROBBERY VICTIM BREAKS DOWN AT INQUEST." "PETERSEN CHILD HOME FROM HOSPITAL." "ISLIP SUSPECT DETAINED, RELEASED." This last clipping included a picture of a huge, malevolent-looking black man flanked by officers.

It had gone on for weeks, and she had photocopies of every mention, culled from libraries and newspaper morgues.

The last entry in the family tragedy was another headline, from about six months later. There was a large reproduction of the photograph of the happy family in front of the house, another of Bert alone, and photos of the sailboat—unmanned, its tiny dinghy trailing behind—being towed into a harbor. The headline read "ISLIP ROBBER'S LATEST VICTIM. PETERSEN HUSBAND APPARENT

SUICIDE." The smaller lines continued, "Boat Found Floating off Virginia Coast. Anchor Missing. Searching for Body. Left Note to Daughter." They had photographed the note, found in the boat's cabin, pinned to a table with a small knife. "Darling," it read, "please forgive me. Be brave for me. Mommy and I will see you in Heaven. Daddy."

The doctor looked over at Margaret. "Where's the original of Mr. Petersen's suicide note?"

She winced. "Among my papers, in a safety-deposit box at my bank. She can have it when I'm gone."

He nodded and turned the page.

And stared.

A chill crept slowly up his spine as he studied the rest of the pages of the album. More yellowing clips, some copies and some cut from actual newspapers. Sensational headlines, shocking photographs of pain and suffering and death. One violent image after another. Other, unrelated cases from all over the country. Several pages devoted to one particular case ten years ago in Hawaii, uncannily similar to the Petersen affair. As in Islip, there had been a rash of local burglary/murders, culminating in an incident involving a well-known socialite. The husband had returned home to find his wife murdered. The clippings included photos of the dead woman in a pool of blood and the grieving husband with his blank face emptied by shock. And exactly as in Islip ten years before, the perpetrator or perpetrators had escaped.

Clippings from Louisiana and Wyoming and Arizona and several other states. Break-ins, assaults, murders.

Case after case: some solved, some open, many involving whole families. A grim, relentless obsession.

He shut the album, placed it on the desk, and went to stand over the woman who sat on the bed. "Have you ever seen that scrapbook before?"

"No. What's in it, aside from—what I saw?"

He waved a hand. "Other cases, not unlike her own. Not related. I think she uses the clippings as a reminder, as a fantasy of some sort. To prove she's not alone, that what happened to her happens to a lot of people. I doubt she'd ever commit violence, considering her own experience of it."

The woman slowly raised her eyes and regarded him thoughtfully. There was a troubled expression on her face.

"Doctor," she said quietly after a long moment of deliberation, "I think I should tell you something. Something I've never told anyone else."

He watched her face, waiting.

Margaret looked down at the blue-bedspread, apparently unable to continue eye contact with him. Her voice was a whisper. "Are you familiar with the particulars of the attack on my sister?"

"Not really," he said. "I've just seen the headlines and photos. . . ." He waved a hand toward the drawer.

Spots of bright pink appeared on her powdered cheeks. Still she declined to look directly at him.

"Sometimes I think I went a little mad then," she said. "If that is so, then I've never fully recovered. Perhaps you should read that first newspaper article. The one in

Newsday the day after—after it . . ." She trailed off, apparently unable to continue.

Dr. Stein returned to the desk and retrieved the scrapbook. He held it in his hands with the *Mythology*. "I'll borrow this, too, if you don't mind." Then, noting her distress, he leaned down to her. "What is it? What do you want to tell me?"

She glanced up briefly before once again turning away. "It's what she said to the mailman when he . . . found them. I've always wondered . . ." Then she shook her head firmly and took a deep breath. "Oh, never mind. I'm just being silly. She was six years old, for heaven's sake—"

At that moment, the telephone rang.

They stared at each other. He watched as Margaret reached for the receiver. She announced herself and listened. Then she raised startled eyes to the doctor.

"It's Robin Trask, the detective I hired," she told him. "He knows where she is! She just called him and invited him to a party!"

NINE

WEDNESDAY, AUGUST 21

ADAM CROUCHED in the bushes on the hillside, peering up through the darkness at the looming black silhouette of the empty house on Skyline Drive. From this angle the house towered over him, jutting up from the steep incline of the hill, giving him the impression that it might at any moment succumb to gravity and begin sliding down toward him. The drive ran along the tops of the mountains near the island's apex. If the house were suddenly to fall, he would be pushed backward down the steep mountainside to fall some nine hundred feet to the town directly below, a thousand lights winking in the dark. He glanced behind him: it was a dizzying prospect. Looking out across the harbor, black now in the night, he could see the brightly illuminated hotel on a faraway point. Just beyond it, a mere pinprick of light at this great distance, was Cliffhanger. After that, the miles and miles of black ocean, isolating the tiny, thirteen-by-five-mile area of St. Thomas from the rest of the world.

He smiled to himself, feeling insular, insulated, cut off from civilization. Here, he mused, I make my own rules. Nobody can see me. Not even God.

He tore his eyes from the breathtaking vista behind him and turned around to focus on the job at hand. Checking to be sure that no immediate neighbors were on their porches or balconies, he crept slowly upward to the building, his black-clad figure moving silently through the tall grass.

Jack Breen and his wife were out tonight, at a party given by the woman who might or might not be Jack's mistress. He smiled in the darkness: only in St. Thomas.

Kay was playing bridge with Stu Harriman at a local hotel: she wouldn't be home until midnight. Diana, at his suggestion, had taken Lisa to the movies at Four Winds Plaza. He'd given them extra money for pizza afterward.

After dinner, he'd waited at Cliffhanger until Stu arrived to fetch Kay, and the others departed in the Land Rover. Then Nola's husband had come to drive her home. As soon as everyone else was gone, he'd left the house and driven here, to Skyline Drive, and parked the Nissan in some bushes about a hundred yards down the road. Keeping away from the road and the other houses on the drive, he'd made his way here through the dense undergrowth on the mountainside. He'd passed directly below three suspended porches since he left the road, and the second one had slowed him down. There were people on the balcony, two men and a woman, drinking and laughing together as they grilled steaks on an outdoor barbecue. The white smoke had billowed out into the black sky above the bushes that concealed him, obliterating the moon.

He figured he'd have at least an hour.

Excellent.

The main entrance to the Breens' house was on the upper floor. The downstairs section, below the road, was a separate apartment, currently unoccupied, a guest room for Stateside visitors. He made his way swiftly up the stairs at the side of the house, which led from the apartment to the parking lot next to the road. The front door and all the windows would be locked, he suspected. It didn't matter. He reached behind him, into his backpack, and pulled out his tools.

There was a large bedroom window on this side of the house, about seven feet above the stairs on which he now stood. He reached up, thankful for his height, attached a medium-size suction cup to the glass near the bottom, and cut a small, round hole. No alarm systems to worry about. Many people in St. Thomas—and Jack was one of them—still thought the island was a quaint, quiet, safe place in which to live. Lock the doors, certainly, but no need to bother with alarms. Robberies had only recently begun to be a problem.

He smiled. There were no alarms at Cliffhanger, either. . . .

He tugged on the suction cup, pulling the circle of glass away from the window. He reached in with his gloved hand and unlocked the window from the inside. Silently, carefully, he pushed it upward. He leapt up and grasped the windowsill. A mighty swing of his body, and he was inside. He made his way across the darkened bedroom to the door, pulling the pencil-size flashlight from his pack. As he went into the living room, he checked the luminous dial of his watch. Five minutes to ten.

Excellent.

He lowered the backpack to the floor, switched on the tiny light, and went to work.

Trish sighed, reaching over as politely as possible and removing Jerry Flynn's hand from her left buttock.

"If you expect me to turn the other cheek, you'd better get me a drink, darling," she said, and the tall, muscular, beaming Irishman trotted dutifully off.

Oh, *yawn,* she thought, glancing around at the other guests in Barbara Conroy's small, cramped living room. The usual suspects. The dreary old Hill Crowd, the tacky Yacht Club Crowd, boring Old Money, obnoxious New Money, conservative Local Black Aristocracy. Snooze. I didn't want to come to this thing, and Kay *would* be off playing duplicate. Oh, well, I'll see her tomorrow, at Lisa's birthday party.

She watched Barbara make the rounds, doing her very best Hostess Bit. She giggled as she watched her consciously avoiding Nancy Breen, her lover's wife. God, that Nancy must be the dumbest thing to actually come to this party, and to bring Jack with her!

Jerry returned to her side, bearing refreshments. She

smiled and thanked him. He really is rather sweet, she thought, in a rough sort of way. Not bad in bed, either. . . .

At that point, the little steel band Barbara engaged for the evening struck up a lively calypso tune, and Jerry asked her to dance. They were in mid-samba when Trish heard the raised, angry voices on the other side of the room, followed by the shattering of glass.

"You didn't like that movie, did you?" she asked her silent young charge as they walked out of the multiplex cinema in the shopping center and headed for the Land Rover.

"No," Lisa moped, not meeting her gaze. "I know I said I wanted a scary movie, but that was a little *too* scary."

In the film they'd just seen, a deranged husband had concocted the perfect plan to kill his unsuspecting new wife and her small son and make off with her millions. Lisa had chosen it, and she'd been unable to change the child's mind.

She herself had barely been able to look at the screen.

She'd watched the actor playing the husband, flaring his nostrils and acting suspicious as hell. Of course, the wife had noticed this and saved herself and her son—with the aid of a hunky, recently divorced cop—just in the nick of time. The wicked husband, wearing a black ski mask and wielding a knife, had been shot dead by the virtuous policeman.

The actress playing the wife, rescued at the last moment, bore a strong resemblance to her mother.

The actor playing the policeman looked exactly like her father.

She'd wiped away her tears as the final credits rolled, before the lights came up and Lisa could notice.

"Adam gave you money for pizza, didn't he?" Lisa asked.

"Yes," she said, "but it's ten o'clock now, and you have a big day ahead of you tomorrow, birthday girl."

"Oh, I'll be fine tomorrow," the child insisted. "We don't even set sail until eleven. Let's get a pizza."

He'd finished with the silver. He was back in the bedroom now, emptying Nancy Breen's jewelry boxes into the backpack. He checked his watch again. Nine minutes after ten.

Excellent.

As he worked, he thought about Diana. She was so lovely, so tall and slender. That dark hair falling down around her shoulders, those dark eyes flashing. He wondered, again, what it would be like with her. He imagined her naked, under him, his face between her breasts, her mouth open as she groaned with pleasure. In the little house on the beach, or perhaps on the *Kay*. . . .

The *Kay*.

He thought of Kyle, probably asleep by now on his little bunk in the cabin. Big day tomorrow: eight adults and six children on the boat. Sleep, Kyle. . . .

He thought, briefly, of Sandra. He'd left her belongings on the tiny, deserted beach, hiding in plain sight. Yet so far they had not been discovered. Oh, well. Nobody seemed to miss her. *He* certainly did not. What a creep she'd been!

He ran the beam of his penlight over the surface of

Nancy's bureau. Something gleamed. Silver-plated hair-brush.

The brush went into the backpack with the other items.

He checked his watch again. Ten-fifteen.

Excellent.

Everyone turned to stare as Nancy Breen, her small, pinched face awash in drunken tears, reached over and slapped her husband as hard as she could. Trish watched her, fascinated. At last, she thought, something's *happening* at this stupid party!

"You *pig*!" Nancy announced. "You absolute *shit*! As if I didn't know why you wanted to come here tonight! To humiliate me again. Well, I've been silent long enough. I'm going home. Give me the keys to the car."

Trish watched, delighted, as Jack mumbled drunkenly and handed Nancy the keys. Good for you, she thought. Hit him again!

As if she'd heard Trish's thoughts, Nancy reared back and did just that.

"Perhaps our *hostess* will drive you home!" she shrieked. Then she turned around and barged through the astonished crowd and out the door.

Barbara, understandably red in the face, signaled to the band, which immediately resumed playing. Trish turned to Jerry.

"Well, that was fun!" she said. "Let's get some food."

They were at the buffet table, about five minutes later, when Trish—and everybody else—saw Jack Breen borrow Barbara's car keys and leave the party.

* * *

There was a pause between sets. Kay glanced over at the table below hers. Their next east-west challengers were finishing up the board. She leaned back in her padded chair and glanced across her own table at Stu Harriman.

"We seem to be doing very well tonight," she said.

"I think so," Stu agreed, grinning over at her. "I'm in a great mood this evening. The insurance came through, so I can start replacing all that jewelry Brenda lost."

"Great!" Kay said.

"Yeah. Brenda's happy. And we're installing an alarm system. In case those bastards come back for more."

"That's not a bad idea," Kay agreed. "I've been thinking about it myself."

Stu Harriman's laugh resounded through the banquet room. "*You?* You're kidding! Kay, darling, who the hell is going to try to rob Adam Prescott? Nobody in their right mind, that's who!"

She shrugged, nodding. "You may have a point."

"Your husband is the biggest, meanest-looking sonofabitch I've ever seen," he told her. "That's better than an alarm system any day! I'm gonna get a beer. Would you like something?"

"Soda," she murmured.

Stu rose and went out to the lobby of the hotel.

She gazed around at the quiet room. Not many tables tonight, she thought. A lot of people must have gone to Barbara Conroy's party. She and Adam had begged off. Adam had wanted the night before the birthday party to stay home alone and read. She'd wanted to play bridge tonight, and she didn't care for Barbara Conroy in the first place.

Lisa had gone to the movies with Diana.

Diana.

She smiled to herself, remembering the phone call two nights before. Diana, with much goading from her, had finally picked up the phone and asked that dreamy young man to go sailing with them. He'd apparently been surprised, then delighted, to hear from her again. Kay had listened to the young woman's end of the conversation, stilted and formal at first, gradually warming and becoming downright friendly. Bob Taylor had apparently said something funny at one point, and Diana had thrown back her head and laughed. She'd done that earlier, too, at the dinner table, when they told Lisa about tomorrow's party. The child had been astonished, and the young woman had laughed.

At any rate, she thought, Bob Taylor would definitely be joining them on the *Kay* tomorrow.

Stu returned with the drinks, and the director arrived with the final boards. Their new opponents moved up to join them. She fanned out her new hand before her and settled back.

Tomorrow is going to be lovely, she thought. Absolutely lovely.

He was going through the breakfront in the living room when he heard the car pull up and stop in the parking lot outside. A door opened and slammed, and a woman—

Nancy, high heels clicking on asphalt, blubbering loudly—came to the front door.

He grabbed the backpack and ducked into the bedroom. He stood just inside the door, listening as keys jingled and the front door was unlocked. Lights clicked on, and the high heels clattered into the living room and stopped. He peered through the crack in the bedroom door. Nancy stood in the middle of the living room, her back to him, in a long, low-cut white dress of some filmy, clinging material, her black curls and pendant earrings glistening as she gazed around at the devastation that had suddenly, inexplicably arrived in her immaculate home: the open breakfront, the displaced furniture, the paintings all askew.

"Oh, my God!" she cried.

What the hell was she doing here? She was supposed to be at that party. His hand reached stealthily down into the open bag and grasped—

Nancy turned slowly around and looked at the bedroom door. She raised a hand to her mouth.

She knows, he thought. She senses that I'm in here. And now she's going to scream. The people next door will be in here in about ten seconds. Everything will be over. Forever.

The hand rummaged frantically. No, not the glass cutter . . . jewelry . . . silverware . . . aha!

He dropped the backpack. Sliding the knife into a back pocket, he forced a casual smile, pulled open the bedroom door, and walked out into the light.

Nancy's eyes—red-rimmed, her mascara smeared from weeping—widened in disbelief. *"Adam!"*

"Hi," he said, grinning sheepishly.

She stared at him for a moment. Then, slowly, they both began to laugh.

"So," the young woman said as the pizza was placed on the checkered tablecloth between them. "I understand you're going to spend Labor Day weekend with your Aunt Frances in Connecticut."

"I sure hope so!" Lisa said. She pulled up a steaming slice from the pie, leaving behind a long trail of mozzarella strands. "I usually go every year, but this year Mommy wasn't sure I should. I'm workin' on her, though. *He's* working on her, too, if you can believe that! I could almost like him for it. *Almost.* Well, I won't say any more: I'm eating his pizza. It's just for five days. I have two cousins about my age, Janie and Keith. They have horses! I love horses, don't you?"

"Yes," the young woman replied. "I think you should go, too. It's good to get away for a little while, isn't it?"

"Yeah," Lisa agreed. "I love St. Thomas, but Connecticut's great, too. Do you suppose you could, you know, throw in your vote with Adam and me? Tell her I should go?"

She smiled over at the child.

"I'll be sure to," she said, and she reached for a slice.

"Well, what do you know!" Nancy Breen cried. "So *you're* the cat burglar! That's wonderful! I don't suppose you need the money—"

He grinned and shook his head. Ten-seventeen.

"Just doing it for the sport," she said, nodding. "A little excitement. Yes. Did you knock over the Harrimans', too?" She sounded more amused than anything else.

Still grinning, he nodded.

"Well, that beats all!" she declared, turning away from him and heading toward the bar in the corner of the living room. "What some people do for a good time! It's this island, you know. The hot equatorial climate. People get crazy ideas."

She arrived at the bar and reached for a glass. Nice figure, he thought. She might be pretty if it weren't for that pinched little face. That dress is wasted on her. . . .

"Well, don't worry, darling," she slurred, still with her back to him. "Your secret's safe with me. You're welcome to anything in this house you can carry. Hell, I'll *help* you carry it! I'm getting the hell out of here. Back to Ohio. Should have done it years ago. Anything I leave behind will just go to that whore of his. Barbara Conroy. Fucking whore. Would you like a drink before we clean the sonofabitch out?"

He came up silently behind her.

"You're drunk, Nancy," he said in a low, clear voice.

She laughed and whirled around to face him. "Well, excuse me for living!"

He moved closer, smiling at her.

"Sorry," he whispered, raising his black-gloved hand. "I can't."

He waited a moment for her to see the knife, for the information to make its way through the alcohol cloud and register. He had to see it in her eyes, that she knew what was happening to her. That was part of it.

She saw. The information registered. She stared, mouth opening, eyes beginning to widen. The crystal tumbler fell from her hand and landed with a thump on the carpet. He allowed himself one more sharp, exquisite second. He could stand here for hours, poised above her, feeling the power. But now he must move, he told himself reluctantly. Already she was acting reflexively, filling her lungs to scream.

In one swift thrust, he plunged the pearl-handled steak knife through her heart.

He jumped backward to avoid the spray. He stood several feet away, watching as she stared at him in uncomprehending horror. Her lips moved, but no sound came. Then she looked down at the knife. The dark stain began to spread across the breast of her bright white party dress as she sank slowly to her knees. She was reaching up as if to pull out the knife when death overtook her. She sagged sideways to the carpet and rolled over onto her back. The body shuddered a moment, then lay still. The pearl handle jutted straight up out of her, gleaming in the light.

In slightly less than thirty seconds, he switched off the lights, retrieved the backpack, and swung his body out through the bedroom window. He ran down the outside stairs and into the brush. He clambered crablike along the steep hillside, slowing briefly under the occupied balcony, to the point just below where he'd left the car. He burst from the bushes and dashed across the road to the place among the trees on the other side where the Nissan was concealed. He was just about to turn the key in the ignition when another car came by along the road. He peered out through the trees and got a glimpse of the car and its driver.

Jack Breen.

He waited a few seconds for Jack to get far enough away up Skyline Drive. Then he started the engine and raced away downhill, in the opposite direction.

As the red Nissan sped through the night on its way home, he glanced once more at his watch. Ten twenty-nine. He'd be back at Cliffhanger before Kay, before any of them. He'd been there all night, reading, in case anyone asked.

But nobody would ask. Why should they?

It hadn't gone as planned, but it had worked out just the same. The burglar had struck again, and now he was violent. More attention. Much more than the Harrimans, who'd barely rated a mention in the local media. This would be on tomorrow's front pages. Everyone would know; everyone would be talking.

The next one wouldn't be a surprise.

Perfect.

When Kay walked into the master bedroom at eleven fifty-six, she found her husband sitting up in bed, on top of the sheets, reading. He was naked, his enormous body dominating the enormous bed. He looked up as she entered and flashed his most disarming grin, white teeth and pale hair glistening.

She glanced briefly at the paperback he held and rolled her eyes in mock disgust. The *Killer Inside Me,* by Jim Thompson.

Still grinning, staring into her eyes, he tossed the book aside and slowly, insolently spread his legs.

Her eyes traveled down his body. Smiling, she closed the bedroom door and locked it.

Lisa came through the swinging door from the kitchen and dashed up the stairs, Jumbi bounding along behind her.

"Good night, Diana," the child called as she ran. "Thanks for the movie. I can't wait till tomorrow!"

She watched girl and dog ascend. Then, glancing at her watch, she called, "Happy birthday." A wave and a giggle from above, the sound of the bedroom door closing, and she was alone in the living room.

She went over to the foyer to turn off the outside lights. Then she moved slowly around the downstairs area, switching off lamps, checking that the sliding doors to the deck were securely locked, removing the keys to the Land Rover from her purse, and dropping them on the coffee table, where they would be found by Kay in the morning. They landed next to a pack of Virginia Slims and a gold lighter that Kay had left there.

Without thinking, without any conscious motivation, she took a cigarette, placed it in her mouth, and lit it. She stood there in the dark, shadowy living room, inhaling menthol smoke and staring at the blackness on the other side of the glass doors. She couldn't see the water, but she could hear it in the distance, crashing incessantly against the rocks far below. Otherwise, the house was silent. She was thinking about this odd dichotomy, and had even begun moving toward the stairs, when she heard the new sounds, the muffled noises coming from the master bedroom to her right.

She stood quite still at the foot of the staircase, straining to hear. She knew what it was: Adam and his wife were making rather loud, passionate love. She could just hear, through the bedroom door and across the room, his moans of pleasure and her sharp, insistent cries.

She moved swiftly, silently up the stairs and down the hall to her room, a shadow among other shadows. She closed and locked her door, leaning back against it, aware that they were now directly beneath her. The sounds of their activity did not come up through the floor, so she resorted to imagining, rather than hearing, the scene.

They would be naked and glistening with perspiration, and he would be on top of her—no; she was sitting astride him as he lay back against the damp pink satin sheets. He bucked his pelvis, thrusting up and in, and she strained the muscles of her thighs to remain one with him, to keep to the rhythm. She stared down at his face, his pale eyes tightly shut in glorious concentration, and opened her throat to rid herself of the little scream welling up within her. She threw her head back, red hair flying, as they rocked faster and faster and moved furiously, almost violently, toward that exquisite, excruciating moment when all consciousness would be lost but for the white-hot, helpless thunder in their center, locked together.

She took another drag on the cigarette and lapsed immediately into a coughing fit. She held the little cylinder out in front of her and inspected it, surprised, wondering how it had got there. She didn't smoke, not anymore. She'd only done so for a brief period, years ago. And even then, they'd been regular cigarettes, not these mentholated things. The mint-tinged taste was foul in her mouth.

Then she was across the room, flinging open the sliding door and bursting out into the chill, crisp salt air. She threw the cigarette from her, over the balcony railing, watching the tiny orange spark streak out and down, remembering her similar action with the brooch three nights before. She grasped the rail and leaned out, feeling the nighttime breeze on her face and in her hair.

They would be finished now, lying side by side in the big bed below her, naked and moist and gasping in mute, breathless pleasure. When they regained their senses, and motion was once again possible, he would reach over in the dark and grasp her waiting hand.

The tremor coursed slowly through her. Damn you, she thought. Goddamn you. It shouldn't be like this. It shouldn't be Kay. Kay has no right! It should be—

The foam caused by the smashing of water against rock was clearly visible in the light of the moon. She stared down, seeing it and hearing it but unaware, anesthetized.

He had everything. He lived here in this gorgeous house on the cliff on this magnificent tropical island, arguably the most beautiful place in the world. He had cars and boats and all the other accoutrements of a perfectly happy, idle, luxurious existence. His pretty, rich wife made love with him and bought him gifts and anticipated his every whim. He made all the right paternal moves with the pretty little girl. He had no reason—she was certain of it—to ever feel a moment's doubt or guilt or discomfort. Yet, unaccountably, he wanted more.

He wanted her.

She tightened her grip on the cold iron rail until her knuckles throbbed, and even then she refused to let go. Remember this, she thought, as you were instructed in acting class. Remember the feeling, so you can recall it when it becomes necessary for you to do so. Study it, examine it, store it deep inside for future reference.

Use it.

The night wind ruffled her dark hair, and the ice-blue moonlight glistened in it as she stood clutching the rail no stronger than her spine, no colder than her heart, resolute, experiencing her terrible, strengthening pain.

TEN

THURSDAY, AUGUST 22

WHEN ROBIN WALKED into the lobby of the yacht club and saw her standing there, a surge of joy suffused him. He'd almost given up hope of ever seeing her again. Yet here she was, lovely and fresh and smiling, a man's white dress shirt draped casually over her turquoise bikini, dark hair falling loose around her tanned shoulders. So pretty, he thought. So very much alive.

"Hello again, Bob," she said. "I'm glad you could join us." She turned to the others. "Everybody, this is Bob Taylor."

He looked around at them all. "No relation." He stood there in his red-and-white-striped jersey, jeans, and Top-Siders, grinning self-consciously and clutching the box of Godiva chocolate.

Kay Prescott and Patricia Manning, whom he'd already met . . . Jerry Flynn in the yellow windbreaker . . . an attractive young blond woman in halter top and cutoffs who was introduced as "Kyle's friend Rita" (he wondered who Kyle was) . . . Pam and Betty Hogan, about twelve and fourteen, not twins but practically indistinguishable from each other (Betty was the younger one) . . . a little black girl named Tina . . . two boys, one black and one white, about fourteen, obviously best friends and obviously trying their best to look cool at a girl's birthday party. He didn't catch their names.

When the pretty girl with the red hair shook his hand, he glanced up at Kay, knowing this could only be her daughter, the guest of honor. He grinned and handed her the candy.

"Happy birthday, Lisa," he said.

The child blushed and giggled. Love at first sight. He winked at her and raised his eyes, at last, to the huge, magnificent-looking man standing behind her.

From the moment their eyes first met, he knew that he did not care for Adam Prescott, and he wasn't immediately sure why. Maybe it was simply that no man should be that gorgeous—a sexist observation, but there it was. He could also see, deep in the pale, clear blue eyes, that the repulsion was mutual. Or perhaps, he thought, this man simply looks at everyone that way, with a thin mask of civility that barely conceals his obvious disdain.

The two men produced mechanical smiles and shook hands. Robin quickly withdrew his hand and turned back to his date.

"I'm glad you called," he said.

She regarded him, smiling. "So am I."

At that point, a muscular, tanned young man with sun-bleached hair, wearing a T-shirt and jams, arrived from the direction of the beach. He spoke briefly with Adam Prescott, who introduced him as Kyle, the mate aboard the *Kay*. Kyle had a firm handshake and a friendly face, and his single earring glinted in the sunlight.

Prescott then turned to his assembled guests. "All aboard!"

There was much excited commotion from the children, who grabbed the birthday girl and dashed out of the lobby. The adults, as enthusiastic if not as energetic as the youngsters, followed them out onto the beach and down to the dock, where the sloop awaited them, dazzling white against the vivid blue of the Atlantic.

Adam was the first to leap aboard, followed by the mate. Robin watched from the dock as the big man, clad in white jeans and an open short-sleeved shirt, took complete charge: shouting orders to Kyle, stowing the enormous cooler he'd brought, leaning over to help the children onto the deck.

Then Robin turned to the girl at his side. She stood there, watching intently as her employer hauled the kids aboard. He noticed her face: something in her expression as she stared at Adam Prescott and the children made Robin decide, then and there, to stay very close to his date for the rest of the day.

They followed the others. The moment Robin's feet left the solid dock, he began, ever so slightly, to tremble. He made his unsteady way over to a cushioned seat in the cockpit. Straining to appear casual, he grinned around at the others. The *Kay* was about sixty feet long, he figured, and it seemed awfully cramped for so large a group. Still he continued to grin, wondering inwardly which peril— seasickness or claustrophobia—would get him first.

He dug his nails into the plastic cushion as the motor sprang to noisy life beneath his feet. He watched as Kyle jumped onto the dock, untied the craft, and leapt aboard again. Then he turned to the young woman sitting next to him, concentrating on her face and her polite small talk as the boat glided away from the dock and out into the water.

She asked him if he'd ever sailed before, and he said that he had not. She explained that as soon as the sloop cleared the points to port and starboard and entered open water, Adam and Kyle would cut the inboard and hoist the jib and they'd really be on their way.

Robin watched the sail rise up the mast and billow out as it caught the wind. Then he held his breath and screwed his eyes tightly shut as the entire vessel lurched suddenly sideways.

She laughed at his expression, reached over, and took his hand firmly in hers. At the same moment, the vessel began to move smoothly forward across the surface of the water. He felt the pressure of her soft hand and opened his eyes. His respiration returned to normal. He looked around: everyone else was laughing and chatting.

"Are you going to be all right, Bob?" she asked.

He inhaled the scent of flowers, saw the dark hair

dancing in the breeze. He relaxed, settling back on the seat and grinning over at her. "Hey, no problem."

And there *was* no problem. He had caught up with her, and she was beautiful, and everything was going to be just fine.

Landlubber, Adam thought with disgust.

The young man sitting next to Diana was white as a sheet, and she was holding his hand to keep him from passing out. Just what I need, an idiot like that. Some beard! He glanced around at the others. A couple of Lisa's friends were obviously nervous, but you'd expect that of children. Not a grown man. Well, he was Diana's problem: Adam had something else to think about.

He'd managed to get Kay and Diana to the club and onto the boat without either of them seeing a newspaper or hearing the gossip that even now must be spreading like fire throughout the clubhouse. Trish and Jerry seemed to have missed it as well.

He's been the first to arrive at the table on the sundeck where Nola was laying out the breakfast things. The *Virgin Islands Daily News* was in its usual spot next to his place setting. He'd looked down and seen the bold headline: "SKYLINE DRIVE MURDER—HUSBAND HELD." He'd handed the paper to Nola, who'd taken it into the kitchen. When Kay joined him, rested and relaxed and blushing from last night's activities, she never noticed its absence.

He studied his passengers. No, nobody was yet aware of the incident. The children were playing some sort of game, pretending to be sailors or pirates, under Kyle's watchful eye. Trish was helping Kay hand out drinks, and the two of them were discussing women's fashions with the girl Kyle had brought along, a waitress from some bar. Adam grinned to himself when he regarded her: he couldn't remember her name, and he wondered if Kyle could. Kyle was like that about women.

Someone had given Bob Taylor a can of beer, which might bring a little color back to his pallid cheeks. Diana sat close to him—a bit too close for Adam's liking—and the two of them laughed a great deal as she pointed around the boat, explaining the rudiments of sailing. The young man, he noticed with irritation, could barely take his eyes from Diana's face.

He gripped the wheel, his back to the others, and gazed out toward the horizon. Soon they'd get to St. John and drop anchor at Trunk Bay for the picnic lunch.

Jack Breen, he thought. Goddamned Jack Breen. Nancy *had* to leave the party early, and Jack *had* to follow her. The argument had been witnessed by everyone else at Barbara's house, according to the *Daily News*. He glanced behind him at Trish and Jerry: they'd been there. They must have seen it, too.

When Jack found his wife on the living-room carpet, he'd apparently fainted. He'd come to several minutes later—about the time Adam was arriving home—and called the police. He told them that the house had been robbed and Nancy murdered, probably by the same burglar who'd knocked over the Harrimans' house.

Of course, nobody believed him. Everybody knew about his relationship with Barbara, even the police. They'd called her to verify the Breens' times of departure from her house, and she'd gotten hysterical. Nancy's tirade had been mentioned, and the cops took it from there. It was obviously a domestic crime, they reasoned, and Jack had robbed his own house afterward to lay the blame elsewhere.

As far as they were concerned, there was no burglar.

Jack Breen's bumbling could ruin the plan.

Diana. He turned around and regarded her as she talked and laughed with her alleged date.

He remembered her on this boat ten weeks ago. It had been her suggestion—and he was still trying to figure this out—to rob local houses in the weeks beforehand. Make it look like part of a random pattern, she'd said, rather than a specific, premeditated act. Be away from the island when the real action went down. She'd figured out disguises and flights and car rentals: after a while he'd relaxed and left it all to her. He was astonished at the way her mind worked. She was a brilliant young woman.

But she did not know about Nancy. She would not approve of that, he thought. She didn't yet know about the others, and she wouldn't approve of them, either. There might be a scene.

The children cried out in delight as St. John appeared before them. Kyle manned his station and they tacked, setting a new course along the north coast of the smallest U.S. Virgin Island. Soon they would sail past Caneel Bay and into Trunk Bay.

Everyone was looking over at the vivid green landmass looming up out of the water on the starboard side of the

Kay, and Diana was pointing toward the top of the closest hill. Adam looked up. The statue of Christ towered over them, smaller than but similar to the one above the harbor of Rio de Janeiro. The so-called Son of God stood smiling, vivid white against the blue sky, arms extended outward in kindly, amaranthine benediction.

His gaze fell from the statue above them to Diana's face. She was leaning against the starboard rail, looking up. She closed her eyes briefly and moved her lips in some silent prayer. So, he thought, her Greek and Roman fascination is insufficient: she puts stock in *this* mythology as well.

Even as he watched her do this, he knew that he was not going to tell her about Nancy Breen. She might not react well: their original blueprint had been only for robberies, not anything else. She didn't know about Sandra—or Greg, for that matter. He understood the necessity of their disposal, but her stunt with the statue of Christ only proved that she was still bound by earthly laws. If anything were to upset her at this stage, it could endanger the plan.

He would write the Breens off as a loss and try again. He'd let Jack take the fall; he didn't give a damn about him anyway.

Kay arrived next to him at the helm. She put her arm around his waist and rested her head against his shoulder.

"Thank you for today," she murmured. "Lisa is in heaven, and so am I."

He leaned over and kissed her lightly on the forehead. No, you're not, he thought. Not yet. . . .

He placed his arm around his wife's shoulders and smiled at her. The burglar would have to strike again, and soon. Labor Day was only ten days away.

"So," Robin said, "what do you do for the Prescotts?"

She was leaning back, her blue bikini standing out vividly against the red cushions. Her smooth, tanned skin glowed in the sunlight.

"Au pair," she said. "Companion. That sort of thing."

"Lisa seems like a really nice kid."

"She is."

"So how long will this go on?" Robin asked, feigning the most casual interest.

"I'm not sure," she replied, brushing a lock of dark hair away from her eyes. "I like it here. It's so beautiful, so pleasant. Not at all like New York, in case you haven't noticed. I guess I'll have to go back soon, but at the moment I'm enjoying myself. How about you? Will your business keep you around for a while?"

"Looks that way," he said.

"Do you have a family waiting for your return?" she asked.

"Not really. I'm not married or anything. My parents live on Long Island. I have a co-op on West Seventieth. I just moved in, so there isn't even any furniture yet."

She laughed. "I'll eventually have to find an apartment in Manhattan myself. My long-range plan is to be an actress. I've been studying for some time now—"

"Oh? Where?" he asked before he could stop himself.

"HB—that's Herbert Berghof Studios to you," she said.

"Oh, wow! That's—um—very interesting." He smiled and nodded, biting his tongue. Dumb. You're supposed to be in real estate, he reminded himself. Bob Taylor has never heard of HB and could care less. Margaret Barclay's report hadn't mentioned that the girl took acting classes. He sat there, smiling vacuously at her, amazed that they had so much in common and frustrated because he couldn't let her know that. Hell, he knew at least five students at HB. The two of them probably had several acquaintances in common.

"Show biz must be a tough profession," he observed, playing the disinterested outsider. "Are you sure you're cut out for it?"

"I'll soon find out, won't I?" she murmured.

Much later, he would look back at it all and realize that this had been a lie. At that point she had no intention of trying her luck as an actress. She had other plans, but at the time he had no way of knowing that. He only knew that he was beginning to like her.

And much later, when he looked back at it all, he would also realize that it was the near-fatal accident on board the *Kay* that afternoon that had proved to him that he was capable of very strong emotions where she was concerned. This beautiful young woman, this aspiring actress who studied at an acting school he'd been thinking about enrolling in, this enigma who for some reason was calling herself Diana Meissen: he was quite capable of falling in love with her.

Yes, he would later realize, it was the accident that had changed everything.

* * *

He's really very nice, the young woman thought. Good-looking, of course, but open and friendly and funny as well. I never seem to take up with men like him. They're always around, I guess: there must have been nice guys at college, in Hawaii and San Francisco, even in Glen Cove. This one is from New York. The world is obviously full of them. I just don't pay attention.

She smoothed her hair and grinned as he took yet another photograph of her with the little camera he'd brought along. He was snapping everyone: Kay, Trish, Kyle and Rita, Lisa and the other children. She noticed, smiling, that he carefully avoided photographing Adam, even in the one shot he took of the entire group. The two men obviously disliked each other.

She was feeling better, calmer, now that they had arrived at their destination. The shock caused by her initial sight of that big white statue on the hill had unsettled her, made her briefly forget herself. An impulsive reaction, she now determined—the result of too much childhood exposure to nuns and chapels and the hushed, unquestioning adoration of what were, if she looked at it honestly, mere inanimate objects. But she hadn't been thinking rationally when the mountain loomed up out of the water, dominated by that huge, spectacular presence. Some quirk, some uneasy combination of the image of Christ towering above her and the dark, guilt-tinged thoughts that now possessed her constantly, had prompted the automatic response. *Pater Noster, Qui es in Caelis, sanctificatur nomen Tuum. Adveniat regnum Tuum. . . .*

They had sailed into Trunk Bay and dropped anchor. Kay and Trish were laying out the lunch things as they were brought out from the cabin. There were sandwiches and cold chicken and salads and potato chips. There was also a chocolate cake stashed somewhere out of sight: she and Kay had helped Nola with it yesterday.

My God, she thought briefly. I stood there in this woman's kitchen, helping her make a cake for her daughter's birthday.

The children, excited by the sight of the perfectly white strip of beach before them, were cavorting around the deck, getting in the way of the grown-ups. Kay looked up from her chores.

"Diana," she called, "could you be a darling—"

"Sure," she answered immediately. "Okay, kids. All ashore who's goin' ashore! Stay close to Mr. Taylor and me in the water." She turned to him. "You don't mind, do you?"

"My pleasure," he said, grinning as he put away the camera, kicked off his shoes, and shed his jeans and striped jersey.

Very nice, she thought, regarding the muscular torso in the black Speedo. She'd seen him like this before, but she hadn't really noticed.

She whirled around and dived over the side, followed by Bob Taylor and six laughing children.

It happened on the return trip, in open water, shortly after they'd weighed anchor and set sail for St. Thomas.

He and the girl had played with the kids on the beach

and led them back to join the adults for lunch on the boat. The cake was produced and devoured, with the obligatory singing and blowing out of candles. More gifts were produced: cologne, compact disks, a Nancy Drew novel, more candy. Lisa accepted all of them with uncontained delight. It's fun to watch her tear into the packages, he'd thought. She really is a lovely little girl.

The wind had changed while they were in Trunk Bay. The water was choppier than before, and huge dark clouds had materialized in the sky. St. John receded in the distance behind them, the tiny white spot that was the statue of Christ growing smaller and smaller and finally disappearing completely. The *Kay* pitched and rolled, rising up on waves and crashing down again. The children had gone below to play Sardines in the cabin, and the other adults in the cockpit appeared unconcerned with the rather violent voyage. Adam Prescott was standing at the wheel as if he hadn't a care in the world. Robin was beginning to feel queasy.

What happened next drove all thoughts of seasickness from his mind. It also very nearly cost two lives.

The young woman named Rita, sitting next to Kyle in the stern, asked Kay for one of her cigarettes. Kay picked up her pack, found it empty, and crumpled it. She then rose and went down into the cabin, announcing that she kept spare cartons there.

The boat had been running before the wind when the wind's direction changed yet again. Adam whipped his head around to Kyle and shouted something over the sudden roar. Kyle jumped up and went to join Adam. The two men prepared to come about.

Through the open cabin door, Robin saw Kay reach over the children piled on Kyle's bunk and grab a cigarette carton from the shelf above it. She shook out a fresh pack, replaced the carton, said something to the children that made them all laugh, turned around, and climbed the three steps back up to the deck.

Kyle, the sheet clasped in his hands, shouted to everyone to keep their heads down. He and Adam looked up at the sail, which began to flap as the bow crossed the wind. . . .

Kay arrived on deck, laughing as she brandished the pack of Virginia Slims. "Kyle! Stop mooching my smokes. That carton is practically empty." She moved toward the stern.

As he boat turned, the boom began to swing over the deck.

Trish shouted a warning and pointed at the sail, but Kay didn't seem to hear her. . . .

Robin felt the fingernails dig into his forearm as the girl at his side looked up and realized what was about to happen.

Adam had turned away to grab the wheel. . . .

The wind hit the sail, filling it.

At the last possible moment, Kay turned to see the boom coming toward her. The cigarette pack fell from her hand. She stood staring, frozen in shock. . . .

From that point on, it seemed to Robin that everything had shifted into slow motion. He saw faces contorting and everyone shouting, but he couldn't make out the words. He was aware only of the girl, and of the roaring in his ears as the blood rushed to his head.

She rose—slowly, slowly—from the seat next to him and lurched forward, raising her arms before her as she moved. In a long, graceful action, she closed the gap between herself and Kay Prescott. She pushed the startled woman down onto the deck. Just as she was beginning to drop down next to Kay, the boom smashed into the side of her head with a sickening thud.

It happened in seconds, he later reasoned, but it seemed to take forever. The impact lifted her from the deck and sent her flying sideways. She soared out over the rail and fell—ever so slowly, ever so gracefully—into the churning sea.

He must have stood up. There must have been a moment in which he consciously decided to move. If there was, he would never remember it. He was leaping, and he was plunging downward, and he was in the water.

The ocean, unlike the bay in which they'd been swimming, was freezing cold. The *Kay* was moving away from him at a rapid rate, leaving him behind, but he was not aware of this. He was paddling with his hands to keep his head above the giant waves as he looked frantically around him for the girl. A wall of water crashed into his face, submerging him for a moment, and he fought his way back to the surface.

He burst up from the water, gasping for air. When his vision cleared, he saw her head bobbing in the waves about thirty feet in front of him. He brought up his arms, already numb with cold, and began to swim toward her. He had to fight for every inch that brought him closer to her inert form, and several times he was pushed backward by the relentless current. Still he struggled on, unthinking, motivated only by his instinct, his overwhelming need to reach her.

She disappeared at one point, only to rise up at the next moment on an enormous wave ten feet before him. He stroked and kicked with a power he had never known he possessed, a power born of panic. Five more feet, he thought. Three. . . .

Then his hand made contact with her arm. He seized her in a mighty grip and pulled her to him. He held the unconscious woman up with one arm, paddling furiously with the other to keep them both afloat.

When she came to, she nearly drowned them both. She was in shock, he knew, and unaware of her actions. She woke to find herself in rough water, screamed and thrashed for a moment and then reached out with both hands to grab him. What she grabbed was his throat.

He shouted her name and reached up with his hands to remove the crushing pressure, but her grip was like iron. The moment he stopped paddling, they both began to sink. Another gigantic wave crashed over them, sending them down under the surface. She squeezed his neck more tightly as he flailed with his arms. His lungs began to burn as he fought to resurface, but she was weighing him down. In one last, desperate effort, he grabbed her hands and wrenched them from his neck. He held her hands tightly in front of him and kicked, sending them both upward.

He thrust his face up out of the water and inhaled. He held her, coughing, and flailing, close to him as the dark spots danced before his eyes. He was just beginning to wonder what to do next when a large, round, white object splashed down into the water next to them.

Thank God, he thought the moment he saw it. Thank God thank God thank God.

Then he was straining to grasp the life preserver, and strong hands were reaching down for the terrified girl, and Adam Prescott was hauling them into the Boston Whaler.

When he saw that she was all right, Adam relaxed again. It had been close: the boom had struck her with a tremendous force, and she had been in the cold water for nearly fifteen minutes.

That stupid young man had acted quickly. Idiotically, but quickly. Adam grimaced, acknowledging reluctantly that he really ought to be grateful for Bob Taylor's bravery.

No. He was grateful for nothing, beholden to no one. If Taylor had not leapt to her rescue, he himself would have delivered her.

He smiled through the interminable dinner at the restaurant, picking at his lobster and pushing the second birthday cake around on his plate. He kept up his end of the conversation, with everyone's concern for Diana being the main topic. He watched her across the table. She laughed and shook her head, dismissing the whole incident as being over and done with. There was a slight bruise on her left temple, but the doctor at the club had examined her and Taylor and pronounced them none the worse for their ordeal.

The young man was making much too much of it. He clung to Diana, patting her arm and pouring her wine and practically cutting up her food for her. Adam cringed inwardly as he watched the jerk reach over to pull a single red rose from the centerpiece and present it to her. What a horse's ass the man was!

Stupid girl, to jump to Kay's defense like that. If anything had happened to Kay, he could have lived with it. Labor Day would no longer have been necessary; true, it would not have been half as exciting, but it would have been a genuine accident. He would rather that nothing happen to Diana, however. Not before Labor Day, when she would at last feel free to come to him. Not before he'd had her, made love to her.

After that, well . . .

"Thank you," the young woman said.

Robin smiled and squeezed her hand. Then he watched as she got into the Land Rover with the Prescotts and drove away.

He took his time driving back across the waterfront to his hotel. Along the way, he gazed around at the thousand tiny lights that shone so brilliantly against the black shapes of the town on his left, the harbor on his right, and the hills that rose up, up above everything. There was a nearly full moon, and its reflection in the water added to the fairy-tale quality of the view. He had the impression that he was infinitesimally small, a minute being traveling slowly across the bottom of a velvet-lined jewel box. Tropical evening, he thought, smiling to himself. St. Thomas at night.

The events of the afternoon seemed somehow ludicrous, melodramatic, when seen from this remote, romantic perspective. Thrashing around in the violent ocean, holding her up, both of them nearly drowning: had that really happened? It was so far away, already forgotten.

Almost. There was something else, nagging at the corner of his consciousness. What was it? Something had happened that should not have happened, that would never have occurred if it hadn't been for the bizarre accident. He had the distinct feeling that he'd made a mistake somewhere during the day, committed some error.

He would have to call Margaret Barclay and report everything, relive for her the whole crazy day. He would shrug it off, put her mind at ease. They knew where the girl was now, and what she was doing. She was all right. That was the important thing, wasn't it?

As he pulled into the parking lot at Bolongo, he made a conscious decision not to tell Miss Barclay that he was in love with her niece.

The young woman filled the glass from her bathroom with water, set it on the table next to her bed, and placed the rose in it. She lay back on the bed, gazing up at the ceiling, recalling every moment, every detail of the day.

Something was wrong. Terribly wrong. Somewhere in that strange, terrifying series of events, one specific thing had happened that endangered her. Adam. The plan. Everything.

She'd got through the rest of the party, assuring Kay and Trish and the others that she was fine.

But she was not fine.

She reached up with her left hand and gingerly touched the bruise on her forehead. No, that wasn't. It was tender, but the slight pain would be gone in a day or so, just as the scar had vanished from her palm almost overnight. What bothered her, hurt her, about the bruise on her temple was not the pain itself, but what it reminded her of. Something that had nothing to do with now. . . .

The photographs. Bob Taylor had taken pictures of them all, all but Adam. She didn't like having her picture taken: cameras told too much. Oh, how she knew that! She didn't even care for the snapshots of her early life, the ones in the scrapbook in her desk at home. She kept them only to remind herself that once, long ago, her life had been safe and sane and comfortable. It was important for her to remember that. No, not the photographs.

Saving Kay Prescott. Another tie, another emotional link to the woman, like the amethyst.

Don't be silly, she thought. That certainly wasn't it. Kay Prescott deserves what's coming to her. I can still go through with the plan without batting an eye. No, it wasn't Kay Prescott.

What was it? Why this sudden anxiety, this foreboding?

She sat up and glanced over at the bedside alarm clock. Midnight. Then her gaze traveled from the clock to the red rose in the glass next to it. She almost realized then. Almost.

There was a moment of confusion, of something being not quite *right*. She stared at the blood-red petals, remembering the handsome, desperate face as he reached out for her in the water. She had been barely conscious. The shock of the blow and the falling and the angry, bottomless water had dulled her faculties. She couldn't remember much of it clearly, but she was certain that something was wrong. Somewhere, in the boat or the water or the restaurant, *something* had happened that should not have happened.

She shook her head to clear away the nagging thoughts. She stood up and walked over to the window to look out at the silent, moon-flecked water. Beautiful moon, she thought. A circle of icy silver in the dark Atlantic night.

If she'd had more experience with love, she might have recognized the symptoms. But she had never really loved anyone, not the boys in school or Clem, the father of her almost-child, or Warren Burton, her married lover at Harvard. She had loved only one man in her life, and she thought about him now.

Adam.

With a long sigh, she left the window, turned off the lamp, and fell across the bed. Her sleep, when it finally came, was fitful.

It was late in the evening in the quiet house on the quiet street in Garden City, Long Island. The only light came from the little lamp on the desk in Dr. Stein's office.

He'd made his way slowly and carefully through the scrapbook, from cover to cover. The Hamilton had been easier: she'd highlighted the relevant pages. What he'd concluded was disturbing because it wasn't a conclusion at all. Just a series of random, seemingly disparate facts. He had no idea what they all added up to, if anything.

He did not understand the young woman.

The grandfather clock in the living room across the hall chimed for the first hour of the morning. He removed his glasses, rubbed his bleary eyes, and took a long sip of club soda. Europe in just a few days, he reminded himself. But now, this.

The yellow legal pad stared up at him. He stared back. After a while he picked up the black felt-tipped pen next to it and began to write, referring to both books. By two o'clock he had discovered a pattern.

He did not sleep that night.

ELEVEN

FRIDAY, AUGUST 23

THE OLD MAN moved slowly, methodically down the beach, poking and sifting the sand in front of him with a stick. Every time he arrived at a fresh patch, he would lean forward and scrutinize it with his sharp eyes, then carefully rake the sand, watching for anything unusual that might rise to the surface. When he was satisfied that the area had been thoroughly examined, he would step forward to the next.

The sun had risen about forty-five minutes before: this was the perfect time of day for his work. The beaches were deserted at this early hour, and this particular cove was rarely populated even at midday. Few on the island ever ventured here. Teenagers, lovers, the occasional adventurous tourist: just enough to make the sand interesting, if not a potential goldmine, like the strips of beach in front of the resort hotels. Of course, the problem with the more famous beaches was that somebody was always chasing him off them. But nobody would bother him here, he thought. Too isolated, and too damn early. With a sense of satisfaction and anticipation, he continued on his quest.

So great was his concentration that he didn't see the little pile of clothes until it had arrived at his feet, materializing like manna in the barren earth before him. He stared down at the trove, feeling the excitement grow within him. A white blouse, a pair of sandals half buried in the sand, and a large straw bag, the kind sold in all the gift shops downtown. A design of flowers wove into the sides, and "St. Thomas, Virgin Islands" written beneath it. He wanted very much to see what was inside the bag.

He stood there in the sand about ten feet from the little mound, trying to appear as nonchalant as possible. He went so far as to pretend for several minutes that he had taken a sudden, passionate interest in scanning the distant horizon, all the while keeping watch on his discovery out of the corner of his eye.

At last, when he could stand it no longer, and one more quick check revealed a still-empty beach, he closed in. Walking directly up to the pile and dropping to his knees, he dipped both hands down into the bag, scooping up its contents with his long, bony fingers.

The glossy magazines were accorded a cursory glance and immediately discarded. Likewise the compact, perfume atomizer, chewing gum, tampons, Kleenex, and envelope.

The little red leather wallet was at the very bottom, under a layer of discarded tissues with lipstick smears on them. A swift search revealed a driver's license with writing but no picture, several photographs of old people and babies, and what appeared to be a library card. The billfold section held what he'd really been looking for: three twenties, a ten, and six singles. Seventy-six dollars!

With another quick glance around the beach, he pocketed the bills. He was about to rise and run from the scene of his crime when he noticed something interesting. The wrinkled, medium-size manila envelope lying next to the magazines was covered with writing. He picked it up and examined it, felt its overstuffed bulk. He shook it tentatively. Nothing: it was obviously filled with paper. He held the envelope up close to his bloodshot eyes and worked his way slowly, laboriously through the writing on its surface.

First there was a name, written in large capitals with a drippy fountain pen. "D-I-A-N-A M-E-I-S-S-E-N—B-O-L-O-N-G-O." This was followed by seven numerals, obviously a phone number. Under that, smaller letters read "N-o-t h-e-r r-e-a-l n-a-m-e. L-a-b-e-l s-e-w-n i-n p-u-r-s-e." Next to these words was an arrow pointing to the right, where more words were written on three lines, one below another. The first word of the top lines was illegible, the fountain pen having dripped and smeared across it. The second and third words were "P-E-T-E-R-S-E-N B-A-R-C-L-A-Y." The second line read "1-3-6 S-h-o-r-e R-o-a-d." Under that was written "G-l-e-n C-o-v-e, N.-Y. 1-1-5-4-2."

It was the names and the address that reminded him. This bag and these clothes belonged to someone, someone who had placed them here and was not here now. Someone who might be in trouble. He looked down at the little pile, then out over the smooth, empty surface of the water.

He had a quarter in one of his pockets, and there was a pay phone up by the main road. He would call the police. Then he'd come back here and keep an eye on the stuff until they arrived. Who knows? he thought. Maybe there'd be some kind of reward.

"I think I know what 'Diana' means," the doctor said.

Margaret looked up from the roses to see him standing over her. He had arrived in her garden unannounced, but she wasn't particularly surprised to see him. The first thing she noticed about him was that he apparently had not had much sleep. Then she saw the scrapbook and the *Mythology* under his arm.

He reached down and helped her to her feet. They stood facing each other for a moment.

"Well, then," she said. She turned around, walked immediately over to the wrought-iron table on the patio, and dropped into a seat. "Perhaps you'd care to join me for lunch."

They waited while Mrs. O'Rourke produced sandwiches and iced tea. As soon as the food was on the table and the housekeeper had returned to the kitchen, Dr. Stein leaned forward and tapped the books with his finger.

"Are you familiar with Greek and Roman mythology?" he asked.

Margaret glanced over at the Hamilton and shrugged. "Working knowledge. I certainly read that somewhere along the way. Is this going to be a quiz?"

He smiled and opened the book to a page at which he'd inserted a bookmark.

"Diana is a common enough name," he began, settling back on the wrought-iron patio chair. "It would mean nothing if we didn't know two other things: she loves mythology, and she loves word games. Scrabble, anagrams, crosswords, and that word-association game that probably has a thousand names—I seem to remember that in my neighborhood we called it Botticelli. Don't ask me why. So we know the way her mind works."

"She's always been rather melodramatic," Margaret observed.

He nodded. "Exactly. 'Diana' could mean anything, until you consider the other alias, Selena Chase. I think the second name is fairly easy: Barclay, Chase—they're both banks. But it's a double entendre as well, just like 'Selena.' "

Margaret stared. "What on earth are you talking about?"

The doctor pointed down at the open book. The yellow highlight markings covered most of the page.

" 'The Goddess with Three Forms,' " he read. "Artemis/Diana, goddess of the hunt, or *chase*. Twin of Apollo, god of the sun, and known sometimes as Selena or Luna, goddess of the moon. Diana, Selena: two names for the same divinity."

"And where," Margaret asked, "did she come up with 'Meissen'?"

He looked away. "I'm not so sure about that. She obviously isn't referring to expensive china. The only thing I could find in any reference books at home that was even close is some valley in Germany. Meisen, with only one *s*. A steel center at one time, apparently. The unusual thing about it was its role in World War Two. There was a prison there—"

"You mean a camp?"

He shook his head. "No. It was for German officers, Nazis accused of betraying the cause. Many were detained at Meisen for the duration of the war, and several never left. I don't know if that has any kind of psychological connotation for her. . . ."

Margaret pushed away her untouched plate and leaned forward.

"This is all very interesting, I'm sure," she said. "But there's one thing you haven't mentioned."

Dr. Stein nodded, second-guessing her.

"Why?" he said. "Yes, that's the vital question. What could all this possibly mean? I had no idea, Margaret, until about two o'clock this morning. I was reading through this." He tapped a finger on the album. "Here's what I noticed. First of all, let me relieve your mind on one count. As I was leaving here the other day, you mentioned what the child said to the mailman on the morning after the murder: 'Mommy's dead. I killed her.' All these years, you've wondered if a six-year-old could do something like that."

Margaret lowered her eyes from his piercing gaze. When she spoke, her voice was barely a whisper. "It's just that, well, she's so *strange* sometimes. No, I never really believed it was possible, any more than the police did." She raised her face again. "But that isn't what you wanted to tell me. You've found something that bothers you. What is it?"

The doctor nodded. "It isn't about what anybody said. It's about what they *didn't* say. I can't tell you what went on in my sessions with her, but I'll go so far as to say that neither of you, in relating to me the story of the tragedy when she was six, ever mentioned a young woman named Karen Lawrence."

Margaret stared at him. Karen Lawrence. She slumped back in her chair and closed her eyes. Oh, God, she thought. I never expected to hear that name again. The newspapers—of course. It would all be in the clippings. The girl must know as well. Several moments passed before she became aware that the doctor was speaking.

". . . away from the house that night. He told the police he was at sea on a merchant vessel, but a routine inquiry shot a hole in his alibi. For a while there, they suspected that Bert had returned to the house and murdered his wife. Then a woman named Karen Lawrence came forward and admitted that Bert had been with her during the time in question. They'd been having a casual affair, she said, for several months."

Margaret nodded wearily. "She used to baby-sit for them. She testified at the initial inquest, before they found that suspect. The man with the robbery record.

When he turned up, they lost interest in Bert and Karen Lawrence and focused on him. I can't say I wasn't relieved. They let him go for lack of evidence, but I've always assumed he was the—"

Dr. Stein raised a hand, cutting her off.

"Yes," he said. "I know what you assumed. But neither of you ever mentioned that your brother-in-law, her father, had been unfaithful to his wife."

She stood up then. She moved quickly, almost automatically, in the direction of her rosebushes. Her comfort, her pride . . .

"He's dead, Dr. Stein. Madeleine was not a—a very passionate woman. . . . Oh, well, I'm not going to defend the man! But his daughter adored him, and he had nothing to do with—what happened. He was with *her*—with Karen Lawrence. I can't imagine his remorse, what he must have gone through in those next six months before he . . . He started drinking. I heard he went to Atlantic City and gambled away half the inheritance. He apparently couldn't face the child; she came to stay with me. And then, finally, he went out in his sailboat, and . . ."

He had risen and followed her out into the garden. Now he stood behind her and spoke softly.

"Yes," he said. "He killed himself. But I'm not interested in that right now. I'm interested in Karen Lawrence."

Margaret whirled around to face him. "Why?"

"There aren't any pictures of her in the clippings," he explained, "but the papers described her as an 'attractive redhead.'"

"Yes, that's right," Margaret said.

"How old was she, Margaret?"

She thought a moment. "I don't know, about twenty-five. . . ."

"And what happened to her, after the murder and Bert's suicide?"

Margaret shrugged. "I—I have no idea. I never saw or heard of her again."

"Did she attend Bert's funeral?"

"There wasn't a funeral; they never found him. It was a memorial service. Bert's parents were dead, and I don't think he had any other relatives back in Montana or Minnesota or wherever it was. I arranged it, and I took the child. And there was some young man there, one of his mates from the Merchant Marines, who was very upset about Bert's death. Charlie something. I've forgotten his last name. No, she wasn't there. So?"

He gazed down at the red roses, nodding to himself.

"No," he repeated softly, "she wasn't there. She'd already disappeared." Then he raised his eyes to hers. "Come back to the table, Margaret. I want to show you something."

The red rose in the glass next to her bed had opened slightly, the soft petals loosening and stretching in the morning sun. She leaned down and breathed in its scent, thinking briefly of her aunt in Glen Cove.

Then she remembered the face of the man who had given her the flower the night before.

Then, as ever, she thought of Adam.

Today was Friday. Next Friday he would leave her, but

only for a while. He would deliver his stepdaughter to her mother's sister, getting her out of the way, and then he would fly to Florida to visit an acquaintance who had recently moved to Palm Beach.

He and the acquaintance, Roger somebody, had won several local races as a two-man team on Roger's sailboat before a business opportunity had required Roger and his wife to move to the mainland. There was a race in Florida the day after Labor Day, and Adam had contacted Roger two months before and suggested they enter it. The other man had been delighted by the idea, and now Adam had a perfect cover for the plan. He'd stay in a hotel in Palm Beach for a few days, visiting with the man and his family as much as possible before the race. High visibility, he called it.

Nobody would miss him for nine hours on Labor Day, he'd assured her. He'd be back in Palm Beach in time for Roger's barbecue party that evening, receiving the news of his wife's tragic death in the presence of many witnesses.

All she had to do was be sure that Kay was alone in the house at two o'clock on Monday afternoon.

She stepped out onto the balcony and gazed around at the bright-blue seascape. The little town across the water to her right seemed to be dozing in the sun. She leaned against the balcony railing, allowing the warmth to enter her skin.

No one could connect her to it, she thought. Any of it. That was the best part, the vital part. Otherwise . . .

She would be away from the house all day, she'd told him. The original idea had been for her to go out on the

Kay with Greg on Labor Day. Of course, Greg had disappeared since the plan was first formulated, but there was always Kyle. She could ask Kyle to take her sailing, take him out for dinner and dancing, and return to Cliffhanger late that night to discover the robbery and murder.

She'd met Kyle yesterday on the *Kay*, and he'd paid no attention to her. Besides, he apparently had a girlfriend, Rita.

But now Bob Taylor had arrived on the scene. The next time she got Adam alone, she'd tell him her new, improved idea.

Things were falling into place.

With a little sigh, she went back into the bedroom. Kay had taken Lisa into town to buy some things for the child's trip to Connecticut. She almost smiled, remembering how easy it had been to change Kay's mind on that count.

"Well, if *you* think it's best, Diana . . ."

Oh, she *did*, she assured the woman.

Done.

She checked herself in the mirror. Yes, the hair was holding, and she was actually getting used to the eyes. Then she turned around and glanced over at the closet door. The locked suitcase was in there, behind the clothes. The scrapbook, the dress, the wig, the Kouronos: everything.

The others would be home soon, and there was still one more item on her agenda. She left the room and went downstairs. Nola was about somewhere, so she'd have to be careful in the kitchen. There was a large package of hamburger on the second shelf of the refrigerator. She'd noticed it there this morning.

It was time to do something about the dog.

"What is this?" Margaret asked.

She was again seated at the table on the patio, and the doctor stood beside her, leaning over. He had just placed the scrapbook in front of her, open to the final page of clippings about Bert's disappearance at sea. Then he turned the page. She was looking down at a new set of headlines, dating from ten years ago. Some sort of murder case in Hawaii. She shrugged: what was the doctor getting at?

"This," he said, "is something else she obviously found fascinating. Notice the similarity. A rash of robberies in Hawaii. Darlene Bishop Phillips, the Bishop Hotels heiress, is stabbed to death during a robbery attempt at her home on Kauai. Husband away at the time. That's the fellow, there."

He pointed. Margaret looked down at a grainy, yellowed photocopy of a front page. A dark-haired man with a beard sat slumped over in a tropical-looking living room, his face buried in his hands, his eyes glazed with shock. Standing behind him, leaning down with her hand on his shoulder, was a tall, slender woman.

"It turns out," Dr. Stein continued, "that the husband, Drew Phillips, was with this woman at the time of the incident. Her name was Kimberly Brown, an attractive, red-headed widow who lived on Kauai with her baby daughter. She was Drew Phillips's mistress."

Margaret looked down at the album with new interest.

"Yes," she said. "I vaguely remember this. Bishop Hotels—wasn't the husband eventually murdered as well?"

"Look," the doctor whispered, pointing down at the album. "She's saved all the clippings."

Margaret glanced briefly through the four pages of cut-out news items. The last headline, dated three years after the first incident, read "FIRE AT SEA: Yacht Explosion Kills Bishop Murder Husband." The remains of a man believed to be Andrew Phillips, husband of Darlene Bishop Phillips, had been "partially retrieved." His mate, a young man named Stephen Ingalls, also of Kauai, was missing. A search of Drew Phillips's property revealed that his several bank accounts had recently been cleared out.

"The bank accounts they mention were a fair chunk of the Bishop girl's fortune," the doctor said. "About three million. What kept people speculating was the fact that Kimberly Brown and her baby disappeared at about the same time."

Margaret shook her head and leaned back in the chair.

"Very interesting," she said, "and very sordid. I suppose the Brown woman and the mate killed him and made off with his money. She and the mate could even have killed the wife in the first place. A long-range plan. But what's the connection?"

He went around the table and sat across from her. Leaning forward, he made sure she was watching him before he went on.

"Your sister was killed, and her husband later died mysteriously. Nearly half of their money disappeared, as did Karen Lawrence, the attractive redhead in her midtwenties who was your brother-in-law's mistress. Ten years later, in Hawaii, another rich woman is killed in amazingly similar circumstances. Again the husband dies mysteriously, and a lot of money disappears. And again there is an attractive redhead in the story—a widow this time, with a baby, a woman in her midthirties. Kimberly Brown. Please note the presence of boats in both stories as well.

"I keep thinking about the tall figure with the black stocking mask. The child heard a noise coming from her mother's bedroom in the middle of the night, and she went to investigate. She saw her mother's body and the figure standing over her. Then the assailant struck her on the head with a heavy object and fled."

He leaned even closer to her.

"Is it possible," he asked, "that the figure the child saw that night was a woman?"

When Kay pulled into the driveway, she saw someone kneeling beneath the tamarind, and for a moment she didn't recognize who it was. Then, as the car drew nearer, she saw that it was Diana, sitting back against the trunk, and that she was not alone. The dog was stretched out on the grass before her, quite still, its head in the young woman's lap.

As she swung around to park in front of the house, she experienced a brief, inexplicable chill, an undefined, parenthetical moment of disquietude. The figures had not looked up, had not in any way acknowledged the arrival of the car. The shade was too dark, the figures too still, the humidity too close and heavy. . . .

As Kay and Lisa got out of the Land Rover, the young woman raised her hand from the dog's head and waved to them. Jumbi, as if released from a magic spell, jumped to her feet and bounded out of the shadows and across the grass, black and tan coat flashing in the sun, barking her usual ebullient greeting.

"You seem to have made a new friend," Kay told the young woman as they walked up to her.

"Yes," she said, rising. "I decided it was time for Jumbi and me to put our animosity behind us."

"Come see, Diana," Lisa said, grabbing her hand and leading her out from under the tree into the sunlight. "The packages are in the car. Let's take them up to my room. I got a new dress and a pair of jeans and . . ."

They ran off toward the Land Rover ahead of Kay, the dog at their heels. Looking beyond them as she neared the house, Kay saw Nola standing in the front doorway.

"Telephone, Mrs. Prescott," the housekeeper called. Then, lowering her voice, she added, "It's the police."

She saw the dog prancing on the lawn, heard Diana and Lisa giggling together as they unloaded the car, and noted the worried expression on Nola's face.

She stood in the living room for a long moment, staring down at the receiver resting next to the base of the princess phone.

The police.

At last she took a deep breath and raised the instrument to her ear.

"Hello," she said. "This is Kay Prescott."

"Miz Prescott?" The thick, musical calypso accent belonged to the local chief of police, an elderly native man named Potter. What is it? she thought, and why is the chief himself calling me? Oh, God. . . .

"Hello, sir," she said, trying to keep her voice casual.

"Sahree tuh be bod'rin' you, Miz Prescott, but we gaht ouhselves a prahblem heah. A missing puhson—"

Missing person, she thought. Oh, God. Adam! He was out sailing again today. . . . "What's happened, Mr. Potter?"

She clutched the receiver, bracing herself.

"Well, ma'am, we ain't shuah. Ol' Digger Joe, you know him? Well, he be out combin' de beaches dis mahnin', lookin' fo stuff—"

Oh, Christ, this man was so old! This could take hours. She bit her lip, knowing it was fruitless to protest, to insult an ancient West Indian gentleman when he was telling a story.

"—an' he be dahn at dat li'l cove neah de yacht club, pokin' heah and deah in de sand, you know, like he does, an' he come upon dese clothes an' dis puhse lyin' right deah on de beach—"

Clothes? Purse? What was the man babbling about?

"—an' he look in de wallet—you know Ol' Digger Joe, Miz Prescott, always lookin' fo' rum money—an' he fin' a dribuh's license wid dis name on it"—he paused a moment, obviously reading from some report on his desk— "dis name, Sandra Franklin. An' we done brung it heah to de Fort. Now, I see dis name an' I says to myself, Sandra

Franklin. Wasn't dat de young Stateside geahl up by Cliffhanguh?"

A guilty sense of relief flooded through her. It wasn't Adam. It was something else entirely. Sandra.

"Mr. Potter," she said as firmly as possible, "has something happened to Sandra?"

"Ah!" the chief exclaimed. "I wuz right. She *does* wuhk fo' you."

"She *did* work for me, Mr. Potter. She left my employ about three weeks ago, and I haven't heard from her since."

There was a pause on the line as the old chief processed that information. "Well, ma'am, Ol' Digger Joe, he find huh clothes and puhse. An' huh cah is pahked neah de cove, but ain' nobody know wheah de geahl be. We tink maybe she done drahned."

Drowned. Sandra. . . .

"That's terrible," Kay said. "Is there anything I can do?" My God, she was thinking. First Jack and Nancy Breen, now this. What next? These things always come in threes. She tried to concentrate on Mr. Potter, who was speaking again.

"Do you know how we c'n get in touch wid huh fambly?"

She stared out at the sundeck, searching her mind.

"No, sir, I don't," she said at last. "Sandra never mentioned a family."

"Hmmm. Miz Prescott, we don' know nuttin' 'bout dis geahl, only what we find in huh puhse. Could you come dahn by de Fort dis aftuhnoon? Maybe you can tell us sometin' dat can help us."

She sighed and glanced at her watch. Poor Sandra, she thought. Well, I can show Potter the reference I got from Joan Hirsch, her previous employer. Maybe Joan knows something about a family.

"I'll come now," she said.

Margaret raised an imperious hand.

"Enough," she said. "So according to your theory, we're looking for a tall red-headed woman, about forty-five years old. Someone the girl is—" She broke off, unable to think of a word.

"Tracking," the doctor suggested. "The woman may have a child between the ages of"—he calculated—"eleven and fourteen. And it's entirely possible, given Karen and Kimberly, that her first name begins with the letter K." He leaned forward in his seat and spoke in a low, clear voice. "Your niece had always been very troubled. Suddenly, ten years ago, about the time of the murder of the hotel heiress in Hawaii, she became calm, serene, as if she'd just solved some major problem. This incident made national headlines, and this photo"—he pointed down at the picture of Drew Phillips and the woman named Kimberly—"was in every paper in the country. She was in boarding school at the time, but she could have seen it and recognized her mother's assailant. For the next three years, she didn't know what she was going to do with her knowledge, but she at least knew where the woman was. Then, seven years ago—about the time the husband's yacht burned and Kimberly Brown disappeared—your niece did something very interesting."

Margaret felt the chill moving slowly down her spine. She swallowed, trying to soothe her suddenly parched throat.

"She quit her job," she whispered, "and went to—"

"—Hawaii," the doctor finished. "Looking for clues, perhaps, to the woman's whereabouts. When she realized that Kimberly Brown was gone without a trace, she may have lapsed into a state of despair."

"She met those flower children, or whatever they were," Margaret continued, "and went with them to a commune in San Francisco. . . ."

The doctor nodded. "And the rest, as they say, is history. Abortion, suicide attempt—and all in a time when she didn't know where her mother's killer was, when she again believed that the person who had destroyed her life would go forever unpunished. Then, three years ago, she began her second period of unexplained serenity, and a few months ago she took off for the Caribbean. Now she's back there."

Margaret stared at him. "I don't understand. What could possibly make her—"

Dr. Stein reached down to the scrapbook and riffed through the heavy vellum pages to the final entry at the back. It was a single clipping from the *Virgin Islands Daily News*, dated June 7 three years before, centered on the last page of the album. Some sort of society-page notice, announcing the marriage of local widow Kay Belden to a man named Adam Prescott, an international sportsman new to the island. What was unusual about the clipping was not the article itself but the blank space next to it. The newspaper border was still cemented to the page, but a two-inch square, probably a photograph, had been carefully cut away.

Margaret gazed down at the tiny newsprint and the gaping hole beside it. Then she closed her eyes and shuddered. Kay Prescott. Her daughter had just celebrated her thirteenth birthday, according to—

"We can clear this up fairly easily," she said. And with that she stood up and went into the house.

Dr. Stein rose and followed her into the living room. She walked over to the piano, picked up one of the framed pictures on top of it, and handed it to him. It was a photograph of a young red-headed woman, standing with the child in front of the house in Islip.

"That's Karen Lawrence," she said.

She proceeded across the room and into her office. By the time he joined her there, she was already speaking into the phone.

"Robin, I'm so glad I caught you. Listen, those photos you mentioned yesterday, the ones you took on the boat . . . yes, well, is there a—what do you call it?—a fax service on the island?"

Kay walked slowly out of the police station in the old stone fortress on the Waterfront at the edge of town and made her way down the hill to the lot where she'd parked the car. She glanced at her watch. Go home, Kay, she thought. Time to go home.

She wandered into the parking lot, playing back in her mind the scene in Chief Potter's office. He'd been extremely kind, even solicitous. Joan Hirsch had joined them, but she was unable to shed any light: all she'd had from Sandra was the recommendation of an employment agency in the States. A long-distance call revealed that the agency was no longer in business. Dead end.

Potter had asked questions and listened politely as Kay answered them. She had noticed his interest as he watched her examine the personal belongings on his desk: clothes, shoes, bag. . . .

Oh, Sandra, she thought. You poor, unlovely, unloved young woman.

Then she thought about Diana Meissen. She told herself that what she was beginning to suspect was not possible. It was really too far out even to consider. . . .

She had passed the Land Rover, walked right by it toward the other end of the lot. She stopped, realizing, turned around, and retraced her steps.

Go home, Kay.

The young woman sat there, her eyes on the child who perched on the couch next to her, hearing but not listening to her breathless, girlish monologue. She was concentrating, rather, on those other noises that provided a constant soundtrack in the house on the cliff: the whistle of the trade wind through the glass doors facing the ocean, the odd cry of the gulls, and the rhythmic, muffled, faraway crashing of the breakers against the rocks below. The ever-changing but never-ending sounds of the island.

". . . and they have another horse, a mare named Mrs. Ed—she's Mr. Ed's wife—and Mr. and Mrs. Ed have two children, Dancer and Starface. I always ride Starface; she's the gentlest . . ."

Where was Kay? It was nearly dinnertime, and she had not yet returned from—wherever. Adam had returned from his sail a half hour ago: he was in the master apartment now, showering and dressing.

The living room was bathed in amber light from the golden sunset outside. Through the wall of glass she could see a vast expanse of bright, wheat-colored sky. The water in the distance appeared light brown, with a million yellow highlights.

". . . a party on Labor Day with all their friends. We ride the horses and have a picnic near the golf course in Greenwich. I hope they're planning that this year. Do you play golf, Diana? Aunt Trish does, and Daddy used to . . ."

It was this last random statement that brought her back from her woolgathering and focused her attention on Lisa. She watched the girl for a moment, and when Lisa at last paused to draw breath, she inserted a question.

"Do you think about your father a lot?" she asked.

"Oh, yes," Lisa whispered. "Every day. He was wonderful. He always made me laugh—and Mommy, too." She paused before adding, "What about you, Diana? You never mention your parents. Do you see them a lot?"

She felt the dry tightness at the back of her throat and the stinging at the corners of her eyes as she regarded the child's innocent, upturned face. She doesn't know, she thought. I've never told her. I've never mentioned it to any of them.

"No, Lisa," she said quietly. "I lost both of my parents a long time ago."

They sat facing each other in silence as the last golden sunlight slowly faded from the room. Then Lisa, in an act that contradicted her thirteen years and flashed forward to the graceful woman she would become, nodded once and reached out gently to take the young woman's hand in her own.

The door under the staircase opened and Adam arrived in the living room. He was fresh from his shower, in a starched, short-sleeved white shirt and faded jeans. His platinum hair glistened in the dying light of day. Perhaps sensing the mood in the room, he went silently over to the opposite couch and sat.

She turned her attention from Lisa to Adam, aware— for the hundredth time—of the acute, overwhelming sensation she always experienced when this man came into her presence. It was a sharp, clear, naked emotion, so powerful that for a brief second, she wondered if Lisa could pick up on it. Oh, God. . . .

A moment later, the sound of the approaching Land Rover reached them. The three listened as the car was parked and Jumbi ran into the driveway from the garage to bark a greeting. Then they turned to watch as Kay and the dog came in to join them.

Kay looked around at them all, her gaze finally coming to rest on the young woman on the couch.

"Lisa," she said in a quiet voice, not looking at her daughter as she spoke, "run upstairs and get ready for dinner."

Without a word, the child obeyed. Jumbi followed her up the stairs. When they were gone, Kay dropped wearily down next to her husband.

Adam touched her arm. "What is it, Kay?"

She shook her head, still gazing over at the other woman. "Bad news, I'm afraid. I've just been down at the Fort with Chief Potter. Sandra's disappeared. They think she's drowned."

There was silence in the room. Kay's words traveled slowly across the table and crashed into the young woman's consciousness. Drowned. Had she said *drowned*?

Kay resumed the story, explaining about the clothes and the bag on the beach and the Jeep parked among the trees. Sandra had been traced to a guest house downtown, where she'd been staying since her inexplicable departure from Cliffhanger, and the landlady there had not seen her for nearly a week. Potter had shown Kay the girl's possessions: the clothes and the bag. . . .

The bag. At the mention of it, the young woman very nearly gasped aloud. The manila envelope with the money. Was there any way for the police to trace it to her?

Adam was watching her intently. She glanced up, startled by his intense gaze. She knew he was thinking what she had been thinking. Carefully, as unobtrusively as possible, she met his eyes and shook her head once. No, she communicated. If the silly girl had actually kept all that cash rather than putting it in a bank, there was nothing about the bills or the envelope that could possibly connect them, herself and Adam, to any of it. I was careful, her eyes told him. I did as you instructed. Large bills, from a bank in New York several weeks ago, and a plain, unmarked envelope.

She couldn't breathe. There as a pressure in her chest, a tingling in her knees. She leaned back, the nails of her right hand clutching the arm of couch. Drowned. . . .

Impossible, she thought irrelevantly. People don't drown; not really. Not so very conveniently. . . .

Why did Kay Prescott continue to watch her? What was it about the woman's attitude? Natural curiosity at how Sandra's successor was taking the news? Or was it suspicion? Had they found something? Did Kay *know* something? Had that silly girl written down her name and her phone number at Bolongo for possible future extortion?

Her purse. Oh, God: she'd left the table at Sparky's for several minutes, gone to the ladies' room. She hadn't taken her purse. Had Sandra . . .?

She willed herself, forced herself, to look directly at Kay. She studied the woman's face. I can't read your expression, she thought. I don't know what you're thinking. . . .

"It was rather pathetic, really," Kay said, turning her gaze at last from the young woman across the room to Adam, on the couch next to her. "There was just a blouse and a scarf and a pair of sandals. The bag was full of fan magazines. An empty wallet and some makeup and a pack of gum—and those damned, silly magazines. The poor thing." She shook her head absently and reached over to take her husband's hand.

On the other side of the coffee table, the hand that clutched the arm of the couch opened, relaxed. The young woman leaned back against the cool leather and raised her hand to her eyes, weak, powerless with relief. It washed over her in waves, one after another. Kay doesn't know, she thought. It's all right. It's all right it's all right it's . . .

Holding his wife's hand tightly in his own, Adam looked across the table and smiled.

Kay, noting the girl's apparent distress, leaned forward. "What's the matter, Diana? Are you feeling ill?"

The young woman regarded Kay for a moment before replying, and in that moment another facet of the plan was put in action.

"I suppose," she sighed, smiling rather weakly. "A bit of a headache. I haven't been sleeping well the past few days. I wonder, could you give me the name of your doctor?"

Margaret sat at her desk, staring down at the pictures.

It had been nearly six o'clock when they arrived back at the house from the stationery store in the next town, the nearest fax service of which Margaret was aware. She now possessed three eight-and-a-half-by-eleven sheets of paper displaying eight remarkably clear color reproductions of snapshots Robin Trask had taken in St. Thomas the day before. Robin had compiled quickly and efficiently from his end, and he hadn't asked any questions. For that Margaret was grateful: she would fill him in later if necessary.

Dr. Stein had driven her in his Volvo. As he drove, he broke the news to her of his impending vacation. On Monday, he told her, he and his wife were flying to Europe for three weeks. Three weeks, she'd thought as they parked and entered the store. Too long. If his suspicions are correct, something will have to be done before he returns. And I will have to do it. Alone.

She wondered what his wife was like. Was she the sort of woman who would put off a long-awaited vacation for the sake of one of her husband's patients? It hardly mattered: Margaret would never ask. She'd imposed on him quite enough. Besides, the girl was no longer his patient.

Now, examining the photographs with a magnifying glass, she wondered if there was really anything to worry about in the first place.

She'd spread the pictures out across the desk. On the left was the framed photograph of Karen Lawrence. In the center was the page from the dismantled scrapbook, the newspaper shot of Kimberly Brown with Mr. Phillips. To the right of this were the pictures from St. Thomas. Their eyes traveled from left to right. Twenty years ago. Ten years ago. Yesterday.

Margaret held the glass over the final series of photos. A cloudy day, rough water in the background; in the foreground, the crowded cockpit of a medium-size yacht. Happy, smiling people. The central image in all of the pictures was a lovely little red-headed girl grinning into the camera: the birthday girl. More children, flanking the star.

Her niece, looking rather peculiar with dark-brown hair, smiling self-consciously into the lens, as if she'd really prefer not to have her pictures taken. A handsome young man pulling on a rope, or sheet, or whatever it was called. A young woman with him, what Margaret's mother would have called an obvious blonde. A large, beefy, red-faced man of about fifty, probably Irish and certainly friendly, his arm around the tiny waist of an elegant, exotically beautiful, fiftyish former-model type. A rich woman, Margaret decided. Well-bred, globe-trotting *femme du monde*, definitely underweight. She wondered, briefly, who these people were.

But the face that she and the doctor were now scrutinizing so closely belonged to a tall, slender redhead in her forties who appeared in four of the photos. There was only one really clear shot; in the others the woman was either turned slightly away or hidden behind a large pair of sunglasses and a low-brimmed straw hat. In the single good picture of her, Kay Prescott stood next to her daughter in the cockpit, grinning into the camera. Behind them could be seen the back of someone's head: a tall, platinum-haired man at the helm. Mr. Prescott, presumably. The woman had temporarily removed the hat and sunglasses, and she had her arm around the child's shoulders. It was a perfect shot.

And that was the problem.

"No," Margaret said at last, speaking for both of them. "This is not the same woman."

She hadn't yet progressed to the next step, considered the implications of this simple, irrefutable fact. She only knew one thing, and it filled her with a sense of great relief. Karen Lawrence and Kimberly Brown and Kay Prescott were three different women. There was a resemblance—a strong one—between the first two. There was even a chance that, given ten years and a different hairstyle, they *might* be one and the same. But neither woman looked anything like the woman in St. Thomas.

"There goes that theory," Dr. Stein said, grinning rather sheepishly as he went around the desk and sat across from her. He reached up and rubbed his eyes.

Margaret put down the magnifying glass and looked up at him. "What now?"

The doctor leaned back and emitted a long sigh. "Now I apologize for worrying you, and I go home to dinner. And now you relax and accept one other possibility, a possibility *I* should have considered. Maybe—just maybe—she's not doing anything. Maybe she just likes the Caribbean, likes the idea of changing her environment and her physical appearance, likes living with a picture-perfect family"—he waved a hand at Robin's photos—"in whatever capacity. I thought there must be a pattern, a method in all of this—some outrageous plan. And so did you. We were both perfectly willing to believe my theory of elaborate revenge against some shadowy—and, as it turns out, nonexistent—woman. Don't you see? We were willing to believe that of her because that's the *impression* she gives. I've studied her professionally, and you've known her since she was born. We both know she's capable of it.

"But it's obvious I was wrong," he continued, and his voice changed again. Now he sounded certain of himself.

"I think she's simply trying to get her act together, if you'll excuse the out-of-date lingo. A change of scene, a change of outlook. Maybe this is her way of putting her past behind her. She'll be back, Margaret, and soon. You must know that. You are her only steadying influence. You always have been."

He looked down at the pictures on the desk, then over at the little gold-framed photo that rested permanently on one corner of the blotter. In it she was wearing a cap and gown, staring sullenly out at the world, the lovely hair falling down around her shoulders. High school graduation. He shook his head, grinning ruefully down at the photograph.

"She really is an extraordinary young woman," he said.

They sat in silence for a long time. Then, as Margaret watched him, the doctor rose to leave. He reached across the desk to shake her hand.

"I'll call you when I get back from Europe," he said.

She walked him to the front door. He was out of the house and heading toward his car when she finally stopped him with the question she'd been wanting to ask for the past several minutes.

"Dr. Stein," she called from the doorway.

He turned around on the front walk.

"What would you have done," she asked, "if your theory had been correct?"

A slow smile spread across his face.

"It's not what *I* would have done," he said. "What would *you* have done?"

Then, with a nod and a wave, he turned and walked into the early-evening shadows.

She closed the heavy front doors and leaned back against it, listening as the car started and drove away. She gazed ahead of her into the living room. It's getting dark, she thought. Time to turn on the lights.

What would she have done? A very good question.

And she would have to figure out the answer, she realized, moving slowly toward the kitchen to see what Mrs. O'Rourke had left for her dinner, switching on every lamp she passed until the entire house was ablaze with light, belying the darkness that pressed in against the windows.

The doctor was mistaken. She was certain of it; she had never been more certain of anything. His initial theory, erroneous though it had turned out to be, was still closer to the actual truth, whatever that was. Her niece was up to something. Something dark and secret and wrong.

And she, Margaret, was on her own.

Nineteen thousand, four hundred, and seventy-six dollars! The old beachcomber couldn't believe his luck. He counted it all again just to be sure. He glanced nervously up and down the beach, half expecting Chief Potter himself to drop out of the nearest sea-grape tree and clap him in irons. He reached inside the filthy, tattered jacket and pulled out the pint bottle of rum he'd swiped from the bar he'd been begging in last night. He unscrewed the cap and took a good, long pull.

No more begging, he thought. Not ever.

He sat down in the sand and smoothed out the bulging,

wrinkled envelope on his knee. In the dying light of sunset, he worked his way once more through the lettering scrawled across the front.

This is not good, he thought. That last part is a name and address, probably of the money's owner. If anyone finds this, they'll take the money away. Even now, he knew, the police could be looking for him. It wasn't until after he'd placed the call to them that he'd looked in the envelope and seen its contents. He'd taken it and made his escape before they arrived.

His sister in Dominica. That was the answer! Tomorrow morning he'd make his way down to the Waterfront and find a fishing boat heading for Dominica. Agnes had four children and no husband: she'd know what to do with the money. Yes, he'd go home tomorrow. But first he'd get rid of this envelope.

He removed the bills, stuffing great handfuls into the pockets of his jacket and pants. Then he unscrewed the cap of the bottle and dumped its remaining contents over the manila paper. He fished a pack of matches out of his knapsack and set the envelope on fire. He held the burning paper until it nearly singed his hand, then he let the smoldering corner fly away on the wind.

With that, Old Digger Joe stretched out on the cool sand, made a pillow of his knapsack, and drifted off to sleep.

TWELVE

MONDAY, AUGUST 26

THE YOUNG WOMAN was halfway down the winding path to the beach when she heard the sudden snapping of a twig in the woods behind her. She paused, listening, wondering what it could be.

It couldn't be Lisa, she thought. She'd only left the child minutes ago back at the house, padding up the stairs in her bathrobe to dress. Adam and Kay had left the house separately immediately after breakfast, she to meet Trish downtown and he, a few minutes later, to the yacht club. It was then that Lisa had suggested they draw pictures on the beach today.

"Go on ahead, Diana," she'd called as she went up to her room. "I'll get the sketchpads, and Jumbi and I will meet you there."

It was a fine morning for such a venture: the sun bore

down on the island, glimmering through the branches, and a cool breeze rattled the leaves above her head. But even the rustling all around her did not conceal the loud crack of the twig. She had just begun to list in her mind the several possible wild creatures that might be responsible—another iguana, perhaps—when she was possessed of a horrible certainty. It crept swiftly up through her, rooting her, suspending everything. She was not alone, and whatever had joined her was human. Someone was standing quite close, on the path above and behind, watching her. She could feel the eyes.

She stood there frozen, unable to move forward or turn around. How far was she from the house? Would anyone hear her if she cried out? Who could be lurking here, on the grounds of Cliffhanger, unknown to its occupants?

This last thought made her panic subside. Don't be silly, she told herself. Cliffhanger was, after all, private property, and she really had no reason to feel that she was in any danger. Whoever stood behind her among the trees was trespassing. Perhaps it was someone lost, unaware that he or she had wondered out of public territory.

Then she heard the second twig snap, and the footsteps approaching from behind. She closed her eyes, helpless, all rational thought flying from her in the deep, piercing thrill of her fear. She waited, listening to the footsteps and the quick, ragged breathing. . . .

The darkened bedroom. The lamp lying on its side on the floor, casting off weak light at strange angles, illuminating the blank face of the child standing frozen in the doorway. The moaning from the white-clad figure on the floor. The dagger lying on the soft white carpet, now stained dark red. The cold, rough feel of it in her hands as she bends slowly down to pick it up. The bloody hand, outstretched, reaching for her in supplication or recrimination or . . . warning. The footsteps approaching from behind, and the quick, ragged breathing, hot breath on the back of her tiny neck. The smooth, black leather-gloved hand grasping her shoulder and whirling her around. One brief glimpse of the mask. Darkness. . . .

The ungloved hand grasped her shoulder and whirled her around. A lurch of sheer terror engulfed her as she stared up into his eyes.

Then, as quickly as it had come, it was gone. The roaring in her ears subsided, and her vision cleared. She caught her breath and returned from the past, peering up—here, now, on this path in these woods in St. Thomas, Virgin Islands—at his handsome face.

"Adam!"

He stood before her, holding her arms, grinning down at her. His hand reached up to touch her dark hair. Then the shock of the memory was replaced by the shock of the present as he leaned forward and pressed his lips to hers.

Adam kissed her in the early-morning shadows of the forest below the cliff. Then, without a word, he took her by the hand and led her down, across the sunlit beach, and into the cool, dark interior of the boathouse. Once inside, he kicked the rickety door shut behind him, pinned her against the uncertain wall, and kissed her again. His large, rough hand reached up to caress the soft expanse of flesh just below her throat. Leaning forward, he buried his face in her hair and breathed in the clean, flowery, fleshy scent that always seemed to be there, wherever she was.

Pressed against her, his eyes tightly shut, he fought off a wave of something that was almost dizziness as the warmth of her body flowed outward toward him. Her heart was pounding furiously: he felt the vibrations against his chest. He reached down with his free hand and grasped her firmly around the waist, grinding against her abdomen, letting her feel through their clothes the burning heat she aroused in him.

She pushed at his shoulders with her hands, wriggling against the planks of the wall—"No!"—but he was having none of that. He clamped his mouth down upon hers, cutting off further protest. Awkwardly, keeping their lips together as he moved, he began to maneuver their bodies away from the wall and across the room to the pile of pillows and blankets in the far corner. At last he picked her up in his arms and sank to his knees next to the blankets.

This time she stopped him. She shoved away from him and fell with a thud onto the pillows. She rolled away to the corner, taking in a gulp of air to form the shout: "Don't!"

He watched as she huddled against the wall, pulling her knees up under her chin, facing away from him. Then he rose to his feet and stared down in consternation.

"What the hell is wrong with you, Diana?" he barked as the heat left him and the cold anger flooded in.

"What's wrong with *me*?" she gasped, still fighting to regain her breath. "Lisa will be down here any minute.

What if she came in here and found us? You've not even supposed to be here. She thinks you went to the club a half hour ago. So did I, for that matter."

He looked down at the young woman gazing accusingly up at him. At last the humor of it sank in. He began to laugh, and after a moment she joined him. He reached down and pulled her to her feet.

"Sorry," he said, chuckling. "Temporary insanity. Your beauty and all that."

"Well, control yourself," she said, but there was humor in her tone.

They laughed together again, but it was all he could do to retain the appearance of casualness. Oh, God, he thought. I want this woman. I want her almost as much as I want—

"What are you doing here, anyway?" she demanded, leaning back against Fred Belden's dusty worktable and regarding him evenly.

He grinned. "I wanted to get you alone, so I parked on that little dirt road halfway down the driveway and came back. I was heading for the house when I saw you come out and go off down the path through the woods. I figured you were coming to the beach. And what better rendezvous? We can talk now. I've been worried about you, Diana. Ever since the other day, when Kay came back from the Fort and told us about Sandra. It's too bad about her, of course, but you looked like you were going to faint! What the hell happened to you?"

* * *

She turned away from him slightly and shook her head. She reached out behind her to grasp the table firmly, grounding herself. Close call, she thought, but I'm all right. She would have to be very careful now. Proceed with caution.

"I was thinking about your money," she said. "I did just as you said: plain manila envelope, lunch in a crowded tourist place. Five thousand to leave Cliffhanger and ask no questions."

She'd added fifteen thousand of her own, fifteen thousand he didn't know she possessed, to clinch the deal. How arrogant—and how typical—of this gorgeous, impractical man to think that a person's cooperation in what would eventually turn out to be murder could be bought so cheaply!

"You see," she continued, "I didn't know whether she still had that envelope at the time of—well, you know. How horrible that must be. Drowning."

Adam came to stand before her, leaning close.

"Actually," he said, "I understand it's rather a pleasant way to go."

She looked up at him then, into his eyes. Not liking what she saw there, she shook her head again and went on. "Well, at any rate, she didn't have the money. It wasn't among her things. Kay would have said something. Imagine if the police had found all that cash in her purse! It would have looked pretty suspicious."

He leaned even closer. She could feel the hot expulsion of breath on her cheek as he spoke. "What do you mean, 'suspicious'?"

She stared, remembering her recent acting classes. He'd delivered the line wrong, she thought. Much too quietly, much too intently. It was her first inkling, and the slow, dull shock of it emanated outward from the pit of her stomach, causing every muscle to contract. Oh, God, she was thinking. Is it possible . . . ?

With tremendous effort, concentrating as the instructor at the Studio had shown her, she shrugged and smiled. Casual, she thought. That's the proper way to play this. Not really very interested at all. . . .

"Oh, I don't know," she fairly sang, fixing him with her easiest grin. "Guilty conscience, I suppose. I mean, it's not as if *we* had anything to do with her drowning. Well, water—if you'll forgive the atrocious pun—under the bridge."

Adam laughed. He roared with amusement, and the precarious structure that housed them shook dangerously at the sound.

She went over to open the door and looked out at the base of the path leading up to the house. No sign of Lisa, not yet. Enough of this, she decided. Whatever he had done, whatever she was beginning to suspect of him, would have to be sorted through and figured out later. Now there wasn't much time. Down to business.

"Listen," she said, whirling around in the doorway. "I've altered part of my agenda. I won't be with your mate on Labor Day. I'm going to be with Bob Taylor, somewhere away from the house. When you call Kay from Florida the night before, tell her you'll call her again at two that afternoon. She'll wait here for the call, and I'll be . . . elsewhere."

This sobered him, she noticed with something approaching amusement, wiped the smile from his face. He came over to her, peering down, his face a study in suspicion.

"Bob Taylor," he said. "Why? What's the matter with—"

She cut him off. "Kyle just spent a whole day with me, and he never once looked in my direction. He has a girlfriend. Bob Taylor, on the otherhand, is obviously interested. So what would be more natural than my dating him? Don't get all weird and jealous about this, Adam. Let's use it to our advantage."

She had reached over during this exchange and placed a hand on his arm. Now he pulled roughly away from her touch and turned to face the other side of the room. When he spoke, his voice was barely a whisper.

"She's not his girlfriend," he said.

"What?" she demanded. "What are you talking about?"

He took a deep breath, trying to control his sudden rage.

"Rita," he said. "Kyle. She's not his girlfriend." He turned to face her. "Is this necessary, Diana? Do you have to actually go *out* with that creep?"

He noted the flare of defiance in her eyes.

"He's not a creep," she said. "As a matter of fact, I'm having dinner with him tonight. He's a perfectly nice, perfectly harmless—"

"*Harmless!*"

"Oh, Adam, for God's sake! Isn't that just like a man! As if I hadn't heard *you* in your bedroom the other night—"

"Kay is my wife, Diana. I'd hardly compare that to—"

"Stop it!" she cried. "There isn't time. Lisa will be down here in a few minutes. Just listen."

She paused for a moment, watching him. He went over to lean against the edge of the table next to her. When he'd made it clear that she had his attention, she continued.

"There's a potted plant in the foyer, a spider palm or some such thing, just inside the front entranceway."

He nodded. She leaned closer, lowering her voice despite the fact that the two of them were quite alone in the cottage. "I'll put what you'll need in there, buried in the dirt, okay? You park the rental car in that little turnaround place where your car is now. When you come in the front door, just look in the pot."

He nodded again. She really is amazing, he thought.

"Right," he said. "And I'll be quick. You've given me less than two hours on the island before the flight back to Miami."

"I thought that would be enough," she began, but he stopped her.

"Yes, it *is* best. Don't worry, I'll be on that plane. Just be sure you don't arrive home until about five hours after I take off. I want to be at that party when you call."

She turned her face and looked up at him. They were leaning toward each other, and the little smile at the corners of her lips was somehow irresistible to him. He bent to kiss her and was pleased when she closed her eyes and returned the pressure, raising a hand to touch his hair.

"Jumbi!"

The cry came from far away, from somewhere on the path halfway up the hill. It was followed by a sharp, distant bark.

Still leaning together, they stared into each other's eyes.

"We're going to do it," she whispered, playing with the hair just above his ear. "It's going to work, and then we'll be together. Always. Always, my darling."

He reached up to remove her fingers from his hair and gave her a gentle shove toward the door. "You'd better go out there and meet her. Take her down to the other end of the beach so I can get back to the path without her seeing me, all right? And for God's sake, hold on to that dog!"

She brushed his lips once more, briefly, with her own.

"I love you," she whispered.

And then she was gone, across the room and out the door and running lightly, feet barely touching the fine white sand, hair flying out behind her, through the trees. He watched her go, his heart and body fairly bursting with pleasure at the sight.

The young woman came out of the trees into the light and paused for a moment, feeling the warm sun bearing down on her upturned face. It soothed her, calmed her ragged nerves.

Acting, she thought, is a lot more difficult than it seems. The acting had been in her attitude throughout the scene in the cottage—well, after the grappling part, anyway—in the nonchalance, the ease she appeared to feel when she was alone with him, when, in fact, the opposite was true. But she mustn't let him know that, or the whole plan would be ruined.

What worried her about him was the possibility that her behavior might somehow give away the fact that she was onto him. Ever since the news three days ago of Sandra's apparent fate, she had become slowly more convinced that her first, ridiculous suspicion was probably correct. People don't just drown: she'd told herself that a hundred times over the weekend. Certainly not when it would be so incredibly *convenient* for them to do so.

No, she thought. Don't say things like that. Don't even think them. That isn't the kind of person you are, the kind of person you want to be. Especially now when every day, every minute, is so precious.

She spared a brief thought for Kay Prescott and her daughter. Perfectly nice, well-meaning, innocent people. They had never done anyone harm, had never wished anyone ill, as far as she knew. Yet now their whole orderly, safe, charmed existence was coming to an abrupt end. An end brought about by her, the young woman who stood on the beach gazing up at Cliffhanger. She had plotted the course of the tragedy that hovered now in the warm tropical air above the house on the cliff, waiting for the moment next Monday afternoon, seven days hence, when it would settle down around them all. A cloud, a miasma of pain and sorrow such as they could not imagine. When she was through with this family, nothing would ever be the same.

Yet, she had long ago convinced herself, in the end it would be for the best. The best for her and for Adam. Besides, soon it wouldn't matter. Soon all would be one.

She shook her head to clear it. Friday, she thought. Please, God, just get us all through until Friday. Then Adam and Lisa will be off to New York, and the plan will really, truly be under way. I didn't even know Sandra: I can't afford to waste tears for her now. After Friday, well . . .

She glanced up at the sky. It hadn't all been her fancy, she reflected. There really were dark clouds gathering. The weather had been so clear only moments before! Now everything was turning gray.

The slowly fading sunlight continued to wash over her, its healing, almost pharmaceutical effect causing her to smile with genuine pleasure at the sight of the little girl and the dog bursting from the forest and running toward her across the sand. Enjoy this, she told herself. Enjoy it while it lasts, while the sun is still here. The clouds are forming already: the rain won't be far behind.

There isn't much time.

Adam's eyes followed them as they ran off down the sand toward the rocks at the farthest end from the path. Wait a few moments, he thought. Give them time to settle down with paper and pencils, and for Jumbi to stretch out at their feet. Then you can make your move.

Time for the next phase.

Diana knew, he told himself. She had all but said that she suspected what happened to Sandra. It wasn't much of a stretch of logic from that to Nancy Breen. Not that he'd told her the identities of his "robbery" victims. The papers were reporting Nancy's death as a crime of passion. Diana had certainly heard about it by now, but she had no reason to connect it to the plan. It didn't really matter: Diana knew part of the story about Sandra, at least, and she had remained silent about that. Silence was tacit consent. She was leaving that aspect of it to him.

Good, he thought. There is more to be done. Now. Time for the next accidental victim. And I know just where that victim can be found.

He peered out through the gap between two uneven boards in the warped, rotting wall. Yes, they were sitting on the rocks now, leaning over the sketchpads, lost in concentrated creativity.

Excellent.

Just before he left, he glanced around the shed and smiled. I'll be back here soon, he thought. Thursday, the night before I leave for the mainland. An assignation, one in which that pile of blankets will figure prominently.

Perfect.

He glided swiftly out the door and off through the trees. Just as he reached the base of the path, he heard the first, faraway roll of thunder.

THIRTEEN

MONDAY, AUGUST 26

(CONTINUED)

"DO YOU THINK," Kay asked, "that certain things are fated to happen? That they're somehow—I don't know—preordained?"

Trish stopped in the act of lifting her coffee cup. The delicate pink and white Belleek seashell froze in midair some three inches from her lips. Another woman, one who did not know Kay as well as she, might have said, "I beg your pardon?" and, raising an eyebrow, "What on earth are you going on about?" or "Have you been reading Shirley MacLaine again?" Something frivolous and clever and obnoxious. Trish said nothing. She had long ago grown used to Kay's serious moods, and this question obviously signaled one of them. She lowered the cup.

"Yes, I do," she said. "I think a great deal of what happens to us is part of a pattern. Don't ask me what sort of pattern, or who I think is responsible for it, but yes. What is it, Kay? Are you thinking about something specific?"

She watched as Kay lit a fresh cigarette and gazed down at the roofs of the houses below them. From Gladys Bellamy's terrace, perched on this hillside above Charlotte Amalie, they had a dramatic view of the town and the harbor at the bottom of the hill. The buildings crowded down to the water, which stretched out, dull and choppy, as far as they could see. The distant mountains on the other side of the curved bay were a misty, indistinct green in the muted light of the overcast afternoon. The angry, pewter-colored clouds hung down, obliterating the topmost points of land. Tiny cars crawled along the waterfront roads far below, and ant-sized people walked on the esplanade at the top of the seawall that ringed the harbor. The everyday bustle of life was apparent wherever they looked, yet not a sound reached them. The silence of the island was as thick, as oppressive, as the gathering storm.

"It always amazes me," Kay said, "how suddenly the weather can change here. It was so beautiful this morning. I hope it doesn't rain before lunch, or they'll have to move all that inside." She waved an arm, including the buffet table Mrs. Bellamy had set up at one end of the patio. The linen tablecloth flapped in the wind, held down by the huge silver platters of ham and chicken and salad. The two white-jacketed housemen flanking the feast looked nervously at the sky, then at each other.

Five other people stood or sat about the little garden in front of the big gray Danish plantation house, a relic of an earlier, more romantic St. Thomas. Every month the Arts

Council had lunch at the home of one of its members. Mrs. Bellamy, the current chairperson, a large, imposing native woman in a brightly printed dress, was regaling the others with a story from her long-ago days as Gladys Rollins, a rather well known opera singer, before she returned to the island and married one of its wealthiest citizens. They were, Trish thought, an oddly mismatched cross section of island society. The current panel included herself, Kay, Mrs. Bellamy, a young native man who was a talented sculptor, an elderly native man renowned as a Calypso singer under the name King Caribbean, and two young men from New York who had been dancers on Broadway before coming to St. Thomas and opening a men's clothing shop.

"You haven't answered me," Trish said, reaching for the cup. "You seem to be preoccupied today. Tell me what's going on before La Gladys drags us over to the trough."

In spite of herself, Kay giggled. "Hush! One of these days she's going to hear you calling her that."

"Big deal. Maybe she'll think twice before she decides to favor us with 'The Bell Song' again at the next talent show. I swear, if I have to sit through that one more time—"

"All right," Kay said quickly, glancing over at the others and raising a hand to nip Trish's monologue in the bud. She rose and went over to the railing at the edge of the terrace. "I was just wondering, why Diana Meissen? I mean, what role does she play in my life? Everything was just going along, you know, okay but uneventful. Then, all of a sudden, Sandra takes off and this new girl arrives, and the most extraordinary things are happening. I felt a little competition from her, so I guess I made an extra effort in the way I look, and now Adam is . . . responding to me much more strongly than he has in a long time."

"You mean sex?" Trish leaned forward, eyes wide.

Kay reddened slightly. "Uh-huh. That young man takes an interest in her, and suddenly I'm playing matchmaker, trying to get them together. Lisa has never behaved so well. Hell, she even got Jumbi to like her! And then on the boat the other day, she saved my life." She turned to look at Trish, lowering her voice. "Then this bizarre thing happens to Sandra. I mean, it's awful, really. Nobody should die so senselessly. But, funny thing: all I could think was that it was all somehow *meant* to happen. To prove to me that I was doing the right thing. That I was *supposed* to meet Diana when I did and take her into our lives. I was in the Fort Friday, looking through Sandra's belongings, and when I came out and went to my car, something very strange happened to me. Oh, God, this sounds so weird. . . ."

Trish stood up and went to stand beside her friend. She raised a hand and placed it on Kay's arm, cringing slightly as their privacy was briefly invaded by the piercing mezzo-soprano giggles of the former Gladys Rollins on the other side of the terrace.

"God, she even *laughs* in High C! What, Kay? What is it?"

Kay emitted a long sigh. "I suddenly thought, yes. This *is* right. This marvelous young woman has taken me out of myself. She's taken charge of the house, of my finances, of Lisa. She's brought Adam and me closer together. She's put ... *something* back in my life that I never even noticed was missing. I walked right by my car: if I hadn't remembered myself, I would have walked all the way home." She shook her head slightly as if to clear it. "Are there really people like that, Trish? Or am I just imagining it? You know, it's almost funny: at first I thought she was after Adam. Isn't that silly?"

Trish decided that the question was rhetorical and wisely remained silent.

"Come on, you two!" the resonant, pear-shaped tones of their hostess called to them, breaking the odd spell.

"Ah," Trish sighed. "Her nibs awaits. Let's get over there pronto, before she breaks into the third act of *La Bayadère*."

Kay laughed. "That's a ballet, not an opera."

Trish glanced over at the rotund figure of the former diva. "Even worse! What do you feel like doing after the meeting?"

"Sorry," Kay replied. "You're on your own this afternoon. I have an appointment."

Trish, Great Friend, understanding confidante, brushed off the dismissal. She grinned. "Race you to the table," she said.

And did.

Margaret told herself that she had every right to be here in this room again, but she didn't believe it. She felt odd, out of place, vaguely embarrassed, despite the fact that there was no one to witness her transgression. Mrs.

O'Rourke had gone on her weekly trip to the supermarket, so she was alone in the house. She sat on the blue chenille coverlet at the very edge of the bed, as she had one week before, when Dr. Stein brought her here.

All right, she corrected herself, *I* brought *him* here. No sense in laying blame at another's doorstep. I am responsible for my actions. I alone.

Her gaze traveled slowly around the room. With an effort, she cleared her mind of everything that had been raging through it for the past five weeks, ever since the morning when the girl kissed her lightly on the cheek and fairly danced away down the sidewalk to the waiting taxi, bound for—

For what? For an island in the Caribbean, nearly three thousand miles away. For a family she'd apparently never met before, a woman named Kay Prescott and her husband and child. For a paid position, a job as a governess or companion, little more than a domestic. A servant.

If she looked at it truthfully, it was this fact that most bothered Margaret. The idea that a Barclay would place herself—willingly—in a position that was subservient, ignominious, déclassé. Was this how the girl defined happiness, the extent of her ambition? The depth and breadth and height her soul could reach? A servant.

Enough, she commanded. It's time to think calmly, rationally, as much like the girl as possible.

She nearly laughed aloud at the irony. Calm? Rational? Since when were these appropriate words to describe the machinations of her niece's mind? Edith Hamilton's *Mythology*: that was her bible, the creed to which she subscribed. The goddess whose name she had borrowed, Medea, Clytemnestra, Electra, Antigone. Women who strapped on armor and marched into battle, who murdered their husbands and butchered their children, who went happily to their deaths defending their family name, who loved and hated and avenged themselves with a passion not even guessed at by ordinary mortals. These were her heroines, her originals, the people with whom she somehow identified herself. Goddesses, queens, princesses—and nary a governess among them. Nothing so low as a paid companion.

Wrong. Something was wrong. She had taken for herself the name of Diana, goddess of the moon and of hunting, protectress of women. What had Dr. Stein said? Something about three forms . . . the goddess in three forms, whatever that meant. She didn't understand it, but it sounded very grand. Hardly a suitable allusion for the hired help.

She stood up and went over to the desk. She scanned the shelves of books above it, her gaze resting at last on the end of the bottom shelf, where the *Mythology* had been replaced next to the volumes of Greek plays. Yes, these things were important to her niece. But why?

Without really thinking about it, preoccupied with thoughts of Sophocles and Aeschylus, she reached out and pulled open the lid of the desk. Distractedly, she let her hands roam over the contents of the little shelves and pigeonholes. Letters—no, she would not read them: that was too degrading, too much a violation. Tax returns and check registers—quite a few of them, going back several years.

Check registers.

It occurred to her, then, that she knew very little about the young woman's finances. The two of them had never really discussed money. Margaret had paid for the girl's education, of course, up to and including her unsuccessful attempts at college. She had been provided with food and clothing, and Margaret's insurance policy included her as dependent, but there were things of which even Margaret was not informed.

Margaret and Madeleine had inherited a considerable fortune: about twelve million, divided equally between them. Madeleine had barely had an opportunity to touch hers. In the six months after her death her husband had gone crazy, reportedly gambling away huge sums. By the time Margaret was officially put in charge of the child, six million had dwindled to three million. This had been placed in trust for the girl, who had never mentioned it until shortly after her sixteenth birthday. At that time she'd asked Margaret, her guardian, to help her to obtain access to the interest. This Margaret had done without asking questions: it was, after all, the girl's money, and Margaret, for all her devotion, was not her true parent. Independence and privacy were two rights that had been encouraged in Margaret, and she could do no less for the girl. Even later, when she realized that drugs and liquor and the fateful trip to Hawaii and San Francisco had been among the girl's purchases, she could not find fault with what she, Margaret, had done. But those things had come later, after the girl was of age and would have had the funds in any case. Only now did it occur to Margaret to wonder why she'd needed money when she was sixteen.

The girl's first act on obtaining an allowance had been to open a checking account, and all the information was here. A small stack of register booklets, records of checks written, going back ten years. Margaret flipped through them until she found the earliest one. It was the one on the bottom, of course: with her methodical mind, the girl had even stored all of these things chronologically. She had written the dates and numbers of the first and last checks recorded in the booklet on the cover in her small, neat hand. After a moment's hesitation, Margaret sat down at the desk and opened the passbook to the first entry.

Cash. Cash. A local restaurant. A theater ticket agency. Cash. Macy's: a rather large sum, nearly two thousand dollars. She noted the date and cast her mind back. Yes, about two weeks before the girl had left for the final boarding school, Miss Stanton's School for Girls in New Paltz. Extra clothes, probably.

She didn't particularly notice the unfamiliar name until she had passed it three times as she scanned the columns. When she saw it a fourth time, she stopped.

Mr. Carson Fleming, three thousand dollars.

Margaret stared down at the entry, racking her brain. The girl had never mentioned anyone named—

She went back a page. Yes, here it was again: Mr. Carson Fleming, three thousand dollars.

The first payment to Mr. Fleming had been made in the third week of September, just after the sixteen-year-old arrived at Miss Stanton's School. The second was almost exactly three months later, in December. Then March, June, September.

She raced through the next register book, and the one after that. She flipped through the pages, the nail of her right index finger sliding down column after column. Five books in all, including the current one. She dropped the last book on the little pile before her and sat back in the desk chair, staring down.

Mr. Carson Fleming. Three thousand dollars, every three months for the past ten years. One thousand a month; two hundred fifty a week. For ten years.

That was not all. Five days after the first payment, ten years ago, while the teenager was allegedly settling in at the exclusive upstate boarding school, she had written a check to Pan American Airways for nearly twelve hundred dollars. Four entries later, she had paid some fifteen hundred dollars to the Kauai Sunset Hotel. The next check had been made out to the South Seas Rent-a-Car Agency, for three hundred seventy-five dollars and change. She did the math in her head: a round-trip ticket and perhaps one week, with food and transportation, in a tropical hotel.

Margaret shook her head absently from side to side as she stared distractedly down at the escritoire that had once belonged to her mother, slowly taking in, processing the awful information. The clear, undeniable fact.

Her niece—or *someone*—had been in Hawaii ten years ago, at or about the same time that Darlene Bishop Phillips was murdered.

There were two options, as far as she could see. She could sit here, stunned, allowing the shock to carry her into cardiac arrest, or she could move.

She moved. She reached forward and rummaged

through every crevice and cranny, pulling out every piece of paper, every envelope, every scrap of information she could find. She heaped it up before her and began—willing herself to slow down, to be thorough—to sift through it all. At some point in the next forty minutes, she took a page of the girl's creamy blue stationery and a pen from their pigeonholes and began jotting down dates, amounts, names. There was no diary or journal of any kind, but she had her own clear memory of the girl's actions through the years to help her.

She finished making her last note on the back of the sheet of stationery, which was now covered with writing. Then she stood up and began replacing everything where she had found it. In minutes, the desk was once again pristine, the neat, orderly workplace of the neat, orderly young woman whom Margaret really did not know at all.

Carrying the paper, reading as she moved, she went out of the bedroom and down the stairs. She did not hobble now; she did not even reach out for the banister as she descended. Her leg, despite the threatening rain outside, did not bother her. She walked into the living room and stopped, rereading her notes and arranging the facts sequentially in her mind.

Fact: the girl had been paying—retaining?—someone named Carson Fleming for the last ten years.

Fact: the girl had, indeed, been in boarding school at the time of the trip to Hawaii. She'd managed, with effort, to struggle through her junior and senior years there, and Margaret had received full reports of her progress from the faculty. She had not made good grades, and she'd been described as dreamy and distracted, but no one had ever mentioned a long absence. Certainly not in the first few weeks of her stay. No, she had not gone to Hawaii— but she had financed someone else's trip there.

Fact: at eighteen, upon inheriting, the girl had obtained credit cards, Visa and American Express. She had charged her own trips to Hawaii and San Francisco when she was nineteen. She had charged several other things as well, things that didn't make much sense, notably not one but *two* round-trip tickets to St. Thomas—in addition to her own two. The first dated from three years ago, when the girl had been living in this house and going to work every day. *She* certainly had not gone to the Virgin Islands and stayed at the Frenchman's Reef Holiday Inn for several days—but *someone* had, and she'd paid for it. The second sojourn—same hotel, same rental-car agency—had occurred some five months ago, fully one month *before* the girl's own first vacation in the West Indies. She had sent somebody to the Virgin Islands. Twice.

Fact: eleven weeks ago, just after her return from her first trip to the West Indies, the girl had paid nearly twenty thousand dollars to the South Bay Gables Rest Home in Brookhaven, Long Island. Her copy of the contract was among her papers. On June 5, the home had admitted one Carson Fleming, age seventy-seven, for permanent residency. He had arrived there in an ambulance from Southside Hospital in Bayshore. He had apparently suffered a stroke shortly before, and the girl had admitted him to the home. She had paid for everything, or at least a considerable percentage of everything. She'd signed the admittance forms and left a number, unfamiliar to Margaret, for the staff to call in case of emergencies concerning the patient.

She went over to the princess phone—now clear of its temporary interception device—and dialed the number indicated on the document from the rest home. She had no time to wait, to wonder what she would discover when the phone was answered, and what that might mean. It was picked up almost immediately. A woman's voice; low, Brooklyn-accented, bored.

"Service. Name of account, please."

Margaret hung up at once. She stood there in the middle of the living room, staring out through the open door as the first raindrops began to land softly on the roses. Odd, she thought, that her flowers should be so well provided for, at this of all junctures. Another cloudy day, another gentle fall of rain. . . .

Who, she wondered again, is Carson Fleming?

Kay walked across the patio to the far end, holding the flowers gently, carefully, in her hands. She stepped off the flagstones onto the soft grass and moved through the first brake of palms and birches next to the cliff's edge. As she arrived in the tiny clearing, she looked up sharply as a thunderclap rolled across the ragged Atlantic sky.

The twin headstones stood silent sentinel. The Harbingers, Samuel and Clara. She afforded the graves a brief glance as she passed: they were clear of weeds and leaves, unsoiled by droppings from the gulls that made the cliff their home. A second, smaller group of thin palms separated the couple from the other marker, the lone granite rectangle standing some fifteen feet from the precipice.

She went over to stand at the foot of the grave, staring down at the words. The name, the dates, and the quotation she had chosen, the final couplet of his beloved Shakespeare's eighteenth sonnet:

> So long as men can breathe or eyes can see,
> So long lives this and this gives life to thee.

The breeze preceding the approaching storm whisked past her as she stood there in her green silk Lunch With The Arts Council dress, the cold, wet wind whipping through her hair and stinging the back of her bare legs. When there was a lull, she went around to kneel down on the soft grass beside the grave and reached out to place the little bouquet in the center of the mound. A large rock lay nearby; she picked it up and rested it gently on top of the bunched, rubber-banded stems. A little security, she thought. These flowers will remain here for a while, at least.

The house was behind her, invisible through the trees. There was no one on the rocks below or on the points and beaches she surveyed from the cliff. Looking out over the angry, windswept sea, she was not surprised to find it devoid of life. Small-craft warning. There was nobody anywhere. She might have been the only living thing in the world, alone here with her husband. It was a melancholy feeling, but not a particularly unpleasant one. There was something almost cozy, reassuring, about it. She knelt there for a long time, looking at the headstone, out over the water, up at the imminent sky. After a while she began to speak.

"Lisa mentioned you again yesterday. I heard her telling Diana about the time you took her downtown during Carnival. About the Ferris wheel, and the cotton candy in her hair, and how you brought her home and washed her up before I found out about it. You always did spoil her so. She doesn't really care for Adam; I'm aware of that. She's always going on about you, though. I hope it isn't wrong of me not to discourage that. . . .

"I wonder what you'd make of Diana if you were here. I think she has a lot in common with you. The two of you have the same kind of power, I think: the ability to change everything around you for the better. I don't know what to call that, exactly. The power of positive thinking, good vibes—something awful and insufficient like that. But my life was better with you, and I think it's going to be better now that she's here.

"So I've come to a decision. I've decided to make a go of it with Adam, and to see that Lisa has everything. And I want Diana around—for a while, at least. I think she needs someone to love her. I've been doing a little matchmaking. He's a nice young man named Bob Taylor—no relation, as he's always so quick to point out. He rather reminds me of you. They're perfect for each other, really. I hope they realize that. Love is not an easy thing to come by."

She looked out from the clifftop at the clouds sinking lower over the water. Another cold, damp breeze washed past her.

"I have to go now," she said. "I'll be back to see you

soon." Kneeling down toward the stone, she whispered, "Love you."

She reached over briefly to caress the flowers with her hand. Rising to her feet, she heard the distant laughter of her daughter and her friend—guardian, benefactor—as they came up from the beach and crossed the lawn. Just in time, she thought; a few more minutes and they would have been forced to seek shelter in the cottage. It isn't safe there. Glancing guiltily down at the grave, she told herself for the thousandth time that she really should see about having it demolished. Sorry, darling, she thought as she turned to go, but it is really for the best. . . .

The first large, heavy drops of rain smashed down onto the flagstones as she hurried across the patio and into the house.

For the tenth time in the last hour, Margaret reached for the phone, picked it up, and almost immediately replaced it in its cradle. She sat on the burgundy velvet couch, huddled in the sweater she'd finally thought to fetch from the downstairs closet, staring down at the notepad on the coffee table before her.

She couldn't do it.

On an impulse, she stood up and walked into the kitchen. The rain poured down onto the lawn outside the big window over the sink. She stood there looking out, listening to the constant splashing against the other side of the panes. She dropped her gaze to the neat row of shiny tins on the counter. The largest held flour, the next sugar, the next coffee. She was actually reaching for the third container when her arm, as if of its own accord, dropped listlessly to her side. I don't want coffee, she thought. I don't want anything. I'm stalling.

Do it, she commanded. They can't have you arrested for calling. They won't even know who you are unless you tell them.

I can't.

She measured coffee into the filter tray, attached it to the automatic coffeemaker, and poured water into the well at the top. Then she flicked the switch at the base of the appliance and walked back into the living room.

I must.

She reached for the phone, paused momentarily, grasped it firmly in her hand, raised it, and dialed. No need to refer to the notepad again; she'd memorized the number.

It rang three times. In those few seconds, she thought seriously of putting the receiver down again. Maybe there was no one there to answer phones at this hour. Even if they answered they wouldn't tell her anything. There must be regulations about that sort of thing, especially with a stranger on the phone. Besides, instructions might have been left prohibiting the disclosure of any information about—

There was a sudden click and, before she could expect it or be even remotely prepared for it, a cool, efficient female voice spoke softly in Margaret's ear.

"South Bay Gables. May I help you?"

Kay hadn't played Scrabble in years. She'd even forgotten that she owned the game. Fred had loved it and sometimes they'd even allowed little Lisa to play with them long past her bedtime. The three of them would make popcorn and drink ginger ale and laugh together for hours, seated around the card table in the corner of the living room, late into the night. Or on rainy afternoons, when the view of the harbor and the rest of the island was obscured, as it was now.

Kay watched, amazed, as the beautiful young woman across from her put down her tiles, move after move, spelling out the most brilliant words. And they always seemed to end up on the red squares, tripling their value. Even Lisa, usually so ebullient, maintained a respectful silence. It was uncanny: the young woman could take the most ordinary letters—the same ones Kay and Lisa had in their trays—and arrange them into anything she wanted.

The ceiling fan whirled lazily above their heads. Jumbi, anesthetized by the inaction of the silent humans above her, stretched out to her full length on the cool floor beneath her young mistress's feet.

Kay Prescott looked around her, satisfied. Her daughter was absorbed. Her house on the cliff was watertight. Her husband would be relaxing at his clubhouse, safe from the storm. Her other husband had fresh flowers on his monument. And her champion, her knight in female armor, was winning the game.

Margaret wandered back into the kitchen. The downpour outside continued unabated. Perhaps it would rain all right, she thought.

Saturday. Five days. . . .

The carafe in the coffeemaker was steaming, filling the room with a rich aroma. She stared, perplexed, wondering how the coffee happened to be there. She must have made it herself, she supposed, but she could not remember doing so. She pulled the sweater closer about her shoulders.

The woman on the phone had been remarkably forthcoming. She had not even asked who Margaret was, or which patient she wanted to see. She had simply told her, in that soft, efficient institutional drone, that visiting days were Saturday and Sunday, from one o'clock until dinnertime. If visitors wished to arrive at any other time, arrangements must be made with the patient's attending physician. The woman had not actually used the word *patient;* she referred to South Bay Gables' inmates as "residents." The next time "residents" could "receive guests" was Saturday at one o'clock. Margaret had thanked her and hung up.

She reached for her mug and poured coffee. Holding it up before her, she smiled, remembering. It had been a birthday gift from her niece. Across the white china was printed the caption *World's Greatest Mom,* in black letters. Beneath the words was an enormous red heart. It was her most valuable possession. She would trade her house for it, and her car and her stock portfolios and her bank accounts. She would trade everything for this one silly, ordinary object and what it represented.

"I love you," the young woman had said as she handed Margaret the present. Strange, Margaret thought now: there are some people who can say that with such sincerity, with a complete lack of affectation. The people who mean it, who have no trouble whatsoever vocalizing their emotions. And yet this same straightforward, honest person was now living a lie. She'd dyed her hair and adopted a new name, assumed a new identity. Now she was Diana Meissen, alias Selena Chase, alias—

Margaret paused, staring down at the bright-red valentine that adorned her priceless cup.

Alias who?

It was there, in that book, or so she supposed. Dr. Stein had mentioned it, referred to it, several times. And never, not once, had she thought to ask the obvious question.

She set the cup down on the counter and left the kitchen. Then she ascended the stairs and walked slowly down the hall toward the blue bedroom.

The Scrabble board had been put away, Diana having won three games out of three. Now they were all in Lisa's bedroom, trying to make method out of madness.

"Do you need this?" Kay asked, holding up a red jumper.

Lisa groaned.

"No, Mother," she enunciated carefully, turning back to sift through an assortment of carefully preripped jeans.

Diana, who was folding a multicolored sweater into a suitcase, smiled over Lisa's head.

"That's for school, Kay," she said kindly, "not for a week with her cousins in Connecticut."

Kay shrugged and dropped the jumper on a chair, unable to fathom the secret code that Diana seemed to have mastered, as she had mastered Scrabble. The young woman knew instinctively what Lisa would and would not want to take to the States. She was so efficient, Kay observed, so tuned into the world of a young girl, as she was tuned in to Kay's own wants and needs: it was almost magical. Mary Poppins, she thought.

Diana glanced up from her labor. "Don't forget the CDs."

Lisa's eyes widened. "Oh, yeah. Thanks. Janie would kill me if I forgot those."

Kay watched, fascinated, as Lisa dropped what she was doing and reached over to pick up a small pile of plastic boxes on her dresser. Diana knows everything, she thought. Everything about my daughter's world. I, on the other hand, do not.

With a laugh and a final shrug of bewilderment, she walked out of the bedroom and went downstairs, leaving the experts to their work.

Margaret had brought the book down to her office. Her niece's bedroom was now the scene of her crime, as she considered it, and she no longer felt comfortable there. She got a fresh cup of coffee from the kitchen and sat down at her desk.

It was nearly dusk, she realized. As if that mattered: the sky had been so dark all afternoon that the world outside her windows would slip almost imperceptibly into night. The heavy rain was still clattering against the house, showing no sign of letup. She had added her heaviest bathrobe to the layers of clothing in which she was now bundled. Even in midsummer, she thought, I am always cold. An uncomfortable byproduct of advancing age. With a sigh, she reached for the book and began her search.

She found the chapter she wanted, then the subsection. The passage she sought had been highlighted with a yellow felt-tipped marker. She read through it once quickly, then went back and reread the final part more carefully. As she read, she was aware of an odd sensation: the temperature of the already chilly room seemed to be lowering. That cannot be, she reasoned. The coldness is not in the room, but in me. In the marrow of my bones.

Artemis/Diana, daughter of Zeus, goddess in three forms. By her common name, she was goddess of the hunt. As Selena/Luna, she was goddess of the moon. But according to Edith Hamilton, the later poets had assigned this elusive deity a third, paradoxical identity. This name was so famous, so universally recognized, that there had been no need for the Romans, after the Greeks, to come up with another. It was the same in both religions.

A flash of lightning lit up the gray landscape outside, and the thunderclap that followed shook the house. She stared down at the information, trying to grasp it, to comprehend. The coldness pressed in, freezing her heart.

The third identity, the final form of the divinity.

The goddess of darkness and of dark things, commandress of the night. Her time was midnight; her familiar, the cat; her domain, the deepest, most secret, most dangerous recesses of the human soul. Down the centuries, all those who worshipped Evil called out her sacred name.

Hecate.

FOURTEEN

MONDAY, AUGUST 26
(CONTINUED)

ADAM STOOD in the shadows of the rainy nighttime beach, watching his next victim dress for dinner. The sliding glass door leading to the small second-floor balcony afforded an excellent view of the brightly lit room, and the curtains had not been drawn. The possibility of a Peeping Tom—or, he mused, a Peeping Adam—had not been entertained. The weather and the usual emptiness of this place after sundown had assured a false sense of security—definitely false, for here, against all odds, he was.

He measured the height of the balcony with his eyes: eight, perhaps nine feet, no more than that. Modern construction, he thought, smiling. He could leap and swing himself up with little difficulty. And the sliding door, he could see from here, was slightly ajar. Excellent.

The slick, belted black raincoat and black fisherman's cap served double duty, keeping him relatively dry as they hid him from the light. He stood next to a large palm, ready to crouch behind it should the need arise, should his quarry glance down toward him.

As it turned out, he had no cause for worry. The clothes were donned, the lights extinguished, the room emptied. He watched the distant figure emerge from the building and cross the parking lot, illuminated by the nearby streetlight. After a moment there came the roar of an engine. By the time the two little red taillights began to move toward the street, Adam was already out of the shadows and heading swiftly for the red Nissan that waited in a dark thicket beside the road some fifty yards away.

He would watch and wait, and when the time was right he would strike. A great deal depended on his victim's plans for the rest of the evening. Oh, well, waiting was half the fun. . . .

There was only the one long, relatively straight road leading away from the beach, and at this hour it was practically deserted. Picking up the trail was a snap. The lone set of taillights receded before him, glowing steadily ahead like a beacon, urging him to follow.

She was wearing a skin-tight, strapless, knee-length, blood-red dress—what Robin believed was called a sheath—and her dark hair fell loosely around her bare, tanned shoulders. She grinned across the tiny patio table, jangling gold earrings and bracelets. The vague, tantalizing scent of flowers that he had come to identify exclusively with her floated toward him on the cool air of the dark, wet, torch-lit terrace.

The rain had stopped just as they arrived at the restaurant, so the outdoor tables and chairs had been quickly wiped off and the torches lit by industrious employees to allow the dinner crowd to spill out of the bar and take advantage of the momentarily clear evening. The illuminated swimming pool gleaming in the darkness and the silent white facades of the guest-house buildings on two sides enveloped them, cutting them and this place off from reality. Above all, the massive round stone tower mere yards away completed the impression of an otherworldly, fairytale garden. The pianist in the room behind them was playing "Isn't It Romantic?"—a rhetorical question at best. The sparkle of the flickering torchlight on the drenched flagstones and palm fronds surrounding the table; the golden glow on her face; the laughter in her eyes; the moist, full, pink promise of her lips: he had almost been beguiled into some hazy, trancelike state.

Almost.

"Penny," she said, lifting her champagne glass.

He blinked and focused on her. "What? Oh—I was just trying to remember the last time I did this."

She grinned again. "Did what?" She managed to make it sound charmingly suggestive.

"Oh, you know, *this*." He waved a hand to encompass the terrace and the pool and the large open doors leading in to the noisy bar. "A restaurant, with a woman. . . ."

"About three weeks ago, if I remember correctly."

He had the grace to blush. "Oh, that. Yes. . . ."

They smiled together, remembering his imposition at Bolongo. Then they'd had lunch on the beautiful beach; now they would dine at this beautiful hilltop guest house. Their meals together, he mused, were nothing if not picturesque.

Blackbeard's Castle dominated the top of Government Hill on the west side of town, and the dining deck above the bar, where they would soon be shown to a table, commanded a stunning view of the harbor at night, the lights against the black background stretching out below them. Floodlights concealed in the foliage around the patio dramatically underlit the huge, conical brown stone structure here in the center of the compound, the one that gave the place its name. Far from being a castle, it had once been a sugar mill, one of several to be found in various spots on the island. But that was prosaic: sugar mills, in St. Thomas, were a dime—or perhaps a doubloon—a dozen. As for the great pirate's involvement with the site—well, what the tourists didn't know wouldn't hurt them. Romantic legends sprang up so readily in this part of the world: the locals could just as easily have claimed that Beethoven had composed his Fifth Symphony in the shadow of this edifice, named it Ludwig's Castle, and created the same effect. It would have been accepted as gospel—as, indeed, everyone accepted the concept of this mill's having once been a den of thieves.

Artifice. The word occurred to him as he looked around, trying in vain to picture a gang of hearty, rum-soaked rascals lolling at the base of this tower, sabers in

teeth and patches over eyes, wooden legs and talking par-
rots and all the rest of it, singing a rousing chorus of—

"*. . . Isn't It Romantic?*" The soft, plaintive voice of the
pianist, a young, blond Stateside man in a dinner jacket,
wafted across the terrace.

Artifice. Robin's gaze finally came to rest on the lovely
young woman across from him, whose name was not Diana Meissen, whose hair and eyes were not dark brown,
whose agenda remained unclear. He tried to imagine what
she was thinking as she sipped her wine and smiled at
him, but he quickly gave it up. The pirates were more
accessible, more easily comprehended.

Artifice. He was an actor, and he was currently em-
ployed by this woman's aunt as a detective. He was traveling under an assumed name, shadowing another human
being, reporting on her actions. For this he was being paid
a great deal of money. . . .

Two people waiting for a table in a restaurant, the evening waiting ahead of them, an evening in which they
would normally be getting to know each other, finding out
if they did or did not enjoy one another's company. Picking up on, responding to, one another's sexual tension. Yet
here they sat, both using false names and false identities,
neither one who he or she claimed to be. And only one of
them knew that. He had a sudden vision of the two of
them sitting there, both wearing those instant disguises
sold in novelty shops, the thick black glasses with false
noses and mustaches attached that made whoever wore
them look like Groucho Marx. The image should have

amused him, but at the moment he didn't find it remotely funny.

He sighed. Sex was the least of tonight's tensions.

"So," he offered into the odd silence, "how are things at Cliffhanger?"

Something like a frown floated across her face for a moment. In that brief instant she appeared to be ill at ease, troubled. Then she raised her glass and emptied it.

"Great," she said, extending the glass toward him for a refill. "Adam—Mr. Prescott—and Lisa are leaving Friday morning for New York. She's visiting some relatives in Connecticut, and he's delivering her and going on to Florida to be in a Labor Day regatta or something. Which reminds me: why don't you come to the house Thursday for dinner? It's a little going-away party—well, hardly; they'll only be gone a few days—and Kay wants to have some people there. Her friend Trish will be there with her boyfriend, the guy you met at the birthday party."

"Jerry."

"Yes, Jerry. Would you like to come? You haven't seen the house yet."

"What do you mean? I just picked you up there."

She grinned. "You didn't even get out of the car. I mean, you haven't seen the *inside* of the house."

"No," he said, "I haven't. I'd like that."

She smiled again. "Good. I'll tell Kay you've accepted."

He nodded, thinking that even their dialogue sounded like lines in a play. He couldn't think of anything to say to her that wasn't a shallow pleasantry. He remembered the dossier in his hotel room: there were so many subjects to

be avoided. But, he mused, I can't spend all evening
avoiding them. I've got to get her talking, find out—

She smiled over at him. He forced himself to smile
back.

Artifice.

Then the waiter arrived to lead them in to dinner.

Adam watched as they followed the waiter in from the
terrace and up the stairs. She looks so beautiful tonight,
he thought. That red dress. . . .

He was sitting at the end of the bar farthest from the
doorway, on the other side of the room from where they
passed through on their way up to the dining area. The moment they entered, he turned his face away from the door
and leaned down behind the bar, as if he'd dropped something. Then, as they ascended, he slowly straightened, smiling to himself. They had not seen him: they were too intent
on each other's presence.

The smile died on his lips as he pondered that fact.
The way she leaned toward him as they walked, his hand
lightly holding her arm, guiding her, their heads bent together. Her sudden, musical laugh as they climbed the
stairs.

He glanced at his Scotch. He was gripping the tumbler
tightly in his fist: a little more pressure and it would shat-
ter. Slowly, methodically, he relaxed his grip on the glass.
He raised it to his lips, drained it and signaled to the bar-
man for another.

Bob Taylor.

Goddamn Bob Taylor to hell. . . .

He was just beginning to wonder what he should do next, how to continue his surveillance of his victim upstairs without drawing attention to himself, when, as if by magic, the solution presented itself. Jack Breen—pale, nervous, and more than slightly drunk—came into the bar and looked around. The moment he appeared, there was a pause, a brief hush in the room as everyone caught sight of him. *Oh, look, darling, it's Jack Breen, out on bail; he killed his wife, you know. . .* The words were whispered, or transmitted in mere glances, before the inevitable nods and smiles were offered and conversations resumed.

Adam grinned. He raised his arm and waved, beckoning to the other man. Jack, with visible relief, crossed the room and plopped gratefully down on the empty stool next to his old friend.

Adam slapped him on the back, shook his head, and bought him a drink.

The artichokes had been cleared away and the lobsters placed before them when Robin decided to try being a true detective.

"So," he began, pouring chardonnay for both of them and placing the napkin-covered bottle back in the bucket at his side, "you said you were from New York. Whereabouts, exactly?"

She looked up at him, fingering the silver nutcracker beside her plate. "Long Island."

His look of surprise was a credit to at least one of his chosen professions. "Oh, wow! Really? I was born and raised in Merrick. Tell me we live next door to each other!"

"Not exactly," she replied. "I'm from—farther out. Suffolk County, actually. Um, Islip."

He feigned just the right amount of indifference. "Oh. I'm not familiar with it. Do your parents still live there?" He controlled his urge to wince as he heard himself saying the words. Just what, he wondered, am I trying to prove?

She was staring at him. He noticed, while picking up his utensils and preparing to dig in, that her eyes seemed to have grown larger, her pupils to dilate. As he watched, she ran her tongue quickly over her upper lip before she spoke.

"My parents are . . . I . . . no, they don't."

Stop it, he commanded himself. Don't do this to her.

"So," he said, "where are they?"

She sat very still, apparently contemplating the view of Charlotte Amalie beyond his shoulder. Then her gaze came to rest once more upon his face. If he wasn't mistaken, she seemed to have made some sort of private decision.

"My parents are dead," she whispered. "They both died when I was little. The woman I call my mom is actually my aunt, my mother's sister. You saved my life the other day."

It was his turn to regard the view. He did not answer her immediately: what answer could there be to that? If he thought for a moment, he knew he could find the connection, the theme that linked together her seemingly random statements. What could his saving her life—if, indeed, he *had* saved her life—have to do with her telling him that her parents were dead? Well, he decided, at least she's told me something, something I know to be the truth.

He raised his wineglass to his lips, intrigued by the notion that had suddenly materialized in his mind. What if? he thought. What if I were to lean across this table right now and tell her everything? My real name, and what I'm really doing here, and what I know of her? I could start with her true identity, address her by her actual name. Just lean over and take her hand and say, "I know your name is—"

"Hello, you two! Fancy seeing you here. Small World department."

They both looked up, surprised. Trish Manning loomed above their table, clad in something long and shiny and green that looked suspiciously like a sarong. A large white gardenia dominated the left side of her sleek head, resting in a field of tightly coiled black hair. She grinned down at them and reached out to grasp the hand of the man at her side.

"You remember Jerry, don't you? Don't get up, Bob. We're just wafting by on our way out. I see you're having the lobster. Delicious, isn't it? You look stunning, Diana."

"So do you," the younger woman replied.

Trish glanced from Jerry to Robin, then turned back to the girl with a knowing smile.

"Of course I do," she drawled. "If we don't look stunning for them, they'll simply find women who do. Men are such pigs, don't you think? That's a joke, boys. Anyway, the two of you are such *attractive* pigs. Well, we mustn't intrude. See you Thursday, Diana."

"You'll see him, too," the younger woman said, pointing to Robin across the table.

Trish beamed down at him. "Lovely!"

"Oink," Robin replied.

Everyone laughed. With a final flutter of her dramatically manicured fingernails, Trish led her escort away and down the stairs.

Robin regarded his companion. She was watching the others disappear, a little smile on her lips. Then she turned her attention back to him.

"I like her," she said quietly, reaching out for her wineglass. "She's a good person."

Before he was aware of what he was doing, he reached over and covered her extended hand with his own. For the briefest of moments he felt the warmth of her soft skin against his.

She stared. Her eyes widened in surprise and she quickly jerked her hand away, lowered it to her lap. He sat there, awkward, immobile, his arm stretched out before him. He watched as the bright-red blush spread across her face.

"Sorry," she whispered. "I didn't mean . . ." Her voice trailed off, stopped.

He withdrew his hand and looked away from her, out at the lights of the town rising up the mountains behind her. They sat there in uncomfortable silence for several moments. Then, with an effort, he forced himself to look at her again, thinking briefly of what he'd been considering before Trish interrupted them. He'd actually been toying with the idea of letting her know everything. The sight of her face, grave once more, told him that he would not do it. Not now, not ever. And not merely for the sake of Margaret Barclay, or for the money. He knew, looking at her, that this woman was unhappy. He could not bear the thought of causing her more unhappiness. It was too high a price to pay for her secrets, whatever they were.

It would be so easy to fall in love with her. But that, he knew, would bring with it an awesome responsibility, and he was probably not the man for the job. Hell, he didn't even know what *he* wanted; what could he possibly do for this woman?

He returned to his meal. The decision was made: he would do what had to be done. He would watch her and report her actions to her aunt in Glen Cove. Then he would leave her alone. He would leave her to her melancholy.

Suddenly she looked up at him and broke the silence.

"By the way," she said, "what are you doing on Labor Day?"

"I don't understand it, Adam. Why would anybody do that? I mean, stealing the stuff is understandable, I guess, if you're poor, or greedy, or whatever. But why Nancy?"

Adam shrugged, watching Jack Breen down his third drink. "I guess she caught them in the act. I'm sorry. It's such an awful thing to happen."

"They suspected *me,* for chrissakes! I spent the night in

a cell. A cell! My lawyer couldn't even get me out until the next afternoon. At least Martin waived bail. There's something to be said for belonging to the same yacht club as the judge. But I couldn't even go to her funeral in Ohio. I can't leave the island! I'm a prisoner here until this is over."

"There's no evidence against you," Adam pointed out. 'Besides, there were the Harrimans. It seems there's a burglar—"

Jack waved a dismissive hand. "I don't want to hear about that. I just hope I never meet the prick face to face. I'll *kill* him, Adam, I swear to God I will! With my bare hands."

"Shhh."

Jack lowered his voice. He leaned toward Adam, his bloodshot eyes searching his face. "I loved her, you know? I wasn't really serious about Barbara. Now what do I do? What would you do, Adam? What if it had been Kay?"

Adam managed to keep a straight face. He even went so far as to look shocked.

"I can't imagine," he whispered.

"Adam Prescott! Well, the woods are full tonight."

He looked up, startled by the voice. Trish and Jerry had arrived beside them at the bar. He regained his composure swiftly, watching with amusement as Trish's eyes traveled from him to his companion and Jack Breen's identity registered on her. Her smile disappeared, and she lowered her voice.

"Hello, Jack," she said, placing a hand on his shoulder.

"I'm so sorry about ... everything. If you need anything—"

Jack reached up and covered her hand with his own.

"Thanks, babe," he said, smiling wanly at her and Jerry.

Jerry leaned down to whisper in Adam's ear. "Good of you, Adam. Awful decent of you, to come and baby-sit like this."

Adam nodded, not correcting the false impression. If they thought his meeting with Jack was prearranged, so much the better. Alibi.

"What are you folks up to?" he asked.

"We just dined above," Trish said, pointing directly upward. "Now we're off to that new piano place down on the waterfront for a nightcap. Then I'm going home. Golf, crack of dawn. Stu and Brenda. Snore. But Jerry's meeting some people later. Aren't you, darling?"

Jerry nodded. "Yeah, at the Reef. Dancing, I think. Why don't you guys meet us there?"

"Sure," Jack slurred. "I can't stand the idea of that empty house."

"How about you, Adam?" Jerry asked.

"Oh, I don't know, Jer. Kay's playing bridge tonight, and—"

"Oh, yes," Trish observed, "and Diana's upstairs with that divine Mr. Taylor. Lisa must be home alone."

"No," Adam said, thinking swiftly, amending his plans. "Lisa's spending the night with some friends down the road. Slumber party."

Yes, he thought. Dancing, Perfect.

He raised his eyes to the others. "I'll call Kay and see

if she wants to meet us there. But I'll have to go home and change. Could you manage . . ." He trailed off, indicating Jack, who was now practically slumped against the bar.

"Done," Jerry said.

"Come on, Jack," Trish said, taking his arm and pulling him gently up from the stool. "Jerry's going to drive you. You can leave your car here tonight and come back for it tomorrow."

"Fine," Jack mumbled as she led him away across the bar.

Jerry followed them, turning to wave.

"Hope to see you at the Reef," he called back across the room, loud enough for several other patrons to hear him.

"I'll try," Adam replied.

He waited a moment after they were gone. Then he went to call the hotel where his wife was playing bridge. He waited several minutes while the front desk transferred the call to the game room off the lobby, and several more for the message to be conveyed to Kay's table and the caddy to return with her reply. She would meet him at the Reef in about two hours.

He glanced at his watch. Perfect.

Then, the little smile widening on his face, he went upstairs to the dining room.

Bob Taylor watched him silently as he approached their table.

"Hi, kids," he said as he arrived. "Trish said you were up here having dinner. I just came to say hello, and to tell you, Diana, that Kay and I are going to the Reef later to-night, so we won't be home until late."

He watched, amused, as Diana processed that information.

"Fine," she said at last. "I won't expect you, then."

Adam looked from her to the young man across from her, who seemed to be annoyed by the intrusion. Good, he thought.

"So," he said as lightly as possible, "what are you two doing after dinner?"

He hadn't meant it to sound insinuating, but he could tell from the brief flash of anger on Bob Taylor's face that it had been interpreted that way.

"After this, Bob's taking me home and returning to his hotel," Diana said. She was enunciating carefully, looking directly into his eyes.

"Yeah," the dreary young man offered to the conversation. "I'm expecting a phone call from the States in about an hour. Got to get back to Bolongo."

Taylor was looking at the girl as he said this, Adam noted. The extraneous information was apparently for her benefit. So, he thought, the romantic date isn't going so well. Good.

"Bob's coming to Cliffhanger for dinner on Thursday," Diana said, still watching Adam intently.

"Great!" Adam enthused. "I'll see you then. Have a nice evening." He raised his eyebrows, smirking at the young woman. "See you back home, Diana."

She nodded, conveying a message with her eyes. Don't

do this, she was obviously thinking. Not in front of Bob. We mustn't be suspected. . . .

He beamed down at them. Then he turned and sauntered away from the table, aware of their eyes following him back across the dining room. He grabbed their waiter as he hurried past and told him to take them an after-dinner drink, and to put it on his bar tab downstairs. The waiter nodded. Then Adam went back downstairs and across the patio to the parking lot, chuckling to himself. An after-dinner drink, he thought. A last few awkward moments together. Excellent.

Now that he knew exactly where everybody was and where they would be in the next hour, his surveillance was no longer necessary. The irony of his good fortune was not lost on him. Diana and Bob, Trish and Jerry, Jack Breen: all in the same place tonight. And a new, improved alibi. Excellent.

He checked his watch: nine-fourteen. He would go back to Cliffhanger now and change for the rest of the evening. Then he would run ahead and wait for victim to come to him.

Just as he reached the Nissan, the sky opened again, and another crash of thunder echoed across the harbor below. He got in and started the engine. Before he pulled away, he reached down with his hand to feel under the passenger seat. Yes, he thought. He'd found it in an empty boathouse at the yacht club. A good, solid crowbar that couldn't be traced to him.

Perfect.

* * *

Robin and the young woman sat in his rental car, silent, listening to the patter of the rain on the roof and looking off in opposite directions. She was gazing at the front door of the house, he at the huge tamarind in the center of the circular drive. The porch light and the floodlights aimed up at the tree were indistinct, wavering, seen through the wet windshield. Their evening was over; it was a few minutes after ten o'clock.

"Well," he said.

"Well," she echoed. Then turning to glance over at him, she added, "See you Thursday."

With that she was out of the car and running quickly across the path to the front door. She turned around briefly and raised an arm in final salutation. Over the rain, he could hear the distant sound of a dog barking. He waited until she was safely inside the house and the barking ceased. Then he drove away.

What the hell was that all about? he wondered as he made his way back down the drive and through the stone portal to the main road. They had been doing fine until that moment at the dinner table, when he touched her hand and she pulled away. That moment, he thought now, when I realized that no matter what Margaret is paying me, I don't have the *right* to further invade this woman's privacy. The moment I knew I couldn't tell her who I really am or what I'm really doing in St. Thomas.

Yes, he thought, that dropped a wrench into the proceedings. My morality. *She* can call herself Diana Meissen, or Selena Chase, or Greta Garbo, if it comes to that.

Dye her hair red or brown or green. Whatever. I can't. And I can't go on pretending I don't know who she is.

I can't pretend I'm not falling in love with her.

I can act on a stage: I can do this when I'm Hamlet, or Stanley Kowalski, or even Chucky the Clown. Not when I'm me.

He would tell Margaret now, tonight. He would go to dinner at Cliffhanger on Thursday, and he'd take her out sailing on Labor Day, just as she'd requested at dinner. But that was it. No more. After that, the girl could stay here and be Diana Meissen or go someplace else and be somebody else. He didn't care—or if he did, he wasn't going to admit it. He had offered her his hand, his help, and she had refused. She had made that, if nothing else, perfectly clear. The woman of mystery had elected to remain mysterious.

So be it. The day after Labor Day—next Tuesday—he was out of here. History. Aloha. Time to get back to New York, furnish his condo, grab a copy of *Backstage* and hit the audition trail. Tell Yakimadoro that from now on he'd only accept easy assignments, like infiltrating the Mafia. Find a nice, friendly dog. Or maybe a cat.

Some actor, he thought as he drove through the rain on his way to Bolongo. And some detective. Some fucking detective.

Adam stood in the rain on the balcony, just outside the sliding glass doors to the bedroom, waiting. In his left hand, under the black raincoat, he clutched the crowbar.

It was nearly ten-thirty. Soon, he thought. Soon. Any minute now.

It was always the anticipation, his favorite part of it. The waiting, the knowing that soon he would be in complete control. The thrill of pure energy, the surge forming deep inside, imbuing him. No drug, no mere physical act, however pleasurable, was like this, now. This moment.

Yes, he thought as he waited, I'm ready now. Ready for God. Not that vague, intangible presence that was believed in and prayed to by the ignorant, the impotent, the ordinary. Mine is the real power, the one true God.

He heard the sound of a car door slamming in the distance, followed by the splash of feet running in the rain. Stepping back into the shadows of the balcony, he closed his eyes and drew in a long, deep breath. The crowbar burned, ice-cold, in his almighty fist.

FIFTEEN

THURSDAY, AUGUST 29

KAY HELD the enormous knife up in front of her and brought it suddenly, violently down, piercing the outer layer of skin and cutting cleanly through. Then, without pausing, she brought up the sharp, heavy blade and smashed it down again. And again. A series of swift, efficient strokes, one after another. At some point she slipped from conscious effort into automatic routine as her mind wandered away from the task at hand, blinded by the pain and anger she'd kept inside for several days. Now, in this action, she had finally found a physical outlet for it. Her rage, her acute, overwhelming sense of violation traveled down her arm and into the blade, communicating itself in the grim satisfaction she felt as she sliced through flesh and the blood flowed, oozing from the gaping wounds.

This, she thought as she once more raised the knife and stabbed, is for Trish. And this, and this.

Trish. Oh, God, Trish. . . .

Kay had practically been living at St. Thomas Hospital for the last three days, haunting the waiting room and the nurses' station, sitting next to the bed whenever possible. She'd only just now returned from today's vigil, to make dinner for the others. Nola and Diana hovered nearby, getting the pot ready for the noodles and chopping vegetables for the salad. But Kay was supervising the Stroganoff herself. It was her mother's recipe, and she trusted no one else to make it properly.

She wielded the cleaver once more, cutting the beef into small, perfect cubes, glancing over at the labels of the two bottles of burgundy that stood uncorked on the other counter. Dinner, at least, would be fine.

Jerry Flynn would be there, and Bob Taylor. Now that Trish's condition had improved from critical to stable, there was really no point in putting off the original plan. Kay could use the distraction, to say nothing of Jerry.

Adam had been wonderful throughout the ordeal: sitting with her and Jerry for long hours at the hospital, insisting on the best doctors, taking care of medical and insurance forms, even offering to cancel his trip to the States. But Kay had insisted that he keep his promise to Roger Bartlett in Palm Beach, and they had both decided it would be best for Lisa to go to Connecticut. Kay would be fine here, she insisted, with Diana and Nola. And the doctors said Trish would be all right. She'd probably be out of the hospital in a few days, and the decision to have her recuperate here, at Cliffhanger, had been unanimous.

Kay set the meat aside and reached for an onion. As she did so, she glanced briefly over at the young woman on the other side of the counter. Diana looked up, smiled, and returned her attention to the cutting board before her. She really is amazing, Kay thought as she worked, treating the onion more gently than the beef as her anger dissipated. Trish had not suffered any permanent damage; Kay had been assured of that.

Trish.

The thief had struck Trish on the back of the head, one powerful blow with a blunt weapon of some description. Trish hadn't seen anything. She had just entered her dark apartment, was in the act of reaching for the light switch, when something crashed against her skull and she pitched forward into oblivion. When she came to, hours later in the hospital, she was unaware of exactly what had happened to her. Kay had told her, Kay and Chief Potter. Her jewelry and her silver—like Brenda's and Nancy's before her—were gone. The concussion was bad but not life-threatening: Mr. Potter had remarked that the blow seemed to have been designed to do the job while creating the least amount of damage. The robber had obviously wanted to hurt her, to neutralize her temporarily, but not to kill her. The chief had been certain of that, and no one had seen any reason to argue with him. Certainly not Kay, who'd been trying not to think about it at all until just now, when she held the cleaver in her hand and her outrage manifested itself physically. The sonofabitch hadn't had any such qualms about killing Nancy.

Jack Breen had been with Jerry and several other people at the Reef at the time of the attack on Trish, which had pretty much exonerated him of any involvement in the robberies and the death of his wife. Kay went over the evening in her mind: dancing with Adam; laughing with the others at the big round table at the club; removing the glass from Jack's hand and insisting that he switch to ginger ale. Then later, at home, making love with an unusually excited Adam, and the phone ringing. . . .

Jerry had left the club at two-thirty, dropped Jack at home, and gone to Trish's condominium. He'd let himself in with his own key and nearly tripped over her.

She closed her eyes and reached for the pasta. Diana placed the last of the chopped vegetables in the huge wooden salad bowl and came around the counter.

"That's done," she said quietly. "I have to get ready now."

Kay nodded. As the young woman passed her on the way to the door, Kay reached over briefly and touched her arm.

No words were spoken. They regarded each other for a moment, and then Diana smiled and nodded and went out of the kitchen.

The young woman sat at the vanity table in her little bedroom upstairs, staring at her face in the mirror.

It would all be over soon.

She reached down into the top drawer and pushed

aside the cosmetics: the perfume and the makeup and the dye. There, at the very back, was the small prescription bottle she'd obtained the day before. Good. She closed the drawer and reached for her hairbrush. She watched her actions in the glass as she catalogued her list of new secrets.

Adam had murdered Sandra Franklin.

Adam had murdered Nancy Breen.

Adam had very nearly murdered Trish Manning.

One hundred strokes, as she had done all her life, as her mother had done for her when she was small. One hundred strokes to make it soft, to make it gleam.

And what, she wondered as she brushed, had happened to Greg? She had forgotten about Adam's former mate, the only one who could link her to Adam before her present visit to the island. She had forgotten him as conveniently as he had disappeared, to be replaced by the ignorant Kyle. As conveniently as Sandra Franklin, the only other possible witness, had drowned.

If she was honest with herself, she would have to admit that she'd been aware from the outset that others would be harmed, that her private passions would lead, step by fateful step, to this obvious eventuality. That her happiness, her ultimate fulfillment, would exact a price. But she had made the choice. She had decided long ago that it was a price she was willing to pay. It was, perhaps, her greatest secret.

Stroke, stroke, stroke of the brush as the new secrets were added to, and mingled with, the old. She stared at the face before her, thinking, I am living a life of secrets.

Those I've kept from Mom. And Juana. And Kay and her daughter. And this interesting new character Bob Taylor. And most of all, Adam.

Adam, who thinks nothing of using murder to get what he wants.

Then, gazing at herself, she discovered the irony, the macabre humor, in that. How very alike we are, she realized. I think nothing of it, either. Adam doesn't know that about me, but he will soon enough. Until then, I will remain silent.

The tears had come quietly this time, unheralded. She stared at her reflection, watching as one heavy drop rolled slowly down her cheek, followed by another. She lowered her head, biting her lip and staring sightlessly down at the surface of the table. After a moment, she raised her chin and willed herself to look once more at the frightened, unhappy woman in the glass. Then she put down the brush and reached for the lipstick.

Passion's Promise.

The three men waited in the living room for the women to arrive. Adam looked over at the other two, wondering what in God's name he could come up with to break their silence. Jerry and Bob had arrived almost simultaneously, and he had greeted them and led them here. He'd handed out drinks from the bar in the corner. Only the young man had sat down; Jerry remained standing near the doors to the deck, staring out over the dark water. Adam hovered between them, aware of the discomfort he always felt when he was forced to be with people whom he found boring. Which, he mused, was practically everyone.

Where the hell is Kay? he wondered. What could possibly be taking so long in the kitchen? And why doesn't she just show Nola how to make her precious beef Stroganoff? That's what servants are for.

Then another thought occurred to him, and he raised a hand to his mouth to hide his wry smile. Too bad Trish won't be joining us, he thought. Oh well, she'll be out of the hospital in a few days, and no real harm done. He had seen to that. He had constantly reminded himself, as he prepared and executed this latest phase of the plan, that Trish could not be sacrificed. That would have ruined everything. Kay would have been inconsolable, and he would not have been able to leave the island. Running off to a race in Florida mere days after the murder of his wife's closest friend would have appeared suspicious, even to him. So Trish had been spared. The crowbar, now resting deep in the Atlantic, had replaced the weapon of choice, and the silly woman had a mere bump on the head as a souvenir of the mysterious bandit who was roaming St. Thomas, preying on the rich.

Excellent.

There was a sound from the upper floor, and all three men turned to look. Diana stood on the balcony above them, gazing down. She wore a gauzy white blouse and pleated navy skirt, and her dark hair hung straight to her shoulders. Adam stared as she came slowly down the stairs, marveling at the fact that any woman so simply dressed could be so breathtakingly beautiful. He glanced over at Taylor: the young man seemed rooted, stunned by the vision. Then he turned his attention back to the object in Taylor's enraptured stare as she arrived at the bottom of the staircase.

"Good evening," she said. She bestowed a quick smile upon the smitten Bob Taylor before turning her full attention, and a dazzling grin, toward Adam. Even the melancholy Jerry had discontinued his contemplation of the distant waves and fixed his gaze on the lovely young woman. She seemed to have that effect on everyone. But her heart, Adam knew, was his. She was beautiful for him, and him alone.

Yes, Adam thought as he stepped forward to greet her. Perfect.

Jerry Flynn went home almost immediately after dessert, and the rest of the little group dispersed temporarily throughout the house. Kay sat next to the phone in a corner of the living room and called the hospital. Adam Prescott excused himself and disappeared into the master bedroom. Lisa ran up to her room, accompanied by her dog. Robin took this opportunity to go outside and join the young woman who stood at the railing on the deck, gazing steadily out at the moonlit water.

He stood in the doorway behind her for a few moments, watching her dark hair move gently in the evening breeze. So lovely, he thought, Then, remembering their dinner date three nights before, he forced himself to look away from her and over at the lights of the hotel on the next point of land across the bay. No, he reminded himself: this loveliness is not for me.

If she was aware of his presence behind her, she gave no sign. She leaned against the rail, apparently fascinated by the way the moonlight burnished the sea. The long, wide streak in the water below the moon sparkled as if with inner fire. He followed her gaze to the ribbon of ice-blue light, wondering—not for the first time, not for the last—what she was thinking. His focus returned to her hair, the back of her neck, the rippling white blouse, and he emitted a long, low sigh. It was this that announced him. She abandoned her vigil, or whatever it was, and turned around, a little smile forming at the corners of her mouth. He went over to stand next to her at the railing.

"Penny," he said.

Her sudden laugh transformed her, changing the moment from quiet and contemplative to something warm and light and unaffected. She gave herself over to it, throwing back her head and shaking with merriment. He grinned in the darkness next to her. So, he thought, she can be spontaneous. She should try it more often.

They both bent over the rail, shoulders touching, looking out at the nighttime view.

"That's my line," she replied, still giggling. "I stole it from Noël Coward."

Now he, too, was laughing. "Are you sure it wasn't Philip Barry?"

The moment, lovely as it was, disappeared in an instant. He felt the sudden tension in her arm where it pressed lightly against his. Then she pulled away and turned her face to him. Her smile was gone. He watched as her mouth tightened and her brows moved closer together. Something was puzzling her.

Oh, he thought as it dawned on him. Oh, great! How many real-estate salesmen would possibly know . . . dumb, Robin. You are truly dumb.

It was, he would later realize, his second big mistake.

Now, on the deck, he merely blushed and turned away from her piercing gaze.

"I'm a fan of old movies," he mumbled. "Philip Barry wrote *The Philadelphia Story*."

There was a slight pause before she said, "Yes, I know." Then, as if sensing his distress, she moved the conversation away from early-twentieth-century playwrights. "So, are we on for Labor Day? You will come sailing with me, won't you?"

His laugh was half amusement, half relief. "I promised, didn't I?"

"You did," she said, "and I intend to hold you to it. No begging off with a sudden headache. The only way to conquer fear is to get back on the horse—or, in your case, boat."

They were both laughing now, and their bodies were once more leaning together at the railing, once more relaxed.

"Oh, come on!" he cried in mock exasperation. "I'm not *that* scared of boats."

"Good. You'll need all your courage for the cat."

"The . . . cat?"

"Catamaran," she sang, grinning innocently up at him.

"You know, two pontoons with a sort of net stretched between them. Kind of like a trampoline. You sit on that, and—" She broke off, smiling. "Something wrong, Bob?"

He was gripping the rail, shuddering.

"Why don't I just jump off this cliff right now?" he muttered, leaning forward and looking down into the black abyss. "It'll save time. . . ."

"Hi, kids. Having fun?"

They both whirled from the railing. Adam Prescott stood in the doorway, grinning, holding out a silver tray.

"Coffee's being served in the living room," he said.

The moment he saw Prescott, Robin knew that there was something peculiar going on. They had just eaten dinner, and Jerry Flynn had already gone home. They'd have coffee now, and then Robin would leave as well. Prescott was at the end, not the beginning, of his duties as host. So why, Robin wondered, had the man changed his clothes? He'd removed the suit he'd been wearing; now he was clad in jeans, sweater, and sneakers. And there was something else. . . .

As they followed Prescott inside, the girl spoke up. "Bob is taking me out sailing on Labor Day, Adam. Isn't that nice of him?"

Prescott set the tray down on the coffee table and straightened, facing the two of them. Robin felt the involuntary discomfort as the unnervingly handsome blond giant raked him up and down with the gaze of his washed-out blue eyes. Then he looked from Robin to the girl. "Oh? Labor Day, you say?"

"Yes," she replied, meeting Prescott's gaze with her own. "Labor Day."

He smiled, and his too-white teeth glistened. "Excellent!"

He glanced over at his wife, who was still on the phone in the corner. Then he leaned down to pour. He handed a cup to the girl and filled another. As he approached with the coffee, Robin realized what it was that he'd noticed on the deck moments before and found to be so odd: Prescott fairly reeked of freshly applied bay rum. Robin studied his face as he leaned toward him. Yes, he thought, very strange. Not only has the man changed his clothes; he's shaved as well. Now, why would any man change clothes and shave at ten o'clock in the evening? Why would I do such a thing? Only one reason.

They sat in a semicircle around the table. As he added cream to his cup, Robin noticed the strained, rather intense exchange of glances between Prescott and the girl. Prescott grinned, and the girl blushed. Robin put down the creamer and reached for the sugar bowl, thinking suddenly, incongruously, of Margaret Barclay.

She sent me here for information, he thought as he stirred the coffee. It never occurred to me until this moment that maybe—just maybe—that information is something I'd rather not know.

Kay hung up the phone and went over to join the others.

"Trish says hello," she announced, sitting next to her husband and accepting the cup he extended to her. "Thanks, darling. She's feeling much better, but she can't see through all those bandages. The doctor says they'll come off in about three days, and she may actually be out of the hospital on Tuesday. Let's see, that's the day after Labor Day. . . . I'll bring her straight here, of course." She smiled proudly around at everyone.

Her husband reached over and slowly, lovingly, began twirling a lock of her bright-red hair between his large fingers.

"Diana," she cried, alarmed by the odd look that had suddenly appeared on the young woman's face. "Are you all right?"

"What? Oh, yes. Yes, I'm fine," the girl whispered, and she slowly raised her cup.

Robin was halfway down the drive to the main road when his curiosity got the better of him. His curiosity, yes—and something else. Of course, he could justify what he was about to do by convincing himself that it was part of his job. But he knew better.

Pausing to analyze it was not a good idea, he knew, even as he noticed the little dirt turnoff in the beam of the headlights. It was this track branching off among the trees that really swayed him, made his idea a reality. He swung the car off the drive, parked in the turnaround at the end of the track, and left the car. Moving quickly and as silently as possible, keeping out of sight among the trees that lined the main drive, he walked back up the hill toward Cliffhanger.

He emerged from the trees at the end of the lawn. The huge tamarind in the center of the circle shone silver in the moonlight. Checking to be sure there was nobody at any of the lit windows of the house, he crouched and ran as swiftly as he could across the open ground. He made it to the base of the tree in seconds and flattened himself against the enormous trunk. In the absolute darkness beneath the thick, fruit-laden branches, he waited.

Adam waited until he was certain that Kay was asleep. It didn't take long: the past three days of worrying about Trish Manning had taken their toll on her nerves, and as far as sleep was concerned, she had a lot of catching up to do.

Just to be sure, he had earlier stolen two sleeping capsules from her medicine cabinet and mixed the contents in the cups of coffee he'd handed her and Diana. The moment Bob Taylor had departed, Diana had disappeared upstairs and Kay had come into the room and fallen into bed. Now her breathing was deep and steady.

Excellent.

He switched off the lights and left the room.

The young woman waited in the shadows of the darkened upstairs hallway, listening for sounds elsewhere in the house. She'd left the bedroom door ajar in case the need arose for a quick retreat, and for the past thirty minutes she'd been standing here, straining her ears to detect any noise below. She leaned back against the cool white stucco, peering out through the wall of glass before her at the moonlit front lawn. Her vision blurred from time to time. At one point a few minutes ago, she'd fancied she saw something moving among the shadows under the tamarind tree. Then she'd blinked, and the night had once again been still. Why was she suddenly so tired?

Her mind was working more efficiently than her other faculties. Behind her heavy eyelids, her thoughts were racing. How would she follow him if he took the car, which he was almost certain to do? The keys to the Land Rover would be in Kay's purse, wherever that was. Her bedroom, presumably: that was no good. And where the hell was he going, anyway? She knew he was up to something: the change of clothing and the shave immediately after dinner had tipped her off. Kay, of course, hadn't noticed. She'd been too busy worrying about her friend and about Adam and Lisa's impending trip to the States.

Her sudden, inexplicable fatigue was apparently stronger than her anxiety. And she was anxious, not only about Adam but about Bob Taylor. For the second time in a week, Bob had made her feel uneasy, wary. What was it about the man that so disturbed her? He'd saved her from drowning; she should be grateful. He was certainly attractive, even sexy; that should prompt certain responses from her, too. Yet she was aware only of being uncomfortable whenever he was around.

Tonight, for the second time, he'd confused her. That remark about Philip Barry: even people in show business didn't remember him. But this young real-estate broker certainly did. It had made her feel odd, as she had felt last week after the birthday party. *Something* he'd said or done during the birthday party. Something not *right*.

Her eyes were blurring again, and she stifled a yawn.

Wake up! she commanded, remembering the coffee she'd barely touched and wishing she'd drunk it all. Fighting off the weariness that threatened to overcome her, she made a decision. She would wait here in the hallway to see if and when he departed. That was all she could do. She'd have to trust him after that: tonight's activities could very well be part of the plan. She wished, not for the first time, that he'd told her more of his agenda. But of course, that would have required his telling her about Sandra and Nancy and Trish *before* the fact. Perhaps it was better to play by his rules after all.

To calm herself—and to keep awake at her post—she concentrated on the scrapbook. She did this whenever she felt frightened or began to lose her resolve. She had only to conjure the yellowed pages with their screaming text and grainy photographs, and she was immediately filled with a renewed sense of purpose.

She'd only photocopied the first twenty-eight pages for the second scrapbook, the duplicate she'd brought to St. Thomas. The original, locked safely away in the grandmother's escritoire in her bedroom at home, contained an entire second section that, while comforting to her, was not pertinent. Random cases, from all over America, of people in situations similar to hers. Now, pressed against the wall of the upstairs hallway at Cliffhanger, she thought only of those first twenty-eight pages. Her baby pictures, and her mother and father, and the woman in Hawaii. . . .

The sudden sound broke through her reverie. Somewhere just below her a door quietly opened and closed.

Then she heard the muffled sound of rubber-soled shoes padding lightly, carefully, across the living room to the foyer. The front door now, slowly opening and softly shut. She stepped forward toward the glass wall, looking down. Adam came into view below her, moving quickly away from the house, toward the two vehicles parked in the drive. She glanced down at her watch: eleven-thirty.

She was just about to turn around and go back into her bedroom when Adam did something extraordinary. Just as he reached the drive where the Nissan stood waiting, he turned and walked off across the lawn toward . . . toward . . .

She ducked into the bedroom, kicked off her high-heeled pumps, and fumbled in the darkness for her sneakers. Finding them under the bed and tying the laces cost her several minutes, but at least she knew he was on foot, and where he was obviously going. She pulled on a dark sweater over her white blouse and ran back out into the hall. In a flash she was down the stairs and heading for the front door, her mysterious lethargy instantly forgotten.

Robin crouched behind the tamarind, watching Adam Prescott stride across the lawn and into a gap between the trees near the edge of the cliff. He did not hesitate for a single moment. Silent as the shadows to which he clung, he moved forward to follow.

There was a path at the place where Prescott had disappeared, parts of which were dimly illuminated by the moon. He could just make out the shape of the other man moving through the foliage ahead. The wind whistled through the leaves, strong enough to muffle any slight sound he might make. His quarry was bolder now that he was a safe distance from the house. He strode purposefully—and rather noisily—down the hill.

Robin kept back, maintaining a distance of some fifty yards. As they made their way farther down, the roll of the surf grew stronger. By the time Robin's shoes left hard earth and sank into sand, the sound of the nearby breakers was surprisingly loud.

He stood quite still at the end of the path, listening for sounds ahead of him in the darkness. His eyes had adjusted somewhat, and the moonlight here on the open beach was strong. He caught a brief glimpse of a large, dark shadow leaving the sand and entering the trees about halfway along the beach. He heard the heavy footsteps crunching on what must, by the sound of it, be fallen palm fronds dried by the sun.

Then he saw the light. The strong nighttime trade wind suddenly rustled the trees between him and Prescott, and among the moving branches he noticed a flicker of brightness, as of a lamp or candle. Prescott was obviously heading toward it.

He heard the distinct sound of a door opening on a rusty hinge, and the light grew. It emanated, he now saw, from some kind of small building set back in the trees behind the beach. Slowly, carefully, holding his breath, he moved closer to the light.

Prescott was standing outside the open doorway, looking into the room. The sound of his low-pitched laughter traveled through the trees, and after a moment he entered, closing the door behind him. The soft light continued to gleam through the gaping cracks between the vertical boards that formed the walls.

Robin was just beginning to steel himself, to actually contemplate the prospect of moving closer to the hut, when he became aware of the faint sound behind him. He froze, listening intently. Then, when he realized what it was, he moved silently, instinctively to his right, away from the base of the path, deeper into the shrubbery, and ducked down behind a trunk.

Someone else was coming down the path to the beach.

He watched from his secret vantage place as she came by. She was looking straight ahead of her, heading toward the light that shone dimly through the forest. Her hands were clutching her upper arms as if she were cold, despite the heavy sweater she wore. He could not see her face from this angle, but he heard her soft, ragged breathing.

She came to a halt at the bottom of the path, not twelve feet from where he was concealed. He fancied he could almost hear her thinking. After a long moment, she apparently came to some sort of decision and stepped cautiously forward into the trees.

He risked rising to a standing position, the better to observe her. She neared the boathouse, slowing even more as she reached the place where the dead, dried fronds barred her way. She bowed her head and stepped carefully through them, peering down into the darkness at her feet. She glided across the final distance and directly up to the side of the building.

As he watched, she bent forward and looked through a crack between the boards. She stood there, frozen, for one full minute. Then she turned around and faced in his direction, her back to the boathouse. She raised a hand to cover her mouth, slowly shaking her head from side to side. At last she lowered her hand and, with one swift backward glance, retraced her steps through the trees to the base of the path, gaining speed as she put distance between her and the little hut. By the time she passed his hiding place, she was running. She flew by him, a blur of dark sweater and dark hair and pale white face, and up the path toward Cliffhanger. Even with her frantic pace, he had not failed to see the expression in her eyes, or the tears that streamed down her bloodless cheeks.

He knelt in the darkness behind the bushes, watching her go, wondering why the sight of her desolate face should move him as it did. And why was the chilly seaside forest suddenly so warm? He could feel the heat as she ran by, almost as if it emanated from her body, sending a wave of warmth outward into the night air. He watched her, squinting into the gloom, straining to see her until that last possible moment when the forest and the darkness enshrouded her.

He waited until the sound of her headlong flight had faded away up the hill. Then he stepped out of the shadows and walked silently, cautiously through the trees to the wall of the boathouse. Holding his breath, he leaned forward and peered inside.

Well well well, he thought, staring. What do you know?

* * *

Kay was awakened by the slamming of the front door. Her sleep had been fitful, and as her mind struggled up from its deep stupor she realized, with a vague sense of alarm, that she was drenched in sweat. She had the impression that she'd been dreaming, and that the dream had not been pleasant, but she could not remember a single detail of it. She lay between the moist sheets, gradually becoming aware of the sound of running footsteps. She heard them flying across the living room and up the stairs. By the time she forced herself to rise from the bed and stagger out into the hall, the only thing left to hear was the shutting and locking of a bedroom door above her.

She stood in the center of the dark living room, gazing up, wondering if she should investigate. The cold floor shocked the soles of her bare feet, and her gauzy nightgown flapped in the draft that gushed through the open doors to the deck. Her mind was unaccountably fuzzy, and her arms hung heavily at her sides. If she didn't know better, she would swear she'd taken a sleeping pill. No, she would certainly remember if she had.

Where had Diana been at this hour? And why had she come running into the house like that? Kay thought she'd gone to bed when Bob Taylor left.

Bob Taylor.

A slow, knowing smile came to her lips. So, she thought. A rendezvous, arranged previously—perhaps when they were alone together after dinner, when she went to call Trish.

She raised a hand to her parched throat as another wave of weariness washed over her. She must get a drink of water and return to bed. She would have to be up early tomorrow, to see Adam and Lisa off at the airport.

Adam.

She looked around the dark, empty room, wondering where her husband could be. He apparently wasn't in the house. He must have gone out somewhere, to meet Jerry or Jack Breen or some of his buddies from the club and hoist a few on the eve of his trip to Florida. One of those mandatory, all-male send-offs to the Day after Labor Day Regatta. My, she thought, I certainly missed a lot when I fell asleep so quickly tonight.

Even in her exhausted state, that line of reasoning bothered her. Adam didn't seem to have buddies, really . . . . Oh, well. Maybe he's making an effort. Good for him. And Diana is apparently making an effort as well. Good for her.

Had she been another kind of woman, Kay Prescott might have suspected something. She might have gone to the front window and seen the Nissan parked behind the Land Rover in the driveway. She might even have gone so far as to ask her husband, the next morning, where he had been the night before. But she did none of these things. She was an honest, trusting woman who loved her husband as well as she could, though not as well as she had loved the man who instilled such trust in her in the first place. If innocence can be regarded as a fault, it was Kay Prescott's only one.

With a yawn and a shake of her heavy, drug-tinged head, she went back to bed—thus, in an odd way, setting the stage for the final act of the tragedy. The scandal. That Cliffhanger business.

SIXTEEN

SATURDAY, AUGUST 31

MARGARET CAME OUT of the house into dazzling sunlight and walked briskly toward the garage. Lovely day, she thought, inhaling deeply as she fiddled with the remote control device. The heavy garage door shuddered into its long, slow ascent with a small shriek of rusty protest. She made a mental note to ask Mrs. O'Rourke to get her husband to come over someday soon and attend to it.

My mind is wandering again, she realized as she got into the gray BMW. Funny how it does that whenever I'm worried, when I'm trying not to think about something. The overload, no doubt: the surfeit of worries that suddenly seems to be laying siege to my life.

She smiled ruefully as she drove in the direction of the Long Island Expressway. Perhaps I'll go mad, she thought.

Perhaps my terrors will rise up and choke what's left of my mind. Someone—as if I don't know who!—will put me in a place, some glorified hospital not unlike the one I'm visiting today. Then I'll be out of it, and it will all be somebody else's problem.

No, she told herself, I will not go mad. I will handle this—whatever it is, whatever it turns out to be—as I have handled everything that fate has thrown my way. I am that self-possessed, at least. I can do it.

The Expressway was, mercifully, less crowded than she'd expected it to be on the first day of the holiday weekend. She looked at her watch: yes, she'd be there by two o'clock. She could even stop for lunch in Bellport or Brookhaven and perhaps get some flowers or a box of candy. Some such prop, the better to pass any inspection there might be by the authorities at the rest home. She had already decided to announce herself as what she was: the mother, legally speaking, of a friend. She could only hope that Carson Fleming would accept that and agree to see her. If not, she would simply return to Glen Cove, and no harm done. An afternoon's drive, nothing more. A small price to pay for a chance, slim as it was, to satisfy her curiosity.

Carson Fleming, Carson Fleming. . . .

She searched her mind again, as she had done constantly for the past four days. The name was vaguely familiar. Somewhere in the past she had seen it or heard it, but where? He was seventy-seven, and he'd suffered a massive stroke.

He may not be there at all, she reminded herself. He may very well be dead.

No. He was alive: she was sure of it. If not, there would have been something among the girl's papers to indicate his passing. If her niece had paid for the convalescence, she would almost certainly have paid for the funeral.

Of course, there was another, realistic possibility. Carson Fleming, whoever he was, could be comatose or, at the very least, physically and/or mentally disabled.

She reached over and switched on the car's air conditioner. She was wearing her lightest summery flower-print dress and sandals, but she could feel the beads of perspiration gathering. It wasn't particularly hot today, and yet—

Oh, stop it, she commanded as the green, white-lettered sign sailed by on her right: "You Are Now Entering Suffolk County." Just go there and do what you can.

Resigned, she gripped the wheel tightly in her moist hands and pressed her foot more firmly on the accelerator.

The young woman couldn't feel anything. No, that wasn't the truth: actually, she was feeling so many different things all at once that she was unable to come to grips with any of it. Everything seemed to be pressing in on her, restricting her breathing and her circulation. It was a massive, oppressive weight.

She'd awakened this morning as if from a drugged sleep, forced herself to go downstairs to the kitchen for coffee, and brought the cup back here, to her room. She hadn't eaten anything: the thought of eating made her feel queasy, and it would require energy she was not certain she possessed. Now she sat at the foot of her bed, staring listlessly out past the balcony at the bright blue, glistening, hyperactive Caribbean. The gulls swooped and soared, circling the sailboats and motor craft, leaping upward into the sun and dropping back to skim the surface for food. Their piercing cries of hunger and victory and frustration reached her where she sat, enervating her, forming around her a shell of dull inertia.

This, she supposed, is shock.

The beach the other night had been the beginning of it, but it was by no means the biggest surprise she'd experienced. In fact, when she thought about it, it wasn't a surprise at all. She'd gotten over the first, reflexive horror almost immediately. The long run up the hill to this room had knocked it from her body as it had winded her. By the time she made her way to the bathroom to splash cold water on her face, the feeling had passed. No, the boathouse was the least of it.

She shook her head, dismissing the beach. I must concentrate on the real problem, she thought. I must figure out what to do. If not, Adam will be lost to me. Forever.

The real problem: the one that had struck her like a blow to the stomach the night before as she prepared for bed.

They'd gone to the airport yesterday to put Adam and Lisa on their plane. She'd taken charge of the tickets and the bags, leaving the others to say their good-byes in private. There had been much hugging and kissing between Kay and her family: she'd been relieved to have something to do, busywork, while that was going on. When boarding time arrived, she'd briefly embraced the child and shaken Adam's hand, careful to avoid eye contact with him. At last the plane had taken off, and she and Kay had driven into town for some shopping and a huge lunch in Kay's favorite restaurant. The afternoon and evening had passed uneventfully.

The two of them had sat up late together in the living room, lounging on the couches and sipping cold drinks, Jumbi asleep on the floor between them, Kay in a fuzzy pink bathrobe, smoking cigarettes, her face slick and shiny with cold cream. A slumber party: that was what Kay had laughingly called it. They'd talked about Trish in the hospital, and the apparent crime wave, and clothes and jewelry and cosmetics and scents. Then, as with every slumber party in history, they'd eventually gotten around to discussing sex. Well, Kay had, at any rate.

She'd sat back on her couch across from Kay Prescott, watching her, smiling and nodding and making all the proper noises to orchestrate what was, essentially, a monologue. Yes, she'd murmured, it's terrible about Trish: thank God she's all right. . . . No, she didn't like hats, either, had never felt comfortable wearing them. . . . Yes, too much eyeliner *did* make most women look like hookers.

On and on, until suddenly Kay was launched on a new tack, about Adam and her late husband and some boy in high school back in Connecticut. College men: Yale versus Harvard versus . . . Athletes. Football, hockey, lacrosse: the three sports to avoid when considering boyfriends in college. Date-rapists, every one of them. . . . Drama majors: the best-looking men on campus, *always*, and safe dates. Of course, half of them were gay, but . . .

She'd flinched when Kay made that last observation, but she said nothing. It was amusing, really, to see this forty-five-year-old woman gushing and giggling and carrying on as if she'd been magically transported back to Vassar. She was just beginning to notice the dramatic change in Kay's demeanor in the twelve hours since Adam had left the island. Much more relaxed, much less—she studied the woman's face, searching for a word—*guarded*. That was it. She could almost like this woman under other circumstances. They might have become friends. Thinking of the amethyst brooch, she blinked and turned her gaze away.

Then, inevitably, the topic had rolled around to Bob Taylor. Kay had somehow changed horses in midstream. One moment she'd been evaluating swimming teams and lifeguards; the next, she was recalling the accident on the boat and Bob's heroics in the water. He hadn't hesitated for a moment, Kay remembered, but plunged into the water and fought his way through the waves.

She had closed her eyes as Kay spoke, thinking back on the incident. She could remember clearly now the panic she'd felt when she awakened in the ocean, and the intense look on Bob's face as he swam toward her, reaching for her, shouting to her—

"I think he's in love with you," Kay had said.

She opened her eyes then, staring. "What?"

"In love," Kay had repeated. "Bob Taylor. With you, Diana. Don't you think so?"

She'd had to think about it. She didn't care about Bob Taylor one way or the other, she privately insisted, and her civility toward Adam's wife—toward this woman she actually liked—was beginning to wear thin. Time to go upstairs, she'd decided. To be alone, to relax, to think. Enough of this "slumber party."

"Oh, I don't know," she'd murmured, rising. "I'm not very good at knowing when men are in love with me—or when they're not, for that matter. It's late, Kay. I must be getting to bed."

"Of course," Kay had said, watching her as she walked over to the stairs. "I didn't realize the time. I'm going to visit Trish tomorrow afternoon. Would you like to come?"

"Sure," she'd called back as she ascended.

Then, just as she'd reached the top of the stairs, the other woman's voice had stopped her. "Oh, and, Lisa—"

She'd turned around on the balcony and looked down. Kay stood looking up at her, blushing, grinning feebly through her expression of distracted surprise.

"Oh, for Heaven's sake!" Kay had cried. "I just called you Lisa! I meant to say Diana. *Diana,* Nola will be off Sunday and Monday this week. Labor Day. If you want her to get you anything special from the supermarket tomorrow, leave a note for her in the kitchen. Otherwise, you'll have to wait till after the holiday."

She'd nodded, said good night to Kay, and made her way down the hall to her bedroom. She'd gone to the vanity table and sat down, reaching automatically for the brush to begin her nightly hundred-stroke ritual, and looked up at her face in the mirror.

That was when it had happened.

It was difficult now, the next morning, to remember exactly what had triggered it, whether it had been the talk of Bob Taylor, or her memory of being in the water, or Kay looking up at her and calling her Lisa. Or had it been the sight of her own image, the dark eyes and alien hair, before her? All of these things, probably. The combination, the sudden juxtaposition. She didn't know for sure now. She only remembered the horrible, wrenching surprise. It arrived in a huge, violent rush, blinding her, washing over her skin and piercing her nerve endings. She sat there gasping as her eyes adjusted and the image in the mirror came slowly back into focus.

He knows.

The words had entered her consciousness as she sat staring at her reflection.

Bob Taylor knows.

Her dark hair had hung down limply to her shoulders, and the creases had deepened at the corners of her eyes as her pupils began, ever so slowly, to dilate.

Bob Taylor knows who I am.

Then, in that awful moment last night, she'd done what seemed to most natural thing. She'd picked up the brush and begun the hundred strokes.

And only one person can have told him.

When she was finished with her hair, she'd turned off the light and fallen across the bed. She had lain there in the darkness for several hours, assessing it, going over it all in her mind. What he knew; what he might know; what he could not possibly know.

He? No, not he. Not merely he.

They.

It had been nearly five o'clock when sleep, the exhaustion of frustration, overtook her. She'd awakened hours later to find that she was still lying on top of the covers, fully clothed.

Now, in the brilliant light of morning, it seemed to her that there was only one recourse, only one solution. It was eleven o'clock, and soon Kay would be ready to go to the hospital. She must act quickly, before she changed her mind.

She rose from the foot of the bed and left the room. At the bottom of the stairs she turned, went over to the telephone in the corner of the living room, and slowly raised the receiver.

It was a large, imposing old Long Island mansion, set back from the main road on a flat headland next to the bay just outside the village. The pillared, white wood structure of the original three-story residence had been augmented on both sides by long, low, more modern-looking wings with louvered windows and flat roofs, which were in rather violent contrast to the gingerbread and latticework—not to mention the eponymous gables—at the center. But it was the huge, yellow-lined parking lot off to the left that, more than anything else, announced to the world that this once-gracious home was now an institution.

Arriving shortly before two o'clock, Margaret followed the metal signs and luminous arrows around the drive to a space in the lot marked "Visitor" and crossed the neatly mown lawn to the front entrance. She walked quickly, purposefully, hoping that her own momentum would keep her from faltering. She was a friend, she insistently reminded herself as she entered South Bay Gables; she had every right to be here.

Her trepidation was short-lived. The moment she walked across the small, empty lobby and confronted the pretty girl in the starched white uniform and nurse's cap behind the desk, she knew everything was going to be all right. No stern doctors or sinister matrons or security people: merely a little blond girl, barely out of her teens. This she could handle. She took a swift inventory of the girl's visible attributes, singled out the most remarkable one, and plunged.

"Good afternoon," she gushed, grinning across at the girl and holding up her brightly wrapped candy box. "I'm here to see Carson Fleming, I'm an old friend, I'm in a bit of a hurry, can't stay long, you know how it is—my, what beautiful earrings! Where on *earth* did you get them?"

The young woman blinked, processing all the information she'd just been given and obviously wondering which statement required a response. To Margaret's infinite relief, she chose the last.

"Why, thank you!" she giggled, raising a nervous hand to the garish chandelier dangling precariously from her tiny right earlobe. "They were a gift from my fiancé. He's an intern over at Nassau Medical. We're getting married in November."

Margaret, following the ancient ritual of female etiquette, dropped her gaze to the fourth finger of the girl's left hand. "My *dear*! Hang on to him!"

The nurse looked down at her minuscule diamond and laughed with proprietorial glee.

"I intend to," she purred. "Of course, Gus—that's his name, Gus—wanted to wait until his internship was—oh! I'm sorry. You said you were in a hurry, didn't you? Calvin!"

This last was called over her shoulder to a large black man in a green orderly's uniform, who sat on a couch in the station behind her, idly watching a tiny television set. He jumped to his feet and came over to them.

"This lady is here to see Mr. Fleming. He should be out on the lawn now, in his usual chair." Turning back to Margaret, she said, "He'll love the candy, I'm sure, but don't expect him to—well, you know. . . ."

Margaret, who did not know, nodded as if she did and followed Calvin from the lobby.

They made their way down a short corridor and across a rather crowded day room. The patients—"residents"—looked up with varying degrees of interest as she passed. The majority of them were elderly, she noticed, and obviously infirm. They sat on couches, in rockers, in wheelchairs, some watching television, others playing cards. Most of them, it seemed to her, were doing nothing in particular—just sitting by themselves, unattended, gazing vacantly ahead of them. A few had visitors today: young, well-dressed relatives with gifts of food and flowers. Restless children, in Sunday clothes they hated, sat uncomfortably still on uncomfortable couches, being fondled and fussed over by frighteningly old grandparents. This is it, she realized. The place I fear most, filled with the sort of people I most despair of becoming.

Her anxiety came creeping back, despite her triumph at the front desk. Why am I here? she wondered, staring around her with ill-concealed horror. What am I about to find? What connection could my niece possibly have to anyone in this place?

Carson Fleming, Carson Fleming. . . .

She followed Calvin out to the patio at the back of the complex. More chairs and couches outside; more patients, basking in the sun, attended by friendly nurses and silent orderlies. A huge lawn rolled away from the buildings, down to Great South Bay, which lay, majestically blue, a hundred yards before them.

The sun bore down on her as they crossed the sloping green lawn toward the water's edge. There was an enormous willow tree here, its wide limbs dropping leafy tendrils nearly to the ground, providing a carpet of shade. In this cool, dark haven several old-fashioned, white wooden lawn chairs had been placed, facing the bay, for the comfort and enjoyment of the inmates.

Calvin pulled aside the curtain of leaves and motioned for her to enter. She walked past him into shady darkness and stopped, looking around. There were four chairs under the tree, but only one was occupied. An old man sat with his back to them, apparently looking out over the water. Margaret could see the back of his white head and the bony, withered hand resting on the arm of the chair, clutching the corner of the blanket spread across his knees. As she watched, the orderly went around and knelt in front of the figure.

"You have a visitor," he said, "and she's brought you something. You just have a nice visit with her, and I'll be back later so's we can get you on in to dinner."

If the old man understood or even heard what was said to him, he gave no indication. With a nod to Margaret, Calvin left the arbor and walked away across the lawn. She was alone now, alone with the man in the chair.

She stood there behind him, looking down. So, she thought, this is he: this is Carson Fleming. This man in this chair is one of the most important people in my niece's life.

There was no going back. The thought entered her mind at that moment, as she looked away from the back of his snowy head and out through the leaves at the blue water and the white sailboats and Fire Island, hazy in the distance. She heard the faint buzzing of grasshoppers and the muffled sound of faraway voices, laughter from the patio.

Then she walked around the chair and turned to face him.

He sat hunched over, the blanket tucked around his shrunken form, staring down at her feet. Then he slowly raised his head and looked up at her face.

Margaret stared. She clutched the candy bar tightly to her chest as she looked down into the clouded, uncomprehending eyes, remembering them, feeling the rush of the years crowding in on her and the stab of stark, long-ago pain. Her lips began to move, seemingly of their own accord. She made a bad attempt at speaking, but nothing would come, so great, so profound was her distress. When at last she found her voice, it emerged as a single hiss of cracked sound, half word, half whisper:

"You."

As she watched him, breathless with surprise, she saw—or imagined she saw—the faintest flicker of recognition on his face. His eyes widened almost imperceptibly, and his tongue moved slowly across his parched lower lip. His right hand came up slightly, and the trembling fingers uncurled, seeming to point themselves directly at her. Looking at him, she fancied she saw a brief mirror of her own fear. For one odd, frozen moment, she thought he was going to speak.

Then, as she stared, the old man lowered his gaze from her face to the view of the water behind her, and the spark in the eyes went out. She leaned forward to study him. No, nothing. If her presence, or even her identity, had briefly registered, the moment had definitely passed. His expression was devoid of intelligence, of life. He didn't know she was there.

She whirled around and stood with her back to him, her left arm hugging the box, her right hand clamped over her mouth lest she cry out. The ocean flowed before her, implacable, eternal, host to the gulls and sailboats that even now flashed white against it.

The ocean. Sailboats.

Then, in that horrible moment, she knew.

He could tell her nothing, this old man in the chair behind her. His part in it was over. Forever. He sat there, incapable of speech or even of reason. She would not learn from him why he had gone—twice—to St. Thomas, or why he had been sent to Hawaii.

She must have turned around again, though she would never remember having done so. She must have reached forward with her trembling hands and placed the candy box in his lap. She might, for all she knew, have even taken a last, brief look at him.

Then she was running. Out from under the willow tree, up the sloping lawn, and around the side of the building to the parking lot. Curious, mildly astonished faces. Fumbling in the pockets of her dress, searching for her keys. The ignition turning and the engine roaring mercifully to life. The blur of the gravel drive and the winding main street of the town as she searched frantically for the signs that would lead her to the Expressway and thus home, to the comfort of her house, to the reassurance of her roses.

Robin pulled on a T-shirt over his faded jeans, ran his fingers through his hair, and went out on his balcony to wait for her. Almost five o'clock, he noticed: she'll be here any minute.

Her call had surprised him. He hadn't expected to see her again until Monday, the day after tomorrow. He'd promised her a Labor Day sail, and he'd keep his word. But he'd already packed most of his things and called American Airlines to reserve a seat on the Tuesday-morning flight to New York.

Now all he had to do was tell Margaret Barclay.

He looked back into the room at the phone on the bedside table, next to the Chablis and the two glasses he'd ordered from room service. No, he thought, it can wait until tonight, when she calls me for the daily report.

The daily report. His last two installments had been briefer than usual, because he had decided—for reasons he himself was unsure of—not to tell Margaret everything. Ever since the dinner party on Thursday, which he'd related in the most general of synopses. Very nice, he'd said: beautiful house; good food; the wife and the child were nice, but the husband was kind of strange. A going-away party for the husband and the child, she to relatives to Connecticut and he to a regatta in Palm Beach.

And how, she'd inevitably asked, is my niece?

Oh, fine, just fine, he'd said. Big lie. But he hadn't any qualms about it, because he had no real concern about the girl. She was silent and secretive, but she seemed to be relatively happy. Well, as happy as she'd probably ever be. . . .

As for the end of the evening, he'd thought about it a lot and come up with a theory that explained her behavior. She liked the woman, Kay, and the little girl, and she was, naturally, concerned about their welfare. She'd obviously concluded—as Robin had—that Adam Prescott was too good to be true. When he started behaving suspiciously, changing clothes and shaving after dinner, she'd pulled a Nancy Drew and followed him down to the beach, where her suspicions—and Robin's—had been confirmed. What they'd both seen was no big deal as far as he was concerned, but then again, he didn't know these people. He had no emotional connection to them. The girl would just have to live with her knowledge: he couldn't imagine her getting involved in a private family situation. If Adam Prescott and his mate, Kyle, were lovers, it was really no business of hers. But she certainly had been disturbed when she saw the two men together in the boathouse.

Enough, he decided. Just do your job.

So, on Tuesday he'd return to New York, after he went sailing with her. And maybe kissed her.

He was thinking about that, fantasizing about what it would be like to go to bed with her, when he heard the low, tentative knock on his door.

Perhaps that explained what happened when he opened it.

There could be no more putting it off: Margaret had run out of excuses. She'd watered the roses and run the dishwasher and sorted the laundry she'd found in the basket in the utility room. She'd made a pot of coffee and emptied all the downstairs wastebaskets into the big plastic garbage can in the garage. She'd actually begun to mop the kitchen floor before she remembered that Mrs. O'Rourke had waxed it only the day before. She stopped and leaned on the mop in the middle of the kitchen, staring down at the bright, immaculate tile. Had it been another day, any other day of her life, she would have laughed at her folly.

There were no more chores, no more busywork tasks to keep her from thinking about it. She was going to have to confront her worst fears. Now. Carson Fleming, the staring, drooling revenant, had seen to that.

It was a magnet, that little blue bedroom at the end of

the upstairs hallway. A mystical, irresistible lodestone that even now was filling the house with the sound of siren music, the music of those stories in those books that the girl so cherished. And it could no longer be ignored.

Sighing, bracing herself, Margaret put away the mop and pail and walked across the living room to the bottom of the stairs.

Afterward, the young woman sat up in bed and looked around her, adjusting her vision to the gloom. The sun had set at some point, and the faint light coming in through the open doors to the balcony did little to illuminate the situation. She peered into the gathering darkness, gradually making out the tangled sheets, the half-empty glasses on the table, the clothes scattered recklessly about the floor. At last she leaned back on her elbow and turned to look down at the man who lay next to her.

He was lying on his back on top of the sheets, a dark, well-muscled arm folded back behind his head. His hair and skin were damp, and one blond lock hung lankly down across his forehead. His eyes—so friendly, so different from Adam's!—were staring up at the ceiling. As she leaned over him, he turned his head to look at her, and his hand came up to touch her hair. She grasped the gentle fingers and pressed her lips to them. He grinned up through the darkness.

She'd heard, or read somewhere, that this was the ideal time of day for love. Not morning, when every part of you is still half asleep, and not the more traditional bedtime, when the average person is reasonably exhausted from some sixteen hours of activity. The perfect time was now, in the late afternoon, the middle of the day; when physical stamina and sensual awareness were at their peak.

Well, she thought, smiling down at him, there's truth in certain rumors.

Then, remembering at last why she was there and what she must now do, she stood up and began retrieving her clothes from the various places where they had fallen. She felt his gaze on her as she dressed and was grateful for his silence. She pulled on her sandals and reached for the nearly empty wine bottle. She filled her glass, picked it up, and went out onto the balcony.

The beach was deserted. A few lights shone from the empty bar and dining area, and the underwater lamps cast moving shadows on the turquoise walls of the pool. The roll of the surf a hundred yards before her was the only sound in the world. She leaned against the railing and sipped the cool, dry wine and wondered how she was going to get rid of him.

There was an explanation for what had just happened, she told herself, and it had nothing to do with love. It had to do with last chances, and with the need, in light of recent events, to feel desirable, desired. This afternoon had been the end of a long, silent, invisible process. She hadn't anticipated it, hadn't known it was going to happen. Yet every step she'd taken in the past few weeks had brought her here, to this bizarre yet somehow inevitable juncture.

She had come here to talk, to tell this man—what?— some lie or other. To fob him off. But then he had opened the door, and she had looked into his eyes and seen something that she recognized, that she understood too well. Without thinking, without hesitating, she had stepped forward—hungrily, desperately—into his arms.

And now, she reminded herself, it's over. I must act, and quickly. Otherwise—

"Penny," he said.

She looked back over her shoulder. He was leaning against the door frame, watching her, his rumpled hair and the brightly striped sheet he'd wrapped around himself giving him a silly, comical appearance. The sheet concealed his entire body from the neck down, even his arms; a white and pink and blue striped cocoon. It could almost be an African ceremonial robe, she thought. The sight of him like that filled her with a sudden surge of warmth, of tenderness. These were not the emotions she needed for this scene; she immediately turned back to face the view.

"Listen," she said, looking out, her back to him, her concentration entirely on what her acting teachers had called emotional memory. "I'm only going to say this once. You seem like a nice man, and we've had a lovely time together, especially today. You saved my life. But I'm going to leave now, just the same, and you and I will not meet again."

There was a pause, and then he said, "Just like that?"

"Yes," she answered, maintaining her detached, rather icy tone. "Just like that."

Another pause. She felt the first chill of evening and shivered slightly as she waited. He would not leave it at that, she knew. No one would.

Presently he said, "Are you going to tell me why?"

She shook her head. "I think you know why." She heard

the soft hiss, the expulsion of air. Impatience, perhaps, or exasperation. Good: he was playing the scene with her.

"No, I don't," he replied. "I don't understand you at all. I really don't know the first thing about you."

From somewhere deep within her she summoned a low, cruel laugh.

"Oh, yes, you do," she drawled, amazed at the sound of her own voice.

Then he supplied her with the necessary cue. "Diana—"

She whirled around then, fists clenched, hair flying, her face a perfect mask of rage.

"Don't call me that!" she screamed. "Don't ever call me that! I'm not Diana! There's no such woman, as if you didn't know! Don't you dare call me Diana!"

He rushed forward, extending one arm from the folds of the sheet, his face registering his confusion. "What the hell—"

"Oh, please!" she cried, recoiling from his attempted touch. "The other day, when I woke up in the water and saw you coming toward me, reaching out to me. You called my name. Do you remember? *Not* Diana. My *name*! Don't stand there pretending you don't know it, Mr. Robert Taylor—or whatever your name is!" She leaned forward, shouting into his startled face. "Just do me a favor, okay? Go back to New York. Go back and report to your *employer*! Tell her I'm fine, never been better. Tell her I have a job I like, with people I like. Tell her that I do *not* appreciate what she's done; that I don't want her sending her lackeys to spy on me; that I'll come home when I'm good and ready. Go *now*, Mr. Taylor, and stay the hell away from me!"

Done, she thought. That's a curtain line. Now for the exit.

She glanced at his face, which was now bright red with embarrassment. As well it should be: he obviously hadn't realized his mistake in the water until this moment, when she told him about it. I must get out of here, she thought, before I lose the momentum, before my real emotions take over and I decide not to hurt this perfectly nice man.

He was between her and the door. She barged forward, bringing up her hand to push past him. At the same moment, he reached out and grabbed at her shoulder with his exposed arm.

"Wait," he began. "You don't understand. Please, I must—"

It was as far as he got. She slapped his hand away and thrust herself forward, knocking him aside, her shoulder actually pushing, rather hard, into his chest. The collision of their bodies sent him staggering away toward the railing.

She was already through the door and inside the room when she heard the awful sounds behind her: the dull thud as his body hit the railing, and the strangled cry. She whirled around in the doorway to see him lurching out over the rail, his body imprisoned in the sheet, trying desperately to reach back and grasp the wrought iron with his one free hand.

She saw it happening an instant before it happened. She even moved, lunging toward him with outstretched arms, trying to grab him, or at least the sheet, with her hands. Too late. She saw his hand reaching back, grasping air, and a brief flash of his startled, terrified eyes. There was one dreadful second of frozen time as the reality of it overwhelmed her senses.

Then he fell. His body slid over the rail and down some twelve feet to the patio in front of the hotel room below. She arrived at the rail to see him drop, twisting once in midair as the sheet finally came free of him. He landed almost squarely on a white-cushioned chaise longue directly underneath the balcony. Almost: there was a glass-topped, metal-rimmed outdoor table next to the chaise, and she winced as she heard the sound of his forehead striking its edge, and the shattering of glass. His head snapped back, and he uttered a soft moan as his body bounced on the chaise and tumbled sideways to the patio. He landed facedown, arms splayed, one leg bent up behind him, half on, half off the chair.

She stood there paralyzed, staring down at the naked white body that lay unnaturally still among the shards of frosted glass. As she watched, the pink and blue and white striped sheet fluttered down to land, light as a feather, on the gray concrete beside his bleeding head.

The two discoveries in the blue bedroom were very nearly simultaneous.

Margaret was sitting in her niece's little desk, gazing down at the scrapbook and the sheets of paper that lay beside it. The tiny desktop lamp provided the only illumination in the room, a little pool of dim light that washed across the surface before her, an island in the darkness.

She knew what she would find, had known before she entered the room. It seemed to her, now, as she sat here, that she'd figured it all out in that strange moment this afternoon, as she stared down at the old man in the chair by the water's edge. Coming here was merely an act of reinforcement, to prove to herself beyond any doubt that her awful suspicion was correct. Only with this act could she silence the siren music.

She reached up with her shaking fingers and opened the book. She leafed slowly through the now-familiar first pages, letting the whole terrible story from Islip twenty years ago play once again before her eyes. The headlines; the pictures of her sister and her brother-in-law and the little girl and the mailman and the innocent suspect; the long columns of newsprint recounting every sad detail. Then, at last, the final entry: the empty boat and the facsimile of the heartbreaking note in Albert's careful, legible hand.

Then, with a massive, incalculable effort, she willed herself to turn the page.

And there it was. Obvious. Indisputable. Unmistakable. Hawaii, ten years ago. The newspaper had turned nearly brown with age, and the grainy photograph had never been clear in the first place. But now, as she looked at it again with wiser eyes, she recognized it at once. She'd seen this picture several times in the past few days, but always she had been looking in the wrong place. She'd been studying the face of the woman. Just beyond the figures in the picture was a huge open doorway through which could be glimpsed a grove of palms, with a tiny dock at the edge of the ocean in the background.

The ocean. Sailboats.

When she could tear her eyes away from the sight, she

looked over at the pages of reproduced photos next to the scrapbook. St. Thomas, one week ago. She leafed through them, searching faces. A long shot of the sailboat, and one of Kay Prescott, and the little girl, and her niece, and—

There was only the one picture, on the bottom page, and it was not distinct. Only the back of a head and a shoulder, blocked by the smiling people in the foreground. But she was certain.

The ocean. Sailboats.

She sat there in the dark bedroom, her body slumping, huddled over the dim lamp as if for warmth. She slammed the scrapbook shut and pushed it away from her, to the corner of the desk. With a sweep of her arm, she sent the faxed pages fluttering to the floor. This action revealed a final piece of paper, a lined sheet from a yellow legal pad that had lain hidden underneath the others.

At first she didn't notice it. She shut her eyes tightly and bowed her head, giving herself over to her despair. The sound began as a low rumble deep within her, growing to a moan as it forced its way up from her soul. It rose in pitch and volume as it rushed past her lips and out into the room, a high, keening wail of desolation that vibrated on the windowpanes and echoed from the pale-blue walls. Finally, when all her breath was gone, the anguished scream subsided, stopped. The siren song—the jangling, buzzing noise inside her head—was still. Silence.

When at last she opened her eyes and the real world came slowly back, she found that she was staring down at a sheet of yellow paper. Two words, scrawled across the top in large capital letters with a black felt-tip pen.

DIANA MEISSEN.

She stared, pulling the memory from somewhere that seemed a long time ago. Oh, yes, she thought. Dr. Stein had made notes. He'd pointed out the significance of Diana, the goddess in three forms. And he'd told her something else, something about a valley in Germany. . . .

Diana. The Greek goddess, from the stories her niece so loved. She loved mythology, and drama—anything theatrical. And puzzles: Scrabble . . . word games. . . .

Anagrams.

The second shock was as violent as the first had been a few moments before. She gaped down at the yellow paper as the word jumped up at her, rearranged itself in midair, and struck her in a single, overwhelming rush of crystal clarity.

And she was on her feet, knocking the chair over backward in her surprise, in her flight across the little room to the night table next to the bed, to the telephone on the table, and No, her mind cried over and over as she fumbled with the dial, No! It isn't Germany, it isn't a valley at all.

The young woman ran from the room and down the stairs to the beach, calling into the office as she passed. Please come quickly, there's been an accident—something like that. She wasn't aware of her words, only of her frantic need to get to him, to see if he was all right. By the time she rushed around to the front of the building, the night manager was right behind her.

She stopped at the edge of the patio and raised her hands to her face, staring down. The manager, a large, capable-looking man, pushed past her and knelt beside Bob Taylor. He placed his fingers lightly on Bob's neck at the base of his throat, then lowered his head until his ear was next to Bob's mouth. He stood up quickly and ran back toward the office, shouting to her as he passed.

"He's alive. I'll call the hospital. Cover him with that sheet. Try to keep him warm, but don't move him. Understand?"

She nodded absently, listening as his running footsteps receded. Then she stepped forward and dropped to her knees. She lifted the striped sheet from where it lay and placed it as gently as she could across his body. She leaned over him as the man had done, straining her ears, barely able to make out the shallow, ragged breathing. But it was there. It was definitely there. . . .

Reaching over, she took his outflung hand gently in her own. She remained there for a long time, whispering quietly to him, unaware of the manager's return and the gradual assembling of two or three other guests around the patio, the low murmurs and concerned glances, the hot tears that streamed down her cheeks and dropped softly onto the sheet. She didn't know, would never remember, what she whispered to him, whether encouragement or endearment or confession. All three, perhaps. She would only remember that at some point, somewhere in the long, anxious minutes that she knelt there waiting for the ambulance to arrive, in his room behind the balcony above her head the telephone began to ring. It rang and rang and rang, and then was silent.

PART THREE

GODDESS OF THE DARK

SEVENTEEN

SUNDAY, SEPTEMBER 1

"HI, MOMMY."

"Hello, darling. How's Connecticut?"

"Oh, it's super! I wish you and Diana could be here. They have two new horses!"

"That's lovely. Have you been riding yet?"

"Sure, we did that first thing. We've been twice now. Aunt Fran is taking us to the movies tonight, and tomorrow there's a big picnic at their school."

"Well, sounds like you're going to be busy. I'll see you Thursday, sweetheart. Say hello to the kids for me. Now put Aunt Fran back on, all right?"

"Okay. 'Bye, Mommy. I love you."

"I love you, too, darling."

* * *

"Bolongo."

"Hello, I wonder if you can help me. I've been trying to reach one of your guests, but he's not answering his phone. Robert Taylor, in room—let me see, I wrote it down somewhere—"

"Robert Taylor? Umm—well, ma'am, Mr. Taylor—one moment, please. . . ."

"Hello, this is the hotel manager. You were inquiring about Mr. Robert Taylor?"

"Yes, I—"

"May I ask to whom I am speaking?"

"This is Margaret Barclay. I'm calling from New York, and I've been trying to reach—"

"Are you a relative, Ms. Barclay?"

"A *relative*? I—umm—is something wrong with Mr. Taylor?"

"Ma'am, are you a relative?"

"I don't—yes, I'm a relative. I'm—I'm his mother."

"Oh. I'm sorry to have to tell you this, but there's been an accident. Your son is in St. Thomas Hospital. There weren't any papers among his things, and we weren't able to ascertain—"

"Excuse me, what sort of accident? Please, is—my son—all right?"

"I really—let me give you the number of the hospital, ma'am. They'll be able to tell you more than—"

"Yes, but what happened?"

"He fell, Ms. Barclay. From the balcony outside his room. I believe he has a concussion, and a broken leg, but they seem to think—"

"Fell? Was he—oh, God—was he—how?"

"I'm sorry, ma'am. The doctors can tell you more. Or perhaps Ms. Meissen."

"Ms. Meissen?"

"The young woman who saw it."

"She *saw* it?"

"Yes, ma'am. She was with him when it happened. Here's the number of the hospital. . . ."

The young woman replaced the receiver in its cradle and wandered away from the phone booth, down the walkway in front of the tourist shops of Havensight Mall, toward the piers where two cruise ships were docked.

So, she thought. That's that. The end.

She hugged her upper arms with her hands, regretting her decision not to wear a sweater. Evening in St. Thomas could be so chilly: she should know that by now. At the moment she didn't seem to know anything, couldn't think clearly.

Car: poor, sweet, wonderful Car, my dearest friend. Gone.

There was a bench near a row of little palm trees in front of the entrance to the dock. The shopping center was nearly deserted at this hour: the stores were closed, and the passengers aboard the ships would be sitting down to dinner now. She was alone in the tiny park. She sat down and leaned back, staring up at the enormous liner before her. Lights shone through the portholes, and she could hear faint music and laughter from the decks above. Her eyes traveled slowly along the majestic hull to the prow. She squinted through the gloom of dusk to make out the name of the vessel: *Song of Norway*. Lovely, she thought vaguely. A beautiful name for a beautiful ship. *Song of Norway*: that was the title of a Broadway musical, the story of Grieg. Car used to play the original cast recording on his stereo. The two of us would sit in his living room together for hours, listening. "*Strange music in my ear. . . .*"

Car. Carson Fleming. Gone.

Margaret had never known about him. He had been her secret. He had visited her twice when she was in the hospital, bringing candy and flowers. Once his wife had been with him. After that she hadn't seen him again for eight years, but every year he'd sent her birthday and Christmas cards. Then, when she was fourteen, the day after her first expulsion for fighting with the other girls who teased her about her parents, she'd gotten on a train and gone to see him at his home in Suffolk County. His wife was ill by then; she died the following year, just before . . .

It was difficult to describe the bond that existed between herself and Car. She'd read somewhere about the Japanese custom of indentured servitude: if you saved someone's life, you became responsible for that life. Car apparently subscribed to that theory, even though he hadn't technically saved her from anything. But he'd unwittingly played a part in the most terrible event of her life, and their fates had become inextricably intertwined.

She'd sneaked out of the house almost every day in the weeks after Mrs. Fleming succumbed to cancer, tending to the shattered, lonely old man. They would have seemed an odd pair if anyone had observed them: the fifteen-year-old girl making meals and cleaning up after the elderly widower, who sat in the big, battered chair in his dingy living room, staring at the walls. But nobody did see them. Their friendship had remained a private matter.

In their mutual isolation, they had reached out to each other. She had visited him at every opportunity, often coaxing him out of his house for trips to the movies or the park or the shopping mall. She always paid for everything: his meager pension had been depleted by his wife's long, costly illness. She even took to giving him an allowance of sorts. He always accepted reluctantly, promising to pay it back. He never had, of course. Even at fifteen, she was wise enough to realize that he drank too much. Never in her presence, but she knew just the same.

He had returned his young friend's charity with a far greater gift. It was Car—not the doctors or the priests or Margaret—who had slowly convinced her that she had done nothing wrong on that awful night all those years before. She had been traumatized, and the shock had served to blot out the entire incident from her memory. All she remembered was a face wearing a mask, and the moment, the next morning in her mother's bedroom, over her mother's body, when she blurted out her macabre confession.

"Mommy's dead," she'd whispered to an astonished Carson Fleming. "I killed her."

For eight years, until she met the mailman again, she had actually believed her own words. She thought she had somehow caused her mother's death and her father's subsequent suicide. The old man had helped to banish **that** misconception. It had taken him the better part of two years.

Then, when she was sixteen, on the eve of her departure for boarding school upstate, exactly ten years to the day after the nightmare in Islip, he had again come to her aid. She would never forget that day in the beginning of September when she had risen as usual and gone downstairs for breakfast with Margaret. She'd been in the act of lifting a spoonful of cereal to her mouth when she happened to look up at the open newspaper Margaret was perusing. There, across the table, four feet in front of her face, was the front page with the photograph and the lurid headline: "HOTEL HEIRESS SLAIN." Her idly curious gaze had traveled down from the young woman standing beside the rattan chair in the well-appointed tropical home to the desolate face of the victim's grieving husband.

And everything had stopped. Been changed. Forever.

It was the eyes: she'd recognized them immediately.

As soon as she could get away, she'd stumbled onto the train and made her way—blindly, automatically—to Car's house in Islip. With trembling hands, she'd held out the newspaper for his inspection. He'd stared at the photograph, not at all convinced. But she had been adamant, and finally—for her peace of mind more than for any other reason—he'd agreed to her hastily drawn-up plan: she would go off to school, and he would be her "legman." That was what he'd called himself. She'd paid for everything, even putting him "on retainer," which she'd continued to pay every three months for the rest of his life. And he'd actually gone to Hawaii. . . .

Five days later, she'd been summoned to the telephone in her dormitory in New Paltz and heard his hoarse, incredulous affirmation of her worst fears. He had seen the figure in the mask. He had stood ten feet away, on the steps of a courthouse in Hawaii, staring, looking past the black hair and beard at the face of Andrew Phillips.

The face of Albert Petersen.

The next time they met, weeks later at his house in Islip, she'd made it clear to Car that they would not go to the police. They would wait and watch. But she rested easier in that time because she knew, at last, the identity of the figure in the mask.

And she knew where he was.

Then, three years later, the yacht in Hawaii had blown up and the body had been found. The woman and her child and the mate from the yacht all disappeared, along with the hotel woman's fortune. Only two people in the world could guess what had really happened. She'd been nineteen then, and she and Carson Fleming had known, even as the story broke, that the remains on the yacht were mostly likely those of the mate, and that the mistress, Kimberly Brown, and her child were probably at the bottom of the sea.

Remembering her own childhood, she'd told Car her suspicions about her baby-sitter, Karen Lawrence. He'd agreed with her this time: Lawrence was presumably dead. She'd even wondered whether the friend from the

Merchant Marines—Charlie something, who'd carried on so at the memorial service—might have been involved.

The next day, she'd quit Nassau Community College and flown to Hawaii. By the time she arrived there, the figure in the mask had once again disappeared. Her frustration, her despair of ever finding him again had prompted the reckless drink- and drug-soaked excursion to San Francisco. She'd blocked out the following months just as she'd blocked out the night of her mother's murder. When she came to her senses, she was strapped into a bed in a rehab center on Long Island. The baby that had been growing inside her had been taken away from her, and with it her will to live. Then her half-hearted excursion to Harvard and the suicide attempt, and Juana Velasquez, and a vague new idea of becoming an actress. Not for fame or fortune, however: she knew innately that if the phantom who plagued her ever turned up again, her best chance was to play by his rules.

Which was exactly what she'd eventually done.

Car had been frantic all the time she was in California and at the clinic on Long Island. He'd received the usual money every three months, in envelopes postmarked San Francisco, but he had not otherwise heard from her. He'd even considered the possibility of approaching Margaret Barclay, but then—wisely or unwisely, he was never certain—changed his mind.

Upon her release from the clinic, she'd immediately gone to see him. He had been overjoyed to find her again, and he threw himself into the role of "legman" with even more energy. He decided, privately, that it was his sacred mission, his quest, to find her enemy again in whatever new lair he had chosen. He had the idea in his head that this intense young woman was in need of a champion of sorts, a protector, and he would play that role.

He and the girl had at least one lead in their quest for the man in the mask: their quarry's positive mania for keeping to old patterns. They knew that their search would probably end in a place somewhere in America, near the ocean and sailboats. And money. An oceanside playground with plenty of attractive, rich, available women. That had narrowed the field considerably.

While she went off to Harvard, Car took to collecting daily newspapers from the most likely locales. Every day—thanks to old acquaintances at the post office—he received some thirty newspapers, and he spent a good portion of every afternoon and evening scanning the society pages. Her dismissal from Harvard and her attempt at suicide spurred him on, bringing an even greater sense of urgency to his search.

He eliminated New York and Hawaii and anywhere close to them: their quarry was not insane—not in *that* respect, at any rate. He eliminated lakes and rivers: a serious boat person seeks only open water. He eliminated colder, northern reaches such as Maine and Washington and Canada. The Gulf Coast and the Caribbean were the most likely suspects. . . .

He slowly became aware during this time—and he mentioned it to the girl—that he was beginning to think like their quarry. This filled him with an odd satisfaction, gave him the truest pleasure he'd experienced since the death of his wife. He began to realize that he was actually enjoying it.

Florida. Louisianna. Texas. Southern California. Cape Cod. Chesapeake Bay. The Carolinas. Puerto Rico and the Virgin Islands. The papers arrived, were perused and removed. Once or twice in that long, long time he felt a fleeting sense of despair, but he suppressed it and soldiered on. There would eventually be a new wife, he reasoned, and that woman would definitely be rich—the sort of person who occasionally made headlines.

The headline—and the all-revealing photograph—had appeared on the society page of the *Virgin Islands Daily News* one day in June, three years ago: "LOCAL WIDOW MARRIES SPORTSMAN." He'd passed it on to the girl, and she'd pasted the notice onto the last page of her album, but the sight of the happy, smiling people had upset her so much that she'd removed the photograph and destroyed it. But now they knew: his name was currently Adam Prescott, and he was living in St. Thomas, Virgin Islands.

Car had left immediately for St. Thomas. A few days later he was back, with names and addresses and a now-familiar story. A rich widow, a yacht, and a house near the ocean. This woman, Kay Belden, now Prescott, had a child. A girl named Lisa.

She'd thought about all of this for a long time. Car had left her alone, waiting for her to decide what they were going to do with their new knowledge. He was all for going to the police, but he knew his young friend would not agree with him. She would probably come up with some other plan.

As, indeed, she had. She'd gone to work every day in the little dress shop in Glen Cove and enrolled in acting classes at the Herbert Berghof Studio. She'd had to audition for a place in the class, of course. Uta Hagen herself had been her monitor. She'd never been so nervous—well, almost never—but she relied on her instincts and trusted in her material.

For the audition she had chosen *Antigone*. Not the speech she'd declaimed so melodramatically in school; this time she used the final scene of the play. An audacious, presumptuous move: Miss Hagen had probably played the part herself at some point, and she'd be familiar with the interpretations of Katharine Cornell and Irene Papas and Genevieve Bujold and Heaven knew which other illustrious colleagues in both the original version and the modern retelling by Anouilh. But it felt right—it was a role that she alone understood completely.

No toga this time, just street clothes. She'd stood in the classroom before the great actress and allowed the emotions to flow through her. She had been condemned to execution for attempting to bury her brother, defamed as a traitor. She spoke of duty, of honor, of the sacred demands of blood. Of her need, regardless of the pronouncements of kings, to bury her dead and thus preserve the name of her family. Her crime had been one of necessity, beyond the petty laws of men, and the gods, she knew, would forgive her. As the soldiers bound her hands and led her away, she turned at the last moment to the watching, weeping chorus.

"Behold me," she'd commanded, "what I suffer. . . ."

And so her acting training had begun. She'd studied, storing every lesson of characterization and carriage and makeup, waiting for the day when they would be put to excellent use.

She'd waited for almost three years. She knew that Kay Prescott and her daughter were safe for the present, though she did not share that knowledge with Car.

When she'd asked him, several months ago, to return to St. Thomas, he'd asked no questions. He'd merely gone and observed and returned with the information she needed. Adam Prescott spent most of his time on his yacht, and he did not seem to have a specific girlfriend, though Car had seen him with several women. The mate on the *Kay* was a young man named Greg, a womanizer who hung out every night at a bar called Sparky's. Furthermore, Car had reported, there was a new addition to the household at Cliffhanger, a homely young woman named Sandra Franklin who was the child's companion.

One month after Car's reconnaissance mission, a young woman named Selena Chase had arrived in St. Thomas. An attractive, amoral, green-eyed redhead: it was vital that Selena be a redhead. Karen Lawrence and Kimberly Brown had both been redheads. . . .

What had followed was astonishingly easy. The chance meeting, the sailing trips on the *Kay*, the kissing and cuddling (she shuddered at the memory), and the tacit promise of more—if only his wife were out of the way. It had been Adam, of course, who first mentioned the plan. And Selena Chase had readily agreed.

He was following the pattern, as she'd known he would. She was to return in two months and contrive to replace Sandra Franklin. There would be a string of local robberies, and he would leave the island just before the crucial time. Then, on Monday, September 2, he would sneak back to St. Thomas and murder his wife.

Labor Day. That, she knew, was the pattern. Ten years to the day since Darlene Bishop Phillips. Twenty years to the day since Madeleine Barclay Petersen.

It was her suggestion that he actually leave the island, a definite departure from the original blueprints. In the first two incidents, as far as she could ascertain, the mistresses had merely been used as alibis—though she had no doubt that both women had been in on the plans. This time she would be a sort of stage manager, giving him an alibi two thousand miles away while she made sure that everything at Cliffhanger was in place. He seemed to enjoy her participation in the evolution of the crime: he was not averse to improvements in his pattern, as long as the main rule was observed. It had to be Labor Day. She knew that, and she was relieved to know that Kay would not be harmed prematurely.

So the plans had been agreed upon, and Selena Chase had returned to New York to wait out the two months until the beginning of August, when another young woman—a dark-haired, brown-eyed potential governess named Diana Meissen—would arrive on the scene. A new identity and new coloring, just in case anyone had noticed and remembered the redhead on the *Kay*.

It was then, in New York, that her scheme had very nearly been destroyed. Adam Prescott had been remarkably easy to win over and manipulate, but she had not counted on a surprise opponent: Carson Fleming.

It had been her fault entirely; she was painfully aware of that. She would take it to her grave. Her beautiful plan had been jeopardized, and Car had been irreparably damaged, and all because she had made one incredibly stupid mistake.

She had told him.

She'd lied, of course. She hadn't told him her true agenda, but the lie had been bad enough. She'd sat there on the couch in the little living room in Islip and informed him in a calm, rational tone of voice about Labor Day. About the significance of the date: Madeleine and Darlene Bishop Phillips. She told him that on this anniversary Adam Prescott planned to kill his wife.

Then, without batting an eye, she told him that she was going to kill Adam Prescott.

Now, sitting on the bench among the trees beside the docks, staring up at the *Song of Norway*, she closed her eyes, feeling the hot tears on her face, the anguish in her soul, remembering. Remembering his stunned expression and his automatic sputter of protest. Remembering the jerk of his body as he tried to rise from his armchair, to rush across the room and stop her—physically, if necessary—from achieving her reckless objective. Remembering his hand coming up to the side of his head, his eyes squeezed shut in a grimace of unbearable pain, the little squeal that escaped his lips as he sank to the floor. She remembered the telephone and the white-clad figures that seemed to materialize in the living room mere moments later, and the word spoken by one of them as he leaned over the inert form: *apoplexy*. And she remembered the long, wild minutes—hours, days—in the back of the shrieking ambulance, clutching his hand and searching his vacant eyes and whispering to him, to herself, to God, over and over.

"I'm sorry I'm sorry I'm sorry I'm sorry I'm sorry."

And now Car was gone.

She stood up from the bench and walked slowly through the empty shopping center to the Land Rover.

An orderly had found him late yesterday afternoon. He was sitting under a willow tree, facing the view, a box of chocolates resting on his lap. The candy was from a visitor, a woman who'd come to see him earlier in the day. She wondered who had visited him. He hadn't had any friends, as far as she knew. Since his wife's death, she had been his only contact with humanity. She silently thanked the woman, whoever she was, for her kindness.

I did this, she thought as she got into the Land Rover. I caused Car's death. I caused Bob Taylor to fall from the balcony. Now he, too, is in the hospital. Sandra Franklin. Nancy Breen. Trish Manning. Greg.

And soon, very soon, other catastrophes will be ascribed to me. Kay Prescott and her daughter. Juana, inadvertently involved. Adam, having dinner now in a hotel in

Palm Beach, alone, or maybe with his friend Roger, laughing and joking. Waiting for tomorrow.

Margaret: Mom. Perhaps my greatest victim. . . .

The engine roared to life. With a little shake of her head, she pulled out of the space and headed for the exit. Now, she told herself, there is only one thing left to do. I must go back and prepare for tomorrow. I must be ready to do this, to see it all through to the end.

I must play my role.

Margaret had to wait a long time for the doctor to be summoned to the phone. She sat on the burgundy velvet couch, kneading the folds of her dress with her free hand. The scrapbook lay on the coffee table in front of her, opened to the page with the clipping of the murder in Hawaii: "HOTEL HEIRESS SLAIN." Her nervous gaze flickered constantly back and forth between the photograph and the logotype at the top of the page, the Gothic banner proclaiming the name of the newspaper, with something far more interesting in tiny letters directly below it.

The date.

She had tried calling the detective agency, but all she'd gotten was a recording. A woman's voice—apparently black, apparently middle-aged, and obviously bored by her job—had intoned that Mr. Yakimadoro and his associates were gone until Tuesday, and that messages should be left after the beep. She had not been able to bring herself to leave so vital a message on so impersonal a device, and she had no other number for Mr. Yakimadoro.

She wondered about Robin Trask's family, assuming he had one. Did they know anything? Were they on their way, even now, to St. Thomas? Would the authorities at St. Thomas Hospital be aware that she, Margaret, was not his mother and therefore not entitled to information regarding him?

She had just convinced herself that it was a chance she had to take when she heard a small clicking sound and the doctor at last came on the line.

"Darling," Kay breathed into the phone, "I was just thinking about you. How's everything there?"

"Fine," Adam answered. "Roger and Sally are having dinner with me here at the hotel. They're waiting in the lobby, so I'll keep this short. How are you and Diana holding up?"

"Oh, we're having a high old time," Kay said. "Just girls together. She really is the loveliest young woman. We spoke to Trish earlier. She's much better. She'll arrive here Tuesday, so she'll be ensconced by the time you get back." Then, keeping her voice light, she told a lie: "I spoke to Lisa. She said to send you her love, and to tell you she's rooting for you and Roger."

There was the slightest pause before he replied. "That's nice. Listen, I have to go. Are you going to be home tomorrow?"

"I should think so," she said. "I don't really have any Labor Day plans. Diana's going out sailing with Bob Taylor. She asked if I'd like to join them, but I've a marvelous feeling I wouldn't be a welcome addition to the party."

She smiled to herself as she heard the Land Rover pull up in front of the house.

"Well, good for her," Adam said. "Taylor seems like a nice guy. Tell you what: I'll call you tomorrow, about two o'clock, all right? I'm busy later in the afternoon, but at two I'll definitely be here, near the phone. How does that sound?"

"Terrific," Kay replied, looking up and smiling as Diana came into the house. "Hi. I'm talking to Adam," she told her.

"Give him my love," the younger woman said, dropping onto a couch on the other side of the room.

"I'll expect your call tomorrow," Kay said into the phone. "Around two. Diana sends you her love."

As she grinned over at Diana, Kay heard her husband say, "Send her mine. Good night, Kay."

She said, "Good night, darling. I love you—"

But he was already gone.

She had just replaced the receiver and was in the act of rising when the phone rang again. She picked it up.

"Hello," she said.

There was silence at the other end of the line. Not quite silence: a faint sound of static, and another sound that might have been breathing. She waited a moment.

"Hello," she said again. "Kay Prescott."

The static continued for a few seconds. Then she heard a distinct click, followed by a dial tone. She shrugged and put down the receiver.

"Wrong number, I guess," she murmured as she went to

join Diana, smiling at the prospect of another cozy slumber party.

The moment she heard the woman's voice, Margaret knew that she could not possibly go through with it. She slammed down the receiver and pushed the telephone away from her. Bad idea, she thought, clutching her stomach as the wave of nauseating panic began, ever so slowly, to subside. A very bad idea. . . .

It was the doctor's news that had prompted so rash an act. She would never normally have considered it. But as soon as the full extent of Robin's incapacity had been made clear to her, she had been infused with a fear that had caused her to cut short the doctor's droning diagnosis and call Directory Assistance. Prescott, she'd requested, at a place called Cliffhanger. Without pausing to think it through, she'd dialed the number.

She had known that *he* would not answer: Robin had told her that "Adam Prescott" was in Florida for a sailboat race. If "Diana Meissen" picked up, she'd simply break the connection. She was really expecting Kay to answer, and that was what had happened.

But it was no good. She didn't know Kay Prescott, had not the slightest conception of what sort of woman she was. How could she, Margaret, even begin to tell this story to a complete stranger? That fact, however, had struck her only at the last possible moment, when she heard the clear, low-pitched, cultured voice on the other end of the line. An intelligent voice, she thought, the voice of an educated, well-bred woman. A woman such as I. . . .

And what if it were I? she wondered. What would I do if I picked up the telephone one day and heard a strange woman slandering my husband and my friend, telling me that my life and my child's life were in danger? A disembodied voice, shrill and hysterical, babbling about shocking crimes committed long ago in remote places, involving people I'd never heard of? What would *I* do?

I'd hang up, she realized. Then I'd call the police.

The police. She had only the vaguest notion of what sort of government, what sort of police force, they would have down there. The Virgin Islands were a territory, she knew, one of the three territories belonging to the United States, along with Guam and Puerto Rico. They had governors, she believed, either elected or appointed by the president; she wasn't sure which. There would, presumably, be police: a sheriff, perhaps, or commissioner.

No. She would not call the Virgin Islands police, or the governor, or anyone else. They, like Kay Prescott, would think she was a lunatic.

Robin Trask had only just regained consciousness. He had a concussion and a broken leg, and he had been shot full of painkillers and anticoagulants. He was resting comfortably, the doctor had assured her, and was not to be disturbed. Out of commission. . . .

She even, as a last resort, considered the possibility of calling Cliffhanger again and asking to speak to her niece, "Diana Meissen." Telling the girl that she knew everything, that her plan had been discovered. She was in the act of reaching out for the phone when her hand stopped, drew back.

And then what? she asked herself. What would "Diana" do? Laugh, probably, and hang up. A life might be saved—perhaps more than one—if, indeed, any lives were in danger. But her niece would never, ever speak to her again.

With this thought, Margaret Barclay drew herself up. She rose from the velvet couch and walked out into the cool nighttime air, to the patio, bathed in the blue-white wash of moonlight. To her roses, glowing softly in the darkness.

I will be alone, she thought. But then again, when has it ever really been otherwise? My parents, my husband, my beautiful sister: gone, all of them. And my niece—the coffee cup and *World's Greatest Mom* notwithstanding—is not my own, does not belong to me. She was never mine.

When at last she reached her extraordinary decision, she actually spoke it aloud. Her voice, clear and strong, traveled across the garden, ringing with the weight of her unshakable conviction.

"So be it," she said, and then she turned around and walked back into the house.

Throughout the evening, the young woman constantly caught herself looking over at the telephone.

Don't be ridiculous, she told herself. You're not going to place the call. Even if you did, what on earth could you possibly say? "Stay out of my life"? "Mind your own business"?

"I love you"?

No, she would not call Margaret. She would sit tight. She checked her watch: midnight. Only fourteen hours, and then . . .

She regarded the woman sitting on the couch across from her. Kay Prescott was off on another one of her giggling, gossiping, pointless anecdotes. But they'd shared a bottle of red wine between them since dinner, and the older woman was beginning to slow down. Very soon Kay would yawn and stretch and mention sleep.

That must not happen, she reminded herself. Kay Prescott must not sleep tonight.

As soon as felt she could decently interrupt Kay's monologue, she stood up and reached over for the empty bottle and glasses. "I think we could do with something cold to drink. How about some of Nola's iced tea?"

"That would be lovely," Kay agreed.

"I'll just be a moment," she said, heading for the kitchen.

She went through the swinging door and placed the bottle and glasses on the counter. As she turned toward the refrigerator, her hand slid down into the pocket of her robe and withdrew the little plastic bottle, her prescription from Kay's doctor.

That part of the plan had been the easiest. Doctors, she mused, usually end up giving people exactly what they request, no questions asked. She'd gone to Kay's doctor and complained that she had trouble waking up, getting started in the morning. She'd mentioned that her family doctor back in New York had once given her some tiny white pills that she took upon rising, thereby alleviating the problem. Would it be possible for her to get some of those now?

Of course. Within the hour, she had been in possession of what was essentially speed.

Now, in the kitchen, she opened the vial and shook out two minute tablets. Then, as an afterthought, she got one more.

Perhaps I'll have one as well, she thought as she began to pour the tea.

It's going to be a long night.

EIGHTEEN

MONDAY, SEPTEMBER 2

LABOR DAY

THE PRETTY BLOND Pan American representative at Miami International glanced down at the name printed on the ticket, then smiled up at the dark-haired man with the mustache.

"You're traveling to San Juan with us this morning," she said. "Just the one carry-on bag, right? Is this your first trip there?"

"Yes, it is."

"Beautiful beaches. But I don't suppose you'll be doing much swimming, with that arm."

"Skiing accident. The cast comes off next week. I'll still be on the island, so . . ."

"Good. The sling is the worst part, isn't it? I broke my arm once, when I was a kid. Fell off a trampoline, of all things!"

She giggled self-consciously as she prepared his boarding pass. He's handsome, she thought, in a sinister sort of way. Such intense brown eyes. No wedding ring. Too bad about his posture: he'd look better if he stood up straight. I wonder if that scar on his cheek was part of the skiing accident.

"Here you are. Gate seventeen. Thank you for flying Pan American. Have a nice day, Mr. Phillips."

The man smiled.

"I intend to," he said.

"I can't believe this," Kay said, staring down at the Scrabble board. "That's five games—three to two, your favor—and it's eleven o'clock in the morning! What on earth do we think we're doing?"

She regarded Kay Prescott across the table, suppressing an odd desire to answer her rhetorical question truthfully.

"You'll sleep better tonight," she said at last. Then, because she couldn't resist, she added, "Trust me."

Looking past Kay's shoulder, she saw that the late-morning sun was flooding down onto the deck outside. The deep-blue sky was devoid of clouds. A beautiful day, she thought—as beautiful as I could have wished it to be.

The shriek of a gull swooping by the glass doors brought Jumbi to her feet. She jumped out from her place under the table and ran toward the doors, yapping furiously. She reared up on her hind legs, placed her front paws against the glass, and barked at the birds beyond her reach on the other side.

She watched the animal for a moment, then returned her attention to Kay Prescott.

"Isn't she silly?" Kay was saying, an indulgent smile brightening her weary eyes. "So protective. She fancies herself a guard dog."

"Yes. I've noticed that."

"Amazing," Kay said. "Anytime there's the slightest commotion around here, she turns into Canine Cop! I sometimes wonder what she'd do if there was ever any real trouble. Of course, Fred trained her to obey us, but I suspect he may also have taught her some other things." She leaned forward conspiratorially. "I think Adam's a little afraid of her: can you imagine!"

She smiled at the woman and said nothing.

"Well," Kay sighed at last, "what shall we do now? It's strange, really, that I'm not at all tired. I can't remember the last time I went this long without sleep. Any minute now I'm probably going to keel over and crash."

Yes, she thought. Probably.

Then, forcing a smile, she said, "One more game, Kay. But first I have to call Bob at Bolongo. I'm meeting him at one o'clock, and I want to be sure he rented the right boat."

She got up and went over to the telephone as Kay began picking up the tiles from the board. Keeping her back to the table, she dialed seven digits and carefully lowered a finger onto the cradle, severing the connection. She thought about him for a moment, lying in his hospital bed as she'd seen him when she went there the day before, his right leg encased in plaster and elevated by wires. He'd been asleep then, and she'd been able to spare him only a fleeting glance before ducking back down the hall to join Kay in Trish's room. Of course, neither of the other women knew that he was there, just a few doors down from Trish.

"Hello," she announced into the dead receiver. "Bob Taylor, please, room seven.... Hi, Bob, it's Diana. Are we still on for this afternoon? ... Good.... Did you get the catamaran, the blue one I pointed out? ... Great.... Oh, don't be such a sissy. There's nothing to it. I'll show you how. Okay, I'll see you in about two hours. 'Bye."

She put down the receiver and headed for the kitchen. "I'll get us some coffee," she said. "Just be a minute."

"Fine," Kay called from the table.

She went into the kitchen, spooned instant coffee into two mugs, and filled them with water. While they were in the microwave oven, she reached into her pocket and extracted a second little plastic bottle. Her own prescription, from New York. For her chronic insomnia. She took a small amount of raw hamburger from the refrigerator, dusted it with the contents of one small gray capsule, and rolled it into a ball. When the coffee was ready, she added the powder from two capsules to Kay's cup. She placed the mugs and the meat on a tray and returned to the living room.

"Jumbi," she called, "I have a treat for you."

The dog abandoned her vigil at the glass doors and bounded dutifully over to the table. She swallowed the hamburger in one swift gulp and resumed her original place at Kay's feet.

"I won the last round," Kay said, reaching for her steaming mug. "I get to go first."

The young woman sat down and slowly raised her own cup.

"Yes," she murmured, looking directly into Kay Prescott's eyes. "You go first."

At that moment, the telephone rang.

Mr. Theolonius Gridley of West Horsefoot, Texas, might have been a small-town insurance salesman for most of his fifty-nine years, but he knew a fag when he saw one.

He'd been standing here, minding his own goddamn business, trying to shave off some of the stubble he'd accumulated in nearly twelve straight hours of traveling to get to this godforsaken place that his wife had insisted they come to for their first real vacation in more than ten years. Putting Theo Junior and Betty-Jo through college had nearly bankrupted him, not to mention all those goddamned bills Bertha kept running up at Neiman Marcus.

The airport men's room smelled of urine and cigar smoke and God knew what else, and the tiny plastic disposable razor he'd bought from the vending machine was not very effective, to say the least. He winced as he nicked himself for the third time, cursed Bertha for the hundredth time, and stole another surreptitious glance at the weirdo standing next to him.

When Theo had come in, the guy had merely been spraying something on his hair. He'd parked himself next to the man with a grin and a "Howdy" that the man had ignored. A Noo Yawker, probably. But as Theo was attacking his own beard, the other fellow had produced a tiny bottle and a brush and started painting some strong-smelling, clear liquid on his chin. Then, to Theo's amazement, the guy had picked up a little circle of hair—black, to match the hair on his head—and pressed the false goatee into place.

"Hoo-ee!" Theo had exclaimed. "That stuff stinks to high Heaven. What's goin' on—is it Halloween here in Puerto Rico, or what?"

The black-haired man had glowered at him briefly and said nothing. Then—and this is what had completely floored Theolonius Gridley of West Horsefoot, Texas—the guy had reached into his bag and pulled out an eyebrow pencil. A goddamned eyebrow pencil, just like Bertha used! He'd reached up with the thing and begun painting his mustache and eyebrows.

Fag, Theo decided. He rinsed the residual foam from his now clean-shaven jowls and blotted his nicks with Kleenex as best he could. With a swift, disapproving frown at the other man, he threw away the plastic razor and hurried out of the place before the guy could do something really weird, like make a grab for the Gridley family jewels.

Bertha wasn't gonna believe *this*!

The young woman stared over at the ringing telephone, her hand holding the tile poised above the Scrabble board, her mind working furiously. Then, before the other woman could move, she was up and across the room.

"Prescott residence," she said into the receiver.

When she heard the voice on the other end of the line, she closed her eyes, exhaling in relief. For a moment she'd thought it might be—

She listened a few seconds and said, "Yes, of course. One moment, please."

She looked over at the woman seated at the table. She waited as Kay raised the cup to her lips and took another long sip of her coffee. Then she held out the phone.

"It's for you," she said.

"Sorry to bother you, darling," Trish said into the phone, "but I'm just so *bored* I could scream."

She was lying flat on her back in the uncomfortable hospital bed, and her scalp beneath the bandage was beginning to itch again. Holding the receiver in one hand, she reached over with the other for the button that was supposed to elevate the head of the bed. Nothing happened. Nothing works in this damned place, she thought as she fumbled for the other button, the one that would—allegedly—summon the nurse. Let's see if *that* works, she mused.

"Oh, you're not interrupting much," Kay said. "We're playing Scrabble. We've been up all night, can you believe it?"

"I can believe it," Trish muttered, squirming on the lumpy mattress as she once again depressed the call button. "So why don't the two of you come here and play Scrabble with *me*?"

"I might just do that later, if I can stay awake. After two

o'clock, though. Adam's calling me then. But Diana can't come; she's going sailing this afternoon with Bob Taylor."

"Lucky *her*," Trish replied. "Come visit me if you can. If not, I'll see you tomorrow when you spring me from this joint."

"Hang on, Trish," Kay laughed. "You'll be at Cliffhanger in no time."

"Please, God!" Trish said. *"Ciao."* She put down the receiver and tried to make herself somewhat comfortable while she waited for someone—*anyone*—to answer her summons.

Making the best of a bad situation: that cliché had occurred to her a hundred times in the last few days. She had always relied on her excellent sense of humor to see her through the worst times, and it had been working overtime of late. If she were honest with herself, she would have to admit that she was still very frightened.

That awful moment when she'd reached for the light switch in her darkened apartment, aware of the unnatural silence. The creepy feeling that had washed over her, the feeling of being watched. The spicy, vaguely familiar scent that had filled her nostrils in the second before she heard, rather than actually felt, the thud as something heavy smashed down on her skull. The horrible pain she'd awakened to here in the hospital, with Kay and Jerry and some doctor crowded around the bed, staring down at her.

She moaned, feeling the dull throb in her head as she remembered. I came close, she realized again. I came very close to death. Some grotesque, twisted, evil human being stood in the darkness in my house, in my *home*, waiting for me.

Somebody tried to kill me.

The door opened and a young native woman in a white uniform came into the room. Seeing her, Trish sighed with relief, pushed away her dark thoughts, and smiled, reverting to the famous hearty humor that no longer came naturally to her.

"Oh, honey, am I glad to see you! I can't get this bed to work. Can you possibly raise me to a normal human position?"

"I'll try, Miz Manning," the girl said, reaching for the button. Nothing happened. "Oh, deah. Well, I best be gettin' de custodian to come hab a look at dis ting."

Trish stared at the ceiling and groaned theatrically. "I shouldn't be here. I should be out sailing with Robert Taylor."

The nurse leaned over her. "Robuht Tayluh?"

Trish shifted her gaze from the ceiling to the girl's face, wondering why she looked so surprised.

"Not the movie star," she explained. "No relation."

To Trish's surprise, the nurse burst into laughter.

"I know," she replied. "He jus' be tellin' me dat hisself a few minutes ago, when I took him his lunch. I di'n' know you knew him, Miz Manning."

It was Trish's turn to look surprised.

"There's a *patient* here named Robert Taylor?" she asked.

The girl nodded, grinning. "Right down de hall."

"And he said that? 'No relation'?"

"Yeah, dat's what he say."

Trish stared at her for a moment. She turned her head and stared at the telephone. Then she threw off her covers and stood up, wincing at the sudden stab of pain. She pushed past the astonished nurse and walked out into the corridor.

The dog was already asleep under the table, and Kay Prescott was giving every indication of soon joining her. Twice in the last five minutes she'd dropped tiles onto the floor, and she'd almost lost a turn by misspelling a simple word. Every few seconds her brows shot upward in an effort to keep her eyes open.

She sat across the table from Kay, hands in her lap, waiting. It won't be long now, she mused, watching in fascination as the drug slowly overwhelmed the other woman. Soon.

Two more turns and it was over. Kay picked up two tiles, stared vacantly at the board for a moment, and slowly put them down again. She pushed back her chair and rose unsteadily to her feet.

"Sorry, Diana," she muttered. "I just can't go on another min . . . I . . . I have to lie down. . . . Adam . . . Adam will be calling at two o'clock. . . . I . . ."

She jumped up and ran around the table, grabbing Kay's arm as her body began to sag. Within seconds she had walked her over to a couch and lowered her onto it. By that time Kay had lapsed into unconsciousness.

She straightened up over the woman's inert form and

pushed her hair back out of her face. Twenty minutes to twelve, she noted. Start with the dog. . . .

She managed to pull Jumbi out from under the table and lift her in her arms. Staggering under the animal's surprising weight, she made her way through the kitchen and utility room to the pile of blankets in one corner of the garage. She lay the dog down and came back into the house, locking the garage door just to be sure that Jumbi—in the unlikely event that she awoke anytime soon—could not get back inside. Step One completed: she had gone to the trouble of getting herself on friendly terms with the dog just for this, so that she would accept the drugged meat from her hand.

It hadn't been easy: Jumbi, alone among them, had been wary of her from the moment she first saw her. The dog disliked Adam, and her canine resources had immediately informed her of the primal link between Adam and the young woman. The trust, the friendship that had so carefully been built up had gone against the dog's basic instincts. Yet it had been vital to the plan. If Jumbi were to bark or attack or be in any way underfoot at two o'clock this afternoon, it could prove to be disastrous.

Back in the living room, she walked over to the telephone, lifted the receiver from its cradle, and put it down on the table. Then she went over to the couch and gazed down at Kay Prescott. The woman looked so peaceful in repose—so harmless, so completely innocent. Sleep, Kay, she thought. Sleep. . . .

Now for Step Two.

With a massive effort, more than had been required

with the dog, she leaned down and picked up the unconscious woman in her arms. Dead weight, she realized: the
worst kind. Slowly, stepping carefully, she began her long,
arduous journey.

The flight attendant adjusted the scarf at the top of her
attractive blue and red uniform and walked briskly up the
aisle to the last row of the First Class section. She leaned
over seat 6B and gently shook the sleeping passenger's
shoulder.

"Rise and shine!" she sang. "Welcome to St. Thomas.
You're on terra firma now. Feels good, doesn't it?"

"Yes. Yes, it certainly does."

"The other passengers have gone already. Come with
me and I'll take you into the terminal where we can get
your luggage."

"I don't have any other luggage," the passenger replied.
"Just the bag up there."

The hostess reached up to the overhead compartment
and pulled down the shoulder bag. "Here you are. Now,
follow me and we'll get you off this nasty plane!" She'd
had a great deal of experience with this. Noting the passenger's pale complexion and dilated pupils, she added,
"Will you need some assistance?"

The passenger surprised her by quickly unbuckling the
seat belt and standing up.

"No, thank you. That won't be necessary."

The young woman walked slowly up the hill, across the
lawn, and in through the front door. It was done: there

was no going back now. Soon Adam would come, and all the rest would follow.

She shut the door, leaned back against it, and closed her eyes, listening to the peculiar silence in the empty house—peculiar in that the crashing of the surf and the crying of the birds on the cliff made it anything *but* silent. Yet it seemed to her that nothing in her harsh, violent existence had ever been as still, as peaceful as Cliffhanger was at this moment.

The love she'd felt for Margaret and Carson Fleming and Juana Velasquez had come close, but even that fell short of this. And everything else in her life had been lies, illusions. The nuns, the classmates, the professor at Harvard and her other occasional partners: they had not loved her. Dr. Stein and his legion of colleagues: what was she to them that they should weep for her? The people in San Francisco, including the father of her almost-child: beneath the fringe and the beads, behind the endless talk of love and peace, they had been vapid, selfish children. And Adam—well, her love for him had been the strangest, cruelest paradox of her entire sad, ridiculous, meaningless existence.

Her gaze traveled slowly, lingeringly around the room. Funny, she reflected. It had seemed like a perfectly ordinary place when she first arrived here, nearly four weeks ago. Beautiful, yes, but ordinary. Yet in these four short weeks, how everything had changed! This house, she realized, had been transformed, and she with it, as if the two of them were by some enchantment merging, becoming one. This was what she had been forever seeking: this strange, elusive sensation, this calm. This was home.

Home, she thought. At last. The feeling coursed through her body, tingling, tantalizing, oddly familiar. The thrill was exquisite, voluptuous, and yet she knew—as she had always suspected—that it was temporal. This will not last, she told herself. It never does. I have spent a lifetime dreaming of today, praying for it, needing it as I have needed nothing else. But now that the day has finally arrived, I am aware merely of how quickly it is passing. Perhaps my dream—Antigone's dream—is a false illusion. Perhaps the gods are wise in denying certain wishes. . . .

Then, pushing these thoughts from her mind, she moved. She walked resolutely across the room and up the stairs and down the hall to the bedroom.

"Are you sure that's what Mrs. Prescott said?" Bob Taylor asked.

Trish nodded and sat back in the chair next to his bed. "Yes. She said that Diana was going sailing with you. Now you tell me Diana was with you when you fell off the balcony—please notice that I'm not asking any questions about *that*! So the question is, why hasn't Diana told Kay that you're here in the hospital?"

The young man leaned back against the pillows and shook his head. "I don't know. . . . Mr. Prescott's in Florida, right?"

"Yes. Some race or something. Why do you ask?"

"I'm not sure," he replied. "Why don't you try Cliffhanger again?"

Trish nodded and reached for the telephone. She looked down at his leg, swathed in bandages and elevated by pulleys. That can't be very comfortable, she thought as she dialed. God, it's almost funny: his leg in a cast and my head in a—

Her head. The darkness, and the silence, and reaching for the light switch. The cracking sound, and the pressure at the back of her skull, and the spicy, sweet smell of—

"Bay rum," she said. She had spoken without thinking, involuntarily, and Bob Taylor stared at her blankly: he obviously did not comprehend. Neither, yet, did she.

"It's still busy," she said, placing the receiver back in its cradle next to his bed. "It's been busy for nearly an hour now. I don't understand any of this."

"I do."

The two of them stared at each other, wondering which had spoken. Then they both turned, startled, toward the figure standing in the doorway of the hospital room.

She got the suitcase from the closet, extracted the scrapbook, the black gown, and the wig and laid them out on the bed. She took the box of dye from the vanity-table drawer into the bathroom, turned on the faucets, and wet her hair. The job was quick: she was now something of an expert.

While she waited for the color to set, she carefully removed the tinted contact lenses from her eyes and stored them in their little case. She walked back into the bedroom and laid out the pale-blue stationery and the envelope on the desk. She checked her watch: ten minutes to one.

Finally, she reached once more into the suitcase and pulled out the knife. She stood in the center of the little bedroom in the quiet house on the cliff, staring down at the beautiful Greek dagger, feeling the weight of it in her trembling hands.

The young man behind the desk at the car-rental agency looked up and smiled. "Good morning. Welcome to St. Thomas. May I help you?"

"Yes," said the dark, bearded gentleman in the rather loud flower-print shirt and reflective sunglasses. "I believe y'all have a reservation fuh me. Petrillo."

He showed the young man a boarding pass from LIAT Airlines, with the name written across it in magic marker. Then he handed him the rental agency's receipt, stamped PAID IN FULL.

"Right," said the young man, glancing down at his list. "Your car is waiting in the lot outside. Just show the attendant this." He handed the tall, obviously Southern gentleman a claim chit. "Thank you for using our service, Mr. Petrillo, and remember: we try harder. Have a nice day."

"Why, thank ya! Y'all have a nahce day, too."

At that moment, a boisterous family of four headed by a heavyset, obnoxiously strident woman with a look of grim determination on her face pushed their way up to the counter. With a sigh, the young man turned his attention to them.

Much later, when he was informed of his small part in

the drama, he would barely remember Mr. Petrillo. He would not even be able to come up with a useful description of him. Not that it mattered: by then it was too late to do anything about it anyway.

She put down the blow-dryer and inspected her hair in the mirror. Yes, it was good. Not quite the original shade, but close enough.

She picked up the long, flowing black robe and put it on. Yes; this was good, too. Antigone, in such attire, had faced her tormentors.

Then she piled her hair on top of her head and fitted the wig into place. The final touch. Good. . . .

At last she took the scrapbook from the bed and placed it on the vanity table. She sat down, reached for the stationery with the somewhat odd-looking name engraved at the top, picked up a pen, and began to write.

Adam drove across the island, keeping to the hills and back roads, being careful to avoid the waterfront highway, which would be packed even on this national holiday. There were four cruise ships in port today, and resort towns could not afford to shut down for Labor Day. In St. Thomas, it was business as usual.

Kauai, ten years ago, had been the same: cruise ships and tourists. Fortunately for him, Darlene's beach house, like Cliffhanger, had been far removed from all activity. No one had seen or heard anything. And Islip, not being a resort, had been a snap. The little Long Island town had slept that night twenty years ago, unaware of what was happening in the darkness around them.

He smiled. Islip; Kauai; St. Thomas. Such colorful places, so very, very far from Farnsworth, Minnesota.

He had left *that* place far behind him. There had been nothing to hold him there anyway. His father had wandered off somewhere with some woman, never to be seen again, when he was a baby. His mother, heartsick and silent, had managed for the two of them as best she could. That was what everyone had thought, at any rate: no one had been around to see the abuse, the beatings, or the harness that kept the child a literal prisoner in the house while she went off to work every day.

After she began to drink, she didn't always come home regularly, leaving him bound to the bedpost for days, sometimes, while she was out with one of the ever-growing legion of "uncles." He always knew when there was a new "uncle" around: his mother would cover her blond hair with a bright-red wig and begin behaving in a strange, exciting, overtly sexual manner. Then she would disappear, often for as long as a week.

He would lie on the bedroom floor, wet and stinking from his own urine and excrement, tired and hungry, listening to the sounds of the birds that skimmed the lake behind the house. Birds: those ultimate free spirits. They went where they wanted, when they wanted, with no chains, no harnesses. That, the child on the bedroom floor told himself, was God. No chains, no harnesses. Freedom. From places, from people, from emotions of any kind.

When he was thirteen, he figured out how to get out of the harness when she left and back into it before she returned. Thus he was able to wander about the house, and thus he ultimately found the box in the corner of the attic containing the few possessions his father had left behind. The books with the beautiful pictures of sailboats in them; the pink shirt with the little monogram, AP for Arvil Pederssen, on the pocket; and the knife. The gorgeous Greek dagger. The Kouronos. He would hold it in his hand for hours, feeling its power.

It was the knife that had given him the idea.

He'd started with the birds. He wasn't sure why—not now, anyway. Because they were free, maybe, as he was not. Because they could fly. Because they sang outside the window, sang in the sunlight as only those beloved of God could sing. Because God loved the birds and did not love him. For whatever reason, he'd started there: spreading kernels of popcorn along the windowsill and sitting, silent and unmoving, waiting. He would wait for hours sometimes before one of them swept down from the sky or from the branches of a nearby tree. One would always start it, creeping warily toward him, pecking nervously at the corn; and other always followed. When one of them cast aside its natural fear and came close to him, he would reach out—gently, gently—with his trembling hand. He would hold it firmly, staring down at its little face, studying the wide-eyed fear, and feeling the useless flapping of now-helpless wings against his fingers. He would watch, transported, filled with a power he never understood and could not begin to describe. For as exquisitely long as he possibly could, he would hold its life in his hands.

Then he would use his father's knife.

He'd started with the birds, always imagining they were his mother in her red wig. He'd buried them in the disused flowerbed that ran along one side of the house, heaping dirt over their bodies, waiting for the day.

He'd waited for years, planning carefully, dreaming of it, watching in breathless anticipation for one rare moment when his mother was alone in the house with him, with no "uncles" around.

That opportunity had arrived on Labor Day, exactly thirty years ago. By then there were more than two hundred birds in the flowerbed.

He would never, ever forget the day. He would never forget the thrill of it, that wonderful, helpless expression of shock on his mother's face when she whirled around to see him standing there in the kitchen behind her, the Kouronos in his hand.

He had hesitated, watching her, feeling the power as she stared at her husband's ski mask, the one he'd found at the bottom of the box in the attic. He'd suspended the moment for as long as he possibly could; then, just before she could scream, he had meted out his justice. He had proved his majesty. That glorious experience had been—

Excellent.

Perfect.

God.

Nobody in Farnsworth had been the wiser. How awful, they'd said afterward. The robbery and the murder, and that poor seventeen-year-old knocked unconscious, bound to the bed, unable to remember anything about the intruder except that he wore gloves and a black ski mask.

He smiled now, turning onto the last road, the one that would lead him past Bolongo toward Cliffhanger. The beautiful house on the cliff overlooking the sea, so different from the house by the lake in Minnesota. On his eighteenth birthday, three months after burying his mother, he'd left that place behind for the Merchant Marines and New York, with nothing but his astonishing good looks and his desire. To be rich, to be free, to be a bird on the ocean.

To be God.

Money was his ticket to freedom, and he had no trouble finding rich women to supply it. Madeleine Barclay had allowed him to be God. So had Darlene Bishop.

And now, he thought, turning in through the stone portal with the brass plaques gleaming in the sun, it's Kay Belden's turn. It's time to be God again.

She placed the pages in the envelope, sealed it, and carefully wrote the name on the front. Then she set the letter on top of the scrapbook on the vanity table, picked up the knife, and left the bedroom.

At the bottom of the stairs, she turned and went across to the foyer. She knelt for a moment and did what had to be done, then straightened up and turned around. As she walked toward the sliding doors, she noticed the glare of the sunlight on the glass. Almost two o'clock. . . .

It was fitting, somehow; the perfect time for it. She'd

always imagined that it was at this time of day that Antigone had taken her honor and her fate into her own hands. The harsh Greek sun would have poured down on her, glinting on the shackles that bound her hands. She would have felt the warmth permeating her skin as she walked, erect and defiant, to her courageous destiny.

She strode out onto the sundeck, into the light, and over to the edge. Gripping the railing with her outstretched hands, she stared out at the glistening surface of the sea, not seeing it. Instead she saw the glistening eyes of a hundred sorrowful, black-robed women. She listened: above the roar of the surf, she could hear them as they filled the sky with their lamentation.

Thus attended she stood, erect and defiant, awaiting the entrance of the king.

He stood under the tamarind tree, preparing himself for his entrance. The house was silent, still—almost too still. He thought about that. Kay would be in there, he thought, waiting for his call. The dog, if Diana had been successful, would be asleep somewhere.

He smiled. *If* Diana had been successful: as if he had any doubt of that! She was such a remarkable creature. Every step of the way, he had deferred to her excellent suggestions. Where had she been twenty years ago? Ten years ago? He'd been on his own then. Karen and Kimberly had been such idiots, such dull accomplices. They'd both managed to look bewildered and upset and to babble just the right things to the authorities, but that had been the extent of their usefulness. As for Charlie and

Stephen, well . . . Stephen had been an excellent stand-in on the burning yacht in Kauai. And he'd gotten him to meet him there that day in the same way he'd gotten all the others to do his bidding.

There had been no body on the *Madeleine* twenty years ago, but only because Charlie, for all his love, had been too decent, too conventional in his thinking. So Charlie had not been let in on it; only Karen Lawrence had known, and she and Charlie had never known about each other. Karen had been disposed of, but his lover in the Merchant Marines had been spared. The mental picture he had of Charlie weeping at the memorial service, with Margaret Barclay and that goddamned brat beside him, never failed to amuse him.

Charlie and his daughter. His only living victims.

His daughter.

He should have killed her. He thought he'd struck her hard enough, but he obviously hadn't. His worst moment in the first operation had come when the doctors told him and the sobbing Margaret that the child was out of danger, would live. He'd fallen to his knees and loudly thanked God, while inside he had cursed himself for making such a stupid, costly mistake. When he disappeared, six months later, he'd only been able to take half of Madeleine's fortune with him. The rest had gone to the child. He often wondered where the brat was now, and cursed her existence as he did every day of his life.

He would not make the same mistake with Lisa.

Yes, he thought now, watching the quiet facade of Cliffhanger, there had been several mistakes in the first operation. But not in the second. Kimberly had played her part, as had Stephen, and he'd sat tight for three years, the grieving widower. Then the explosion on the *Darlene*—Stephen had arrived on cue for a lovers' tryst with him—and shortly afterward he'd seen to Kimberly and her little girl. Another brat. And he'd managed to get away with *all* of Darlene's money.

He'd perfected his art with the second operation. But this time, ten years later, he'd begun to wonder just how he'd go about getting rid of Kay. Greg was of no use to him: he wasn't even homosexual, much less in his thrall. And there didn't seem to be an appropriate girl. . . .

Then he'd met Selena, and everything had fallen into place. Greg knew about Selena, which signed his death warrant. The disposal of Greg at sea had gone without a hitch, and he'd cast his eye around for just the right new mate. He'd found him in Kyle, the handsome young hippie that Jack and Nancy had introduced him to at a party at the yacht club. Kyle was interested, sexually speaking. That interest had soon become love: Adam had seen to that. A fire on the *Kay*, with Kyle as stand-in . . . yes, perfect. Kyle knew nothing of the plan, nor would he. He would merely be held in reserve—for another two or three years, maybe—until his charred remains could be useful in the fiery climax of this latest endeavor.

As for Selena, well . . .

She was disposable, too. They all were. She'd gone the longest of any of them without succumbing to his sexual charms, but that would change after today. It was her abstention, he knew—her refusal to do precisely as he wanted—that made her so exciting to him. But she, too, would come around. They always did.

And after that, when he'd tired of her, she would die.

Now. Now was the time. He looked up at the clear, sunny sky beyond the branches of the tamarind and smiled. The energy filled him as it always had, always would: the keen anticipation of proving, once again, his ultimate, unquestionable power.

He reached up and gently pulled the goatee from his chin. Then he dug in his pockets for the gloves and the ski mask. He pulled the gloves on slowly, savoring the feeling of excitement, trying to make it last as long as possible. With a soft moan of pleasure, he pulled the mask down over his head. Then he walked steadily, carefully across the drive and up to the front door. A gentle turn, a gentle push, and he was in the house.

She had decided not to kill him. If she killed him, she would surely go to prison. If by some friendly chance she was acquitted, it wouldn't really matter. She would merely be in another kind of jail; marked, singled out, ostracized. She would be *that woman*, the one who murdered her father, expelled forever from the company of men.

Car was dead. Juana, with the erring Carlos and her child for distraction, had no time for friendship. Bob Taylor—in the hospital bed she'd put him in—was lost to her, as was any man who made the terrible mistake of loving her.

And Margaret, her last, best hope, would be gone. When she learned that her niece had committed the ultimate outrage, she would cast her out. From her house and from her life. There would be no one, no one in the world, who cared.

She very nearly smiled then, looking out over the blue Caribbean. The irony of it: Greek tragedy indeed.

He should have killed me, she thought. I've known it all along, and I have finally come to accept the judgment of the gods. On that night, twenty years ago today, my father murdered my mother and tried to murder me. He should have finished the job.

Now, all these years later, the gods would finally be appeased. There was no way he could make this look like a random act of violence. They would find her here or on the rocks below, and they would find the scrapbook and the letter to Margaret confessing everything, and someone—that little old police chief, perhaps—would put it all together.

Then, at long last, they would have him. And then, at long last, Madeleine Barclay Petersen would sleep.

She gripped the rail and listened to her weeping chorus and waited for the cold, swift plunge of the knife into her back.

He stood just inside the doorway, assessing the situation. The living room was hushed, silent, waiting. A church, he thought. A holy place, awaiting the blessing that I, and I alone, can bring to it. He grinned as he looked slowly around him.

Then he saw her. She was standing at the railing on the sundeck, her back to him, gazing out to sea.

Excellent.

He reached down into the pot of the spider palm next to him and dug around in the loose dirt until he felt it. He straightened, raising the knife up before him.

And stared.

The shock coursed through him as he brought it closer to his face and peered at its shiny, familiar form. A Kouronos. An exact duplicate. . . .

Then he smiled again. Selena really *is* on my wavelength, he thought. Right down to this, the instrument of my justice. What a remarkable woman she is: I may actually be sad to see her go. And I must remember to call her Diana now.

He clutched the knife in his outstretched left hand, feeling its power as an extension of his own. Kay had not moved. She stood at the railing, oblivious, her long black robe and curly red hair moving ever so slightly in the soft tropical breeze.

Perfect.

The sharp, indescribable thrill suffused him as he walked slowly forward across the room, toward the sliding glass doors. He paused in the doorway, watching. The roar of the sea against the rocks below; the cries of the birds outside the bedroom window; his mother standing at the sink in her bright red wig, looking out across the lake.

God.

He stepped silently out onto the redwood platform and moved across it, closing the gap between them. Now, at last, he stood just behind her, looking down. He had to see her eyes: that was part of it. The most important part.

He had to see that she understood, that she knew what was happening to her.

He held the Kouronos up above her in his left hand, prepared to strike. With his right hand he reached out, grasped his mother by the shoulder, and whirled her around to face him.

The hand on her shoulder was more of a shock than the knife would have been. She gasped as she was spun around, and the red wig flew off to fall into the void behind her. She stared up at the black mask, her eyes widening as the platinum hair tumbled down around her shoulders.

This time, however, she was not afraid. Her gaze traveled up his arm to the Kouronos and back down to his startled, pale blue eyes, the mirror of her own. Her surprise was quickly replaced by contempt. When she spoke, her voice was filled with loathing.

"Hello, Daddy," she said.

Then she reached behind her to grasp the rail and leaned back, tilting her head, baring her throat to the knife.

Albert Petersen staggered backward, lowering the knife, away from her—away from this woman who was not his mother, not Kay Belden. He stared, disbelieving, at the pale hair and eyes so like his own, so like—

His lips moved, contorted, as he struggled to speak. Finally, the words came out in a strangled gasp.

"Allie?" he whispered. "Alberta?"

He looked at her, at her head flung back over the precipice, into her mocking, contemptuous eyes. As he watched, she began to laugh softly, her lovely lips curled upward in a sneer.

Then, with a cry of animal rage, he was upon her.

The first cut slashed across her forehead. Instinctively, she let go of the railing and brought her hands up as the blood rained down into her eyes, blinding her. The second stab sank into the base of her neck, just inside the collarbone. She fell to her knees as the pain began to register, overwhelming her, weakening her body and her resolve.

It seemed to be happening very slowly. Her father was the merest shadow now, a dark mass looming somewhere just above her. Through the darkness and the pain and the blood, she barely saw him raise the knife again, barely heard the shout.

"Albert!"

He must not have heard it, either, she thought as she sank lower and he brought the blade once more down into her body.

They both heard the gunshot.

The impact sent him crashing forward. He tripped over the girl and fell heavily against the railing. He heard the cracking sound as the wood splintered, felt the sudden numbness in his chest. The Kouronos fell from his hand and clattered down onto the deck.

At the last possible moment he turned his head and

looked behind him. At Potter holding the gun, and at the woman standing next to him. Into her eyes.

Then the rail gave way, and he was soaring outward into the blinding light, suspended for a moment like the birds outside his bedroom window. He spread his arms and flew, out into the sky and down, down toward the glittering surface of the sunlit sea, where only he ... was ... God.

She felt his leg strike her shoulder, saw him fall against the railing and disappear from her view, but her clouded mind was no longer able to grasp the significance of it. She tried to raise herself up from her kneeling position, but her legs would not support her. She looked up toward the source of the noise she seemed to be hearing from a long way off and saw—or thought she saw—several dark, indistinct figures coming toward her. She swayed, tasting the blood in her mouth, attempting to blink away the curtain of red that now veiled her eyes. In her last conscious moments she reached out to the figures with her hand, moving her lips, oddly aware of the fact that she was making no sound. And yet she had to tell them. She had to communicate it to them. They were her chorus, and it was her final speech.

But all she knew was that she was falling and the redwood boards were rushing up at her and everything was spinning around her and Mommy was waiting and behold me, she commanded as she toppled forward and the last glimmer of light faded, behold me! I have upheld ... that ... which ...

* * *

The little group of people in the doorway moved aside to let her pass. Chief Potter lowered the gun to his side and stood looking over at the still, bloody form lying facedown on the sundeck, slowly shaking his head from side to side. Then he turned to the two uniformed officers behind him and pointed back into the interior of the house. They nodded and followed Trish Manning, who was already dashing toward the master bedroom, calling Kay Prescott's name as she went. A sergeant walked swiftly over to the telephone and dialed. The sounds of running footsteps and doors opening and closing faded as Trish and the policemen moved away through the house, searching frantically for the other woman.

She was aware of the eyes upon her as she stepped out onto the sundeck, aware of the odd impression of quiet despite the roaring of the waves against the rocks below. Her senses had been dulled by the medication she'd taken in order to make the flight, and the succession of surprises she had confronted in her two hours on the island had further impaired her natural reactions. But now it was all beginning to register, becoming suddenly, sadly clear to her.

The police chief watched as she went over to the girl and lowered herself down onto the deck beside her. She reached out as gently as possible to turn the girl over and place her head in her lap. The dark blood trickled down, unheeded, onto her white linen suit.

She pushed the pale gold hair back out of the lovely face and stared down at it, remembering, reliving in mere seconds all the warm, tender moments and words and feelings they had taken a lifetime to create. There were bad things, too: it had not always been easy to love this girl. But only the positive images would come to her, and she wondered at that for a while before she arrived at the explanation. Then, looking down on the sundeck, she knew as much as anyone can ever know about it. Love was never easy. And yet, as difficult as it is, she thought, the very worst of it is easier—oh, so much easier—than living, existing, going on without it.

Holding the girl as close as possible, leaning over until her tears fell down to wash away the blood, Margaret Barclay began, every so softly, to sing. It was the children's song that she had always crooned to the child, as she had sung it, years before, to Madeleine.

Frère Jacques, Frère Jacques,
Dormez-vous? Dormez-vous. . . .

AFTER

KAY STOOD at the gate, staring out over the shimmering runway as she waited for the plane to land. Her friends were just behind her, and she could feel the warmth of Trish's hand on her shoulder. Jerry was saying something, but she wasn't listening, couldn't distinguish the words, so great was her concentration.

She was feeling better now, better than she had in the last week, ever since that awful moment when she awoke, groggy from the drugs and anxious, disoriented, staring blearily around at the crude walls of the little boathouse on the beach. She had come out of the fog as from a nightmare, waiting as the room spun around her, trying to orient herself. And then she had run wildly, desperately up the path, shouting all the way. Across the lawn and in through the open door and straight into the arms of Trish, who had grabbed her and held her and would not let her go.

It had seemed to take hours for all of it to sink in. Trish was there, holding her, and there were others as well. Chief Potter and several policemen and a tall, regal-looking older woman she'd never seen before. Trish was speaking quietly, in an even tone of voice—something about Adam, and about Diana. Adam, they told her, was dead. He'd fallen from the sundeck after Chief Potter shot him. Why? she'd asked blankly. Why had the chief shot her husband? There must be some mistake: Adam was in Florida. And where was Diana . . . ?

Finally, the facts had begun to register. She had been sitting on a couch by then, drinking something warm and sweet, and the older woman was sitting next to her, grasping her hand. The woman was telling her about Diana—whose name, it seemed, was not Diana—and about her parents. Long Island. Some sort of robbery and murder. And something about Hawaii.

She'd sat between the two women, Trish and Margaret Barclay, gradually realizing that the killer, the monster they were describing, had been her husband. Adam. Adam Prescott, alias Andrew Phillips, alias Albert Petersen. On Labor Day twenty years ago, on Long Island, Albert Petersen had murdered his wife, Madeleine, and nearly killed his daughter. The crime spree that had preceded the incident had claimed the lives of two neighbors, and his mistress, Karen Lawrence, had later vanished, never to be seen again. Later still—when his wife's money had run out—he'd turned up in Hawaii as

Andrew Phillips, to woo, marry, and eventually murder Darlene Bishop, the hotel heiress. The robbery/murders of four other residents of the island were obviously also his handiwork. Three other people involved in the second case had also disappeared mysteriously: Stephen Ingalls, Kimberly Brown, and her daughter, age four. In both cases, Petersen/Phillips had apparently died, once by accident and once by his own hand. It was now believed that the charred body on the burned yacht in Hawaii was actually that of the mate, Stephen Ingalls. Three years ago, here in St. Thomas, Petersen/Phillips, now calling himself Adam Prescott, had married Kay. His scenario was the same, right down to the date: Labor Day, exactly ten years after the last one. He'd killed Sandra Franklin and Nancy Breen; he'd attacked Trish; and he'd probably killed his original mate, Greg Billings, as well. Next he was going to murder her, Kay.

His plan had been foiled by the young woman Kay knew as Diana Meissen. Diana, the goddess in three forms: the hunt; the moon; the dark. Protectress of women—appropriate, considering her efforts on behalf of Kay and Lisa. And Meissen, an anagram for another Greek deity: Nemesis, the goddess of righteous anger. The angel of retribution.

His daughter.

She had waited a long time for her opportunity: ten years, ever since the day she read about the Hawaiian Labor Day incident—on the tenth anniversary of her own tragedy—and recognized his photograph in the newspaper.

Diana—Alberta Petersen—had been his final victim.

The young woman had carried Kay down to the boathouse to ensure her safety. She had made certain that Lisa would be away from the island. If Adam had found them in the house . . . Kay had shut her eyes, not wanting to think about it.

Now, as Kay looked out at the tarmac, the sky was filled with the roar of the approaching jetliner.

The next three days had been a blur. She'd slept through most of that time and spent hours lying in her darkened bedroom staring at the ceiling. Occasionally she'd ventured out into the living room to sit with Trish and Margaret Barclay, both of whom were staying there with her, seeing to everything that had to be done. The doctor and Chief Potter came and went, and someone came to repair the railing on the sundeck. Trish and Margaret and Nola took turns hanging up the constantly ringing phone and turning away the reporters from all over America who arrived at the front door. She had only the vaguest impressions of most of it. She was aware, as the dullness was slowly replaced by an acute sense of embarrassment, that she was in what was commonly known as a fugue state. The embarrassment soon caused her odd detachment to dissipate.

She could not believe—*still* could not believe—that she had been so utterly, so titanically stupid. But that feeling, Trish and the doctor informed her, would eventually pass. She nodded and smiled at them, knowing that it would not. It would never go away. She ultimately confided that secret certainty to Miss Barclay as the two of them sat up together late one night. The older woman had smiled ruefully and nodded her head and reached out, ever so gently, to touch Kay's cheek with her cool, soft hand.

The next day they had brought her Adam's ashes. She placed the terra-cotta urn on the coffee table and sat staring at it for nearly two hours. Then she went over to the telephone. The following afternoon a private jet landed at the airport, and she and Margaret were there to meet it. They collected the sole passenger—a quiet, dignified, elderly widow—and took her to Cliffhanger.

Shortly after they got back to the house, Kay had walked out onto the sundeck, flanked by Margaret Barclay and their new friend Amanda Bishop, Darlene's mother, and unceremoniously tossed the urn over the newly repaired railing, into the abyss. The three women watched, expressionless, as the urn soared down—duplicating the path the body had taken—and splashed into the sea. Then they went back into the living room, where Trish was waiting with a magnum of Dom Perignon. It was then, as she drank champagne and spoke quietly with the other women, that Kay knew she would survive this. She would be all right.

One hour later Mrs. Bishop left the island and returned to her home in Hawaii.

That evening, the six o'clock news brought further information. Several people in a tiny town in Minnesota, having seen the news coverage of the events in St. Thomas, had that day come forward with another true story. The man in the photographs, Adam Prescott, bore more than a passing resemblance to Arvil Pederssen, Jr., who had been orphaned in a freak robbery/murder in their town thirty years before. His mother had been stabbed to death by a mysterious intruder, and young Arvil had been the only other person in the house. The date: Labor Day.

Kay had stared at the television screen, feeling nothing. She seemed to be dead inside: nothing was registering anymore.

The next day she had stood here, at this very gate, with Margaret Barclay, watching the men from the hospital carry Margaret's niece up the mobile stairway into a New York-bound plane. After a moment the older woman turned to her, kissed her cheek, and followed. As soon as the plane took off, Kay returned home and placed fresh flowers on her first husband's grave.

Yesterday morning she had gone to the yacht club, accompanied by Trish and Jerry and her lawyer. The little group had walked through the silent, staring clubhouse and down the beach to the dock where the *Kay* was tied. The others lagged discreetly behind as she walked out alone to meet the young man who waited for her. The two of them stood there next to the yacht, regarding each other evenly. Whatever she had planned to say went forever unspoken as she looked into his wet, sorrowful eyes. After a while she shook her head and motioned to the others. They joined her, and the lawyer produced the necessary papers. Witnessed by Trish and Jerry, the astonished Kyle became the new owner of the *Kay* without so much as a penny's changing hands. There was one stipulation, however, to which he agreed: he must take the boat, leave St. Thomas, and never, ever return. She walked away then, but as she stepped off the dock, she turned to look back at the young man who stared after her. She raised her hand and waved to him, thinking that at least she had not been the only fool. She and Kyle had that in common.

And now, as a final, hopeful flourish in a long week of despair, the plane descended from the sky and glided down the runway. She waited as it taxied toward the gate and stopped, and the stairway moved into place. The door opened and the passengers began to descend.

Then she saw her.

With a cry of purest joy, she ran out onto the tarmac, pushing, fighting her way through the crowd. She was so excited, so happy, that she didn't even mind the presence of the reporters and photographers who had followed her here from the house. Trish cried out in shrill protest behind her as flashbulbs popped, but Kay continued running, paying them not the slightest attention. Yes, she thought as she ran, I can survive this: the whispers and the speculation and the sidelong glances. The newspapers and the magazines and the unauthorized true-crime books and the television miniseries that will surely follow. All of it. We will go back to Cliffhanger, to our lives, with Jumbi and our friends to help us.

She stopped on the runway and sank to her knees, opening her arms, laughing and weeping simultaneously. The child let go of Frances's hand and rushed forward. Lisa was grinning as she came toward her mother, and the bright St. Thomas sun danced in her bright red hair, the gift from both her parents.

* * *

Russo helped him into the company car, tossed the crutches into the backseat, and got in behind the wheel. He drove down Broadway, across Fifty-ninth Street, and over the bridge to the Long Island Expressway, remaining tactfully silent. Robin was grateful for that; he needed to think.

Here I am, he thought, going out there, unannounced and uninvited. There is every possibility that she won't want to see me. But I know, after all these days of consideration, of weighing it in my mind, that the attempt must be made. I have to try.

Margaret Barclay had visited his hospital room several times in the few days that she remained on the island. They had not spoken much, but he had welcomed her company just the same. Once he had awakened from a drugged sleep to find her sitting there next to the bed, looking down at him. The day after she left St. Thomas, he had checked himself out of the hospital and returned to New York, to his empty rooms on West Seventieth Street.

His parents were the first visitors to arrive, followed shortly by Russo and Mr. Yakimadoro. His mother had taken one swift, horrified look at his bare living room and the ratty mattress on his bedroom floor and then swept off to Macy's. The next morning a truck had pulled up outside his building. He and Russo had watched from the front window as several men unloaded a queen-sized bed, a couch, two armchairs, and a coffee table and carried them around to the service entrance. He had smiled, knowing that drapes and blinds and kitchen utensils would soon follow. They did. The Oriental rug and the potted plants, however, had surprised him.

His second surprise was the check Yakimadoro handed him from Margaret Barclay. She had paid him the fifty-four hundred she owed him for the five weeks, and she'd added a bonus as well.

Twenty-five thousand dollars.

He'd immediately called her at her home in Glen Cove. She'd listened in silence to his protests, and then she had informed him, kindly but firmly, that she insisted that he keep the money. She had thanked him for all his conscientious effort on her behalf, told him she hoped his leg would mend soon, and hung up before he could say anything more.

That had been three days ago, and in the past three days he'd picked up the phone a hundred times, only to put it back down again. He could not say what had to be said, do what had to be done, on the phone.

He had to see her.

If he went out there, he reasoned, Margaret Barclay would not turn him away. He leaned back against the seat, bracing himself as Russo drove the car down the exit ramp. This journey would probably be in vain, but it was necessary. He was a detective, and he could be an actor, and now he had some money. But that was not enough. There was still the one thing, the most important thing.

And she alone could provide him with it.

* * *

Margaret opened the front door of the house in Glen Cove and turned to say good-bye to Dr. Stein. This was his third visit since her return from St. Thomas, and she was grateful for his interest and his advice. With his help, the whole thing just might, once and for all, be relegated to the past.

He smiled at her and went out, ignoring the lone news van that remained, days after all the others had left, at the curb in front of the house. Margaret watched, grimly amused, as the reporter and the cameraman leaning against the van looked over at the doctor and then turned away. Him again, their expressions seemed to say. She shook her head: as long as they remained in the street and didn't attempt to enter her property, there was nothing she could legally do about it. She could only hope that as time passed and other scandals sprang up to overshadow hers, they would eventually lose interest and go away.

As the doctor got into his Volvo and drove away, another car pulled up behind the van. A stocky, handsome young man with curly black hair jumped out and went around to the passenger side. He opened the door and proceeded to help someone else get out.

Robin Trask.

She shook her head slowly from side to side, smiling to herself as he took the crutches and made his slow, awkward way up to the door. The other man got back in the car and drove away. Clever, she thought. He's thinking that now, with his friend gone, I can't refuse him entrance.

A single flashbulb popped as the photographer got a shot of them together in the doorway. She stepped aside to let him pass and closed the door.

They did not speak. They stood there facing each other, she leaning back against the door and he leaning heavily on the crutches. He still had the cast, she noticed, but the bandage on his forehead was gone. Good.

She asked no questions; there would be time for questions later. She walked past him and led the way across the darkened living room and out into the dazzling sunlight, to the garden. To her roses, and the young goddess waiting.

She watched as he cautiously approached the wheelchair and stood before it. Her niece looked up, wincing at the discomfort of the bandages and the sling on her left arm. Then, to his amazement, the young woman rose slowly, painfully to her feet. Margaret nodded, satisfied: this was the third time in two days she'd gotten out of the chair. Soon, when the stitches were removed and the scars on her forehead and neck and chest mended, she wouldn't need the chair at all. Margaret glanced at the girl's bandages and closed her eyes, remembering in horror how close, how very close the final cut had come to piercing her heart. Only the gunshot had prevented it.

Then she opened her eyes. She watched the two young people regard each other, he with his cast and crutches and she with her sling and wheelchair. This, Margaret thought, is not going to be easy. For either of them. She knows so little of love, and less of trust. He's going to have to get used to that. He'll have to be very patient, very understanding. I hope he's up to it. They have such a long way, so very far, to go.

Just before she turned around to go back into the house, Margaret heard them finally speak.

"Hello," he said, staring at the girl before him. "My name is Robin Trask. Who are you?"

The young woman studied him silently through large, pale blue eyes, her pale blond hair glistening in the sun. Then, it seemed to Margaret, her grave expression lifted briefly, replaced for a moment by a hint of a smile. A beginning: the first tentative step on the journey. She would have to travel slowly, for the way was unfamiliar.

"I don't know," she replied. "I haven't decided yet."